The Retirement Plan

The
Retirement
Plan

A Novel

Sue Hincenbergs

WM

WILLIAM MORROW
An Imprint of HarperCollins*Publishers*

THE RETIREMENT PLAN. Copyright © 2025 by College Fund Productions Inc. All rights reserved. Printed in the United States of America. No part of this book may be used or reproduced in any manner whatsoever without written permission except in the case of brief quotations embodied in critical articles and reviews. For information, address HarperCollins Publishers, 195 Broadway, New York, NY 10007. In Canada, address HarperCollins Publishers Ltd, Bay Adelaide Centre, East Tower, 22 Adelaide Street West, 41st floor, Toronto, Ontario, M5H 4E3, Canada.

HarperCollins books may be purchased for educational, business, or sales promotional use. For information, please email the Special Markets Department at SPsales@harpercollins.com.

HarperCollins® is a trademark of HarperCollins Publishers.

All About Eve © 1950 written by Joseph L. Mankiewicz and *Taken* © 2009 written by Robert Mark Kamen 20th Century Studios, Inc. All rights reserved.

Man on Fire © 2004 written by A.J. Quinnell 20th Century Studios, Inc., Monarchy Enterprises S.a.r.l. and Regency Entertainment (USA), Inc. All rights reserved.

Jerry Maguire © 1996 TriStar Pictures, Inc. All rights reserved. Courtesy of TriStar Pictures.

Love Actually © 2003, *Notting Hill* © 1990, and *Out of Sight* © 1998 by Universal Studios. All rights reserved. Courtesy of Universal Studios Liecensing LLC.

Excerpt from *Magnum Force* © 1973 granted courtesy of Warner Bros. Entertainment Inc.

FIRST U.S. AND CANADIAN EDITIONS

Designed by Kyle O'Brien

Library of Congress and Archives Canada Cataloging-in-Publication Data has been applied for.

ISBN 978-0-06-339801-6
ISBN 978-1-4434-7372-9 (Canada)

25 26 27 28 29 LBC 5 4 3 2 1

For my boys:
Andy
Jack, Luke & Walker
♥♥♥

One

You Don't Need That

Pam licked margarita salt from her lips, looked around her backyard table, and wondered which of her friends would die first. Not that she had a premonition, exactly; she just tended to be a touch morbid that way. Plus, she'd already seen the three other couples' kids graduate and parents buried, so at this stage of their lives it made sense the next event to pop up could be one of their own funerals. As far as she could tell, any of the eight of them had an equal shot of cashing in their chips. Though, if she had any say in who'd be first, she'd prefer it be Andre.

She slapped a mosquito on her neck. Others buzzed the table's citronella candles and the twinkle lights strung around her patio, fighting crickets and Van Morrison for the lead in the dinner's soundtrack. On a steamy night like this, Pam and her girlfriends should have been floating in her saltwater pool and sipping cocktails while their husbands cracked open beers in the hot tub. But they'd had to sell that house.

Pam studied Hank across the leftover burgers and corn on the cob. In the darkness, he was almost handsome again. The table's edge covered his potbelly, and the shadows hid his jowls. She searched for a glimpse of the man she'd married, but he was long gone. Sometimes she missed him.

"Get us another round, will ya, babe?"

He didn't get to call her that anymore, and she shot him a glare he didn't catch. She pushed herself up from the weathered cushion and grabbed four dripping cold ones from the cooler. Hank accepted his and in one motion twisted off the cap and tossed it into her hydrangeas. Larry, Andre, and Dave followed his lead, and Pam made a mental note to collect that trash in the morning.

She padded back to the cooler for the pitcher of margaritas. That was the one good thing about Hank—he still made the best margaritas. Pam dropped a couple of ice cubes in each of her girlfriends' glasses, drained the jug, and stepped over her snoozing dog into her dim kitchen, her skin sticky from the July humidity. She opened the fridge and enjoyed the swish of cool air before reaching for Shalisa's chocolate mousse cheesecake and stepping back outside.

"Nance! Nance!" Larry interrupted his wife's conversation. "Who was . . . ?"

Larry often did that: force Nancy to troll her memory for some detail he couldn't be bothered to find. As though her sole purpose was to be the walking encyclopedia of his life. Nancy tossed back a high school math teacher's name before turning to Marlene. Pam pushed things aside on the table and made room for the dessert.

Dave caught Hank's eye and nodded toward the icy tumblers, drips of condensation sliding over a design of playing cards and dice. "Nice casino glasses, Hank. Stealing merch from the storeroom, are you?"

Hank smiled and shook his head. "New owner, new logo. We were throwing those out, so I brought them home for old times' sake." He winked. "You know I'd never bite the hand that feeds us."

The four friends touched their beers with a clink and took deep swallows.

Pam scowled. These guys. Anything for an excuse to drink—now they were toasting the casino, and two of them didn't even work there. What would be next? Cheers to Larry's bank and Andre's courier service? Seriously.

Dave wiped the back of his hand across his mouth and shifted his attention to the cheesecake. "Whoa. That looks amazing, Pammy." The candlelight hit the gleam of his smile, and Pam caught her breath. She'd forgotten what a looker he was—the way the corners of his eyes creased when he laughed. That's what was different about Dave tonight. It wasn't the dusting of gray at his temples that Pam had just noticed; it was that he seemed almost happy. Pam gave Marlene a quick glance. They weren't fooling around again, were they? Marlene had told the girls that ship had sailed, same as it had for all of them. But had Marlene caved and gone back to giving her husband a good go? Dave interrupted Pam's thoughts. "Is that chocolate?" He licked his lips.

Andre answered, "Sure is. We brought it."

Typical Andre, horning in on the credit. Pam said, "Shalisa made it."

Pam set her hand lightly on Dave's shoulder as she offered him a plate, heartened at the sight of her old friend, but puzzled about his change. If it really was a change. She eyed Marlene, who was giggling with Nancy. Maybe she and Dave were having sex again. She'd ask her later.

Andre waved his slice off and as Shalisa accepted hers, he peered at his wife over the top of his bifocals and said across the table, "Hon. You don't need that."

Pam's head snapped up. She heard Marlene's soft gasp and saw Nancy cringe. The three women watched their friend tamp down her quiet surge of anger. Shalisa leveled her gaze at her husband with the same look that shut down the Curious Cathys who used to sidle up and ask why she didn't have kids. That's how Pam knew Andre's remark had started something he couldn't finish, even if he didn't. Shalisa twirled a slim braid around her finger and fixed her eyes on her husband while she ate every last morsel of her chocolate mousse cheesecake.

Watching, Pam sensed something shift in the night air. As she cleared the dishes, she looked around the table at her husband and the friends they'd made three decades ago, and wondered again which of them would die first.

Two days later, she knew.

Two

Marlene Was Right

It was Hank who found Dave's body.

Monday morning, Pam was standing at the Dutton Realty photocopier, hypnotized by the pinprick beam of light traveling left to right. She was ten copies into the ninety her boss needed when her phone buzzed.

Hank: Don't let marlene or kids go home

What did Pam have to do with where Marlene went? She was probably scraping plaque off someone's teeth over on Stone Bridge Road. Pam checked the copier and decided she had time to investigate. It took Hank five rings to answer. "Hey. Why are you texting me about Marlene's adult children? You realize they all moved—"

"—can't talk. Dave's dead. Don't let Marlene come home."

"Our Dave?" Pam set her hand on the photocopier to steady herself. "Are you sure?"

"Oh, I'm sure, all right. Go see Marlene. Tell her Dave had an accident. I don't know if you want to say he's gone or not. See what you think. But do not let her come home."

The photocopier light traveled left to right.

"What happened?" Silence. "Hank! What happened?"

Hank cleared his throat. "Dave had an accident in his garage. Well, on his driveway. I've gotta go. The police just got here. But don't let Marlene come home. Pam!"

Pam answered in a quiet voice, "Okay."

The light bounced back and started again.

"Wait! Hank?" Pam dragged her eyes away. "Hank! Why are you at Dave's?"

But Hank was gone.

———

Stunned by Hank's call, Pam had forgotten who they were dealing with when she'd agreed to follow her husband's instruction and keep Marlene away. She, Nancy, and Shalisa convened at Marlene's dental office to break the news. The words were barely across their lips when Marlene grabbed her purse and headed for home.

The friends chased after her into the dentist's parking lot, trying to usher her into Pam's van with promises of coffee and consoling at Shalisa's kitchen table. But Marlene pushed past them and unlocked the door of her beat-up Honda. She'd given birth to three daughters in less than three years—her youngest in that same driveway because she'd put off going to the hospital until Dave got home from fishing—and she'd corralled her daughters through puberty and into adulthood without a hiccup. No one put this baby in a corner—or at a kitchen table—when her husband was dead in her driveway.

Marlene spun on them, her blond ponytail whipping around. "I appreciate what you're doing, I really do. But if I want to see my husband, I'm fucking well going to. You are not going to stop me. Got it?"

They got it.

Pam's van was disturbingly quiet. She caught glimpses of boats bobbing in the bay to her left as they wound past the sprawling, historic captains' homes and made their way inland, toward their humbler part of town.

Normally, with all four women on board, Pam could barely concentrate on the road. But on this trip, no one passed her a bag of Fritos, waved their pedicure in her face, or turned up their playlist until she could feel the bass in her bum. Pam snuck a peek at Marlene. Hands in her lap, the new widow stared out the passenger window.

"I'm fucked," Marlene said to the glass.

From the backseat, Shalisa patted Marlene's arm. "No. You're not fucked. We'll get through this."

"My husband is dead and all I can think is, I can't afford to keep my house without him." She turned to look out the front window. "Fucking Dave."

From the backseat, Nancy said, "Fucking Dave? Fucking all of them, Marlene."

Marlene stared ahead. "Well. At least your shitheads can still pay your mortgages." She blew out a breath. "Yep. I'm fucked."

Pam wrinkled her brow. Okay. Granted, considering everything, Marlene wouldn't be your typical widow. But still, Pam expected there to be some sorrow for Dave.

Marlene shifted to face them and leaned on the armrest. "I'm trying to remember the last time I talked to him. We watched *Jeopardy!* last night when he got home from fishing, but I don't know if we said one word to each other. Saturday night, after we walked home from your place"— she glanced at Pam—"he came up behind me in the kitchen, put his arms around my waist, and tried to nuzzle my neck. As if things were normal. I shut that down."

That answered the question Pam hadn't yet been able to ask. Dave and Marlene weren't back to having sex. So why had he seemed so happy the other night? She reached over to pat Marlene's knee, and when she turned the corner, the quiet neighborhood street was abuzz with activity. Two fire trucks straddled the curb, and a cluster of gawkers sought shade beneath a string of maple trees. As Pam inched past the split-levels and ranch-style bungalows with their tidy front gardens, she spotted Hank's car amid the emergency vehicles. The only thing that kept Marlene from jumping out was Nancy saying in a quiet voice, "You can never unsee things, Marlene." Marlene slumped in her seat, released the door handle, and nodded for Pam to go ahead and check things out.

As Pam picked a path up to Marlene and Dave's house, Hank pivoted away from a police officer and charged down the driveway to meet her. He always said offense is the best defense, so Pam picked up her pace to match her husband's, almost colliding with him at the bumper of the coroner's van.

Hank's face was flushed and glistening with sweat. His eyes were red. Five years ago he would have opened his arms and pulled her close, her cheek resting against his chest, like a puzzle piece finding its place. But now he thrust his finger at her. "What did you not understand about not coming—"

"—When was the last time you told Marlene Brand to do anything?" Pam barked back.

Hank's head jerked. He blinked, then said, "Dave always said she's a handful."

"I'll say."

Pam noticed Hank rotated so she'd face into the street. She'd kept her eyes averted as she'd approached the house, Nancy's warning ringing in her ears. She wanted to remember Dave smiling at her over a slice of cheesecake.

"It's graphic. Are you sure you want to know the details?"

Pam nodded.

"Okay. Dave got crushed by his garage door."

"No!" Pam couldn't help herself; she glanced back and saw the bottom of the garage door was raised two feet from the ground. Emergency responders in dark-blue uniforms huddled in the middle, blocking her view. Pam thought she could see, peeking out from under a sheet, a lock of Dave's graying, sandy hair lying pale against a pool of dark liquid.

"You don't want to see." Hank tugged her arm, pulling her eyes back to him. "They think Dave started to pull the garage door down, it hit his head and knocked him out. He fell, and the door landed on his skull and crushed it."

Pam covered her face with her hands. She couldn't believe it.

For years Marlene had been at Dave to get an automatic garage door. Theirs was heavy, manual, and would crash down on its track like a runaway train. Marlene would pitch to Dave, "It'd be easier to take the garbage out.

And maybe we could go crazy and park our car in there like normal people. How's that for a thought, Dave?" But Dave didn't budge, and Marlene would end her tirade by saying, "One day that door will kill one of us."

And now it had.

Pam looked back at her husband. Pam was the kind of person who pondered details until they lined up in a neat row, like Scrabble letters. And some of these tiles were still askew. "Did you see him at the casino today?"

"I told you before, we work in different areas. I never see him there."

"Why was he at home on a Monday morning?"

Hank wiped his arm across his forehead. "I honestly don't know."

"Why were you here?"

Hank sighed. Then shook his head. "I can't right now, Pam. I just can't." His shoulders slumped, he put his hands in his pockets and walked past her, back toward the police.

"Hank. I asked you a question." Pam threw open her arms. As she watched him go up the driveway, two of the officers strained to push the door all the way up. The interior of Dave's garage was the same as the last time Pam had seen it: so full of crap that Marlene didn't have a hope in hell of ever parking a car in there.

Pam took one last look and trudged back to the van to update her friends. She jumped in, doubly relieved to feel the cool air on her scorched skin and to see tears on Marlene's cheeks. After all, thirty years of marriage was still thirty years, and Dave was the father of her children. Surely that warranted some grief.

Marlene blew her nose. "Can I see him?"

Pam scooted across her seat to hug her friend. "Oh, Marlene. I don't think you want to. Let's go to Shalisa's, and we'll figure out what to do."

With her chin on Marlene's shoulder, Pam watched the medical personnel lift Dave's body onto the stretcher. Nancy and Shalisa squeezed forward, embracing their friend as best they could. Marlene whispered into Pam's ear, "Tell me what happened."

Pam tightened her grip and recounted how Hank had found Dave under their garage door. Marlene stiffened, then stopped crying mid-sob. She pushed herself away from Pam and sat straight. Her head tilted, she dropped the tissue from her face, narrowed her eyes, and said, "Are you fucking kidding me?"

Pam shook her head.

Marlene peered at Pam, glanced toward her house, then back at Pam, and gave a short, jarring guffaw. The girlfriends' eyes darted to one another. Marlene covered her face and though Pam feared she'd begun to sob uncontrollably, when Marlene finally dropped her hands to her lap and leaned back against the headrest, the women were all shocked to see Marlene was laughing. Hard—as if she was watching Robin Williams do standup. They exchanged uneasy glances, unsure how to help, and waited while Marlene slowly settled into a soft chortle. Finally, she took a big breath, blotted her cheeks, leaned forward to redirect the air-conditioning vent to blow directly on her face, and tucked her tissue in the edge of her bra. After a moment she shook her head and said, "Let's go. But fuck the coffee. I need a scotch."

Pam didn't know whether to be worried or relieved by Marlene's sudden change of gears, but she was anxious to get out of there, and she eased her van into the street. The coroner's vehicle pulled out ahead and Pam braked to give it distance, cringing at her timing. She reached over to squeeze Marlene's hand.

Marlene's gaze fell on the vehicle carrying her husband, taking him, for the last time, away from the home where they'd raised their three little girls. From the front lawn where he'd posed with each of his daughters on their wedding days.

Marlene squeezed Pam's hand back, then looked down her driveway at the garage door that killed her husband of thirty years and said, "I hope his last thought was, *Marlene was right.*"

Three

Funeral Sandwiches

ook at her. It's like she was made for this." Nancy nudged Pam with her elbow and nodded toward Marlene.

"What?" Shalisa asked. "Widowhood?"

Nancy nodded. "Not to be insensitive, but have you ever seen Marlene look better?"

The trio formed a tight circle, each holding a small plate of triangle sandwiches, and watched their friend, flanked by her three daughters, greet mourners in the receiving line. Marlene looked like a movie star's widow. Her long, blond hair softly framed her face, and a demure smile showed beneath a black fingertip veil. A sleeveless black shift skimmed over her sheer pantyhose above high heels.

Pam had to agree. "She's practically glowing. Do you think she had her makeup done?"

Nancy said, "She must have got extensions. Her hair wasn't that long. Was it?"

Shalisa added, "That dress is new. I bet she's wearing a double set of Spanx. Looks fabulous on her."

As word of Dave's death had spread, Marlene's family had swooped in, and while initially Pam, Nancy, and Shalisa had been in the periphery organizing airport pickups, receiving flower deliveries, and heating up casseroles, on the third day they had retreated to their own homes to leave Marlene and her relatives to await the coroner's official report and plan Dave's funeral.

As expected, given the tragic circumstances, it took a couple of days to confirm Dave had died "an unnatural death resulting from an inadvertent chance happening." In other words, a horrific accident. Dave's female relatives bemoaned what a shame it was for Dave to have a closed-casket funeral; he was such a handsome man with an exceptionally full head of hair—they'd have loved a goodbye peek. Following the service his family and friends gathered in a casino reception room Hank had arranged: a courtesy offered to employees' families so they have one less thing to worry about during their time of loss.

As car doors had slammed shut in the church parking lot, two black limousines had carried the new widow, her three daughters, and their husbands the ten city blocks to the modern structure that towered over the water's edge: the area's sole casino, cornerstone of its bustling tourism industry and anchor to the adjacent one-hundred-room hotel and its conference facility; the complex dominated the shoreline.

One after another, vehicles had pulled to a stop at the circular driveway, dropping mourners off to climb the ten steps to the casino's steel-and-glass-canopied entrance. In the center of the circle, the flag was lowered out of respect for Dave, its fallen employee. It flapped in the salty breeze that blew off the Atlantic.

Pam had known Hank and Larry would already be inside, having raced to Hank's car as soon as the hearse departed for the crematorium. As the casino's director of operations, Hank wanted to arrive first to ensure the details had been taken care of. Andre had driven the women with Shalisa in the passenger seat, and Pam and Nancy in the rear. He had parked in the far parking lot, saying the walk would do them good and they could get their steps in. Nancy had opened her mouth to protest, but Shalisa's head shake had let her know it wasn't a battle worth fighting.

Once inside they had navigated the clusters of tourists in their crisp khakis and the locals in their dark denim. They had made their way through the cacophony of whirring video slot machines, past the quiet *click-click-click* of roulette wheels, and beyond the soft snap of dice bouncing on felted tables, to the escalators where discreet signage had directed them to Dave's reception on the third floor.

There was a good turnout.

Dave's death came at the optimum age for funeral attendance. Young enough that his family and friends hadn't died off ahead of him, and old enough that his daughters' friends had the good manners to be present. Some brought a plus-one.

On occasions like this, Pam missed her daughter, but the cost of air travel kept Claire in New Zealand, on the other side of the world. Pam shifted her gaze to admire Marlene and her daughters. They stood in front of a wall of flowers flanking a poster-size photo of Dave, propped on an easel. Projection screens were dropped down along both ends of the room, and snapshots of Dave's life changed every five seconds. Pam was trying to catch the photos that they'd contributed of Dave with their group of friends, starting years ago at kids' soccer games, then moving to fishing on Hank's boat, hanging out in each other's backyards and family rooms, Christmas parties, New Year's, cottage vacations—but where were their pictures?

Across the bright, primary-colored mosaic carpet, a buffet table ran along the side of the room, anchored at one end by a coffee station and the other by a bar. Scattered in between, tiered trays were layered with sandwiches, crudités, and dessert squares. The women watched Shalisa's husband, Andre, hike up his suit pants, pick up a plate, and travel down the table straight to the vegetable tray.

"That fucker." Shalisa scowled.

Shalisa's sharp reaction to her husband selecting a few carrot sticks jolted Pam. "What do you mean?"

"I think he could be having an affair."

"Who? Andre?!" Pam and Nancy simultaneously snapped their attention back to the tall man with the tight Afro. Dressed in shirtsleeves, his tie loosened, he used plastic tongs to transfer individual grapes to his plate. One rolled to the ground, and he looked around before he toed it under the long, white linen tablecloth with his shiny black loafer.

Pam wasn't sure which was more surprising to her now: that Dave

Brand's handsome face had been crushed by his garage door, or that crotch-ety Andre Murphy had found someone to fool around with. She asked, "What makes you think that?"

Shalisa narrowed her eyes. "He skipped the funeral sandwiches."

Nancy and Pam gasped. In the thirty years the couples had been palling around they'd attended enough of these kinds of events together to know Andre loved a good funeral sandwich. Although usually focused on having a healthy diet, to Andre, funeral sandwiches were a big deal, so he allowed himself this indulgence to offset whatever grief he was going through. His go-to was the squishy, white-bread triangle stuffed with egg salad, not too heavy on the mayo or onions. He appreciated the surprise of a bit of gherkin pickle and a light skim of salted butter. He didn't mind tuna fish if it was done right. But according to Andre, chicken salad elevated any funeral. Finished off with a chewy brownie—not cakey—and Andre's mourning menu was made.

Shalisa kept her eyes on him. "He's always watched his diet, but now he's ramped it up. You saw how he is about his steps. He's downloaded a calorie app, and I found a gym brochure in the car."

"Ah." Pam considered this. "Maybe he's trying to improve himself."

Shalisa raised her eyebrows at Pam. They watched Andre replace the tongs and scratch his ass.

Nancy chuckled. "Who's the lucky gal?" She caught herself. "Sorry, Shalisa." She cleared her throat and reframed her question. "Who do you think he's seeing?"

Shalisa shrugged. "I don't think anyone yet. I think he's still planning—" Her train of thought was interrupted by movement at the entrance, and she pivoted her attention. "Ugh."

Nancy followed Shalisa's line of sight and echoed the sentiment. "Uh-oh."

Pam joined them. "Fuck me."

Sabrina Cuomo stood framed by the reception room doorway. The cool mom who had one-upped them throughout their kids' school years; the first mom to have an Elf on the Shelf and bento lunch boxes. Sabrina wafted into the room, almost in slow motion. Perfect from the tip of her wide-brimmed hat to the toes of her peekaboo slingbacks. A Chanel bag dangled from her shoulder. She could have been holding a negroni sbagliato made with prosecco, and it wouldn't have looked out of place.

Without a word, Pam, Nancy, and Shalisa shuffled en masse five steps to the right and cowered behind a group of tall, dark-suited men. Nancy peeked around the shoulder of one. "She's scanning the room."

"We should be okay. She'll find somebody better than us. She usually does," Shalisa said.

"I'm not so sure." Nancy looked around. "It's mostly Dave's golf pals right now. Uh-oh. She spotted me. She's headed this way."

"Don't make eye contact. Pick up some dishes. Pretend you're helping," Pam said.

Nancy reached for Pam's plate, but Pam wasn't about to let her off the hook and held on tight. Nancy looked Pam directly in her eye and pulled harder. Pam wasn't giving up. "It was my idea," she hissed through clenched teeth.

"Bonjour, mes amies." And Sabrina was upon them.

Begrudgingly, Pam released her plate, and Nancy scooted toward the kitchen while Shalisa headed to the buffet table and elbowed past the startled waitstaff to straighten the cutlery.

Pam, abandoned, tightened her smile. "Been to France, have you, Sabrina?"

Sabrina scanned the room beyond Pam's shoulder. "Just got back. I told my husband, I bet we'll see Pam and the girls at the funeral. So sorry for your loss." Conversations with Sabrina were transitory, lasting only as long as it took her to find someone better. The pickings must have been slim, because she started another sentence. "I haven't seen any of you in ages. Now that Gene is retired, we spend most of the year in Europe."

"Mmm, mmm." Pam mirrored Sabrina's rudeness by watching Dave's slideshow over her shoulder, feeling some disquiet, but unsure why.

And then, without warning, Sabrina threw her sucker punch. "When are you retiring, Pam?"

Pam swallowed. Then pasted a smile on her face and hoped a flush didn't creep up her neck. Whenever someone asked when she and Hank were retiring—a way of combining *man, you got old* and *how successful were you?* into one socially acceptable question—Pam struggled to answer. She found it downright humiliating that she'd worked her entire adult life but couldn't afford to retire. Not now, not in five years, and most likely never. So she did the only thing she could in the situation—she lied. "Oh, we're in no hurry. Hank and I love our jobs."

Pam hated her job. She didn't know how Hank felt about his anymore, and she didn't care. Since he had lost their life savings in that misguided investment five years ago, they'd stopped talking about their work. Full disclosure, they'd stopped talking about most things. Just like Marlene and Dave had. And Larry and Nancy. And Andre and Shalisa. Pam's only solace in the ongoing shame was that misery loves company, and at least her closest friends were in the same, leaky financial boat. All victims of Hank's bad advice. Pam didn't like to dwell on it too much, lest she spiral into guilt and despair. So she'd pulled up her pantyhose and resigned herself to remaining a secretary at Dutton Realty until she died. Under the guise of inclusivity, she had spearheaded the campaign to ensure the office was wheelchair accessible so she'd always be able to get to her desk.

"I recall you were a *secretary*?" Sabrina wrinkled her nose.

"Oh, Sabrina, you have such an awesome memory." Pam wrinkled her nose back, then cast her eyes to the screen in time to see photos of Dave and his family and then his soccer friends flash by. She wanted to tell Sabrina she recalled she leeched off her husband, who one day suddenly seemed to have inexplicably made a killing in an investment, but Pam bit her tongue, fully self-aware she would have been happy to leach off Hank if he'd been leechable. But Hank could barely support himself. That's what happens when you live beyond your means—it catches up with you when you get old. An image of Dave holding golf clubs filled the screen.

Pam had to get away from Sabrina before she said something she might regret. She made an excuse. "I need to check on Marlene—au revoir." But Pam really wanted to find Nancy and Shalisa because something was rubbing her the wrong way, even more than Sabrina.

And now she knew what it was.

A few days earlier, Marlene's daughters had called to say they were putting together a slideshow of their dad's life and asked for shots of the eight friends from over the years. Now, as sunny scenes of Dave's past flashed on the screens, Pam had watched the complete cycle, but where were their photos? She found Shalisa in the kitchen, halfway through a piece of pie.

"You can come out now." Pam waved from the door. "Sabrina found another victim."

Shalisa forked a bite into her mouth and looked for a place to discard her plate. Pam let the door close behind her and turned in time to catch Nancy making her way across the room toward her son, Paul, standing in a circle of young people. Always a great kid, he was over thirty now and dressed in a smart suit and tan leather shoes. He was well groomed with close-cropped hair and a smooth shave. His face brightened when he spotted his mom. He broke away from his friends and Nancy flung her arms around him.

Shalisa joined Pam. "What's with Nancy and Paul? She's hugging him as though he's just back from a tour of duty."

Pam answered, still watching Nancy and Paul, "I was thinking the same thing. Maybe it's just grief. Oh. Here comes Larry. Wonder if he'll join their hugathon."

Larry Clooney turned into the room and stopped at the entrance, his feet splayed, shoulders back, hands in his pockets, probably rattling his change in that annoying habit of his. Pam had to admit Larry had aged relatively well. Although his hair had grayed, his jawline was still crisp, and there was only the suggestion of a paunch above his belt. But he looked lonely, standing there, surveying the room without Hank, Dave, or Andre by his side. Pam saw Larry's eyes land on his wife and son embracing, and he took a half step forward, then stopped, spun around, and left.

Pam said, "Wonder what that's about."

Shalisa drew Pam's attention to the other side of the room. "Who's Sabrina talking to now?" She nodded toward the coffee bar, where their former mom-pal held a cup and saucer and loomed over a diminutive woman in sky-high heels.

Pam answered, "She's cornered Padma."

"*That's* Padma?"

"Where's Padma?" Nancy asked as she joined them.

Pam gestured to where Sabrina was chattering away to Padma Singh, Hank's new boss and the casino's president of operations. She'd arrived from the head office in Mumbai two months earlier. The young woman in her late twenties tucked her long, dark, glistening hair behind her ears, which were heavy with chunky diamond studs.

"I thought she'd be taller," Nancy said.

Pam frowned. "Why would you think that?"

"Everything you said about her. Being so powerful and all. You know. Sketchy, crime boss billionaire mom, MBA, climbing the corporate ladder, coming here to prepare for the big-time casinos in India. I just thought she'd be . . . taller." Nancy shrugged.

Shalisa said, "She wishes she were tall. Why else wear those heels? Look at how she keeps shifting her weight. Her feet are killing her."

Nancy nudged Pam with her elbow. "Have you met her?"

"No, but I want to. As soon as she ditches Sabrina, I'll say hello." Pam turned away to study the screen, her eyes flitting back to keep track of Padma. "Hey. Have you seen any of our photos yet? Any of Dave with us?"

Shalisa shook her head, and Nancy frowned. "Now that you mention it, not a one."

"Huh," Shalisa said. "I wonder if our file was corrupted. But you'd think the girls would have said something."

"Hmm, maybe. Oh! Padma escaped. I'll be right back." Pam thrust her glass into Nancy's chest and moved to intercept Hank's boss as she teetered toward the door. "Padma! Padma! Hi. I just wanted to say hello."

The woman stopped and turned. Pam's stomach flipped. She knew that look. As Pam closed the distance between them, Padma's cool eyes and frozen smile made Pam painfully aware of the one-inch swath of gray that cut a path along her roots. Pam straightened as Padma's gaze traveled down her body, tallying Pam's clearance-rack dress, outlet-mall purse, and ten-year-old funeral shoes. Pam could see the moment Padma was satisfied that her left earring cost more than Pam's whole outfit, and probably everything in her closet, as the young woman's smile widened uncomfortably to reveal straight bottom teeth, and Pam knew she wouldn't be grabbing coffee with Hank's new boss anytime soon. But Padma was now the gatekeeper to her husband's much-needed income, so Pam extended her hand. "I'm Pam Montgomery. Hank's wife." She couldn't help herself and edged a little closer than necessary, towering over Padma's petite figure.

Padma craned her neck to greet her, then asked, "Do you come to all the employee funerals?"

"What? No!" Didn't Padma know Hank was best friends with Dave? Admittedly, no one watching the slideshow would think she and Hank even existed in Dave's life. "Oh, no. Hank and I—"

"There you are!" Hank inserted himself in between them and put his arm around Pam's shoulder. Pam jumped and glanced at Hank. Where had he been since the service and why was he suddenly touching her? His fingers felt strange against her bare upper arm and his shirt was damp. Despite the air-conditioning, beads of sweat dotted his forehead. Was he okay? Pam didn't pay much attention to him anymore, but could he have morphed into a candidate for a heart attack? He was out of breath, as though he'd run to get here. He looked from one woman to the other. "Sorry to interrupt, but Padma, something has come up out front." Hank released his grip on Pam and started toward the door in step with his boss.

Pam watched them go. What the fuck? As weird as Hank had been in the five years since he'd ruined their retirement plans, he'd ramped things up tenfold since Dave's accident. But Pam had read that grief was unpredictable.

Pam turned away and was considering whether she should fill up on more funeral sandwiches so she wouldn't have to worry about dinner, when Nancy and Shalisa fell in beside her. Shalisa said, "You're not going to believe this."

"Believe what?" Pam said. Her eyes found Marlene, still in her funeral veil.

Shalisa whispered, "Marlene is moving."

Pam squeezed her eyes closed. That was fast. Her poor, poor friend. Her husband was barely gone and already she was being forced into a dreary, basement granny flat at one of her daughters' homes. Pam would support her. She'd go see her and invite her back to visit. She braced herself for the details. "Which daughter is she moving in with?"

"Oh, she's not moving in with a daughter." Nancy beamed. "She bought a condo in Boca Raton. Marlene's moving to Florida."

Pam swung around to face her friends. "Boca Raton! How the fuck can she afford that?"

Four

No Harm Done

While his wife had chatted with Sabrina Cuomo at the funeral reception on the third floor, Hank had leaned back in his office chair and wished it would all go away—his debts, their marriage troubles, Dave's murder.

They were only a few weeks from the finish line. Saturday night was the happiest any of them had felt in the last five years. Dave had been joking and smiling—almost his old self. He might have even been getting laid again. Hank forgot to ask him about that when they were fishing, and now he'd never get the chance. What Hank would give to see those girly dimples sitting across from him right now. It had been good to see Dave smile again.

Then this had to happen.

Hank knew who killed Dave. Or more precisely, who ordered the hit. At least, he was pretty sure he did. His best-case scenario was they thought Dave had acted alone, they'd killed him quickly, and they were done. His worst-case scenario was they knew there were accomplices and they'd tortured Dave to get Hank, Larry, and Andre's names out of him before they shot him and crushed his head under his garage door. The guys had held their breath and waited for two things to happen.

First, for the coroner to find the bullet and the subsequent police investigation to erupt. But that hadn't happened. Then Hank realized—when you see a head that bashed in, you don't look for another cause of death. And so far, it seemed he was right. After all, who would want to kill Dave Brand? As far as anyone knew he was merely a low-level casino tech and a lousy golfer.

And the other thing that had Hank popping Tylenol and chewing Tums was expecting a deadly knock on his door from the same guys who'd visited Dave. But that hadn't happened either. At least not yet. But Hank knew they'd be coming.

If they knew about them.

Despite working at a casino all his adult life, Hank wasn't much of a gambler. Right then he wasn't rolling the dice on the probability of any particular scenario and instead was laser focused on keeping them all alive. Even if, by some twisted chance, fortune was smiling on him, and the casino thought Dave had acted alone, they'd still want their money back. So they'd be watching everyone at Dave's funeral.

It wasn't over because Dave was dead. It had just started.

Hank had leaned back in his chair, his feet on his desk, his eyes closed, working to control his breathing until Andre had said, "Oh, look. Pam's talking to Padma."

Hank had surged forward and scanned the bank of closed-circuit TVs on his office wall. He'd found the feed from the reception room, and there in the bottom corner, his wife had been gabbing away to his boss as though they were standing at a church garden party and not his best pal's funeral following his violent death.

Hank had jumped up. His chair had flipped over. He'd pushed by Andre, leaning against the wall popping grapes into his mouth, and Larry, sitting in his guest chair scrolling through his phone. He'd flung open his office door, shot them a look, and their eyes had followed him, their jaws hanging open. Hank had raced down the corridor, past the elevators and straight for the stairs. Was he the only one who understood what was going on? Dave would have understood.

What if Andre hadn't shown Hank the photos before the funeral?

Andre had been working on his laptop when he'd called Hank and Larry over. "Guys. Guys. Come here. You've got to see this."

Hank had been checking on the setup of the casino's reception room before they headed to the church for Dave's service. Larry was doing what Larry did best, watching everyone else work. Andre had connected his laptop to the screens, to display the photo show of Dave's life that his daughters had put together. He had tapped a button and up had flashed a shot of the four of them: Hank, Andre, Larry, and Dave. About twenty years younger, standing side by side on the dock next to Hank's boat, sun bright on their cheeks, their hair tousled by the summer wind—Hank still had enough hair to tousle back then—each dangling a string of striped bass.

Hank could have almost tasted the light, butter-crisp coating Pam had fried them in. They'd sat around the table in Dave and Marlene's backyard and as the sun had set, they'd devoured the fillets, cornbread, and salad made with tiny new potatoes, the red skins still on them, and washed it all down with icy beers and salty margaritas. Afterward he and Pam had walked home arm in arm through the quiet streets, under the canopy of the neighborhood's oak trees. He'd nuzzled her neck and as soon as the babysitter had waved good night from her front steps, three doors down, he'd peeled off Pam's sundress.

Hank had smiled at the memory. But then he'd remembered where they were. And why.

Hank had pushed down the bile collecting in his throat. "What are you doing, bud?"

Andre slid his bifocals up his nose, unwrapped a low-fat granola bar, took a bite, and pressed a few buttons on his laptop. "Just putting together a stellar photo show to honor our pal Dave."

Hank yanked the cable from the laptop, and the screen went black. He'd wound it tight around his fingers. Andre looked up, his mouth open, his bite of granola bar sitting unchewed on his tongue, and he eased his chair back a bit. Larry hurried over to join them. Hank looked around the room, made sure the catering staff hadn't noticed, took a step closer, and kept his voice low. "Are you out of your fucking mind?"

Andre recoiled, pushed the food to his cheek, and asked, "What? What do you mean? It's a great photo."

Hank closed his eyes for a moment. "Yes, Andre. It is a great photo. It's also great proof that I am a fucking good friend of Dave's. Displayed, front and center, at the fucking casino, where Dave and I work, for the colleagues Dave and I work with—and Padma, my new boss, who probably ordered Dave's hit—to see. Let me repeat: Are you out of your fucking mind?"

Andre froze. Larry put his hand on Andre's shoulder. "Andre wasn't thinking, Hank. Dave's death has him rattled. It has us all rattled. He's sorry. Aren't you, Andre?"

Andre nodded while he chewed and swallowed, then carefully folded the foil around the rest of his granola bar and tucked it in his pocket.

"He'll delete those photos right now. Won't you, Andre? All the photos of Dave with any of us. Wives too." Larry looked at Hank. "No harm done."

Hank's eyes darted around the room before he leaned closer, his voice low. "All right. No harm done. But we've got to be smart. We have to keep our heads on. Especially now. Padma or whoever did this is looking for Dave's connections. One slipup, like this, and we're done. You got it? I mean like garage-door-on-your-head done."

———

Now Hank burst through the stairway door and trotted down the carpeted hall to Dave's reception. Hot summer sunlight streamed in through the wall of windows overlooking the ocean to his right, and he felt a trickle of sweat dripping down his back into his ass crack. He slowed his steps to regain his breath.

He needed to put Dave's murder behind him and get back to his A game. When would it end? He'd put out the fire with Andre and the photos only to have this one with Padma and Pam pop up. It was his fault. He should have realized Pam would zero in on Padma and that he'd need to run interference. That was one of the things that had drawn him to his wife all those years ago: the way she would become best pals with anyone in mere minutes. But right now, he had to get Pam away from Padma before she spilled their life story. Or specifically, the part of their life story where he was good friends with the dead guy.

Now was not the time to be connected to Dave Brand.

When Indo-USA Gaming Inc. out of India had taken over the casino six months earlier, Hank and the guys had been worried this new ownership could disrupt the good thing they had going. Hank had poked around the Indian company's Wikipedia page, where it listed its principal investors in blue font. Hank had clicked through to discover associations with Bollywood—which was great. He had envisioned movie premieres and new entertainment in the lounges. But then he'd clicked another blue word and his color had drained.

He'd landed on the page Organized Crime in India, with subcategories on extortion, smuggling, drug trafficking, kidnapping, and murder. His heartbeat had raced. He'd checked his old emails and found the corporate fiscal statement and randomly googled their listed global subsidiaries' names. And too often, he found those companies were linked to news alerts about missing persons. Hank had googled those names too and clicked through to articles about middle managers who had mysteriously disappeared. He'd poured himself a scotch as he read about the ones who were found alive days later, unable to recall precisely what had happened to them. Then he'd refilled his glass with a shaky hand as he'd scrolled through accounts of others who had turned up dismembered and beheaded. Some hanging from a bridge. Goosebumps had rippled up his arms as he'd clicked on link after link. And then he'd realized he was doing all this searching on a company-owned computer. He'd slammed his laptop shut. He knew all he needed to know. He knew if they got caught now, they would upset some nasty people. The type of people who didn't get mad. The type who got even.

So they couldn't get caught. They'd briefly suspended their operation while Hank was vigilant, looking for any change in casino procedure or protocol. Anything that might alter the casino's checks and balances and potentially expose them. But everything remained status quo, and they'd voted to proceed cautiously with the plan, grateful they were almost finished. When Padma arrived, Hank had watched her and finally determined that while she was ambitious, she wasn't a threat—she was more concerned with the casino's color palettes than its profits.

But now Hank realized he may have been wrong about that. Or not. That was the problem. He didn't know.

What he did know was, when Dave was killed, they were twelve weeks from their ten-million-dollar goal. With Dave gone, they had to pull the plug. Now they had to focus on staying alive while they assessed the threat. Since it may have been Padma who unleashed the hounds on Dave, Hank had to keep her off his scent a while longer. Which meant Padma couldn't be talking to Pam.

Hank had wiped his forehead with his sleeve before he had rounded the corner into the reception room.

"There you are!"

Five

They All Do

Used to be when Pam Montgomery thought of her life, it was cleaved into two sections—before and after. Before her parents passed away and after. These days, she tried not to think about the big picture of her life much, but when those thoughts did creep in, her before and after signposts had shifted. Now her life was compartmentalized as: before Hank lost their savings and after. Before, when she didn't clip coupons and could afford Netflix. And after, when she moved to the shitty, rented townhouse a few blocks east of her friends and left the beautiful home where she'd raised her daughter.

Most people in the neighborhood had been to Pam and Hank's house on Glendale Avenue at one time or another. Families, for pool parties; girlfriends, to nestle into Pam's comfy sectional before her wood-burning fireplace and watch a Christmas movie, voting between *Love Actually*, *White Christmas*, or *The Holiday*; or couples, for her and Hank's annual New Year's bash. When the for-sale sign had gone up on her front lawn, so had Pam's wall of lies—we're downsizing, the yard's too big, we want to simplify our lives.

They'd sold the sectional and her grandmother's table—there was no dining room in the townhouse—and gone were the king-size bed and pool table. They'd shoehorned the den furniture into the living room and the guest queen bed into the primary. Pam attempted to squeeze her kitchen table into the breakfast nook, but finally sold it on Facebook Marketplace and found a replacement for twenty-five dollars. She tried to look on the bright side—she no longer had to worry about pool toys or Christmas decor for the mantel she no longer had. The new place was near their old neighborhood, so she shopped at the same grocery store, filled up at the same gas station, and was still minutes from her best friends.

These days Marlene, Shalisa, Nancy, and their husbands were the only guests who regularly traipsed over Pam's worn linoleum kitchen floor. Pam didn't have to keep up appearances with them.

She expected the girls for coffee that morning—a chance to regroup after Dave's funeral and find out what the fuck was going on with Marlene. Pam was straightening up. She still had her pride, after all, and there was no extra cost attached to keeping a tidy home. In her before life, she stashed all the crap associated with household comings and goings in her mudroom, but in her after, in the rented townhouse, everyone came and went through the front door. Pam stood at the base of the stairs with her hands on her hips and grunted in disgust as she scanned Hank's shoes.

When Pam first met Hank, he was living with two other guys in a musty, run-down semi-detached in the downtown core, not far from the college. The house was so bad that when they had donated their sofa to their local Goodwill, it was declined. The guys had left it at the curb thinking someone would want it—no one had. In that god-awful, gross house, the roommates had lined their shoes up along their front entry wall as though they were trophies on a shelf. When Pam and Hank had moved in together, she'd been quick to kibosh that habit. "Use the closet. That's what it's there for," she'd said. Pam found her peace in a clutter-free home, and to keep her happy, Hank had played by her rules.

But that morning, seven pairs of Hank's shoes lay where he'd kicked them off—runners, flip-flops, golf shoes, two pairs of loafers, deck shoes, dress shoes. And even worse, five pairs of dirty socks were strewn about. Her stomach roiled at the sight of them. Who does that? Just strips off sweaty socks at the door and leaves them there to dry and curl. Why? Why, Hank? But Pam knew. The pile of shoes and socks was another "fuck you, Pam."

Pam opened the closet door and tossed in a flip-flop. The next one went in a little harder. By the time the last shoe bounced off the back of the closet wall, Pam was sweating.

"Fuck you back, Hank."

———

"It was a beautiful service." Shalisa threw her arms around Marlene a while later as they gathered on Pam's back patio. "Dave would have been happy to know he had such a great turnout. He did love a party."

"He'd have liked it better if there was dancing. Nothing could keep that man off the dance floor. But it was good for the girls to see how people loved their dad." Marlene pulled out a chair on the shady side of the table while they waited for Nancy.

But Pam had no patience. "So, what the fuck, Marlene? You're moving to Boca Raton?"

After Shalisa and Nancy had dropped that bombshell at the funeral, Pam had been dying to get the deets, but Marlene had been in a constant swirl of people; everyone wanted a moment with the widow. When they were finally alone, Marlene had said she'd be over the next morning to fill them in, and Pam had been further puzzled, because when Marlene had squeezed her goodbye, she'd seemed almost giddy with excitement. Not deflated with grief.

Pam hadn't known what to expect when Marlene let herself in the front door and breezed into her kitchen, but she had to admit she was a touch surprised to see the new widow arrive in full makeup with her hair lightly teased into a flattering bun, wearing heels and a crisp sundress. Not her typical ponytail, shorts, and flip-flops. She had brandished a box of French macarons—from Sabrina Cuomo's gift basket, she'd gushed—and a bottle of chilled champagne she'd picked up on her way over—her treat. Hardly what Pam had expected of a grieving widow, even one who'd spent the past five years being pissed off at her husband. Although Pam had read enough about grief to know not to judge, she was pretty sure she could judge this.

Nancy, perpetually running late, finally called a greeting from the front door, and Marlene bounced in her seat and pointed to the champagne. "Open it, open it, Pam. Shalisa, get some glasses."

Nancy came outside through the patio door and carefully stepped around Pam's lounging, middle-aged rescue dog, Elmer, who lifted his head a couple of inches and thumped his tail twice in greeting.

Once they were all seated around the same table where they'd last been together with Dave, with the inappropriate bubbly before them, Marlene started. "Oh, it's such a relief to be away from all that family." She slumped with a mopey face, then straightened and smiled. "Finally! I can be myself." Marlene picked up her glass and wiggled in her chair. "Cheers!"

Pam, Nancy, and Shalisa exchanged brief glances and offered their champagne in a half-hearted toast, a bit uncomfortable to seemingly be celebrating Dave's death. Marlene was already topping up her glass when Elmer launched himself from the patio and tore across the small patch of grass toward the scraggly line of bushes along the rear fence. Startled, Marlene jarred the bottle, spilling some bubbly on the table. She laughed. "I didn't know Elmer could move that fast."

"Fast?" Shalisa said. "I didn't know he could move."

"Must have seen a rabbit," Pam explained. "I think that's why he's called Elmer. You know, Elmer Fudd."

"He chases rabbits?" Nancy was surprised. "What's he do when he catches them?"

"Oh, he never catches them. Look at him."

They turned to watch Elmer waddle back across the lawn and collapse on his side, chest heaving, on a shady spot of the cement. A few months earlier, Pam's coworker had appealed for an emergency foster home for this scruffy dog they guessed was around eight years old. He'd been spotted scavenging in the streets for weeks before he was caught and brought in to the shelter. No one was adopting him. None of his parts matched. He had a long body and short legs. Most of his fur was a wiry, tawny color but his ears were a silky silver and black.

"Why does his tongue hang out like that?" Shalisa asked.

"He's missing teeth on that side so there's nothing to hold it in."

He'd arrived with several broken teeth and after the shelter had them extracted, he'd needed a home where he could convalesce. Pam had reluctantly agreed to foster him. After all, it was only for six weeks, and she could use the companionship at home, because she sure wasn't getting any from Hank. By the time Elmer was well enough to return to the shelter, Pam had grown used to waking and finding him quietly waiting for her beside her bed. Or by the door to be let out. Or on the other side, to be let in. He never made a noise, and he didn't need attention. You could tell someone had loved him once, and now it was Pam's turn. And it was nice to love again.

Pam turned back to Marlene. "Okay. Spill."

Marlene took another swig, set her glass down on the table, and leaned back. "Well. Did you see that man I was talking to at the funeral? Tall, gray haired, and in a suit?" There tend to be a lot of tall, gray-haired men in suits at funerals, so Pam wasn't sure who Marlene was talking about, but she nodded anyway, and Marlene continued. "He's Dave's insurance agent. Who knew he had one of those? I didn't, that's for sure. Anyway, he came to see me a few days ago. He sat at my kitchen table, opened his briefcase, pulled out a folder, and told me—get this—little ol' Dave, the slot machine tech, was insured to the teeth. Do you believe it?"

No. Pam didn't believe it at all. Dave never seemed to think about anything beyond where his next beer would come from. Although Hank claimed Dave was a mechanical whiz, often tuning up something on Hank's boat, Pam personally had never seen evidence of an aptitude in anything besides having charm and good rhythm. Pam took a moment to relish the memory of being led around a dance floor by Dave. Hank wouldn't dance anymore, and Pam missed it. Even if she could somehow cajole him to the floor, they never dipped or spun at the same time. But dancing with Dave was like being Uma Thurman to his John Travolta.

"What do you mean, 'insured to the teeth'?" Pam asked.

"Dave had the maximum employee insurance at the casino—four times his salary."

Pam did a quick calculation and thought that was probably between two and three hundred grand. Respectable, but not life-changing.

Marlene was counting off her fingers. "And, he had our mortgage and our second mortgage insured, so they're gone. Poof! Bye-bye. I own my house. Outright. Do you believe it?" Pam's eyes were wide. "And he had insurance on our credit cards, so those debts are gone too. And on top of those, you'll never guess what else this guy had to say."

Marlene often did that: say "you'll never guess" and wait until someone answered.

There was a pause, and finally, Shalisa said, "What else did he have to say, Marlene?"

Marlene squirmed with excitement. "Well, the guy in my kitchen said, Dave had another policy. Another one. For a flat one million dollars! They're depositing that—a million bucks—in my bank account—tomorrow!" She threw her arms in the air as though she had just landed a standing backflip at the Olympics.

Her friends looked at her, their mouths slightly open, but no words came out.

Marlene picked up her glass and continued, "It's no wonder we never had enough money, with him paying all those insurance premiums. It's almost as though he knew something bad was gonna happen to him. And it gets better. The casino's HR department called me, and it turns out Dave also gets a pension from the casino. He'd been paying as much as he could into the plan and I get that too. So, look at me. Do you recognize me? I'm your friend . . . the rich bitch." Marlene threw her head back, laughed, then took a swig of her champagne, and choked a bit as she swallowed.

Shalisa and Nancy sat still. Pam toyed with the stem of her champagne flute and watched the bubbles scramble upward for air and release. And just like them, Marlene's money problems were gone.

Marlene said, "So this morning I quit my job. I went in, and everyone was all nice and so sympathetic. They said, 'Oh, Marlene, take as much time as you need. Don't feel you have to rush back.' And I said, '*Rush back?* I'm *never* coming back. Love you all, but this chick is outta here.' My sister, in Boca Raton, told me there's a nice condo on her golf course that just came up for sale. She sent me pictures. You should see the garage! It's spotless. All kinds of organization units on the walls. A hook for every tool. And an automatic door opener! I told her, tell the agent it's sold. I paid the asking price. It closes in two weeks. I'm flying down tomorrow to see it and start things rolling." Marlene looked around at the stunned faces. "Oh! You guys will visit. I'll pay for your flights. It'll be my treat for all your birthdays. It's four bedrooms, you each have your own room. You can come live with me. We'll be like the *Golden Girls*!"

Pam knew they all saw themselves as Blanche, the sexy one. Pam just didn't want to be relegated to being Sophia and have to carry her purse everywhere. And she wanted to be happy for Marlene. She knew she should be. She'd held a sobbing Marlene in her arms when the guys had confessed their investment had crashed and they'd lost everything. The couples' dreams of sunny, side-by-side retirement condos had been dashed. But the only comfort Pam had was knowing she wasn't alone. Misery loves company, and with Marlene's windfall, Pam now had one less companion. Come winter Marlene would be sweeping sand off her lanai and Pam would be sprinkling salt on her icy, northeastern front step. Heck, just weeks from now Marlene would be tracking the sun over the pool in Boca Raton and Pam would still be tracking the Dutton Realty photocopier light left, then right, then snapping back. Pam looked at Nancy, who would still be shelving books at the library, and Shalisa, who'd still be wiping people's chins as a nurse's aide. Marlene continued talking, and something she said perked up Pam's ears.

". . . they all do. Hank, Larry, and Andre."

"What?" Pam asked. "What do 'they all do'?"

Marlene drained her champagne glass. She pulled her chair closer and leaned her face near to Pam's, and said, "They all have one-million-dollar life insurance policies." She straightened.

"How would you know that?" Pam never paid attention to finances; she left it all to Hank, which was probably one reason they were in such a mess. But surely, if Hank had that kind of life insurance coverage, he would have said something.

Marlene refilled her champagne glass. "When Steve, that's Dave's life insurance guy, when he went to the washroom I peeked inside his briefcase." No one feigned surprise; they would have done the same thing. "And he had a letter with all their names. Like, they called him for a joint consultation. So you guys have the same deal. We could all move to Boca Raton!"

That thought hung in the air for a moment, and then Shalisa said, "Except for one minor detail."

Marlene tilted her head and raised her eyebrows.

Nancy finished the thought. "Our husbands aren't dead."

Shalisa picked up her glass and took a sip before adding, "Yet."

———

After Marlene had bombarded them with her tornado of a to-do list and they'd arranged to drive her to the airport the following morning, she'd rushed off to meet with the real estate agent about selling her house, leaving Pam, Shalisa, and Nancy to finish the champagne. Since they'd all taken a personal day, thinking Marlene would need their support after her family left—*ha*, so much for that thought—once the bubbly was drained, Pam opened a bottle of wine. She speculated their taste buds had been dulled enough by the expensive champagne that a screw-top pinot grigio could ride its coattails, and she topped up their glasses.

"She's right." Shalisa played with the stem of her glass.

"About what?" Pam tightened the lid and set the bottle in the shade.

Nancy answered, "Yep. Marlene's right. The only thing standing between us and a Boca Raton retirement condo is our husbands."

"Marlene never said that." Pam lifted her hair from her neck to catch a breeze.

"She might as well have," Nancy said.

"I saw a *Dateline* episode where a wife arranged for her husband to be killed so she'd get his insurance money," Shalisa said.

"Yeah, and she got caught. That's how she ended up on *Dateline*." Pam used her T-shirt's collar to mop up the sweat trickling down her cleavage.

"Too bad we have automatic garage doors," Nancy said.

The women chuckled and sipped their wine.

Pam remembered the question that had been circling her mind since Dave's funeral. "Shalisa? Do you seriously think Andre could be having an affair?"

Shalisa waved the thought away. "No. He doesn't have that kind of energy. But I did think about it a while ago, and I realized the better question is—would I care? And the answer is no. I would not." She shrugged and took another sip.

"You wouldn't?" Nancy prompted.

"Nope. I've decided he can do whatever the fuck he wants. I am done."

Pam thought back to the Saturday night sitting at this same table and the way Shalisa had stared her husband down while she had eaten her chocolate mousse cheesecake, and how Andre, oblivious, hadn't even glanced her way. Pam had watched enough Oprah and Dr. Phil in her day to know sometimes it's not one big thing, but rather a buildup of little things that brings a marriage crashing down. She should know. And Lord knows they all had their share of little things. "I couldn't handle ever thinking if, on top of everything else, Hank was fooling around on me too. I'm sorry, Shalisa. I didn't know things were that bad."

Shalisa sighed. "Well, that's it, isn't it, Pam? No. They're not *that* bad. But is that where I am in life? I'm sixty-three years old and am I supposed to be satisfied my life is not *that* bad? I can't remember the last time Andre and I had any fun together, let alone a good conversation. About anything beyond whose turn is it to take the trash out? Or did I get to yoga today and why do I never ride the Peloton bike he insisted on buying that we can't even afford? If I hear him tell me one more time, if you don't move it, Shalisa, you'll lose it . . ." She shook her head. "You know we haven't had sex in ages. Could be a year. I don't care enough to keep track."

Pam remembered that the last time she and Hank had fooled around, her overriding thought was: Couldn't he have started something *before* she'd made the bed? Other than that, it had been a long dry spell. He'd put his arm around her when she was talking to Padma at Dave's funeral, and she'd felt a jolt. And not totally unpleasant. But, other than that, she didn't know when they had last touched intentionally. She thought back to how she used to reach over in bed and just lay her hand on him. His shoulder, his chest, his hip. Wherever it landed. Just to feel him there. How he'd put his big paw over her small hand and squeeze. Then guide it to his crotch. How they'd laugh at his joke, if it was a joke, and he'd pull her close and wrap her in his arms, and they would make love. Good, warm, familiar, satisfying love. When was the last time that happened? At least a year ago. Maybe two. A wave of loss washed over her. She pushed it away and drained her glass. "Have you thought about leaving Andre?"

"For what? A basement apartment and a bus pass? We can barely survive on our two incomes. We would have been okay if he hadn't cashed in our savings, but now with the mortgages . . ."

Pam nodded in understanding. But at least Shalisa didn't have kids to consider. Even though Pam's daughter was grown and married, leaving Hank would mean officially destroying their family unit, and she wouldn't do that to Claire.

Shalisa grabbed three of her braids and wrapped them around her fingers and then unwrapped them. She sighed. "Yes. I do think about leaving Andre. All the time. I just don't know how. But if he had an accident like Dave, that would be my way out. And if I was left with a million dollars in my bank account at least I'd know I got something out of my marriage." She took a sip of wine. "What about you two? You can't tell me you're happy with Hank and Larry."

Nancy pulled her dark-rimmed glasses from her nose and seemed to be gathering her thoughts while she polished the lenses with her T-shirt's hem. She took a deep breath, then said, "I haven't been happy with Larry since Paul told us he's met someone, and Larry walked out of the room."

Pam gasped, and she heard Shalisa's exclamation. Nancy carried on, "Paul's fallen in love, and I haven't even met his partner. My son is planning the next part of his life, and Larry has cut us out of it. Estuardo's a lawyer. He comes from a nice family. Paul says he has the same sense of humor as Larry, but Larry won't meet him. Larry says it's one thing to accept Paul's gay, but another to actually see him with another man. Do you believe it? It's like we're living in the dark ages."

She returned her glasses to her nose and looked directly at Pam, and then Shalisa. "So, if I had any way out of my marriage, I'd take it. You don't know what it's like to sneak around to keep in touch with your son. I hoped Larry would come to his senses, but he hasn't. Not one bit. Paul was at the funeral. Did you see him? He came to support Dave's daughters, but he respected

Larry and didn't bring Estuardo. But it didn't matter. Larry walked right by him. I hate to say it, but in that moment, I wished it was Larry's head under that garage door. And that was before I knew about the insurance money."

Pam thought of Larry and his beer farts, warm eyes, and long lashes and wanted to smack him. And how was this happening to one of her closest friends, and she hadn't seen it? "I'm so sorry, Nancy. You never said . . ."

Nancy wiped away a tear. "I was so ashamed of Larry I couldn't even talk about it. Honestly, deep down I thought he'd come around and just want Paul to be happy. Isn't that what parents want? But now I've given up, and I've decided I am not walking away from my son. If I walk away from any-one, it's Larry." She looked directly into Pam's eyes. "With a million bucks in my pocket, I wouldn't even look back."

Shalisa leaned forward and covered Nancy's hand. "We're so sorry you've had to go through this. You could have shared it with us."

"I know." Nancy put her own hand over Shalisa's for a moment, pushed her chair back, stooped to give Elmer a quick belly rub, then slid the screen door open and stepped into Pam's kitchen. They heard her blow her nose and open the fridge.

Shalisa refilled their glasses, emptying the bottle. "Now that we're being totally honest—what about you, Pam? You barely said a word to Hank the other night. You used to have so much fun together, and now you hardly talk to him. Wouldn't your life be better without him?"

Pam studied her hydrangeas and saw she'd missed a beer cap when she was cleaning up after their dinner. It had only been what, just over a week, yet it seemed like forever ago they'd sat out here that steamy night. Now Dave was gone. Marlene was excited about moving on, and here Pam was, discovering her best friends had been living with secrets, right in front of her.

Marlene and Shalisa had known each other the longest, having gone to high school together with Dave and Andre. When kids' soccer had brought them all together, even though Andre and Shalisa had no kids of their own they'd tagged along to the games and barbecues. Andre, having played soc-cer in college, had even started coaching. Soon the four couples were a core group. Pam had spent more time with these women than anyone else in her life. What had they been talking about all those hours? Oh sure, they'd chatted about recipes and the royal family. They'd spent hours rehashing whether karma was even a thing if awful Sabrina Cuomo and her slimy husband could come into tons of money and yet they'd lost all theirs. They'd talked about skin care and face shaving, finally believing Nancy when she assured Pam she wouldn't grow a beard if she razored away her fuzzy cheek hair.

They'd liberally exchanged grievances about their husbands such as how when Hank dropped his clothes on the bathroom floor, it looked like he'd been vaporized out of them, how Andre thought every dish needed to soak in the sink even if it only had toast crumbs, and how the airflow on Larry's new CPAP machine was so strong, one night Nancy woke up thinking there was a mouse in her hair. And more personally, canvassed for preferred sexual positions when arthritic knees began to hinder their action—even sharing how that action had subsequently dried up. But now it seemed like they hadn't really talked at all.

Nancy returned to the table with another chilled bottle of wine.

Pam watched as her glass was filled and said, "I look at him and I don't see my Hank there anymore. He changed when they lost the money. He quit. He quit on our retirement plans, and he quit on me." She took a drink. The cold wine felt crisp on her tongue. "Every day for the last few years, I wake up and wonder what it would be like to have a life without Hank. Frankly, I already do. So yes. To answer your question, my life would be better without him. I wouldn't miss him for a minute." She ran her finger around the base of her glass.

The women sat for a moment, the only noise a neighbor's car door slamming and Elmer's snoring.

Nancy broke the silence and said in a quiet voice, "Then why don't we get rid of them?"

Pam's hand jerked and drops of wine splashed over the edge of her glass and landed on the table. She looked at Shalisa, who had cocked her head and was squinting at Nancy. Cautiously, Pam turned back to Nancy. "What did you say?"

Nancy sat straighter in her chair. "I said, 'Then why don't we get rid of them?' Think about it. None of us are happy in our marriages. Marlene wasn't either and now Dave's dead and you saw her. She was practically glowing. That could be us."

Pam's mouth gaped and she stared at Nancy for a moment, then she snorted and sat back. "Funny. You had me for a minute." She smiled and shook her head.

Nancy leaned forward. "No, Pam. I'm serious." Her eyes were wild, as though she were mentally tallying an abacus. "Think about it. Why not? None of us want to be married anymore." She turned sharply to Shalisa. "Do you want to be married to Andre?"

Shalisa shook her head rapidly.

Nancy turned to Pam. "Do you want to be married to Hank?"

Pam blinked. Then blinked again. She tried to speak but couldn't push any words out.

Nancy set her hand on Pam's forearm. "Don't you see? This is our out! We kill Hank, Andre, and Larry, get their insurance money, and say goodbye to our shithole lives." She turned to Shalisa. "Right, Shalisa?"

Now it was Shalisa's turn for her mouth to open soundlessly. Her head jerked in such a way that Pam couldn't tell if she was shaking it no, nodding yes, or having a stroke. Pam had to tear her eyes away and turn her focus back to Nancy. "How much have you had to drink?" Pam held the wine bottle up and inspected it, hoping to find a semi-dissolved remnant of any kind of hallucinogenic. That was the only explanation she could think of behind what Nancy was saying.

Nancy plucked the bottle from Pam's hand and set it aside. "I'm totally sober. Well, maybe not totally. But I'm seeing completely clearly. The clearest I've seen in years." She looked from her one friend to the other, and then said, "I think we should do it."

Pam put both hands up and spoke in a deliberately soothing voice. "Whoa. Just, whoa. Let's take a beat. We've been talking about our marriages, and sure, they're not ideal, but we don't want to be doing or saying anything crazy. Right?" She raised her eyebrows, hoping Nancy would agree with her, but Nancy seemed to be deep in thought. Pam's eyes snapped to Shalisa, who was nodding subtly, as though she was reviewing a checklist.

Pam said to her, "Can you not help here?" She motioned to Nancy with her chin.

Shalisa said, "I'm in."

Pam fell back in her chair and threw her hands over her face. "What am I hearing? Did you two do edibles before you came over? What the fuck is going on?" She sat forward, put her elbows on the table, her fingers to her temples, and squeezed her eyes shut.

She heard Nancy speak. "Pam. You said it yourself. You wouldn't miss Hank for a minute. We can figure out a way to get rid of them. You said your life would be better without him. You said that."

Pam dropped her hands and looked at Nancy. "I may have said that, but I'm not going to do anything about it. He's still Claire's dad."

"When was the last time you saw Claire?" Shalisa pushed.

Pam's heart broke a bit. It had been three years since her daughter had married Dylan and they'd hugged goodbye at the airport when the newly-weds moved around the world to New Zealand. With Claire's busy life and the different time zones, they were barely able to find time to talk. Every lottery ticket Pam bought, she wished she'd win enough for airfare to New Zealand. Not even the big prize—just enough money so she'd be able to hold her only child.

Shalisa tapped her nails on the table and then looked up at Pam. "With a million dollars in insurance money you could travel to New Zealand whenever you wanted. You could quit your shitty job and retire there."

Pam looked from one of her oldest friends to the other. She squinted. "You cannot seriously be suggesting we kill our husbands for their insurance money."

Nancy said, "It's not as though we have another retirement plan."

Pam watched the beads of condensation slide down her glass. She had to admit a life without her husband did sound attractive. But she couldn't do that to Hank.

Could she?

Six

That's What Friends Do

At nine o'clock the following morning Pam sat in her van, her left armpit positioned in front of the air-conditioning vent while Nancy helped Marlene load her carry-on into the rear compartment and then jumped in on the back bench beside Shalisa. Marlene opened Pam's passenger door and jolted to a stop.

Pam looked across the seat. "What is it? Did you forget something?"

Marlene stood frozen.

"Well?" Pam prodded.

"The last time I was in this van I'd just found out Dave had died." Marlene's face scrunched up.

Holy fuck! Pam had watched Marlene keep her eyes straight ahead as she'd locked her front door and given a wide berth to the faint stain on the asphalt where Dave's blood had pooled. But she hadn't expected her van to trigger a breakdown. Pam hurriedly unbuckled, launched herself from the driver's seat, and ran around to embrace her friend, rotating her to face away from the garage. Nancy and Shalisa climbed out, and the four women huddled under the hot sun.

Marlene sobbed. "I'm sorry."

Shalisa patted her back. "It's okay, Marlene. Sometimes the grief is going to hit you like a tsunami. Leaving your home is an emotional moment. You're allowed to be sad."

"Shalisa's right. It's okay," Nancy said, and then over Marlene's shoulder, checked her watch and whispered to Pam, "We're gonna miss our appointment."

Pam flashed a glare at Nancy and whispered back, "Are you for real? Since when have you worried about being on time?"

Nancy steeled her eyes. "It wasn't easy to get four side-by-sides at the last minute. I had to play the new-widow card." She gestured with her head toward Marlene.

The previous day, on Pam's patio, when they were hugging Marlene goodbye, Shalisa had looked down at Marlene's sandals and had shrieked, "You can't go to Boca Raton like that—you'll never make friends with those feet."

Shalisa was right. Marlene couldn't start her new life with raggedy cuticles and cracked heels, so they'd decided to squeeze in an emergency pit stop at the neighborhood nail salon on their way to the airport. Now, after coaxing Marlene into the van, easing her trauma by repositioning her to sit in the rear, Pam drove them along the bay to the nearby strip plaza. She smiled when Shalisa reached between the seats and turned up the volume and once again, Pam could feel the bass in her bum. It wasn't as strong as it used to be, but it was a start.

The nail salon wasn't a fancy place, but it was convenient. They used to be regulars—before—when they could afford to outsource their self-care.

Nancy said from the passenger seat, "Can we swing by my house? I forgot the coupon."

Pam scowled at her. "Two minutes ago you were worried about being late. Do you have any concept of time? Marlene has a flight to catch."

"I'm literally three minutes from here. It's for ten percent off."

"What is that? Three bucks? Surely we can each afford three bucks."

Marlene spoke up from the backseat, "I'll treat for the pedicures. It's the least I can do, seeing as I'm rich now." She chuckled. "You guys can treat me when your husbands are dead."

Pam didn't have to check to know Nancy and Shalisa's eyes were on her. A few minutes later Pam was watching her friends in another mirror, the large one on the salon's wall across from them. They were sitting side by side, vibrating in their massaging pedicure chairs with their feet soaking in tubs of soapy, hot water. Four nail technicians were gathered at the back of the shop in animated conversation.

Shalisa whispered, "What do you think they're talking about?"

Pam answered, "They're probably doing rock, paper, scissors to see who has to take Marlene."

Marlene threw her head back and laughed. "It's not my fault I have bunions. It was all those dance lessons as a kid." Marlene reached out to squeeze Pam's hand. "I'm gonna miss you."

Pam squeezed back. "You're going for two days."

"I know. I mean once I've moved. Permanently."

Pam squeezed again. "We'll Zoom. We'll visit. We're friends forever."

Marlene played with her controls until her cheeks began to jiggle as the chair's rollers worked their way up her back. "You know, I always thought you'd be first, Pam."

Nancy said, "Me too."

In the mirror, Pam saw Shalisa nod in agreement.

"What are you saying? You all thought Hank would die first. Uch. What a horrible thing to think."

Marlene said, "I only mean, you usually lead the way. You know, the first to sign up for fun fair, organize coaches' gifts, sell all your frozen chocolate chip cookie dough. I thought you'd lead us into widowhood too. I never dreamt I'd be first. Well, to be honest, I don't know why, but I always thought we'd do it together. Obviously, I didn't think about it clearly. But whenever I've pictured myself as being old, I'm always with you guys. Never with Dave. Is that weird?"

Nancy said, "No. I think the same thing. It's because we know women usually outlive men. So it's not weird. There's a study that says the happiest people are widows. I think it's because their husbands have given them their children, they've raised their families, and once their kids are grown and husbands are gone, the wives can do what they want."

Shalisa sighed. "Well, since Andre and I never had a family, all I've ever needed him for was to put up the Christmas tree. And last year Nancy found me an artificial one on sale, so now I don't need him at all."

Pam's eyes opened wide. "Shalisa! You're so harsh."

Marlene's phone rang, and she answered. They overheard mentions of open houses and closing dates.

Shalisa leaned forward so she could see Pam and lowered her voice. "Think what you want, Pam. I'm just saying out loud what you're thinking. We do not need our husbands. You and Nancy have had your kids. None of us are having sex anymore. They're not supporting us financially. They're no fun! What the fuck are they, beyond a lump on the sofa and a mouth at the table? If I were a widow, I'd be happy. And rich." She sat back.

Pam was relieved Marlene finished her phone call then.

Nancy said, "I think most women think they'll eventually end up widows. Just depends when. Some are sooner than later."

"Well. I did buy a four-bedroom condo. I hope you guys are sooner." Marlene thumped her chest, coughing a bit as she laughed.

"Me too," said Shalisa.

"Me three," said Nancy.

Avoiding eye contact with Nancy and Shalisa, Pam focused on the nail techs and was thankful when the group broke apart and turned toward them. "Here they come. Let's see who lost and got Marlene."

———

"Bon voyage," Pam called across the check-in area.

"Make friends, but no one better than us," said Nancy.

"At least with that pedicure, now she has a fighting chance," Shalisa said under her breath as she blew a kiss, then called, "See you soon."

They smiled as Marlene waved back one last time, then turned and wheeled her carry-on toward security screening.

Nancy's eyes followed her friend as she traveled through the stanchions. "I'm telling you, that could be us."

Shalisa said, "Don't I know it."

Pam shook her head. "Not me. I'll never wear capris again. They're old-lady clothes. I'm gonna tell Marlene the next time I see her."

Nancy said, "I'm sure she'll appreciate that."

Pam said, "That's what friends do. In our twenties we keep each other from being roofied; in our sixties we let each other know if we're doing old-lady shit and when it's time to pluck our chin hair."

Nancy moved in front to face Pam and Shalisa. "I meant, that could be us—moving to Boca Raton."

"Not this again. I know what you meant." Pam turned toward the exit, looking forward to getting outside and into the fresh air. She stopped, looked around, leaned in, and hissed at Nancy and Shalisa, "I'd like to be moving to Boca Raton too, but I already told you, I am not killing my husband." She locked eyes with one woman and then the other to let that sink in.

Nancy nodded for a moment and then pointed her finger at Pam's chest. "I tell you what, Pam, we'll make you a deal. You go home tonight, and you take a good look at Hank. Tomorrow, if you can tell us one way that he brings an ounce of joy to your life—just one—then we'll drop this, and I swear we'll never talk about it again. Right, Shalisa?"

Shalisa squinted one eye. "Well . . . maybe not nev—"

"Shalisa!"

"Okay. Okay. We'll never talk about it again."

Nancy stretched her arm in front of her, palm down. Shalisa placed her palm on top. Pam looked from one to the other, blew out her breath, then covered Shalisa's hand with her own.

"Fine. Deal."

⸺

Pam opened the fridge and shivered at the coolness. Elmer sauntered into the kitchen and watched her.

"How was your day?" she asked as he plunked down across the threshold.

Pam loved that her dog was indifferent to food. Even if she left a half-eaten ham sandwich on the coffee table, he'd roll by, sniff it, and keep going. On walks, strangers would offer him treats, and she'd be embarrassed when he'd delicately accept it, roll it around in his mouth, and spit it out. She got him a piece of beef jerky, which she knew he approved of, and he took it gently from her hand and carefully chewed it. Pam returned to the fridge.

Two nights ago, still hungry after Dave's funeral, Pam hadn't felt like cooking, so she'd allowed herself a rare treat and ordered in—Hank's budget be damned. She had selected chicken curry for him and, for herself, pad thai. Her absolute favorite food in the world. That was one of the things she missed now that she was poor—that's how she thought of their situation, no point in mincing words. She missed having other people cook for her.

She and Hank had never been rich, but they'd been on their way to a modest retirement when Hank got greedy. That's how Pam thought of it—no point in mincing words about that either. Pam knew Hank didn't mean for it to happen. It wasn't as though he woke up one day and said, "Hey, I'm gonna cash out our retirement plan without consulting my wife and give all our money, our hopes and dreams, to this slimy guy I met golfing. Better yet, let me talk our friends into giving him their money too, and then we can all wave goodbye to life as we know it, together." No. He didn't mean for it to happen. But it had.

Pam pushed those thoughts from her mind. Where was her pad thai? She hadn't had the appetite to finish it that night, so she'd put half in the fridge for later. All day she'd been thinking about heating it up, and she was famished. She could already feel the crunch of the peanuts on her tongue. She was shuffling Tupperware around in the fridge when Hank arrived home and bent down to pet Elmer in the doorway. Pam glanced at him and then went back to the fridge. "Did you see my pad thai?"

"I ate it."

Pam turned to look at him, the fridge still open. "You what?"

"I ate it."

"You ate my pad thai?"

"You were done. So I finished it."

"You finished my pad thai?"

"For fuck's sake, Pam. Yes. I finished the pad thai."

"*My* pad thai."

"*The* pad thai."

"Did you order it?"

"Well, no."

"Exactly. I ordered it. It was my pad thai. I get to eat it. Just because I don't finish it in one sitting doesn't mean it's up for grabs. Available to anyone who strolls by the fridge with a fork. It was my pad thai."

"Whatever." Hank rose, turned to go, then stopped. "And you know what, Pam? I wasn't even hungry."

Pam grabbed the door handle to steady herself. She watched Hank's back as he walked down the hall. After a moment she closed the fridge, picked her phone up off the kitchen counter, and sent a text.

Seven

Whatever Needs Doin'

H ank sat in a row of chairs with his back to the wall, scanning the strip plaza parking lot through the barbershop's storefront window. That's how it was now. Everywhere he went, Hank checked for suspicious faces or vehicles, in case Dave's killers were tracking him. The news reports he'd read about missing executives told tales of the victims abruptly disappearing from the street—being pushed into idling, curbside vehicles or dragged through open doorways. Never to be seen again. Well, at least, not seen *alive*.

Hank had googled *how to spot a tail* but didn't feel overly confident he'd absorbed anything useful. He didn't know who he was up against. With the casino ownership's ties to organized crime in India, he speculated head office could have sent someone from Mumbai. Or Padma sourced someone locally. He didn't know. What he did know was—he had to stay focused on not becoming their next victim.

If there was one thing anyone said about Hank Montgomery, it was that he doesn't go down without a fight. Not that he'd ever really been in a fight. At least, not since he'd played sports as a kid, and even then, he always wore the proper protective equipment. But Hank knew, when push came to shove, he would shove. But Hank also knew he was smarter than the average bear, so really, when push came to shove, he'd look for a way to dodge the push.

He peeled the wrapper off a Three Musketeers chocolate bar and rammed half in his mouth. And on top of everything else, he had Pam on him about pad thai. Fucking pad thai. But she was right, he shouldn't have eaten it. He knew it was her favorite. It was a moment of weakness, and he hadn't even considered what he was doing. He'd stood in front of the fridge with a fork in his hand and before he knew it, he'd eaten anything that wasn't moldy. He didn't know when he'd last had a proper meal, and shoveling the noodles in his mouth calmed his nerves, and these days, his nerves were a mess. He would have preferred a few scotches, but he had to keep his wits about him.

He pulled his phone from his pocket and saw that his daughter had sent him a photo. He clicked on it and smiled. Ran his thumb down the curve of Claire's cheek. She was holding up a fish. He couldn't tell what kind. Probably snapper. She was just like her old man. From the time she was a toddler she loved to join him on the water. He could hardly wait to take her and Pam fishing in New Zealand. It would be just like the old days. Plus Claire's husband, Dylan, would join them. He took tourists scuba diving for a living, he'd know where to find the big ones. What could be better?

Hank put his phone away and stuffed the last half of the chocolate bar in his cheek, tossed the wrapper in the trash, and chewed. After a moment he chased it with a Tums tablet and grabbed a fishing magazine from the dog-eared stack on the barbershop table. He rolled it and unrolled it. Normally, he'd dive into an article while he waited, but today he couldn't even focus on the pictures; they bounced as his leg jiggled. He looked at the empty chair beside him and wished he could see Dave's long limbs stretched out in front of him, his scuffed boots crossed at the ankles. The two of them quietly chatting until they'd split apart if other casino workers happened in. He missed his pal. He pushed the heel of his hand against the knot in his chest that had appeared when he had found Dave on his driveway. Hank wasn't sure if it was grief, fear, or indigestion; he just wanted it to go away.

Finally, Hector finished with his teenage customer, whipped the kid's cape off, and shook out the trimmings. Hank slid into the red leather seat. "Number two all around, straight at the back. And hit the eyebrows."

Hank had been coming to this shop since he and Pam moved to the neighborhood. He thought back ten years to when Hector had become the new owner. How the barber had directed Hank into the chair with a nod, then draped the cape around him with a flourish, like a matador waving at a bull. His dark hair had been slicked back, and his deep-set eyes pitch black. The absence of typical barber banter had put Hank on edge. Silently, Hector had inspected his tools before making his selection and then had snapped open his straight razor and stepped toward the chair. The hairs on Hank's arms had shot to attention.

Hank had sat perfectly still, barely breathing, while Hector had scraped his sharp blade along the edge of Hank's hairline above his ears and the nape of his neck. When the barber came alongside him and lifted his arm, Hank had caught a glimpse inside the sleeve of his guayabera shirt. He had hoped Hector didn't notice his quick intake of breath when he'd spotted the scars—parallel, angry, red, puckered lines scored the tender area under Hector's right arm, as though someone had dragged a rake deeply across his torso. Or branded him with one. When Hector had moved to his other side, Hank had peeked again and seen a matching set on his left. They were so precise that Hank could only imagine what had put them there. What had this man been through? What had he done?

Hank had cleared his throat. "Wh-where are you from originally, Hector?"

"El Salvador."

"You don't say. What did you do there?"

Hector had paused, then said, "Whatever needs doin'."

Hector and Hank had locked eyes in the mirror. Hank had worked to sit still while a chill had slithered down his spine. Hank had read about eyes like Hector's. They called it the thousand-yard stare. Dead eyes. Eyes that had seen too much.

After that first visit, Hank had made a point of keeping his own eyes open when he was in Hector's shop every four weeks or so. He had noted who came and went through the barber's front door, and the back. And while Hector had been discreet, once, when he slid the drawer open in search of a different pair of scissors, Hank had glimpsed a gun. Going to the restroom, Hank had peeked into the tidy office at the back and noticed a safe, much like he would expect at a jeweler's, but overkill for what was needed in a barbershop. In a normal barbershop, at least.

Managing the casino, Hank saw all sorts of people come through those doors. The posers and the real thing. Occasionally, he would look up from his desk and spot Hector's broad shoulders cross the frame of the surveillance monitor while he traversed the casino floor. Alone. Not talking to anyone. With just a touch of swagger. Always unhurried, relaxed. And he would exit. Then invariably, a few minutes later, someone from the casino's To Watch List would leave by the same door, following the barber out. The fact that Hector didn't have his own spot on the casino's list spoke volumes. Hank speculated the barber was deep into something, but so good at it he could still live in plain sight. Hank had decided if he ever had trouble, Hector was his guy.

And now he had trouble.

Hank's hands trembled as Hector brushed the hair from his shoulders, undid the cape, and patted the Bay Rum aftershave on the pink skin at the back of Hank's neck. Hank swallowed and locked eyes with Hector in the mirror.

"Hector?"

The barber raised his eyebrows.

"I think I have a job for you."

"What kind of job?"

"A thing that needs doin'."

Hector nodded while he slowly reached for his straight razor, flicked it shut with one hand, and tucked it into his front pocket.

Hank swallowed. "Someone is trying to kill me, Larry, and our buddy Andre. We want you to kill them."

Hector folded his arms. "Tell me more."

Eight

Recommended Viewing

Pam sat in Shalisa's driveway. She switched off the engine and the temperature immediately began to creep upward. Sweat clung to the hair at the nape of her neck. If she didn't either lower the windows, turn the air-conditioning back on, or drive away, she'd end up a news headline:

Local Woman of Retirement Age Dies in Overheated Car
The stench of Pam Montgomery's corpse was masked by the smell of the rotting lunch she packed for work each day to save a few bucks because she was poor.

Pam only had a couple minutes to decide.

Nancy's compact car wasn't in the driveway, meaning she was late as usual, but at least with that huge juniper blocking the living room window, Shalisa wouldn't have noticed Pam sitting in her minivan debating whether or not she wanted to kill her husband. That unruly bush was an eyesore in front of such a pretty house. Pam knew Shalisa had been pestering Andre for months to get rid of it, and yet there it stood.

Another way their husbands let them down.

Pam studied herself in the rearview mirror. Was she really going to do this? Did she really want to do this? It was one thing to bat around the idea of killing their husbands over a bottle of expensive champagne, two more of cheap pinot grigio, and then at the airport, but it was another to go to someone's house with the sole purpose of meeting to plot a murder. She corrected herself—murders.

If she got out of her van, she was crossing a line she'd never be able to hop back over. Pam pictured herself handcuffed, in an orange jumpsuit with frizzy hair in a jailhouse interview with Keith Morrison, maybe even Lesley Stahl from *60 Minutes*. She imagined sitting at a table with the other inmates, spooning prison hash off a tin tray. Then she remembered her fridge and her leftover pad thai and the casual way Hank had tossed "whatever" at her as he had walked away. And the daughter she couldn't afford to see, being 8,500 miles and sixteen time zones away. Pam collected her purse, opened the car door, walked up the driveway, and let herself in Shalisa's front door.

"I thought Andre was going to cut that down for you." Pam nodded to the juniper.

Shalisa rolled her eyes. "I gave him one hell of an ultimatum the other day, but with everything that's been going on, you know, our friend dying and all"—she smiled at her weak joke—"looks like he's put it off again. Anyway, the way Andre does what I ask him, I'll be sitting in a wheelchair adjusting my oxygen tube before he gets around to it. Maybe now I'll hire a gardener. Come on into the kitchen."

It seemed Shalisa was already spending the insurance money. Pam smiled, thinking her first purchase would be a one-way ticket to see Claire. She'd have to figure out how to ship Elmer there. Maybe she could buy him a seat in the cabin or get him deemed a service animal. That might be a stretch, but she'd cross that bridge when she got there. She followed Shalisa down the hall to her kitchen, remembering the last time she was here they had comforted Marlene around that same table.

This morning the merry widow had texted pictures of her new condo and said that she'd be back that night to officially put her and Dave's house on the market. Pam pulled out a chair while Shalisa poured her a coffee. They'd decided to meet here because there was less chance of a husband dropping in unexpectedly. Andre ran a courier storefront as a one-man show and never left, having to receive and dispatch deliveries all day, whereas Hank at the casino, and Larry at the bank, seemed to have more flexibility, and often popped home for lunch or an errand during the day.

Pam checked her watch. "Nancy knows we said noon, right? I have to be back to the office by one."

Shalisa raised an eyebrow and nodded. Coffees in hand, they sat in silence until Shalisa said in a quiet voice, "Are we really going to do this?"

Pam felt a weight lift from her shoulders, and she could have hugged Shalisa. "No. We're not." Shalisa had committed to the idea so quicky, it was a relief to see she wasn't on board. Pam took a sip of her coffee. "We're just talking about it. It's like that murder mystery game we played for my sixtieth birthday. Just for fun. We're bandying about a crazy idea. That's all. Maybe it'll be the plot for a book we can write. People do that, you know. Reinvent themselves in their sixties."

They heard the front door open and the skitter of Nancy's flip-flops down the hall until she slid onto a chair at the table. "Did I miss anything?"

Pam looked at her watch. "What are you using to tell time these days? A sundial?"

Nancy waved her off. "I had to finish my research."

Shalisa said, "Listen. Pam and I were just chatting. I know we had a couple of bottles of wine the other day, and then we got emotional dropping Marlene off. But we talked about it and all, and just to be upfront about everything, we're not really going to *do* anything. I know—"

"—Oh. We're doing this." Nancy reached into her purse and withdrew folded papers. "Larry made me choose between him and my son, and I've chosen my son. And Shalisa, if you want to know what you mean to Andre, just look at that juniper at your front window. How long have you been asking your husband to take care of that for you?"

Shalisa grimaced.

"Exactly." Nancy unfolded the the papers and pushed them to the center of the table.

Pam glanced at the heading at the top—*OPERATION HUSBANDS*.

"Are you fucking kidding me? You typed this on your computer. When? Right after you googled *how to kill my husband*? Look. Even if we were crazy enough to go ahead with this, we're already off on the wrong foot." Pam tapped the pages with her forefinger. "We are begging to get caught. We are literally *Lucy and Ethel plan a murder.*"

Nancy cocked her head. "I'm not stupid. I did it at the library."

Shalisa squinched her face and asked, "Who are Lucy and Ethel?"

Pam ignored Shalisa and clutched her chest. "Where you work! You realize if someone dies violently, spouses are the first suspects, and the police will do due diligence and investigate us and our computers. Work computers too. That's the first place they'll look in a murder investigation. Don't you watch any TV?" Then she turned to Shalisa. "How did you spend your childhood? The *I Love Lucy* show. You know, Lucy Ricardo and Ethel Mertz."

Shalisa tilted her head. "Wait. Weren't they kind of bumbling—? Ohhh." She nodded slowly.

Pam locked eyes with her. "Exactly." Then turned back to Nancy.

Nancy straightened the papers and tapped her list. "Point number one. Make it look like an accident. No investigation. Look what happened to Dave. He died in a freak accident, and Marlene had the money within the week." She handed them each a sheet.

Pam said, "You made copies! Did you leave the extras in the library wastebasket?"

"No, I did not. And you each owe me two bucks."

Pam recoiled. "Seriously? You're charging us for photocopies?"

Nancy had the decency to look a touch abashed. "Well. I had to pay for them. I'm just trying to keep things fair."

Pam leveled her gaze at Nancy and crossed her arms. "The last time we were together I drove the four of us to the airport. That probably cost eight dollars in gas, so you each owe me two bucks. We're even."

Shalisa sat quietly on the other side of the table as though watching a tennis match, her mouth closed tight.

Nancy put her hand up. "Sorry. Point taken. Sometimes I go overboard."

Pam tapped her chin. "And I'm pretty sure you used my Wet Ones to wipe up the coffee you spilled in my backseat. The coffee that I bought for you and did not charge you for. Those Wet Ones are at least two cents each. I think you used ten."

Nancy squinted. "Well, you did come in pretty hot on that corner."

"What do you think, Shalisa? Or did she use twelve?"

Shalisa shook her head. "Nope."

"Let's leave it at ten. So you owe me twenty cents."

"I get it!!" Nancy said. "I'm sorry. I didn't mean to be so petty."

"Ah." Pam pointed at her and smiled. "That's the word. It's bad enough when you pull out a calculator at lunch, but really . . ."

Nancy scowled at Pam. "Okay, okay. I'm sorry. I got carried away. I've had some money issues the past few years. In case you didn't know. What can I say? Can we please get back to business? I'll pay for the photocopies. Satisfied?" Pam nodded, and Nancy continued. "Okay. So, it may interest you to know, I've taken a couple courses on cybersecurity. We have to, at the library. I used the public-access computers, I did my searches using incognito mode, and just to be safe, I created phony usernames and logins. Anyway, nothing I searched online is incriminating, and I mostly went old school."

Pam and Shalisa looked at her blankly.

"Books. I looked things up in books. No cyber trail. There are only so many ways to kill people, and it hasn't changed much over the years. So the research is done, and this is what I'm thinking." Nancy picked up her piece of paper. "And we'll burn these before we leave here."

Pam and Shalisa looked at each other. Was Shalisa concerned Nancy was full speed ahead on murder highway and they were riding in her backseat? Pam couldn't read her expression, but if she had to guess, she'd say Shalisa was impressed.

OPERATION HUSBANDS

THE PLAN

1. Needs to look like an accident—no murder investigation.
2. Need identifiable bodies—for insurance claims.
3. Need to die in one event—too coincidental for the 3 of them to die separately.

RECOMMENDED VIEWING:

1. Strangers on a Train—Alfred Hitchcock
   Synopsis: Two discontented husbands meet on a train and agree to murder each other's spouse.
2. Horrible Bosses—with Jason Bateman
   Synopsis: Three disgruntled workers hire a hitman who advises them to murder each other's bosses.
3. Bad Sisters—with Sharon Horgan
   Synopsis: Four sisters plot to get rid of the fifth sister's horrible prick husband. They try 5 times.

"Five times!" Pam said. "They had to try five times!"

"Well, it's a TV series. They had to keep it going for ten episodes. They couldn't very well have him die on the first try, could they? That wouldn't be a series—that'd be a movie."

"I guess so," Pam said, and Shalisa nodded.

"But the point is, those women were smart. I won't spoil it for you. But you should watch it. It's really good." Nancy nudged her glasses up her nose. "And it worked."

Pam pushed her paper away. "The only thing I see here that we could use is hire a hitman. I don't know how else we do it. I'm not personally killing anybody." Pam had her limits, and they included poor upper body strength. She knew enough to avoid heavy lifting, and she couldn't envision a way to kill three men that didn't involve moving them. If there was ever a job to outsource, this was it. Especially since their husbands had packed on the pounds in the last few years. She raised an eyebrow at Nancy. "Do you think you can find a hitman on Craigslist?"

Nancy offered a weak smile. Shalisa refilled their coffees and set a plate of chocolate chip cookies on the table. They each took one and started nibbling.

Pam shook her head and looked at Shalisa. "Are we sure we want to do this?" Then she looked at Nancy. "No offense, Nancy. I can see how angry you are with Larry, and I get it. I honestly didn't know he was . . . such a close-minded prick. Maybe we can talk some sense into him. Surely being married to him can't be so bad you've gotta kill him?"

Nancy broke her cookie in half, studied it a moment, and then said, "It didn't used to be. Even as angry as I was at Larry for ruining everything financially, he was still okay to have around. He'd catch mice, change the hallway lightbulb, mow the lawn, and shovel the driveway. Better than doing it myself. But the night he told Paul he didn't even want to meet Estuardo, we were done." Nancy drew her finger across her throat. "From that moment on we were roommates, Pam. Nothing more. And not even good ones. We watch TV in separate rooms, we sleep in separate beds. The only meals we eat together are if we're out with you guys. So now that there's another option in front of me, I want to take it."

Pam swallowed and turned her luck to Shalisa. "Do you really want to do this? There's no turning back."

Shalisa took a bite of her cookie and chewed it slowly before she answered. "You know what I was just thinking?"

Pam and Nancy shook their heads.

Shalisa held her cookie up. "I was thinking this is the first cookie I've eaten in my kitchen in months. Maybe even years. I only bake them when Andre's out, and then I hide them in the back of the freezer, under the frozen fruit. If Andre's home and I want something sweet, I sneak them up to my bedroom. Sometimes I sit on the floor of my closet with a magazine and a stack of cookies. I'm a grown-ass woman and that man is always on me about my diet and keeping active. 'Move it or lose it.' He has me sneaking food in my own home. Hell, yeah. I want to do this. Like I told you, I'm tired of my life being *not that bad*. I'm ready for my life to be what I deserve it to be. Fucking fantastic."

Pam tapped her fingers on the table and then said, "We could just leave them."

They considered that for a moment, and then Nancy answered, "But then we wouldn't have the money. Larry's the one thing I can cash in. Don't get me wrong. I'm not killing him out of spite. I'm killing him for the money. I'm not being vindictive. I'm making a business transaction."

Shalisa said, "Me too. I don't want Andre dead for revenge. In my mind I'm trading him in for a million dollars. And it's a good deal." Then she looked at Pam. "We have to be all in or all out. What about you, Pam?"

Pam cradled her mug and watched a squirrel traverse the branches of Shalisa's backyard maple tree. She thought about how Nancy wanted to see her son. How Shalisa wanted her life to be *fucking fantastic*. What did she want? She sniffed her coffee and remembered how Hank's morning kiss used to taste like roasted chicory. She touched her fingers to her lips and tried to remember the last time she'd been kissed. It's not that she needed to live in the fire of some great love, but did she want to live in the ashes of hers? Could anything be sadder than not knowing when it's time to let go?

Shalisa repeated, "What about you, Pam?"

Would Hank ever again bend down to kiss her cheek as he passed by? Would he?

"No. I mean yes. Yes, I'm in."

"All right, then. Let's get a move on. I have to get back to work and find a hitman." Nancy looked at Pam. "That's how you want to do it, right? We hire a hitman?"

Pam nodded. "I think that makes the most sense. You?" She looked at Shalisa.

Shalisa nodded. "Agreed." And looked at Nancy. "Do you have recommended viewing for that?"

"Just *Horrible Bosses*. It's on the list"—Nancy pointed to her paper—"but in the end, Jamie Foxx didn't work out."

Shalisa took another cookie. "So, where do we find ours?"

Nancy looked out the window and traced her fingers along her lips. Pam drummed hers on the table. Then Nancy turned to them and said, "Hector."

"Fuck. Yeah. Hector," Pam said.

"Hector?" Shalisa said.

"Hector the barber. The guys have been going to him for years. Remember? Hank always said if he ever needed to hire anyone to do . . . how did he put it? To do 'whatever needs doin',' he'd hire Hector," Pam said.

"Oh! Hector!" Shalisa said. "I remember them talking about him. What do they call him?"

"Dead Eyes," Nancy said.

"Right. Hank said when you look at his eyes in the mirror, it's like they've seen too many bad things to have any life left in them," Pam explained.

"I used to take Paul there, but I think that was right about when he was realizing he was more of a salon type of guy."

"Could be. I imagine gay men would probably prefer more upscale after-shave than the one Hector uses. His Bay Rum special reeks," Pam said.

Nancy scrunched her nose. "I can always tell Larry's had his hair cut without even looking at him. Just by that smell."

They sipped their coffees.

"What's the going rate for murder, do you think?" Shalisa said.

"Thirty thousand dollars," Nancy answered.

"You google that too?" Pam said.

Nancy shook her head. "*Mr. Inbetween.* Another really good show. We should add it to the recommended-viewing list. It's Australian. It's about a hitman who's also raising his little girl. In one scene he goes out and knocks someone off—like, violently hacks them to death—and in the next scene he's telling his daughter he believes in unicorns. It's really good. Anyway, he charges thirty thousand dollars."

"Each! For three that's almost a hundred thousand dollars!" Shalisa said.

Pam suggested, "Maybe we can get a deal if they're all together. Kind of like buy two, get one free. Because, really, it's just one job. Let's offer forty-five. That's one and a half times the thirty."

Nancy said, "*Mr. Inbetween* negotiated like that once."

"Where are we going to get forty-five thousand dollars?" Shalisa asked.

Pam thought about her bank account with its three-digit balance and her maxed-out credit card.

"Marlene," Nancy said.

"What?" Pam and Shalisa said at the same time.

"Marlene will lend it to us," Nancy said.

Pam said, "You should add to your list. Point number four: We need to *not* tell anyone else about this. That's how people get caught. We can't tell anyone, especially Marlene. She has no filter."

Nancy shook her head. "We won't tell her what it's for. We'll make something up. Like, tell her you want a hot tub. We'll figure it out." She waved away their concern. "We'll make it a business proposition and offer her interest, like an investment. She knows she'll get it back, eventually. She knows we'll have insurance money coming to us. The guys are going to die sooner or later. We're just making it sooner."

Shalisa nodded. "So, we've got the money, we just need the hitman."

Pam checked her watch. "How do we get to Hector?"

Nine

Depends on You

H ank always had to shower after a haircut. The tiny trimmings that escaped down the back of his collar itched, plus the Bay Rum aftershave Hector slapped on his neck made him smell like the end of a medicated cotton swab.

Pulling into his driveway at midday triggered Hank's memory to his gruesome discovery at Dave's house. He turned his head a bit and squinted as he cautiously checked his own garage. Once he was sure the door was closed, with nothing sticking out, he loosened his grip on the steering wheel. Pam was probably at work, although he might have heard her mention something about taking the morning off. Wherever she was, she wasn't here, so he could go straight in.

Used to be, Hank's mood would brighten when he turned the corner and saw Pam's van in the driveway. She would be inside, waiting for him. There was always something that had happened during the day he'd rush to tell her about. But these past few years, he would need to park and brace himself for the cold temperature inside. Even though there was no air-conditioning in this rental, there always seemed to be a chill.

A few minutes later, Hank stepped out of his shower to find Elmer lying across the bathroom's threshold. "Where did you come from, bud? Were you snoozing when I got home?"

Hank absolutely would have said no if he'd been asked about getting Elmer. But he wasn't asked. One day Pam showed up with this mutt and said he'd be here a few weeks, and then he never left. But Hank had to admit, Elmer was a great dog. He was always there, quietly taking everything in, like a wise old man. And when Hank was alone on the sofa, staring at the TV, wondering what the hell he'd gotten himself into, Elmer would spring up from the floor, land beside him, and rest his head on Hank's thigh, rolling over so Hank would rub his belly. And they'd stay like that for a while: two buddies sitting on the sofa.

Now, in the doorway of the bathroom, Elmer rolled over on his back and Hank fulfilled the familiar request and scratched. Then he wiped the steam from the mirror with his towel and took a good look at himself. How the fuck had he ever gotten here?

Hank was used to firing people. When you're high up at one of the area's biggest employers, people tend to ask for favors. Ninety percent of the time things worked out. Well, maybe seventy. Perhaps sixty. Regardless, everyone understands it's not personal, it's business. He'd had to fire a buddy's son who got caught jerking off in the customer washrooms and had to give final warning to a young father for working under the influence. He'd felt responsible because he'd overseen their hiring. It was Hank's job. From managers to janitors.

So it had been easy for Hank to hire Dave Brand.

They'd been tight for about fifteen years when Dave got laid off from his IT job. One day, when they were out fishing, Dave had told Hank about an employment training program he could take, but if he finished it, he'd be hitting Hank up for work.

"Go for it," Hank had said.

Hank had expected Dave would be great as a video slot machine tech. A bit of a geek, he was smart, resourceful, and reliable. Hank's only caution to Dave had been to not let on how well they knew each other. "Not great for the others to know we hang out so much. They'll look for preferential treatment and see it, even if it's not there."

But there'd been no problems. There were three thousand other employees, and Dave's work was mostly on the casino floor and in the basement maintenance area while Hank was usually upstairs on the second and third floors. When their paths crossed, they were cordial, but not familiar. They'd never been much for going out in public together. Since their friendship had stemmed from their kids, they had gotten to know each other at backyard barbecues and kitchen potlucks, and that's where their socializing had remained. As the kids grew up and moved on, the wives had kept the gatherings going, even after they had lost their money in the investment deal Hank had suggested.

It could have worked. But bad timing and bad markets had made for another story. It had been a financial debacle for them all. Dave, Larry, and Andre included. Hank could have drowned in the guilt. So many times he'd kicked himself for getting the guys involved, but he was generous by nature and had felt it was such a sure thing, he had wanted to share. Another guy in the neighborhood had come out all right on the other side of his investment—that awful Sabrina Cuomo's husband. Surely if good things could happen to that dolt, they could happen to Hank. But being set for retirement wouldn't be fun without the company of his best pals. So he had eagerly brought them in on the deal. But the investment had gone south. Way south. Like to Antarctica, where it died surrounded by penguins and whales—metaphorically speaking.

And now, that financial ruin was only bearable because of those best pals.

As the guys fell into their new reality, they found comfort in each other that they couldn't find at home. There, Hank knew, they each cowered under the shame. Even when their wives weren't vocal, their silence messaged their disappointment loud and clear. And through it all, Dave had shown up for work every day, as Hank had expected.

But Hank hadn't expected Dave to come up with their new retirement plan.

———

Just over four years ago, Hank had returned from enjoying his morning coffee with Andre at his shop and was sitting at his desk when Dave had knocked, his backpack slung over his shoulder. "Got a minute?"

Hank had waved him in, and Dave shut the door behind him. Hank put his pen down and leaned back in his chair, his brows drawn together. Dave never came by his office. Hank gestured to the chair on the other side of his desk. Dave looked around, took in the photos of Pam and their daughter, sat down, and pointed to the bank of surveillance monitors. "Are conversations recorded in here?"

Hank shook his head.

"No cameras?"

Hank shook his head again.

Dave thought a moment, nodded, and then scooted his chair close and crossed his arms on Hank's desk and began, his voice low, "You know those new video slot machines we got in? I found a glitch."

"Wha-at? That's impossible."

Dave raised his eyebrows.

"What do you mean? A glitch?" Hank asked.

"You monitor the cash flow in this place, right?"

"Every day. It's part of my job."

"Have you noticed anything *irregular* the last couple weeks or so?"

Hank thought for a moment. "No."

Dave reached for his backpack. "No cameras, right?" He checked the room's corners.

Hank said, again, "No."

Dave unzipped his backpack and positioned it so Hank could peek inside. Hank's head snapped back. "What the fuck?" Hank stood and stretched across his desk to get a better look. He studied the cash bundles, bound with bands. Not the paper straps the casino used, but the elastic type that holds bunches of broccoli together. Hank looked at his friend and said in a low voice, "What the fuck have you done?"

"Depends," Dave said.

"What do you mean, depends?"

"Depends on you."

Hank started to reach for the desk phone.

Dave lightly touched his wrist. "Well, here's the thing, Hank. What have I done? I've either saved the casino from ever being swindled out of millions of dollars by anyone else who figures out this little programming glitch, or"— Dave paused and looked straight into Hank's eyes—"I've fixed our retirement plan." Dave waggled his eyebrows.

They withdrew their hands from the phone. Dave sat back and smiled.

Hank's head spun. He thought he might vomit in his wastebasket. He hadn't felt like this since he'd watched Pam give birth. His skin had suddenly become uncomfortably cold. He sat down with a thud. Firing that kid for jerking off in the men's room was one thing, but this was different. If Dave went to jail, Pam would make him mow Marlene's lawn and shovel her driveway. Fuck. He looked up.

Dave had zipped up his backpack. "You okay?"

Hank nodded.

"I know. It's a lot. I couldn't believe it the first time it worked. But I've done it five times now. And you're saying no red flags have gone up."

"Five times! Fuck! Dave!" Hank yelled. He lowered his voice. "What the fuck are you doing?"

Dave folded his hands across his flat belly. "You're one of the smartest guys I know, Hank. You're fucking fantastic at your job. Everyone knows that. I lied. I've actually been doing this for a month. I've done it ten times." Dave smiled and, in that moment, Hank understood why women did double takes when they passed him.

Hank raised his hand. "Don't tell me any more. I have to call security. I have to call the police."

"You can call the police if you want, Hank. We'll all be okay. I'll tell them I found a loophole in our security. That I've been testing it out, and I've turned in the money to you as proof." Dave patted his backpack. "This is it. All the money. But do you have to make that call, Hank? Do you? You didn't notice these payouts. And if you didn't notice, no one will."

Hank felt the thump of his heart against his ribs. Sweat prickled his forehead and started to drip down his back. He reached for his bottle of water, but it was empty. He licked his lips. "How much is there?" He squinted at the backpack as though it might explode.

"Thirty-seven thousand dollars."

"What!"

"I could have got more, but if you cash in over five grand at a time you have to show ID."

"You've been cashing in vouchers? In my casino?"

"No." Dave waved dismissively. "I've been getting other people to do it. Marlene's family was visiting, so I used her brothers a couple times. Told them my coworker won, explained employees aren't allowed to play at the casino, told them they had to keep it quiet. Not even tell Marlene. Marlene's brothers were finally good for something. And then they went home." Dave smiled. He looked proud of his ingenuity. "We have a plan, and we know it will work."

"We?"

Dave sat back, crossed his arms over his chest, and winked. "We."

Ten

Don't Be Afraid

Hector Chavez's favorite part of his day was wiping down his barber chair while he waited for his next customer. He loved the smell of Barbicide and the way one pass of a white paper towel across the smoothness of the red leather erased the day's grime.

He wished all his jobs were as easy to clean up.

Hector lifted the no smoking sign off the counter, passed the cloth underneath, and then picked up the desktop calendar, catching a glimpse of the year. More than a decade had passed since Hector had left Ilopango, El Salvador, after the gang truce fell apart. The two years of peace a Catholic bishop and a former guerrilla soldier had negotiated among the local gang leaders had given Hector a taste of the life he had loved to watch on American television, sitting on his mother's battered sofa: dads working in bakeries, auto shops, or barbershops and going home at the end of their workday to happy wives and children. Toasters on the kitchen counter, ice cream in the freezer, curtains on the windows. So when the truce had fallen apart and gang tags had begun reappearing on buildings and bodies showing up in alleys, some young men had started looking for better options. Hector was one of the lucky ones. He got out. He had headed for the nearby resort town, used his good looks to warm a lonely American's heart, and had married his way to a new life.

Coming from the country with the world's highest murder rate, Hector had developed some habits early in life that he'd never shake, like checking if doors locked behind him and if strange people lurked outside. That's why, when he was giving the high school kid a number-one fade on the sides, the van cruising the strip plaza's parking lot caught his eye.

As he moved to the kid's left, he watched the vehicle in the mirror as it slowed and passed by his storefront, circled back to the far end of the parking lot, and reversed into a space. Periodically, Hector checked to find the van still there. The plaza was a two-story strip of eight storefronts with apartments above. Half the structure was occupied by Hector's shop, a bakery, a dry cleaner, and a nail salon. The other half housed a bowling alley that was a popular destination for birthday parties. Hector was used to seeing minivans in the parking lot. They regularly pulled up, and kids poured out carrying brightly wrapped presents. But this was different. There were no kids tumbling from this van. It remained parked while Hector moved on to the next customer and clipped away at the young dad's fringe.

The barber liked doing those kinds of styles best. Anyone can drag clippers over someone's scalp, but to separate and hold strands of hair between your fingers and snip away at your own discretion—that required skill. So when Hector cut one piece too short, his eyes flashed to that van, perturbed by its distraction.

He cashed the dad out, swept his trimmings up from the floor, gathered the garbage, and slipped out the shop's back door. As he moved along the rear of the strip plaza, he crouched, peered around the corner of the dumpster, and zeroed in on the van. He watched for a few moments, then, satisfied, quietly tossed his trash and returned to his shop.

Hector gave one more buzz cut, a two on the side, three on the top, wiped down his red leather chair, and was locking up when he heard the van's motor turn over. As he closed the shop's door he pretended to fumble with his key, giving himself time to watch the vehicle's approach in the door's reflection. This would be interesting. He turned to face the parking lot. The van slowed to a stop in front of him, and its side door slid open.

"Hector, don't be afraid," the dark-haired woman said from the backseat as she pushed her glasses up her nose.

———

From his vantage point behind the dumpster, Hector had recognized the van's driver, the skinny one with the blond bob, as Hank's wife—he recalled her periodically popping her head in to pass on some message to her husband as he sat in the chair. Hector had hugged the brick wall and watched as one of the other women had passed her a box. She'd selected a donut, licked the white powder off her fingers, and had brushed away the sprinkles dusting her T-shirt. He'd thought the dark-haired woman in the back looked like Larry's wife. He doubted she was Dave's wife, as Hector recalled someone saying she was moving to Florida. Too bad about Dave. Not many guys that age could pull off a pompadour like he had. Virtually no recession at the hairline or thinning on the crown, and he'd been over sixty. So if those were Hank and Larry's wives, and Dave's was moving away, then the woman in the passenger seat, with the braids, was most likely their buddy Andre's wife. A big, friendly guy, Andre had his own barber but would occasionally come in to collect one of his pals on their way fishing.

When the van door slid open, the woman added, "We'd like to talk to you. Privately. Would you mind joining us?" She scooted across the bench to sit behind the driver.

As Hector hopped in, he smiled at the women and asked, "Got any donuts left?"

Their gasps of surprise rolled into titters of laughter.

"Oh, you're good," Hank's wife said. "I told you guys he'd be good." She put the van in gear and pulled ahead to park in a spot on the other side of the lot. She lifted her driver's seat arm and pivoted to face him.

The woman on the passenger side released her seat and spun it around, as if she were about to pull out a deck of cards and deal a hand of euchre. She passed him the almost empty box of donuts, and he studied the selection, giving himself time to think. He decided on the sour cream–glazed and to say as little as possible. Did they know Hank had already hired him? Is that why they were here? Were they worried about their husbands' safety and wanted to check that things were on track? His smartest move was to listen. He took a bite and accepted the offered bottle of water.

Hank's wife started. "I think you might have a sense of who we are, but we don't think we should get into that yet." She cleared her throat. "We know you have a very particular set of skills. Skills you have acquired over a very long career. Skills that can make you a nightmare for some people."

Was she quoting *Taken*? Hector took another bite of his donut. He loved Liam Neeson in that movie. Even the sequel. On the periphery he could see the other two women, on the edge of their seats, nodding.

The one beside him, Larry's wife, jumped in. "We'd like to hire that set of skills."

"Skills?" Hector said. His wife had taught him the trick of dealing with people in sticky situations: Repeat their last word. That keeps them talking and they'll tell you more, but it also gives you time to figure out what the fuck is going on.

"Yes, your skills," Hank's wife said. "We'll cut to the chase, Hector. It's just us in this van, and our word against yours if this conversation ever goes any further. Can we speak frankly?"

"Frankly?" Hector said.

"Yes. Frankly. We're going to put our cards on the table." Hank's wife looked at Andre's wife. "You tell him."

"Me?" Andre's wife jumped back a bit.

"Yes. You. It was your idea," Hank's wife said.

"My idea! I don't think it was *my* idea. It was Nancy's idea." Andre's wife looked at the woman beside him on the bench seat.

"I thought we weren't using names," Nancy said. "Shalisa." She looked at the driver. "And Pam."

Okay. His wife was right yet again. Now he knew their names. Hector opened his water bottle and took a swig. His wife had three sisters, and he knew enough to keep quiet.

Pam scowled at the other two women, cleared her throat, and looked at Hector. "Okay. We'd like to hire you to do a hit."

It was a good thing Hector had already swallowed or he might have spurted out his mouthful of water. But he had long ago learned to hold a poker face. Sometimes his wife asked if his facial muscles had died off when he was a teenager. He'd explained to her that a blank face is less likely to get someone stabbed, so Hector had perfected it. And he used it now, but it wasn't easy. "A hit?" he repeated.

"*Hits*," Nancy said. Pam and Shalisa nodded.

"Plural." Shalisa stared at him intently.

Pam took a deep breath, then exhaled. "We want you to knock off our husbands."

Of all the things Hector imagined these women could have said to him in this van, that was not one of them. Hector worked to keep his face still and decided he'd better be careful about his swigs of water. What else could come out of these women's mouths?

Nancy said, "But it has to look like an accident. We don't want a murder investigation, or suspicion of suicide. And . . . and . . . what else?" She and the other women exchanged looks. Nancy fumbled in her pocket and pulled out a piece of paper.

"You brought notes?" Pam said.

"Good thing I did. Lotta help you two are." She unfolded the paper and pushed her glasses to the top of her head. She positioned the page to catch the light and squinted. "Oh yeah. It has to happen all together. Not separate incidents. And bodies." She looked at Hector. "The bodies have to be found."

Shalisa explained, "So we don't have to wait seven years for the insurance money."

Ah. They wanted to kill their husbands for their insurance money. This was like a *Law & Order* episode. "How many?" Hector asked.

"Three," Pam said.

Hank had been right. Someone was trying to kill them. It had occurred to Hector perhaps his longtime customer was suffering a bit of paranoia, brought on by his buddy's death. But Hank had never said outright it was their wives. Sometimes the truth is a difficult pill to swallow. And to say out loud. Even to your barber.

Hector learned a long time ago not to ask about motives. Because people lie about that. And sometimes the motives were fucked up. But he had three wives wanting their husbands dead. And three husbands wanting him to kill whoever it was who wanted them dead. Obviously there was a decision to be made here. He'd have to talk it over with his wife.

"How much do you charge?" Nancy asked.

"Fifty grand."

The women looked pleased.

"Each," Hector added.

"Each!" Nancy said. "We were hoping we could get a group discount."

Hector took another swig of water. "You can hope all you want. One-fifty for the three."

"Maybe we could go to seventy-five," Nancy said.

Hector edged forward to leave.

"Okay, okay. One-fifty." Nancy raised her palms to the other women and said, "It's an investment in our future."

Hector thought for a moment. He should at least try to make them understand what they were getting into. He leaned back in his seat. "Listen. You don't want to do this."

"Yes. We do," they said, pretty much all at once.

Hector grimaced. "No. You don't. Once you do this, there's no turnin' back."

They nodded.

"And you gotta pay."

"We will," Nancy said.

Hector looked at Nancy for a long moment. "Because you really don't want to do this if you're not able to pay. You understand what I'm saying? Not paying is not an option."

They nodded.

"If you do this, you're in another world. And the rules are different there. Comprende?"

They nodded.

"Say it," Hector said.

"We understand," Nancy said.

Hector looked at Pam, and then Shalisa, and they each said, "We understand."

Hector shrugged. "Okay. You pay me fifty now and a hundred after. When are you thinkin'?" He screwed the cap back on his water bottle while the women considered his question.

Nancy spoke. "We were thinking soon." She shrugged at the other women. "Why not? Might as well get on with our lives." She turned back to Hector. "This weekend."

Hector nodded and stepped out of the van. Before he slid the door closed, he looked directly at each of the women one last time, then said, "Don't make me make you regret this."

Eleven

Follow the Rules

Hank was down on all fours, one shoe on, fishing around in the bottom of the front-hall closet for its mate, while Elmer watched, stretched across the kitchen doorway.

"What did she do, Elmer? Stand on the other side of the room and whip all my shoes in here, one by one? Good thing you didn't get decked by a ricochet." He found the one he needed, creaked to stand upright, and then dropped down to sit on the stairs while he tied the laces. He looked at the dog who'd followed everything with his eyes. "Pam likes shoes to be kept in the closet, Elmer. Just so you know. In case you ever get any of your own."

Hank stood, stepped over to Elmer to scratch his ears, and then checked his watch. He had to get back to the casino before Padma missed her tea. Especially now, to avoid suspicion, he needed to keep to that routine even though he no longer had his daily meet with Dave. His chin dropped to his chest as he remembered his pal's easy laugh. He swallowed the lump in his throat before it grew.

———

The morning Dave was murdered, Hank had been doing what he had done every weekday morning for the past four years or so—waiting to commit grand larceny. When Dave hadn't shown up at their meeting spot, or answered his texts and calls, Hank had gone looking for him. He wasn't sure why he had swung by Dave's house; perhaps because he couldn't ask around the casino and he had to start somewhere. He hadn't expected to find him there, and he sure hadn't expected to find him murdered.

Dave's murder. That's how Hank saw it—a murder and a message—because how else could a man come to be found lying in a pool of blood under his garage door, with his head—Hank didn't like to think about that part—and a $1,000 casino chip lying precisely in the center of his chest? The hitmen's calling card. The sight had sent chills slithering up Hank's spine and dropped him to his knees. Once he'd caught his breath, he'd chanced a further look, and that's when he'd noticed Dave's dead fingers were curled around the handle of an ax.

Dave had fought back. Of course he had.

Hank hoped Dave had given them hell. He was tall, strong, and muscular, with so much heart. And his garage had looked like a war zone. But shouldn't there have been blood spatter? Maybe they'd draped a tarp and taken it with them.

Yep. That's how it had played out. The hitmen had jumped Dave when he'd come out to go to work after Marlene had left. The ax was the only weapon Dave could grab. There'd been a struggle, and they'd made a mess of the garage before Dave was ultimately subdued. They'd tried to force him to give up his pals, and when he'd refused, they'd shot him execution style and used the garage door to crush his skull as their coup de grâce. Hank had given a low moan as another thought crossed his mind—maybe they'd restrained him, and the garage door had crashed down while Dave was still alive.

Hank hoped it had been fast and they'd shot him.

The strategically placed chip sent the message—this was a professional casino hit. And a professional hit meant a police investigation. And he and the guys couldn't have anyone investigating Dave's life. The authorities had to think Dave had died in a freak accident. That's why, as soon as Hank could breathe again, he'd stood and then kicked a path through the crap strewn about the garage. He'd pushed away the lawn mower and the Christmas tree stand—who the fuck has a Christmas tree stand in the middle of their garage in July?—he'd grabbed the ax, checked the blade for blood, and finding it clean had tucked it behind a tall, red tool chest where the police wouldn't notice it. He'd returned to Dave and, avoiding the pooling blood, knelt beside his friend's body. He'd rested his hand gently over his still heart, softly patted it twice, and carefully picked up the $1,000 casino chip and tucked it deep in his front pocket. Then, satisfied the garage looked like the scene of a catastrophic accident, he had pulled out his phone and called 911.

Dave was dead, and their message was received.

Hank knew they were in over their heads, so he'd hurriedly met with Larry and Andre, and then gone to see Hector. He had handed the barber enough cash to ensure he was well incentivized to find and take care of whoever was coming for them.

Hank and the guys had one optimistic thought: If Dave had ratted on them, they'd already be dead.

———

It didn't have to play out like this, but Hank didn't have much choice. It was obvious Dave, Andre, and Larry had worked out the details before they pitched him their plan. Hank suspected they may have even rehearsed it.

Hours after Dave had carried his backpack of cash out of Hank's office, the four men had met at the marina with their fishing gear and taken Hank's boat out on the water. It was the perfect night for dusk fishing, but they hadn't dropped their lines. They'd put on some music to mask their low voices, aware sound carries across water; they'd each popped open a can of beer and sat forward in their chairs.

Dave began. "It's a glitch in the system. It's kind of technical but I found a way I can hack the video slot machines and make them think they're getting money deposited so they issue payout vouchers. I service the slots daily, and first thing when I start my shift, I trigger them to spit out the vouchers. Then I do a hard reset. The history is erased. Gone. I've checked and rechecked, and it's clean. Untraceable."

Larry had picked up the plan. "Dave creates three vouchers in three different amounts, always less than five grand so they can be redeemed at the ATMs without ID, and always totaling less than ten grand, because bank transactions above ten thousand dollars are flagged. We can't move more than ten grand a day."

Hank's blood pressure shot up. How long had the guys been working on these details? Larry was a bank manager. A deliberate, planning kind of guy. Not the type who did anything on a whim. It had taken him weeks to commit to their ill-fated investment, and its demise had exacerbated his caution. Nowadays you couldn't get him to golf without at least a week's notice. Preferably more.

Dave said, "I pocket the three vouchers, and then we've got to get them from the casino to the bank. This is where you come in. I take my break and meet you off-site at a prearranged meeting spot."

Larry stepped back in. "No one at the casino knows you two are friends, right?"

Hank and Dave nodded. Dave said, "That's how Hank wanted it, right from the start. And now it works to our favor. If we slip up in any way, no one will suspect we're working together; as far as anyone at the casino is concerned, we don't even know each other."

It was Andre's turn. "For the handoff, we'll have a rotation of fifteen meeting spots. I'll enter the locations into each of your vehicle service records. You open the booklet, check the date, and there will be a code for which spot you're meeting at. It'll be a park, a mall, Walmart. Somewhere public, but not too public." He nodded in response to Hank's raised eyebrows. "In case Dave's ever suspected, the less predictable his movements are, the less chance he has of being followed."

Hank had to admit, if they needed to arrange drop-off locations, it made sense for Andre to pick the spots, since he'd been running a courier service in the area for the past thirty years and knew every nook and cranny in the region. But, holy fuck. Now they were getting into 007 shit. Hank saw a glimmer of hope and looked from one friend to the other. "Am I being pranked? 'Cuz if I am, you guys got me good."

They ignored his question, and the glimmer faded.

Dave continued, "I hand the vouchers off to you and I go back to work. You go about your regular routine, meet Andre for your morning coffee, and leave the vouchers with him."

If he wasn't being pranked, he was listening to a plot to defraud his employer. Hank blanched as he realized how the movements Dave described would implicate him. "Why do I have to take them to Andre? Why don't you just take them there yourself?" Was it just for that reason? So he'd be in deep too?

But no one said that aloud; instead Larry answered, "You visit with Andre most days anyway. It keeps with the routine, but now it also helps with our plan."

Larry was right about that. It was an indulgence of sorts that Hank left his office every day and personally took anything needing to be couriered to Andre's business-supply storefront. He could have sent someone or arranged a pickup, but he liked to get out of the casino, see what was going on around town, pick up coffees, and swing by to see his pal. It had been his routine for so long, it wouldn't arouse suspicion. In fact, if he stopped doing it—that could raise red flags.

Andre said, "You hand off the vouchers to me, and I get them cashed."

"How?" Hank said.

Andre shrugged. "It's the nature of my business in a casino town. Wherever there's a casino, there are people who don't want to cash in their own vouchers. They don't want their wife to know they won, or their boss, or the guy they owe money to. Or they're casino employees." Andre nodded in response to Hank's scowl. "It's a fact of life. I merely provide a needed service. I have guys who will take the vouchers to the casino, cash them in at an ATM—"

Larry cut in. "Again, that's why each voucher is under five thousand dollars, so they don't have tó go to a teller, and they don't have to show ID."

Hank thought of the two hundred surveillance cameras in the casino. "But if the same guy comes too often, he'll be noticed and questioned."

Andre waved dismissively. "I have a never-ending roster of people looking to make quick cash. Pick this up, deliver that, run this errand. Pretty much anyone who gets off a bus in the downtown core and needs an easy buck knows to swing by my shop. They bring the casino cash back to me, I pay them fifty bucks, and they're on their way. Most I won't see again for weeks."

"You don't think they'll run off with the money?" Hank asked.

Larry said, "Some will. That's the cost of doing business"—he shrugged—"and I've factored ten percent attrition into the projection. In our trial run—"

"—Your what?" Hank gulped.

Dave said, "Remember I told you I used Marlene's family. That was just a few times. Then we talked about it and—"

"—What? You guys talked about this without me?"

Larry put his hand on Hank's knee. "We knew what we were asking, and we wanted to be sure, before we asked."

Andre fished four more beers from the cooler and passed them around. "We didn't want to bring this to you if it wasn't going to work."

They popped open their cans, and Hank slugged down half of his and then rested the cool container against his forehead for a minute.

Larry said, "So, in our trial run, we found all but one runner brought the money straight back." Andre nodded. Larry continued, "Then Andre couriers the cash to me, at the bank. And I transfer it to our offshore account—"

"—Wait. *Our* offshore account? You've already opened an account?" Holy fucking mother of God. Hank thought he might vomit overboard. He shouldn't have stuffed down that hot dog at the marina snack bar.

"I open them all the time at the bank, so when I was doing one for a customer, I just added another into the correspondence. I have all your information on file, so I set it up. It's no big deal. Offshore accounts have this fancy cachet"—Larry waggled his fingers—"but you wouldn't believe how many normal people have them. Anyway, the cash arrives, and I wire it to our account. Again, never more than ten grand at a time."

Hank's head was spinning. He took a sip of his beer. These guys were so deep into this plan, they wouldn't be happy if he'd killed it. They didn't *really* need him. His role was pretty much perfunctory, moving vouchers from Dave to Andre. But they'd be robbing his casino, and if he didn't stop them, he'd be just as guilty. But without the money. But they hadn't committed the crime yet. So far, they were just talking. Hank realized there were a lot of *but*s in his thoughts. He looked from one man to the other. "How much are you talking?"

Larry answered, "I figure if Dave prints out vouchers five times a week, at about $9,800 a day, give or take, and we do that for forty-six weeks a year—we'll talk about that logic in a minute—that's about two and a quarter million a year, accounting for the lowlifes who take off with some of our cash. It'll take us just over four years to reach ten million. That's two and a half million each. Then we pull the plug and retire."

"Two and a half million," Hank echoed in a quiet voice.

"It's not buy-a-private-island-travel-the-world wealth, but it's a nice cushion. If we make the right decisions, it can last us. And it's two and a half million more than we have now," Larry said.

Hank studied his empty beer can, then looked up. "Why forty-six weeks?" He noticed the other men's shoulders relax, perhaps relieved that was his only follow-up question so far. They shifted in their chairs, leaned back.

Larry swallowed some beer and crushed his can. "It's one of the rules. My research showed, when people do this kind of thing they get caught if they don't follow the rules. If we're going to do this"—Larry looked from one to the other—"we can't get caught. I'm not going to jail. Look at me. I'm a handsome man with a sparkling personality. I'd be way too popular in prison."

"Not if you packed your cologne," Andre quipped.

The men chuckled. Hank wasn't sure he'd wanted to do this. But he wasn't sure he had a choice. Another sentence with a *but*.

Larry started: "Rule Number One." He pointed to Hank and Dave. "Continue to keep your friendship on the down-low at the casino. Less chance of getting caught if people don't know you're friends."

No problem there. That was just maintaining the status quo.

"Rule Number Two. Take your regular holidays. Most workplace embezzlement and fraud scams get tipped off when someone's afraid to leave their post. So you have to take your regular holidays. And not at the same time, referring back to Rule Number One." Larry pointed at Dave. "So you take your three weeks." Larry pointed at Hank. "And you take a different three weeks. Andre and I will take ours when you take yours. That gives us forty-six productive weeks a year."

That seemed reasonable, although Hank wasn't sure how Pam would feel about not being able to holiday with Marlene. But it wasn't as though a Caribbean cruise was in their budget.

"Same goes if you have training or anything that takes you away from your regular duties. People get caught when they get territorial and don't want others to replace them. That raises red flags. So if something comes up, accept it and we'll adjust. Rule Number Three. Spend no extra money. None. Keep the purse strings tight. Tighter even. All the better to avoid suspicion."

Dave said, "Can't we get a little something? Anything? My cash flow is so low . . ."

Andre glared at Dave over his bifocals. "You wanna be somebody's prison fuck bunny?"

Larry put his hand on Andre's arm. "We've got to be smart, Dave. You came up with this plan, and it's genius. But it will take discipline to work. Four years. Just tough it out that long, and we'll be good." He waited for Dave to nod. "And finally, Rule Number Four." Larry leaned forward. "Tell no one. Tell. No. One." Larry looked pointedly at each man. "Not Marlene. Not Pam. Not Shalisa. And not Nancy. Do not tell them. If you think of telling them, picture them in the prison visiting room." He straightened.

As the playlist transitioned between songs, the only sound was the water gently lapping against the boat's hull.

Hank took a deep breath. "Look. You guys have put a lot of thought into this. And maybe it's doable. Maybe we could pull it off. But aside from the logistical aspect of it, stealing from the casino goes against everything I've stood for over the past thirty-one years of my career. I can't do this. Once we cross that line, we can't go back."

Dave kept his eyes on the boat's floor and said in a low voice, "You've already crossed the line, Hank."

Hank's head jerked toward Dave.

Dave looked up. He winced as he said, "I showed you the cash this morning. In the eight hours since, you didn't call security or the police. Instead, you met me on your boat."

Hank scratched his ear and squinted at the setting sun. Had he missed his chance to put a stop to this?

Andre raised his eyebrows. "You owe us, Hank."

And there it was.

The guys never threw it in his face, so to mention it then made the sting sharper.

"Andre's right." Dave grimaced. "We only invested because of you."

"It was our own fault," Larry jumped in. "We're grown men. No one made us do anything. But we followed you into that hole, Hank. You said it was a sure thing. And then said it again. We believed you, and we lost our money. And we lost more. Nancy has barely spoken to me since. I see the way Pam looks at you, Hank."

Andre said, "All our wives look at us that same way. Like we let them down. It's for them. For Marlene, Shalisa, Nancy, and Pam. Without them we have nothing. This is our chance to get them back. But we need you, Hank. We're either all in or all out."

Hank cringed. He had a flash memory of Pam chasing him around their bedroom, trying to plant her morning kiss on him. How he'd finally let her catch him and he'd brace himself as she blew her stale breath in his face. How they'd laugh and he'd wrestle her to the bed, and they'd fuck their faces off. That never happened anymore.

Hank had pushed himself up from the captain's seat and checked the anchor line. Satisfied it still held, he sat down, took another swig of his beer, and then said, "Do you think it would have happened anyway?"

Dave, Andre, and Larry exchanged looks before Larry asked, "What would have happened anyway?"

Hank's eyes followed the flight of a seagull as it soared above them. "That our marriages would have burnt out." He brought his gaze back to his friends. "Do you think it's just because of the money, or do you think things would have turned south anyway?"

After a moment, Dave said, "I don't know about you guys, but for me I'm one hundred percent sure it's the money. Marlene and I were happy. Sure, she can bitch at me like a trucker." His smile opened up. "But if she didn't have to worry about money, you put on the right song, and she starts swiveling her hips and she's in my arms like a sack of iron filings to a magnet. If I can get our money back, I get her back."

Hank's eyes widened at Dave's confidence. He looked at Andre. "And you?"

Andre rubbed his face and fixed his eyes on the horizon. "Shalisa and I've had our challenges. That's for sure. But she loves me. Or at least, she did. I've disappointed her. In a lot of ways." He wiped a tear away and swallowed. "But she is my queen." He turned his head to look at his friends, his eyes glistening, his smile widening. "From the moment I saw her across the gym on the first day of high school. She is and always will be my queen. If we didn't have to worry about the minor details of life—you know, like a roof over our head and eating"—he chuckled—"we'd be solid again." He locked eyes with Dave. "I'd get my queen back too."

Hank scratched his chin, then looked at Larry.

"Well. To be perfectly honest—and I didn't know I was coming to a *Dr. Phil* taping when I got on this boat. But okay. I'll play along. Nancy and I have some problems beyond money. I don't want to get into it. But I will. Soon. It's just sometimes life pushes you to make decisions you never thought you'd have to make. So, I'm not sure. I'm really not sure." He blew out a breath. "But the money would help. What about you, Hank?"

Hank watched the seagull skim along the water's surface and then swoop back up. While he followed its path with his eyes, he said, "She is my everything, and I am empty without her."

The men sat quietly for a moment, and then Andre gave a low whistle and whispered, "That's beautiful, Hank. What song is that from?"

Hank kept his eyes on the seagull and replied, "No song. It's just my thought."

Dave stood up and brought his hands together in slow applause. "Hank Manilow, everybody. Our very own Hank Manilow."

Hank smiled sheepishly and gave a half bow.

By the morning of Dave's murder, they had $9.3 million split between six offshore accounts and were twelve weeks from pulling the plug.

With Dave gone, Larry calculated they had between $2.3 and $3.1 million each—depending on what they decided to do with Dave's share. It was only right it should somehow get to Marlene, but they weren't sure how to go about that yet. Besides, she seemed to be doing okay, thanks to Andre, who had insisted they each have one-million-dollar life insurance policies. He had said they owed it to their wives to be sure they were taken care of if things went off the rails.

And now things were off the rails.

Things were flailing free-form through the sky, and Hank was trying with all his might to get them back on track before it was too late. And his first step in that direction was to drop off Padma's tea and find out exactly how involved his new boss was in Dave's hit.

Twelve

It Takes Vision

C ause and effect: That's what Padma Singh was considering.

The Ishikawa diagram Padma had studied at Harvard Business School was neatly lettered on the whiteboard that hung on the wall across from her desk. At the right end of the horizontal line, Padma had carefully printed *EFFECT—increased profit*. Along the way, she had started to fill in the *CAUSES—average bet, time spent in the casino, casino capacity*. She wasn't exactly sure she was completing the diagram properly. That's how it is when you graduate 892nd in a class of 900; you're not exactly sure how to do things properly. But when your mother is one of *Forbes' Most Powerful Women* and a reputed queen of India's organized crime, no one jots down your class ranking on the corner of your job application. You don't even complete an application. You just tell your mother you want the job.

However, casino profits weren't the problem Padma was focused on right then. At that particular moment, Padma was trying to decide how to *effect* relief on her feet. Below her desk's glass surface it looked like two freshly baked bran muffins were popping out of their Louboutin tins. Not to mention the blister starting on her baby toe.

Padma hadn't intended to be on her feet that long. Working the room on a weekday morning was different from a Saturday night. On Saturday nights, casino patrons were partying and eager to chat with the president of operations, take a selfie, and have their comped cocktails upgraded to premium. But Wednesday mornings at ten a.m., anyone at the tables just wanted the dealer to shoot them the cards, pay the bets, and shut up. They weren't looking to chitchat with the boss.

An hour earlier, Padma had taken the service elevator down to the main level and had worked her way through the kitchen, past the rows of stainless-steel equipment manned by chefs and prep cooks outfitted in crisp, white uniforms and hairnets. She'd discovered the kitchen's activity was the best barometer to indicate how busy the floor was. If there was hustle and bustle at the grill, the gaming tables and machines were packed. But on this week-day morning the busboys had been leisurely polishing coffeepots as she'd headed straight through, out the doors, around the corner, and on to the floor.

Padma always felt a bit like Sharon Stone making an entrance in *Casino* when she took her first steps on the bright, mosaic-patterned carpet. Although no one had turned to watch. And the clientele wasn't as glamorous as in the movie—at that moment there'd been a lot of elastic waistbands and orthopedic inserts in the room. Still, her heart had pumped faster, driven by the sounds of roulette wheels spinning, slot machines dinging, the murmur of bets being placed, and the quiet cheer of money won. That din and the pulse of lights had melded together in a stench of hope, and desperation.

Padma had made her routine sweep past the slot machines when she smelled it. She hadn't been sure at first. She'd paused and sniffed. Circled a second time, backed up a couple steps, and sniffed again. She'd looked around, and the only machine in operation had been manned by a wizened, white-haired lady sitting on the padded stool in front of a $1 denomination option.

Padma had approached her. "Excuse me, ma'am."

The woman had shot her a glance and hit play.

Padma had noted her $75 credit and buck-a-spin bets. Her wrinkled, age-spotted hand with pointed red nails had pushed the button again, and her credit had risen to $85.

"Excuse me, ma'am," Padma had repeated. "Don't you think you should go to the restroom?"

The woman had shaken her head. "I can't leave now. It's gonna hit. I can feel it."

"But, ma'am. You must use the facilities." Padma had concentrated on breathing through her mouth so the pungent smell of urine wouldn't overwhelm her. She'd scanned the casino floor for a security guard and pondered her life choices. If she'd taken the posting at the Mumbai tech startup her mother had arranged, she wouldn't have been standing beside a woman who'd been peeing her pants all morning. But Padma was tired of being pushed around by her mother and had plans of her own. So there she had stood, sidestepping a puddle of pee. She'd spotted security, raised her hand, and in seconds two staff had arrived at her side. She'd left them to deal with the pee lady and hobbled to her office.

Padma was prepared to suffer for success. Her mother told her high heels project a more professional persona, and that Padma needed all the help she could get in that department. So for the past two months Padma had been squeezing her pudgy feet into four-inch pumps. And it wasn't going well. Padma's low center of gravity and chubby toes weren't built for the physics of stilettos.

Now, back in her office, she longed to kick off her shoes, but she'd found out the hard way that once those dogs were freed, they'd puff up like blowfish in a shark tank, and she'd be stuck until the swelling went down. Instead, she gingerly tucked them under her desk and tidied the surface, straightening her keyboard, water bottle, and phone. She picked up the small pile of casino equipment brochures and tapped them on the desktop, aligning their edges. She set them next to the small tray that held the set of chips she'd signed out from the casino bank the previous week.

She should return them, but she found the touch of their cool smoothness to be almost therapeutic. She picked one up and rubbed it between her forefinger and thumb. It was a bit sticky, so she spat into a tissue and wiped it clean before stacking it with the others. It was probably dried coffee. On her way into the casino bank, she'd brushed by some idiot employee in the hallway, and he'd left splashes of his coffee on the tiled floor. If she'd gotten a better look at him, she would have had his manager write him up. His carelessness had almost killed her because moments later, when she'd returned to the hall with her tray of chips, her stiletto heel had slipped in the puddle of his fucking coffee. She could have broken her neck. As it was, she'd had to crawl around on her hands and knees to collect the scattered chips. She'd heard footsteps approaching from around the corner and had scrambled to rise, aware being found on all fours with her bum in the air wasn't her best look.

She'd hurried to her meeting, where she'd spun those chips like dreidels on the boardroom table and lobbied the design team to reimagine them infused with glitter. She spun one now, and then another, and another until they were like a row of spinning tops. Her mother had a miniature Zen garden on her desktop. A small tray filled with pristine sand, littered with a few semiprecious stones, and a tiny rake that she sometimes toyed with to smooth out the surface, mesmerizing an employee while they waited for her to make a decision.

What could be a more fitting desk toy for a casino boss than a tray of chips? Padma laid the chips down in a row, restacked them, and then lined them up again, reordered by denomination: one each of $25, $50, $100, $500—she left a space where the $1,000 chip would have gone—and finished the row with the $5,000 and $10,000. It was a lot of money to casually display on her desk, and it made her a touch giddy. She imagined they sent a subliminal message of power. Maybe she would keep them. At least, as long as she held on to them, she wouldn't have to reimburse the bank for that thousand-dollar chip.

A glimpse of movement from the wall of closed-circuit monitors to her left drew her attention, and she saw Hank turn the corner and head down the corridor toward her office, his shoulders hunched. Lately, he looked like he was carrying the whole world's problems on his back. Padma hurriedly straightened. She glanced at the row of chips, slid the brochures on top of them, and began randomly tapping on her keyboard before Hank came through her door.

Even though Hank was an old and out-of-touch boob—she wouldn't be surprised if one day he showed up for work wearing a clip-on tie—Padma appreciated that he did the heavy lifting of the day-to-day operations. That gave her the leeway to focus on more important things—like her career path and glittery casino chips.

"Morning, boss." Hank crossed the room, set her tea on the desk, and took a seat across from her for their daily chat.

Padma smiled as she reached for the cup.

Admittedly she didn't have a lot of experience with colleagues; she'd finished her MBA only a few months earlier, and this was her first real job. She wasn't sure how to best manage Hank. She'd arrived as his superior with the intention to fire his ass for a youthful replacement she knew she could control. But then he'd started bringing her a morning tea when he'd returned from getting his own coffee. Padma had appreciated both the show of respect and not having to make the trip to the refreshment station down the hall to fetch her own, so she'd decided to keep him around a bit longer.

She held her warm paper cup between her hands and studied him for a moment. There was a crease between his eyes as though he was worried about something. Although she couldn't be sure. Two months after meeting Hank, Padma knew as much about him as she'd read in his file that first day: exemplary employee, had started thirty-one years earlier as a dealer, then moved to pit boss, then pit supervisor and games manager. Finally landing as director of operations fifteen years ago. He oversaw every department, and the managers reported that he did it well. Impressive, considering he didn't have an Ivy League MBA like her. At least now, with her at the helm, the Indo-USA Gaming Inc.'s casino and her mother's investment were in properly educated hands.

Padma started, "I want to talk to you about the slot machines."

"Do you mean Donna? Yeah. That was unfortunate. She normally outfits herself in diapers, but . . . she got caught short. It won't happen again."

Padma stifled a gag at the memory and carried on. "That funeral last week was for our head slot tech, and I wanted to touch base before you hire his replacement."

"Right."

Hank lowered his eyes, and Padma saw his forehead's crease deepen as he looked at her puffy feet. Self-conscious, she tucked them under her chair, and as the shoe's leather pinched her blister, she winced. "Did you know him?" She drew Hank's eyes back to hers.

"Who?"

"The slot tech." She couldn't ignore the stab of pain as her shoe ravaged her tender toe. Her lips twisted into a tight grimace.

Hank held her eyes and answered, "Not really."

"His file says you hired him." She let out a controlled breath.

"Does it? Probably did. But he didn't report to me."

"He was a very handsome man. And it seems as though he was well liked. People were lined up out the door to speak to his widow."

"He was a great guy." Hank coughed into his hand. "So I hear."

"I know you're doing some hiring. A couple dealers, a new director of security, and now the slot machine tech. I wanted to let you know you don't need to replace him. I've decided to change out our slot machines."

Hank's head snapped up. "You what?"

Padma noticed Hank's knee started to bounce. She straightened, and so proud of what she was about to say, she did her best to suppress her smile. "I did an analysis of our slot machine payouts and compared to the other casinos in the Indo-USA Gaming family, our machines pay out about $2.5 million more a year."

She'd heard other people talk like that at business school and never dreamt those types of words would come out of her mouth. In that order. If she could have high-fived herself, she would have. She wished she'd recorded this meeting so she could send it to her mother. That would show her Padma was on top of things. Even if it was a fluke that she'd figured any of this out. If it were even true. Padma hated numbers and only looked at the books after her original project crashed and burned.

When she first arrived, she had big plans to make over the casino decor in cream tone-on-tone with pops of fuchsia. She had thought that color scheme would elevate her customers' gambling experience to be serene and relaxed. Practically spa-like. She should have known something was off when her mother had agreed it was a fabulous idea.

Hank had listened as she described her vision and then set up a meeting with casino consultants. They'd presented Padma with a study on the psychology of gambling, and evidence that calm didn't pry money out of people's hands, chaos did. And busy, colorful carpets promoted spending and hid stains; cream with pops of fuchsia did neither. Padma had shelved her project, realizing her mother had set her up to fail and Hank had saved her from a career-killing misstep. She still planned to fire him, just not yet. But with nothing else to do, Padma had opened the books.

Accounting bored Padma, so she had lined up the summary pages of other casinos the company owned side by side on her computer screen and had noted the numbers on the bottom line matched—except one. The slot machine payouts at this casino were higher. A lot higher. It had to be obvious, or Padma wouldn't have spotted it. Even she knew that.

Looking at her now, across her desk, Hank was silent for a moment. "How long ago did you notice that?"

She thought Hank would ask how she found out and congratulate her on her discovery. But instead, the boob was wondering *when* she had realized it. He probably felt responsible, and he should. Until two months ago, he was running things.

"Hmmm. Last month, I guess."

"Did you share your findings with anyone?"

Another weird question.

"Just some people at head office when I went on that corporate retreat." Padma had intended to keep her cards close to her chest until she had concrete numbers to report, but standing around at the pre-dinner mixer, she'd become fed up with the other division heads looking down their noses at her—figuratively and literally—so over her cosmopolitan she had let it slip that she had found a leaky hole on the casino's tight ship. After all, anyone can reshape a floundering operation, but it takes vision and talent to pinpoint the cracks in a seemingly well-run machine. Stanching the slot machines' overpayments would increase company profits. That alone would prove Padma belonged; she wasn't here merely because of her mother.

Padma tried to keep her connection to her mother quiet, even using a different surname. She'd heard the whispers about her mother being one of India's notorious mob bosses. Strong women gangsters were legendary in her home country: the Godmother, the Bandit Queen, Bela Aunty—and even though her mother had a master's in engineering and a trail of successes in Silicon Valley, it was true that she did what was necessary to protect her hard-earned fortune. Her mother spent most days ruthlessly navigating

India's rocky infrastructure, but to Padma's chagrin, these days she was more focused on navigating her daughter's love life.

The maternal titan of India's underworld had decided her daughter was to be married in the next eighteen months. Padma could have understood that timeline if she had a boyfriend, but she was decidedly single. So, with no prospects on the horizon, her mother had hired the consultant favored by India's top one percent—The Matchmaker. She was an older woman, outfitted in colorful saris, with a bright manicure, heavily jeweled rings, and an extensive rolodex of bio datas. Padma was not happy.

Padma wanted a love match. To a tall man with a full head of hair and good teeth. Her mother, on the other hand, didn't care about love, height, hair, or dental charts and said Padma shouldn't either. Padma realized she was fighting an uphill battle after her mother had emailed her a study from just a few years back that found only three percent of Indian marriages were love matches. Ninety-three percent of Indian women had arranged marriages. She had no choice but to listen as her mother badgered her, insisting her future son-in-law should have at least two degrees and suitable parents.

Padma hated the word *suitable*.

Padma had been dodging The Matchmaker's calls. Especially after her mother lowered the bar and decreed that Padma was agreeable to consider anyone, anywhere.

Agreeable. Another word Padma hated.

Padma had her own plans.

Gambling was on the rise in India, and since casinos were only allowed in three states so far, the growth opportunities were absurd, and Padma was going to ride that wave. Padma could never be taller than her mother, but she planned to one day not only join her on that *Forbes* list, but to place above her. Way above her. That would show her.

And making this casino more profitable was her first step.

Padma looked past Hank at her whiteboard. She still had to pitch her mother to seal the deal on the purchase of the new slot machines, and Hank was perfect to practice on. She planned to stand while she was on the Zoom call, but right now her feet throbbed, so for Hank, she leaned across the desk, cleared her throat, and recited her prepared lines: "The slot machines are a casino's crown jewels. Every day, each of those machines brings in more money than any of our poker rooms. I'm going to upgrade them to new models with lower payouts and then watch the profits climb."

She crossed her ankles and winced at the shot of pain from her blister. She took a steadying breath and said, "Hank, if head office is happy, we're happy." Then exhaled. She made a point to look straight into his eyes because her mother told her, when presenting to men, being the first to look away is a sign of weakness. Padma held her gaze firm.

Hank blinked and looked at the surveillance monitors.

She'd won. She settled back in her chair.

"When are you thinking of doing this?" Hank asked.

"I've ordered the slots, and they're arriving next week. Take a look." She reached across her desk for the brochures, and as she flipped to the right page, she passed one to Hank. She heard him gasp, and she smiled. "I know. They're something, aren't they?" She glanced up and was about to point out which model but stopped. Hank looked like he'd seen a ghost. His mouth hung open, and his eyes seemed unfocused. Drops of sweat prickled his forehead.

"Are you okay?"

She followed his gaze and saw he was staring at the row of casino chips lined up on her desk. Ah. He'd noticed.

He brought his eyes to hers and held them for a brief moment. Padma tilted her head, and he croaked out, "Sorry. I swallowed a bug. Gotta go." He coughed and, thumping his chest, stood.

As Hank closed the door behind him, Padma squirmed in her chair with excitement. He'd taken that really well. At least until he'd swallowed that bug. Her mother had warned her that men, especially older ones, didn't like women, especially younger ones, taking action without consulting them. But the boob seemed good.

In fact, at the end, his eyes had popped wide open in wonder.

Padma slid her polished fingernail under the first chip, delighting in the *click, click* as she gathered them all together. She enjoyed the smooth heft of the stack against her palm for a moment and then nestled them into the rounded tray, leaving a space for that missing $1,000 chip.

Thirteen

We're Not in Kansas Anymore

Hank closed Padma's office door behind him, leaned against the wall, and clutched his chest. Then he remembered the security camera in the corner, straightened, and concentrated on putting one foot in front of the other all the way down the hall and outside to his car. He texted Andre, wary the message could be intercepted by casino security:

Hank: meet at bank now to firm up r boat loan

Andre would think, *Boat loan? What fucking boat loan?* Then hopefully figure out it was code for: *Get to the bank, fast. We have to talk in person.*

Thirty minutes later, Hank concentrated on keeping his breathing steady while he and Andre waited in Larry's office for Larry to finish with a teller. The chair's chrome arms were sticky in his clammy grip. Hank peeked through the vertical blinds to double-check that the armed security guard was still standing by the front door.

Hank had known he'd be taking a calculated risk dropping off Padma's tea that morning. For all he knew, she might have already uncovered his connection to Dave, and he could have walked through the door, had a black hood whipped over his head, and been whisked away, to be tortured until he told them where their money was. When he had handed her that cup of tea, he didn't know whether she suspected him or not.

But he knew now.

And he needed to fill in Andre and Larry. Through the blinds, Larry was still huddled at the bank's counter. Hank looked at Andre, pacing by the door. "I'm fucking starving. Got anything to eat?"

Andre stopped and nodded to a spot beside Hank's chair. "There's a sausage roll in my handbag on the floor."

Hank exhaled and smiled at his friend. "You're a lifesaver." He looked at the empty floor and then up to Andre. "Fuck. Come on. You know, sarcasm is the lowest form of humor."

Andre let a small smile tug at his lips, then held his arms up. "Well, look at me. Do I look like I'm carrying snacks?" He was wearing khaki shorts and a polo shirt.

Hank sighed. "I thought maybe you had a granola bar in your pocket."

"No. I'm just happy to see you."

The two exchanged a chuckle. Then Andre moved to the desk. "Maybe Larry has something." He pulled open the bottom door. "Bingo." And passed a baggie to Hank.

Hank took half of the ham sandwich and offered the baggie back to Andre. "Want some?"

Andre shook his head. "Carbs." He tossed Larry's apple into the air, then caught it and took a bite.

Moments later Larry closed his office door behind him. He took in Andre and Hank, chewing. His shoulders dropped. "Guys."

Hank swallowed. "Sorry, man. I was gonna pass out. This is good. Is that an aioli?"

Larry ignored him and slumped into his chair behind the desk, accepted the quarter sandwich Hank passed him, and stuffed it in his mouth.

Hank wiped his chin with the back of his hand. "I was right. We are so fucked. Padma figured out the slot machines were paying too much, they know money is missing, and they killed Dave. She had a row of casino chips lined up on her desk, and do you know which one was missing?" Hank dug into his pocket. "This one!" He leaned forward and held up the $1,000 chip he'd lifted from Dave's chest. "She had every other denomination lined up in a row, and there was one empty spot. Where this was supposed to be. If that's not her warning me they're fucking on to me, then I don't know what is."

Larry and Andre stared at the chip for a moment. Their faces still. Then Andre asked, "Why would Padma warn you?"

"I have no idea." Hank shrugged. "Maybe because I bring her tea every day? Maybe because I didn't let her commit career suicide and make the casino *Zen*. But she warned me." He held the chip up again before he stuffed it into his pocket and made himself sit back in the chair and breathe in and then out. "I have to admire what a scheming shark she is. She dropped all kinds of clues. She said to me, 'Hank, if head office is happy, we're happy.'"

Hank looked to Larry and Andre for comprehension, but their faces were blank. "Don't you get it? The wince implied what would happen if head office was *un*happy." Hank made a wincing expression. "And then she looked me right in the eye, for a long time. A real long time. Like, it was getting uncomfortable. I think we were being recorded so she was leaving a lot unspoken. And then, just to be sure I got the message, she lifted some papers up off her desk to show me that row of chips and let me figure out the code."

The room was quiet a moment, and then Larry asked, "How did she find out the slot machines were paying out too much? Dave said he reset them and cleared the memory."

"Padma said it showed up when she compared it to their other casinos. We never had to worry about that because there weren't any other casinos until Indo-USA Gaming took over. And until she arrived two months ago, there was no one to make comparisons. But she noticed our machines pay out way more and she reported it at her corporate retreat. That must be what got the ball rolling."

"Why couldn't they just do an audit like a normal business? Why did they have to start killing people?" Larry asked.

Hank leaned forward in his chair, his eyes wide. "I showed you the company's Wikipedia page. We're dealing with big-time organized crime. Crazy crime. Like, cartel crazy." He sat back. "We're not in Kansas anymore, Larry."

Andre said, "Well, it doesn't matter. Nothing she said is going to change what we're doing. We're already shut down. Dave being murdered did that."

Hank said, "I know we're shut down, Andre. But don't you see? Now it's about keeping the money and staying alive. And maybe not in that order."

Larry walked to the window, scanned the parking lot, and fumbled with the cord as he adjusted the blinds for privacy. "Okay. So Padma or some India casino bigwig figured out something was up with the slot machines. And maybe they did realize it was Dave; it would make sense seeing as he worked on them, but that doesn't mean they know about us. We could still be safe. You didn't notice anyone poking around?"

Hank shook his head. "But they're professionals. I have to think someone is watching everything, even if I don't see them. They're probably tapping my phone. That's why I was careful what I texted. And why would Padma line those chips up like that if she wasn't sending me a message?"

Larry scratched his chin and nodded, as though he'd made a decision. "She was fishing. If they knew it was us, we'd already be dead. So they don't know. Yet. Good thing you kept your distance from Dave at the casino." Larry looked at Hank. "Maybe there isn't anything to link us, and we're worried about nothing. The machines reset, so there's no trail." Larry straightened. "Did she say what she thinks the overage is?"

"$2.5 million a year."

Larry plunked down. "She knew that."

Hank continued, "And she's switching out the slot machines. The ones Dave rigged are being sent back, and they're bound to be inspected. What if Dave slipped up and there's some kind of a trace in the machines? Either way, whether she knows now or finds out later, this could get tricky for us. Real tricky."

Larry leaned forward. "But nothing in the machines would connect to us. Just to Dave. And he's already dead."

Andre shook his head. "But if they confirm Dave ripped the machines off, they won't believe he acted alone. They'll know he had accomplices, and they'll want their money back. They'll figure out they've had those machines for four years and they're looking for ten mil. That's a lot of motivation to keep looking." He turned to Hank. "I think you're right. If she was warning you, it's because she suspects you. You're alive because she just isn't one hundred percent sure it's you. Yet."

Hank nodded. "She did ask if I knew Dave." His heart raced. "Oh my God. She winced when she asked me. Yep. I remember. She looked me in the eye, winced, then asked, 'Did you know him?'"

Andre asked, "What did you say?"

"What do you think I said? I said no! That was Rule Number One. Did you think I was going to crack when I was being questioned by a five-foot-nothing Gen Z? It will take more than that to sink this ship."

Andre squinted at Hank. "What's a Gen Z?"

"Someone in their late twen—Andre! Not now."

Larry said, "Okay. Okay. Calm down. We have to keep our wits about us. Andre was only asking."

Hank looked at Andre. "Sorry."

Andre put his hand on Hank's shoulder. "It's okay."

They were quiet for a moment. Larry picked up a pen and tapped it against his finger. "Did Hector find out anything?"

Hank shook his head. "He said no one's heard of anyone suspicious traveling in and out. No one was looking for a weapon. No one was asking about us. He double-checked what we want him to do if he hears anyone is hiring to kill us, and I told him—deal with them. He asked if we wanted to know who they were first, and I said we don't care who they are. Kill them."

Andre tossed his apple core in the trash. "I think we should give him more money. Just to be sure he's properly motivated." The men looked at each other and nodded. And Andre added, "We've gotta be sure Hector will kill them before they kill us. Whoever they are."

Fourteen

I'll Bring a Salad

Marlene unzipped her purse and slapped the $50,000 in cash onto Shalisa's kitchen table. Pam thought it would be bulkier.

"Took me six trips to the bank," Marlene said as she sat down. "Turns out they don't recommend you withdraw more than ten thousand dollars at a time. The teller whispered I should get it in batches so it wouldn't be flagged to the IRS. Not that I have anything to hide, but who wants to be flagged to the IRS?"

Marlene let out a hearty chuckle and looked around for the others to join her. But Nancy brought her hands to her temples, with her elbows on the table, and watched the pile as though it was going to slither into her lap. She looked at Shalisa and said, "Do you have any wine?"

Shalisa raised her eyebrows. "It's ten a.m."

Nancy answered, "It's five o'clock somewhere."

Pam looked at her watch. "I've only got the morning off. I have to be back at work at one."

"Me too," Shalisa said.

"I don't care. I need wine." Nancy edged her coffee cup away.

Pam caught Shalisa's eye on her way to the fridge. Nancy had pushed for this from the start and then been gung ho with all her research, but could she be having second thoughts? Shalisa offered a reassuring nod as she fished out a bottle of white and pulled some glasses down from the cupboard.

Marlene zipped up her bag and placed it on the floor beside her. "Gawd! You gals look like I've just given you the money for your funerals. Crack open that wine, Shalisa! We need to celebrate. You're finally getting something you deserve. Good golly! Don't look so guilty. I'm happy to lend you the money. And Dave, God rest his soul, would be thrilled to be helping you out. Pam! Chin up, bud. You're getting your hot tub! Hank will love the surprise. Maybe it will spice things up." Marlene winked.

Pam exchanged a quick glance with Nancy and Shalisa. They had made a pact to never tell Marlene why they needed the money, and they had good reason. Marlene was a bad-accomplice trifecta: She couldn't lie, act, or keep secrets. She was exactly who you don't want around when you're committing a crime.

They'd each come up with a reason behind their request—Pam's hot tub, and Shalisa was going to start her own yoga studio. They'd run out of ideas when they got to Nancy, but at the particular moment they were brainstorming, they were enjoying a wonderful cappuccino from the cutest little trailer at a downtown park. Nancy mused aloud how this kind of coffee truck would make a killing at the marina, and voilà, they had their final fake loan request.

For Marlene's protection they'd documented everything in emails, including phony photos and dummy spreadsheets. Pam suspected Marlene hadn't looked at any of it, but if she ever needed evidence that she didn't know what her friends were up to, she had it.

"Listen." Marlene grasped Pam's hand to her left and Nancy's to her right. "I know everyone thinks I'm a bit scattered, and they're probably right. But I know people. And from the moment I first saw you guys at the Fun Fair Bake Sale, I thought to myself, *I could be friends with them.*" Marlene looked at each woman. "You have never let me down. We've had good times and bad, more bad lately, but nothing we can do about that. It makes me so happy to be able to help you out. Dave and I had our problems the past few years, but I loved him. And he loved you guys. Hank, Larry, and Andre were like brothers to him. He'd want me to help you."

Pam avoided Shalisa's eye as she set down the wine and glasses, but she felt Nancy's foot press hers under the table. Pam pressed back. She suspected Nancy and Shalisa felt as shitty as she did about deceiving their friend. Marlene unscrewed the bottle's top and poured, passing the glasses, and said, "I know we had a rough patch the past few years, but now that Dave is gone, I've talked to my therapist—"

"—You have a therapist?" Shalisa asked.

"My sister thinks it's weird that I'm a grieving widow with no grief."

Pam could agree with that observation, but given the blows their marriages had suffered, they'd begun the grieving process years ago.

"Anyway, she set me up with a therapist, and I've decided my path is to focus on Dave before everything went bad. So that's what I do. When he pops into my mind, I dial it back to when we still danced. God, I loved to dance with that man. And back to when we still had sex." She winked at them. "I liked to do that with him too. And when we still laughed. And you know what? I loved *that* Dave. And I miss that Dave. I grieve that Dave." Marlene raised her glass. "So, to *that* Dave."

The others joined. "To that Dave."

Pam loved that Dave too. She recalled the way he'd smiled at her that last night. How she had seen a glimpse of *that* Dave. But it had just been a glimpse. And then it was gone. The husbands they'd married were gone. She swallowed the lump in her throat and noticed a tear roll down Nancy's cheek.

Marlene sighed. "And I just want to tell you guys, especially now that I'm moving away, being a wife and a mom was hard. I know it's easy for some women, but for me it was fucking hard. I wasn't always sure I could be good at it. And I needed to be, for my girls' sake." A sob caught in Marlene's throat, and she toyed with the stem of her wineglass. "But you guys got me through. I don't know where I'd be, or how my daughters would have turned out, if it wasn't for your support. I owe you everything, and I'm so happy you asked me to help you out. You can't know how much that means to me." She let her tears flow.

Here we go. Pam closed her eyes for a second. Marlene had always been a crier. Now they'd get all sloppy and sentimental, and Pam would have to redo her eye makeup before she went to work. She would have loved to let Marlene know she didn't need to give a speech and say a big goodbye—she'd be seeing them all in Boca Raton next month—but instead she rose and hugged her, and Nancy and Shalisa joined her.

Pam leaned into their embrace. She had felt those same arms around her shoulders at funerals, at birthday parties, in emergency rooms, and in conga lines. She and her friends had always picked each other up and held each other up. And that's what they'd keep doing. They'd get through this.

After a couple of minutes Pam pulled away, wiped her tears with her sleeve, and mumbled, "We love you too, Marlene," as they sat back down.

Marlene forced a smile and blotted her eyes. She cleared her throat, took a sip of her wine, and looked toward Nancy. "Now, tell me all about your coffee trailer."

For three women who should be excited about the new opportunities the cash on the table was bringing their way, they drank their wine at a tortoise-like pace. When Marlene finally left to meet her real estate agent, they breathed a sigh of relief. As they closed the door behind her and returned to the kitchen table, Nancy said to Pam, "You never said why you changed your mind and agreed to hire Hector."

Nancy was right. They hadn't talked about what had prompted Pam to text: *I'm in.*

Pam pulled out her chair and sat back down. "Hank ate my pad thai."

Nancy opened her mouth. Then closed it. She pushed her glasses up her nose and finally said, "I don't know what to say to that."

"Hank ate my leftover pad thai, and he wasn't even hungry."

Nancy cocked her head.

"Don't you get it? Hank knows pad thai is my favorite food and I never get to have it anymore. After Dave's funeral, I ordered it and saved half for later. The day we dropped Marlene off at the airport, when I asked him where my pad thai was, he said he ate it. Those leftovers were mine, but Hank just hoovered them down like it didn't matter. Like I didn't matter. And then just threw it in my face that he wasn't even hungry."

"Well. Seeing as you put it that way." Nancy leaned back and folded her arms.

"I mean, he didn't just stab me, he twisted the knife. You don't do that to someone you love. That's when I knew he doesn't love me anymore. When he ate my pad thai."

Shalisa reached for Pam's hand and squeezed it.

Nancy pulled a piece of paper from her back pocket and unfolded it. "Alrighty. Let's take this step by step. The first thing to sort out is how to react when we find out they're dead."

Pam and Shalisa exchanged a quick, relieved smile and leaned forward. Whatever doubts Nancy may have had, she was back.

Nancy flattened the page. "Most likely the police will knock on our doors. We have to be surprised." She referred to her notes. "One of us should collapse to the floor, one should shriek, and one can just shut the door in shock. I'd like to be that one. Pam, can you shriek? Or at least gasp and cover your face with your hands. Maybe fall back against the wall?"

Pam nodded. "I can do that."

"Shalisa, I think you should be the one who collapses to the floor. You do yoga; you can get back up."

Shalisa nodded.

Nancy checked her list. "I don't think we have to cry right away. Although it wouldn't hurt, if you can make it happen. But from what I read—in books, not online—it takes a while for the news to sink in; loved ones are more shocked than sad, so the police won't necessarily expect tears."

Pam interjected, "I was thinking it's smartest if we don't know how Hector's going to do it. So we don't have to *act* surprised, we will *be* surprised. When we meet up to pay the deposit, we have to make sure he doesn't tell us any details."

"You mean, like provide us with a written estimate," Shalisa said.

"You know, sarcasm is the lowest form of humor," Pam said.

"Sorry. I couldn't resist."

"If they're missing before their bodies are found, there might be media attention. We should be prepared for a press conference, so you better re-watch *Gone Girl*," Nancy said.

"More recommended viewing," Shalisa said.

Nancy countered, "It's research. We can't just Lucy and Ethel our way through this. We have to be prepared. I've seen *Orange Is the New Black*, and I don't think I'd do well in prison. I'm attractive with a sparkling personality. I'd be very popular."

Shalisa quipped, "Not if you pack your face masks."

The women chuckled.

Pam said, "Did we settle on a date? I was thinking we should ask him to do it Sunday. Don't you think? We should make plans for the weekend just to be sure the guys don't go away. Overnight fishing or anything. We could get together Saturday night for a barbecue at my place. We can say it's a goodbye party for Marlene."

"Yeah. They wouldn't want to miss that," Shalisa said.

Nancy nodded. "That sounds good. Then we just have to get through the next few days as normally as possible. Sunday, while it's happening, we should do something we'd regularly do. It would be good for our alibis if we were out in public."

Pam said, "Why don't we go to Target? Their security cameras would catch us. I need a new pair of sneakers. And I'm almost out of that trail mix Hank likes. The ones with the chocolate covered caram—" Pam stopped. And swallowed. She stared at her hands. "I guess I don't need to restock Hank's trail mix." Her stomach felt like it had a serving of wet cement sitting at its bottom.

They studied the table for a moment, that detail of their new reality sinking in. No more of their husbands' favorites in the cupboard.

Then Shalisa looked up. "But you should. You should buy his trail mix. It helps with our alibi—that you bought his favorite. You wouldn't do that if you knew he was gonna be dead. Right?"

Nancy gasped. "You're right. That's a great thought. I'll buy Larry new underwear."

Shalisa added, "I'll pick up socks for Andre."

Nancy held her palm up to Shalisa and they high-fived. "Good thinking on that one, Shalisa! Way to crush an alibi."

Pam had a flash of memory of Hank sitting on the sofa, watching TV, munching on his trail mix, and offering the jar to Claire. He would save the chocolate-covered caramels for her. She struggled to smile. Then she flashed back to Hank saying "whatever" and walking out of their kitchen. And she thought of Nancy reuniting with her son and Shalisa's quest for a fucking fantastic life. And then Pam grabbed on to her own fucking fantastic new life and held both hands up ready for her high-fives. "We've got this!"

Nancy said, "You go, girls!"

Shalisa laughed. "We are some badass wives. Don't mess around with us."

Nancy added, "We just have to pay our hitman his deposit, get through dinner at Pam and Hank's Saturday night, and *hel-lo*, Boca Raton!" She looked at Pam. "I'll bring a salad."

"And I'll make my chocolate mousse cheesecake." Shalisa smiled. "I may even eat two pieces just so I can see that frown on Andre's face one last time."

Nancy's phone buzzed on the table, and Pam saw Marlene's big smile and bouffant hairdo pop up. Nancy swiped and said, "What's up, babe?" She listened for a moment, then answered with, "I'll check with the others and let you know."

She put her phone down. "Marlene needs a favor."

Fifteen

Nice Hat

Hector was clipping around the teen's ear when he spotted Hank's big frame lumbering by his front window. The bulge in Hank's back pocket signaled the husbands were upping their ante. Hector wasn't surprised, as these kinds of jobs generally took a turn or two before it was all said and done.

Hank took a seat in the row of chairs lined up against the wall and selected a fishing magazine, but Hector noted he didn't look at it. Instead, Hank's eyes darted about the parking lot, like a hunted animal. Under his arms, circles of sweat inched down the sides of his blue button-down. Hector slowed as he brushed the trimmings off the boy's shoulders, giving himself time to think the situation through. As he tidied his workstation, he took a good look at the parking lot himself. When he went to the storage closet for more aftershave, he locked the back door and set the dead bolt.

Satisfied, he returned, shook out the boy's apron, and draped it over his arm. He slid open the drawer at his station and discreetly withdrew his gun from its place next to his professional-grade clippers and tucked the weapon in the apron's folds. When he joined the boy at the cash register, he set the apron on the counter, the gun beneath it, its muzzle aimed at the front door. Again, his eyes swept the parking lot for anything out of the ordinary and finding nothing, he rang the boy up. Hector watched him leave and then motioned Hank to his red leather chair and set the gun and apron on the rolling tray beside him.

As he climbed into the chair, Hank slid the envelope from his back pocket onto Hector's station. Their eyes met in the mirror. Just then, two men walked by the barbershop window and slowed to look inside. Hector noticed Hank's knuckles whiten on the chair's arms. Hector, his finger on the trigger, rotated the tray so the gun was again pointed at the door. When the men moved on Hank's head dropped in relief, and Hector flung a clean apron around Hank's torso like he had done a thousand times over the years. He was about to grab his clippers, but since he had trimmed Hank's hair just a few days previously, there was no point in going through those motions. Even on Hank's wildest hair days he merely needed a quick buzz to tame the unruly fringe that hung over his ears. Instead, Hector ran the clippers over Hank's neck and then sprinkled some Bay Rum aftershave on his brush and slowly swiped the soft, long bristles along the back of Hank's neck and nodded while Hank talked.

After Hank left, Hector turned the lock, plugged in the closed sign, and turned off the lights as he made his way to the office in the back of the shop. When he opened the door, his wife glanced up from the monitor and smiled. His heart skipped a tiny beat, and he paused a moment to take in her messy bun and the scrunch of her nose. He set the envelope of cash on the desk and sat down across from her. Her eyebrows shot up and her mouth formed the cutest O. She thumbed through the money, then swiveled to tuck it into the safe, then back to him. The light from the screen highlighted her sprinkle of freckles, and her eyes twinkled as though she were sitting in front of one of those social media ring lights. He wasn't sure how, but her dark eyes always seemed to reflect light.

"You were right. He came back."

"I could hear."

"He liked our idea."

Brenda smiled. "I complete you."

Hector chuckled. "I think it's '*you* complete *me*.'"

"Same diff."

"You did have me at hello," Hector said.

"Well, what did you expect? I was just a girl standing in front of a boy—"

"I was standing, you were sitting," Hector said.

"Best day of your life." Her smile slayed him.

"Look at you, telling the truth and it's not even Christmas." Hector beamed.

"Well, I'll tell you another truth." Brenda folded her arms and shook her head. "Some people. Yi, yi, yi, yi, yi."

That was one of the things Hector loved about his wife. Nothing riled her. He could have told her the husbands had decided they wanted Hector to deliver two giraffes and kill a koala bear at sunrise, and Brenda would have the same response: "Yi, yi, yi, yi, yi. Some people." Although she would never, ever have let Hector kill an animal. Not in a million years, for a million dollars. That was a given.

Hector speculated most husbands in his line of work wouldn't share the details with their wives, but they weren't lucky enough to be married to Brenda Palumbo. When he had found her on that El Salvador beach, where she had been spending her day off from volunteering at a local animal shelter, her nose in a criminology textbook, he thought he'd found his golden ticket out of the gangs. That plan had worked for one of his better-looking cousins and three buddies. They had each conned a lonely American into hooking up, convinced them they were in love, and once they were sponsored into a better life in a new country, they'd ditched the heartsick woman.

But there was no conning Brenda Palumbo. She had Hector figured out before she raised her hand to shade her eyes from the sun. By the time he had bought her a hat, she had him committed to helping at the shelter for the rest of her stay and to bringing along a friend.

Before Brenda had even packed up, she had decided she was taking a neutered beagle mix, and Hector, home with her. Part of Hector's immigration process was being quizzed on what you know about the other party. They call it testing "the genuineness of the relationship." And Brenda wasn't about to have her happily-ever-after torpedoed because Hector got tripped up in an immigration interview over details like her birthday, her favorite food, when she last had her period, or her family tree. Brenda had prepared flash cards. In the middle of the night Hector would feel her elbow in his ribs.

"Hec-toro," she'd say. She always called him that. Never HecTOR, or HECtor; always Hec-toro. Like the bull, she had said. One of her first Spanish words. "Hec-toro?"

"Sí?"

"What's my mother's maiden name? Her last name before she was married."

"Ah." He'd have to shake the sleep fog from his head and sift through the strange details Brenda had piled on him, one after another, and finally he'd find it.

"Lucifora," he'd reply.

"Good. How many siblings do I have?"

"Siblings? I don't know that word."

"Sisters, and brothers. That's what siblings are."

"Ah. Three sisters. There's you, Suzanne, Laurie, and Sharon. Two years apart. You're the youngest. And the prettiest. Okay? Can I go back to sleep?"

"One more. What's my pet peeve?"

"Another word I do not know."

"Pet peeve. Um. The thing I hate most."

He'd rolled away from her. "Oh. That's easy. When someone eats your takeout leftovers. Never, ever eat Brenda's takeout leftovers. They're hers. Unless she gives them to you."

She'd curled herself around him, and he felt the warmth of her smile and knew of all the women he had checked out on the beach that day, he had chosen the best one. That's the day their life together had started.

A life of no secrets.

———

There was a quiet rap on the barbershop's back door. Hector and Brenda exchanged glances, and Hector rose to look out the peephole. He nodded at Brenda, closed the office door, undid the dead bolt, and let Pam in. He looked over her shoulder and down the back alley to see the van with Nancy in the back and Shalisa in the passenger seat. They gave him a small wave, and he gave a nod and closed the door. The two stood in the narrow, tiled hallway at the back of the barbershop.

"Nice hat," he said.

Pam touched the brim of Hank's ball cap and raised her sunglasses to the top of her head. "I didn't want to chance being recognized."

Hector had seen that cap on Hank a dozen times. Should he point out to Pam that it was embroidered across the back with *Montgomery*? Brenda would get a kick out of that.

Pam thrust an envelope toward him. "Here it is. The fifty thousand dollars." Her words rushed out. "We don't want to know any details. About how you're doing it. We just want to make sure it happens Sunday. Got that? Sunday."

Hector had learned the less said in these types of exchanges, the better.

"And . . . we don't want them to suffer. Okay?" Pam put her hand on Hector's forearm, then pulled it back. "We want it to be quick. But remember, we need the bodies."

Hector closed his eyes and gave a slight nod to signal agreement. "All right, then. I think we're done." He reached past her to open the door. He held it ajar as she made her way out and was pulling it closed when Pam spun around. He paused.

Pam plucked her sunglasses from the top of her head. "It wasn't always like this. It used to be good. Really good. For all of us. And then a few years ago it just got . . . not good." She looked at the sunglasses as she folded and unfolded the arms. She brought her eyes back up to meet Hector's. "We just want our lives to be fucking fantastic again. You know?" She turned and jogged back to her van.

Experience had shown Hector anybody could justify anything to themselves if they wanted to. And these women wanted to. He closed the door and went into his office. He moved around to the back of the desk, dropped this second envelope of cash in front of his wife and wrapped his arms around her. He buried his face in her neck. "You'd tell me if things got that bad between us before you hired someone to kill me, wouldn't you?"

Brenda smoothed his hair. "Hec-toro. If things got that bad between us, I'd kill you myself."

"That's why I love you." He kissed her cheek and sat down across from her.

She swiveled to the safe and slipped the envelope inside, then swiveled back to face him. "Well. This is an interesting situation you've got yourself into, Hec-toro."

Hector raised an eyebrow and nodded.

Brenda leaned back in her chair. "The wives want the husbands dead for the insurance money. The husbands say someone wants them dead, but they didn't tell you who or why, just that they want you to kill them. We know it's their wives." She cocked her head. "Do you think the husbands know?"

Hector shrugged. The thrum of the air-conditioning unit kicked in.

Brenda continued, "What could those guys have done that was so bad their wives would want them dead?"

Hector shook his finger at her. "Don't be wondering what people know or did. No good comes from that. For all we know they could be running a porn ring. Or sex trafficking. Or into drugs. Or be abusive. We'll never know the full story. Or the truth. So, no point wondering."

She held his gaze.

After a moment, he inhaled deeply, then exhaled. "All right. You think there's more to it, don't you?"

"I do. But you're right—we'll never know the truth. So, what are you going to do?"

Hector locked eyes with his wife. "I'll do what I always do. I'll do what's right for us."

Sixteen

A Hard Truth

Padma was incensed at the irony of it all.

Sixty percent.

If her mother knew Padma's university papers routinely achieved only sixty percent, she would have been apoplectic. Yet now her mother was agreeing with The Matchmaker that Padma should be satisfied to have her future husband meet only sixty percent of her criteria.

Sixty percent.

She may as well marry a corpse.

Padma kept her smile pasted across her face while her mother and The Matchmaker lectured her from side-by-side boxes on her computer monitor. She had humored her mother and agreed to a scheduled call, confident she could dodge any actual matchmaking. And she had to admit, she did enjoy listening to the cadence of the older women's voices. Like her mother, The Matchmaker's first language was Hindi, and the familiar rat-a-tat-tat of their accented English, similar to the drummer of a marching band, brought her back to the rosy memories of her childhood—before she became her mother's biggest disappointment. She snuck a look at the time. It was eleven a.m. here, so nine thirty p.m. in Mumbai. Surely these old gals would be tiring and the call would soon be over.

The Matchmaker said, "You cannot have everything, my dear. That is not how this life works. You must arrange your priorities. And your priorities should be that you find an educated man from a suitable family, of whom your mother approves."

That word again. *Suitable.*

And then, "You must compromise."

Another irksome word. Padma waited to hear *agreeable.*

"You must be agreeable to make adjustments in your own life. You cannot be picky. If you are picky, you will never be happy."

Her mother piped in. "Padma is in no position to be picky."

Padma silently chanted to herself, *I am enough. I am enough.* How did her mother do that? Effortlessly make Padma feel like she was fourteen and inferior all over again? She had to get off this call. She focused on The Matchmaker's red nail polish and hefty emerald ring.

The Matchmaker continued, "I have sent you three excellent candidates for your consideration. Please, have a look at their bio datas."

Padma shuffled the papers. The Matchmaker had emailed the zip file and instructed Padma to print them before their Zoom call. On her glass-topped desk, Padma stacked the dossiers side by side. They were each five pages thick, with four-inch-square headshots in the top left corner of the first page.

"Now," The Matchmaker said, "which of those photographs before you do you find the most pleasing?"

Pleasing? There was nothing *pleasing* about this process. Padma didn't want this old lady and her mother to ship her a husband. Padma wanted to stumble across her Prince Charming in an organic meet-cute like in a rom-com. She took her time in coffee shops, scanning the tables for eligible men, ready to knock their coffees into their lap. But the good-looking guys seemed more interested in the free Wi-Fi than her. Her mother was dissatisfied with her progress and had started the call by reminding The Matchmaker that she intended to host a lavish three-day wedding ceremony in seventeen and a half months. Earlier would be better.

Her mother, pragmatic on many fronts, ignored Padma's argument that normal couples don't set wedding dates before they've met. Period. Her mother had countered that one needed to be proactive in life—especially if one were short and frumpy. The Matchmaker had smiled during this exchange, and Padma was afraid to probe too deeply into her mother's plans lest she discover she'd already booked the honeymoon.

"Padma! Aunty is talking to you." Her mother brought her attention back to the call, referring to The Matchmaker with the familiar term of respect. "And sit straight. You're frumpier when you slouch like that. It's a hard truth."

A hard truth. Right. Her mother wanted her to be the best version of herself, and if she didn't point out Padma's hard truths, who would? So she had said repeatedly over the years. But Padma had read the books and done the therapy, so she knew there should have been some compliments sprinkled in among her mother's *hard truths*. She also knew not to waste her time waiting for them. Time. That was it. Padma needed to buy herself some time. A few weeks could turn into a few months and then, hopefully, never. She looked up from the photos. "I can't decide. Let me think about them and get back to you."

The Matchmaker sighed. "If you can't decide, we could always decide for you."

Padma's heart plummeted at the suggestion, while her mother seemed to be considering it. Padma rushed to cut off that thought. "My apologies, Aunty. I was just admiring the photos and got caught up in the moment. Let me take a closer look." Padma straightened the pages.

Only one of The Matchmaker's prospective grooms provided any peek at a smile. The second looked like a prison mugshot—a beefy man with no neck and a menacing scowl. And the third was completely bald. Of course, he was the scion of India's preeminent bedding manufacturer, and apparently, her mother's frontrunner. She sent Padma a text: *His business is secure. People will always need sheets.*

The Matchmaker's rat-a-tat-tat resumed. "I need to ring off in a moment. I need your decision on whom you would like to see in person, and he will fly over to meet you. We do need to move quickly. As your mother has said, you are not getting any younger, my dear. Tell me which one. Yes?"

Padma held up the mugshot. "I'm sorry, Aunty, but you're sending me sixes. Look at me. I'm a ten."

Her mother interjected. "On a remote desert island of shipwrecked men, perhaps. Padma, my dear, regrettably, you are not a ten. You need to be happy with a six. If you can get that. It's a hard truth."

Padma bit her tongue and thought to herself again, *I am enough. I am fucking awesome.* Her fingers flipped through the casino chips stacked on her desk until she found the one stamped with $10,000. She squeezed it in her palm, hoping the value would seep into her as though through osmosis. "I am enough," she whispered to herself.

Padma's mother continued, "Aunty? Let's have Padma meet the three men you have selected so far. Hopefully one of them may find her not so unattractive."

Great. As if a main dish wasn't bad enough, now her mother was ordering the buffet. But she could tell by The Matchmaker's silence that she didn't like the idea. Padma sat back while the woman tried to diplomatically decline her mother's suggestion. She returned the casino chips to their small tray and absentmindedly flipped through them, one by one. This would be interesting. No one refused her mother.

The Matchmaker sat taller in the screen. "In my experience, madam, too many selections are distracting for the young people. I like to offer one candidate at a time. And then we move on to the next." She folded her red-tipped fingers in front of her.

"Yes. I understand," her mother rebutted. "But Padma is desperate."

Padma's head snapped up. Her internal mantra restarted: *I am enough. I am fucking awesome.*

Her mother continued, "We have a tight timeline."

Timeline. Her mother had reduced her love life to a timeline. Well, at least if The Matchmaker sent all three at once, she'd be out of this matchmaking misery sooner. And she had to give her mother credit—Padma had logged into this call intending to flatly refuse to meet any prospective groom, and now she'd be seeing three. And soon. Her mother had changed the playing field, and Padma had barely noticed.

The Matchmaker said, "All right. I will agree if Miss Padma is agreeable."

Padma wanted to ring off. She had to pee. She glanced at her watch again. Hank would be here any minute with her morning tea, and she didn't want him to catch her being bossed around by her mother. She threw in the towel. "Yes. Send the men from Mumbai. Let them come. All three." Padma looked at the bio datas in front of her. "The big, bald one—"

"And the banker?" The Matchmaker asked.

Padma ran her finger down his bio notes. "Yes, the second one is a banker. I said, all three of them." Padma squeezed her legs together. "Send your men and let them take their best shot." She looked at her calendar. "When can they get here?"

The Matchmaker tapped her pen. "You can expect them to arrive in two days."

"Okay. Two days. Fine. I'll expect to start hearing from them on Saturday. I'm sorry. I really have to go."

Padma rushed off the Zoom call. She would date these men to satisfy her mother, but no one could make her marry them. She hurried to open her door, almost colliding with Hank, holding her tea.

"I'll be right back, just have to go to the restroom."

When she returned a few moments later, Hank was sitting in the chair opposite her desk, texting. His forehead glistened with perspiration and his knee bounced.

She opened her mouth to apologize for keeping him waiting, then remembered what her mother told her: Make sure people know they work for you. She slid into her chair and was elated to see her hot drink on her desk. She stopped herself from thanking him. But when she looked up, she had to ask, "Are you okay? You look pale."

Hank straightened, exhaled, and tucked his phone away. But his eyes looked wild. "Yeah. Yeah. I'm fine. How about you?"

Could he be doing drugs? She'd seen movies where addicts were sweaty. Maybe that's where he went every morning: to meet with his dealer. No doubt about it, it was odd that Hank routinely left the casino every morning, seemingly on the pretense of picking up their package deliveries and her tea. Surely there were better things the boob could do with his time, but Padma got the highest mark of her MBA, a C+, in a Human Resources course, and knew not to micromanage. If running errands for thirty minutes in the morning was how Hank needed to do things—so be it. There were worse things he could be doing.

As Padma reached for her cup, she spotted the bio datas on her desk. An itchy blotch popped up on her neck. She glanced at Hank. He frowned as he studied the surveillance monitors. She hoped he hadn't noticed the dossiers. It was one thing to succumb to her mother's pressure, but it was another for her subordinate to think that a woman as attractive as she was needed a matchmaker. To distract him, she asked, "How did the hiring go?" She slid the incriminating pages under a file folder.

"Good. All done. Even the new director of security. Everything is with HR. The new hires start next week."

Padma took a sip of her tea, and it slipped out. "Thanks for this, Hank. I don't know what I'd do without this tea every morning."

Hank stood. "No worries, Padma. It's the least I can do." He held her eyes for a moment, then headed for the door.

Maybe he wasn't such a boob. She glanced at the stack of bio datas, hidden under the folder. "Hank?"

He paused and turned, his hand on the doorknob.

"How did you meet your wife?"

His shoulders relaxed, and a corner of his mouth turned up. "My mom arranged it."

Ugh.

"Our moms belonged to the same book club. They compared notes and thought Pam and I should meet, so they planned a party and, unbeknownst to us, arranged for us to bartend together. We spent the evening doling out cheap wine to a bunch of old people and sneaking shots." He smiled, but Padma thought his eyes seemed sad.

Padma was curious. "Was it love at first sight?"

Hank looked at the monitors. "Maybe not first sight." His smile spread. "But within the hour. Thanks again, Padma. I appreciate everything you've done for me. I really do." He held her eyes.

Padma watched him close the door behind him. She took another sip of her tea and wondered what that was about.

Seventeen

Tee Time

When Hank had arrived at Padma's office, he'd stopped mid-whistle when he'd heard the voices coming from within. Her tea had been hot, and he'd shifted it to his other hand while he'd hugged the wall and eavesdropped, inching back to be outside the security camera's range.

His heart had stopped when he'd heard those words float out from the crack in her door: "Yes. Send the men from Mumbai. Let them come. All three. The big, bald one—Yes, the second one is a banker. I said, all three of them. Send your men and let them take their best shot."

Hitmen were coming for them. From India! On Saturday. Yep. He was gonna end up one of those missing middle managers he'd read about on the internet. He hoped to God he wouldn't be hung naked from some bridge.

Hank could tell from the strain in Padma's voice that these men were being forced on her. She wasn't even thirty years old. What kind of power could she have, up against whoever was calling the shots at Indo-USA Gaming Inc.? So she did the only thing she could in the situation—she warned him. Again. The first time, to let him know he was under suspicion. But this time, to let him know how it was going down.

As he had waited for Padma to return from the ladies' room, Hank had congratulated himself again for having done whatever it was that had earned her loyalty. He had delivered her tea like clockwork, every morning, so she knew he would overhear her call. Most likely, she had watched him approach her door on the hallway camera. Again, what a calculated move to rush out of her office just as he had arrived and leave the headshots of the Indian hitmen on her desk. She was something else, all right.

He could have scooped her in his arms and hugged her, he was so grateful. Now, thanks to Padma's craftiness, he had a timeline. Two days. Saturday. He had to tell Larry and Andre he finally knew exactly what they were up against.

He texted: *Got us a tee time—it's Saturday!*

He had hoped they'd understand what that meant. He'd have to connect with Hector, so the barber would have time to prepare.

Hank had sat in Padma's office, his heart thumping, his leg bouncing up and down. Thinking. What to do next? Out of habit, he had straightened his tie, and an image had flashed across his mind. Would the next person to touch his tie be a funeral director, adjusting it in his coffin? He knew he tended to be a touch morbid that way. Would he even need a tie? The way things were going he'd most likely have a closed-casket funeral just like Dave's. He had shaken off the thought and returned his focus to not ending up in a coffin.

When Padma had returned from the restroom, Hank had gone through the motions of updating her on the hiring status, then headed to his office. He had closed the door and leaned against it. He couldn't remember walking down the hall, but there he was. He looked at the photo atop his credenza, of Pam and their daughter. Would he ever see Claire again?

He knew he had to talk to Larry and Andre and then get to Hector. Fast. The barber needed to know the new timeline.

Why had Padma asked about his wife? Had she been warning him that Pam wasn't safe either? No. Pam had to be safe. She didn't know a thing. None of the wives did. That was Rule Number Four. Tell no one. And they'd made damn sure they'd all obeyed it. Hank had always hung on to the hope that when they had their ten million and he was finally able to tell Pam what they'd done, his wife would forgive him for losing everything, and come back to him. And they'd reunite with their daughter.

If only he wasn't too late.

Eighteen

Fri-Yay

Pam unloaded the groceries on the kitchen counter as Elmer watched, his body stretched along the floor, only his eyes moving. Pam used to love Fri-yay late afternoons. That lull between a busy week of work and the burst of weekend social activity. That was always a special time for her and Hank.

She missed it.

She would usually arrive home first, and on a hot day like this, she might uncork an icy, thirty-dollar bottle of pinot grigio and pad across her flagstone patio to make sure there were a couple of imported beers in the outside beverage fridge, for him. She'd dip into the pool, and when she heard the garage door close, and the familiar cadence of his footsteps through the house, she might slip out of her bathing suit, thankful for the privacy their tall hedges provided. When the screen door slid open and he stepped outside, she'd hold on to the side of the pool, waiting until he approached and saw what she was offering. She loved it when his lips gave that little pop of surprise; his eyebrows would shoot up, and a smile would spread across his handsome face. Hank would hold open a towel and dry her off and they'd either head to their covered patio or inside and make love, his warm touch so sweet against her water-cooled skin. Afterward Hank would whip up margaritas, and they'd sip them until it was time to meet up with their friends for a Friday evening boat ride.

But that was before.

Before they had to sell that house, and its pool.

Now, on a hot Friday afternoon, Pam locked the oscillating fan so it could blow directly on her as she put away the shopping. Sure, you don't need a pool or air-conditioning to have a sex life, but you do need some sort of attraction.

Before they lost the money, when Pam looked at Hank, a shot of electricity ran between them. She'd touch his arm lightly, and he'd grab her fingers with his other hand.

After. She tried not to look at him anymore.

Well, she wouldn't have that problem for much longer. They were really doing this. What would it feel like to know he's never coming home again? She poured herself a glass of water from the tap and looked out the window at her hydrangeas while she drank. This time next week she'd be free. And rich. She tapped her fingers on the laminate countertop. She'd get granite in Boca Raton. Maybe even marble. It wasn't the best for wear and tear, but she could indulge in that finicky surface now that Hank wouldn't be around to spill his hot sauce on it. That marble would stay pristine forever.

She checked her watch. It was eleven a.m. Saturday in New Zealand. What would Claire be doing? She picked up her phone and texted:

Hey. Hope things r good. Would b great if ur dad and I could facetime with u. Are u free in an hour? Or let me know what time tmr would work.

It was the least she could do. Give Claire a last conversation with her father. She heard a car door slam and glanced at her watch again. Elmer's ears twitched, and Pam said to him, "Hank's home early. What do you think he's up to?"

Hank burst through the door and stopped short when he saw her standing in front of the fan. Elmer's tail thumped.

Pam sniffed. "Did you get your hair cut?"

Hank stooped to pet Elmer and ran his other hand over his scalp. He looked like he wasn't sure. Was she imagining things? Last night, when she crawled in between the covers, she could have sworn the slightest hint of the barbershop aftershave had wafted over to her side. But Hank had his hair cut just the previous week. Maybe a few molecules had clung to the pillows, and they were stirred up and released into the air. But now, there was that smell, again, this time in her kitchen. Perhaps it had rubbed off on her own clothes when she had last seen Hector.

She talked to Hank's back while he opened the bottom cupboard and set their large thermos on the counter. "Listen. Thank you for doing this. Making us margaritas."

Hank straightened and looked directly at her, something he didn't do much anymore, and said, in a quiet voice, "It's no problem, Pam."

He checked the fruit basket on the table and, finding it empty, went to the fridge where he pulled out a bag of limes. Pam followed his path with her eyes. She'd try to connect. For old times' sake. "How are Larry and Andre doing?"

Hank opened the cupboard above the fridge and pulled down the tequila.

"Hank?"

He turned, the bottle suspended midair, and raised his eyebrows.

"I asked you a question."

"Oh." He reached for the salt. "Sorry. I thought you were talking to Elmer. You talk to that dog like he's a human being."

"Why would I ask the dog about your friends?"

"I don't know, Pam." He blew out a breath and rubbed a lime between his palms. "I don't know why you do anything, anymore." He rolled the green sphere along the cutting board and cleaved it in two with a practiced stroke.

What was that supposed to mean? Pam watched as he reached for another lime, thought a moment, and then responded, "Why I do anything these days, Hank, is because I feel like I don't have a choice. In anything. Anymore."

Hank's knife hung above the second lime. And then he halved it and reached for a third.

"And I wish with all my heart that I did." Pam turned and left the room.

Nineteen

We'll Be Fine

A re you fucking kidding me?" Larry slammed his trunk closed in the marina parking lot.

"Careful." Andre looked around at the other boaters unloading their supplies for a dinnertime cruise, or maybe even the weekend if they had a live-aboard. "We don't want to attract attention."

Larry scowled at him, but lowered his voice to hiss, "With all that's going on, you think this is a good idea? When did you find out?" He stood with his hands on his hips, his beer cooler and fishing gear at his feet.

Hank moved a few steps closer. "Pam asked me last night," he said, in a low voice. "Pick up your stuff." He looked around, scanning the marina parking lot again, as had become his habit. "Seriously, let's get to the boat. Andre's right. We don't want to attract attention. Pick up your stuff and let's get to the boat."

The men walked down the dock, Hank in the lead, careful not to hurry, looking straight ahead. He was afraid to glance over his shoulder lest he find Larry and Andre tiptoeing behind them like the *Pink Panther* cartoon character. Better not to see. Hank stepped over the gunwale and dropped his gear on the seat while he unlocked the cuddy cabin.

Larry caught up to him. "You could have said no."

Hank lifted his head to face him. "Could I have? Larry? Really? If you could say no to Nancy, would you be wearing those shorts?" Larry winced but didn't look down at his pastel, quilted, patchwork-design Bermudas, embroidered with tiny whales, that Hank speculated Nancy had plucked out of a bargain bin, in probably some sadistic way to wreak revenge on her husband for whatever problems their marriage bore. Hank continued, "We have to look like everything's normal. Marlene wants to scatter Dave's ashes tonight, and nobody's gonna say no to that. We'll take the girls out, have a drink, dump Dave, and bring them back to the dock."

Dave would have gotten a kick out of his remains being "dumped."

Larry pointed his finger close to Hank's chest. "I want to go on record that I think this is an egregious error in judgment."

"Noted."

There was no point in telling Larry he wasn't about to say no to Pam about anything right now. He didn't know what the fuck was going on with her anymore, but earlier in their kitchen she seemed to be giving him some kind of doomsday edict, when all he was wondering was why had she stopped keeping the limes in the fruit bowl. She had to know they weren't as juicy when they were in the fridge. And then she'd gone on some philosophical rant about *wishing with all her heart she had a choice.* Fuck. Just put the limes in the fruit bowl, Pam. There's your choice.

He turned back in time to hear Larry ask Andre, "Do you think we should all be together, right now? The three of us are fucking sitting ducks, and now our wives are fucking sitting ducks with us. When those hitmen get here, it'll be like shooting fish in the fucking proverbial barrel. They'll take us all out." He dropped into the cushioned captain's chair like a deadweight, his neck craning this way and the other.

Hank grinned at him. "What are we, Larry? Ducks or fish? Make up your mind." Then he disappeared into the cabin.

Now Andre scanned the marina grounds. "Once we're out on the water we'll be fine."

Hank stuck his head out the cabin door and held out a jar of roasted peanuts. "Snack?" When Larry and Andre waved it off, Hank poured some into his palm and then popped them into his mouth. "I already told you," he said, with his mouth full. "They're not coming until tomorrow. We'll be fine."

"Like hitmen are reliable when it comes to scheduling. If they got an earlier flight they could come at us anytime." Larry picked up a pair of binoculars and turned them toward the parking lot. "And you told Hector, right? About these guys from India?"

Hank took another handful of peanuts and screwed the lid back on the jar. Now Larry was going to ride him. No, Hank hadn't told Hector that, specifically. He didn't want to get into it with Larry and Andre right now, but if he'd told Hector hitmen were coming from India, then Hector could make the connection to the casino. And then he could make the next connection—that there could be a lot of casino money floating around. Hank didn't want Hector making those connections, so he'd been vague. Hector didn't ask a lot of questions, and Hank liked that about him.

But Hank knew Larry and Andre wouldn't like that answer.

So instead, Hank repeated what he'd told Larry the last time he asked. "I told Hector to kill anyone who's after us. We don't care who they are."

Twenty

Bad People

Brenda Palumbo-Chavez watched her husband sweep the last of the hair clippings into a neat pile. "You're sure the wives said it's for the insurance money?"

"That's what they said."

"Hmm." Brenda picked up a cloth and passed it over the counter. "And the husbands want you to kill whoever's after them?"

"That's what they said."

"Do you think they know it's their wives?"

Hector stopped sweeping and leaned on the broom. He smiled to himself. This was the second time she'd asked him that. Funny how she accepted the wives were killing their husbands but couldn't fathom that the husbands could kill their wives. He watched her wipe a spot on the counter. He understood her confusion and congratulated himself. She knew he could never harm her. Ever. His mother would be proud of him. Brenda turned to face him, her eyebrow raised in question. He shrugged. "You know how it is, amor. Some things we'll never know."

Brenda looked out the window. "There's a Reese Witherspoon and Ashton Kutcher movie on Netflix."

"Oh yeah?" Hector smiled.

When Hector had first moved to the States, his ESL teacher suggested he watch movies to improve his English. Every day, when he wasn't job hunting, Hector planted himself on the sofa and turned on the classics: *Goodfellas, The Godfather, Pulp Fiction, Get Shorty, Snatch, Scarface.* But when Hector had started calling money "dough" and when passing the dessert tray to her dad urged him to "take the cannoli, leave the gun," she'd stepped in. She'd prepared a list for Hector's recommended viewing, and they'd sat side by side and watched those movies until they could practically recite the lines aloud. Yet another thing they enjoyed doing together.

Jerry Maguire, Notting Hill, Love Actually, When Harry Met Sally, and *Sleepless in Seattle* were the tip of the iceberg. Hector knew his wife appreciated his soft spot for Reese Witherspoon—*Walk the Line, Legally Blonde,* and especially *Election.* For a while Hector spoke with a bit of a Nashville twang.

Brenda folded the cloth by its corners. "Remember *Sweet Home Alabama*? Remember the misunderstanding when Melanie thought Jake didn't love her anymore, but really everything he had done was for her, she just didn't know it. Jake had this hope he could get her back—"

Hector put up his hand. "Stop right there, amor. First of all, ninety percent of rom-com plots are that same misunderstanding, and secondly, I'm not going to look for some rom-com analogy to justify these people. I know you look for the good in people, and I love that about you, but sometimes . . . people are fucked up."

"I guess."

Hector put his broom aside, walked over to his wife, and cradled her face in his hands. "In my line of work, it's either bad people doing bad things to other bad people"—he shrugged—"or sometimes, it's good people doing bad things. Either way—it's fucked up."

"Could be. Well, if nothing else, you've got yourself the perfect double dip."

"I do not know this term."

"It's when you're paid for two jobs but only have to do one. A double dip. That's what this is. The husbands want what they want. The wives want what they want. They're both paying you. But you only have to do one of their jobs."

Hector nodded slowly. "Because the dead ones won't know I didn't finish their job."

"Exactly."

Hector mulled that over for a moment, then said, "That's obviously an American term. Because in El Salvador we do the job we're hired for. To completion." He kissed her forehead.

Twenty-One

Goodbye, Dave

"F ucking Hank. Again."

Pam stood at the back of her open van and stared at the boxes of casino glasses Hank had scooped up when the logo changed. She'd let him use her van to bring more home, but the deal included unloading this crap. Yet another way he'd let her down. She checked her watch. She closed the back, went around to the passenger side, and carefully placed her foil-covered charcuterie board on the front seat. Pam hadn't been sure what type of snacks to pack for an ash scattering, so she'd gone with cured meats and cheese. And carrot sticks and hummus for Andre.

She looked at her dashboard clock. She was okay for time. Before, when she still lived in her comfortable home on Glendale Avenue, she wouldn't have to factor in the extra minutes it took to reach her friends. Before, she would have backed out her driveway, made two rights, and been at Shalisa's door. Now she'd have to wait at three lights.

Pam pulled up to Shalisa's, and as Shalisa slid in, Pam lifted the tray, set it back down on her lap, and said, "The first thing I'm gonna do when we get our insurance money—I'm hiring someone to cut that down for you." Pam pointed toward the offending juniper bush.

She reversed onto the street and saw Nancy waiting at the curb a few houses down. Andre had once joked he'd heard the city contractors complaining they had to replace the sidewalk connecting their homes because the two women had worn a trough in the cement, creating a tripping hazard.

Nancy climbed in, and a moment later she leaned forward between the driver and passenger seat and pushed her glasses up her nose. "I was thinking, if we get back early from the boat, maybe after we drop Marlene off, we could swing by Nordstrom. They're having a big sale, and I'll need a new black dress for the funeral. Maybe two, if the visitation is a different day. Three if it's two days."

It was a good thing Pam was already stopped at the red light, because if she'd been driving her snacks would have flown through the windshield when she slammed the brakes in shock. Pam closed her eyes for a moment and pinched the bridge of her nose. She glanced at Shalisa and was reassured to see her squinting at Nancy apparently also in disbelief. Good. It wasn't just Pam. "Nancy, if we were spotted shopping for black dresses two days before we knew we needed them for our husbands' funerals, how would that look to the police?"

"Ohhh." Nancy sat back in her seat. "Sorry. I didn't think about that. You're absolutely right. I saw seventy-five percent off and got carried away."

Pam drove another two blocks and turned into Dave and Marlene's driveway like she had a thousand times before. Marlene came down her front steps holding a white cardboard box. Pam riffled through her Rolodex of memories until she landed on a few previous times she'd sat in this same spot, with Hank in the driver's seat, to pick up Dave and Marlene and then head over to Shalisa's, or Nancy's, or the marina. The times Marlene had skipped ahead to join them in the car while Dave had locked up and then made his way down the driveway, his hair gelled, carrying his cooler of beer. So vibrant and alive. He'd climb in the front seat, turn around, and offer her a wink and a "Don't you look nice tonight, Pammy," and then turn to chat with Hank.

He was a good guy. And now he was in a box on his wife's lap.

Marlene patted the smooth sides. "Oh, it's not all of him. It's only a quarter. I saved some for each of the girls." She pulled the box closer. "I hope I got his hands. He had great hands."

They were silent the rest of the drive to the marina and the walk down the dock. Before she climbed on board, Marlene passed Dave to Hank. Pam watched her husband falter as he took his friend's remains in his hands and brought them to his chest. The color drained from his face as he carefully carried the box into the cabin and placed it under the bow. For a fleeting second, Pam wanted to rest her head on Hank's shoulder and her hand in the middle of his back. But just for a second. She shook her head—no— and went straight to where the cooler was stowed and found the thermos of margaritas Hank had mixed for her and the girls. Pam almost hadn't asked him to make them, leery of piling on another favor, but a Friday night on the boat wouldn't be the same without Hank's signature cocktail. Hank always said if he had chosen a different path in life, it would have been bartending.

Larry and Andre undid the lines, and Hank headed his boat out the channel to the open water of the Atlantic. The sun was still high in the sky, but the wind had died down and the water was smooth as glass. It was like the old days. For a good stretch of time, once the kids were off on their own on Friday nights, and before their lives fell apart, this had been their regular routine. If the weather was good, they would meet at the dock, load the boat with drinks and snacks, and head out. On really hot nights they'd swim off the stern. But most often there was enough breeze that they were comfortable just sitting, bobbing on the subtle swells. Drinking, eating, talking, and laughing. There was always so much laughter.

After their lives changed Pam had fought with Hank to get rid of the thirty-foot Sea Ray Sundancer and its expenses, but he had held firm against her. It was paid for, he said. And they needed some joy in their lives. Yet Pam and the wives never stepped on it again. Why? Why had they stopped? They had loved doing this, and there was no price tag attached; the only investment was their time. Why hadn't they spent it here?

Pam looked back on the shoreline as they headed through the buoys. Hank pointed the boat south and ran full throttle for a few minutes. Pam sank into the rhythm of the bounces as though five summers hadn't passed since she had last been here. Behind her sunglasses she studied Hank. His ball cap on backward so the wind wouldn't rip it away. His hands, strong and tanned on the wheel. He wore khaki shorts, and although his belly hung over the waistband, his legs and bum still had definition. From behind, he could be thirty. She remembered how she would come up behind him and wrap her arms around his waist, resting her cheek between his shoulder blades, against the sun-warmed, soft cotton of his T-shirt. She remembered the smell of sea salt mixed with their laundry detergent and his sweat. She closed her eyes and turned away.

Hank eased up on the gas, and the boat slowed. He cut the motor, and they gently bobbed. Larry went to the bow, dropped the anchor, and tied it off. Andre connected his iPhone to the sound system and hit play. Pam didn't have to ask, she knew he'd select the guys' mutually curated playlist they titled *Fun Depressing*. And it was. A bit of sentimental, a bit of rock, a bit of country. John Prine, Alabama Shakes, Van Morrison, Bruce Springsteen, Tom Waits, Wilco, Johnny Cash, Steve Earle, and Miss Etta James.

It had started with a mixtape of a handful of songs, and once Hank created an Apple Music account, he and the guys had taken years to expand it, one song at a time. The process had often played out before her. They'd be sitting around, anywhere—a restaurant, a car, someone's home—and a song would come on. Hank would stop talking, cock his head, listen for a moment, and ask the room, "What is that?" One of them would reply, and another would google the artist. They'd talk about it for a bit, and then came the thumbs down or up—"Add it to the playlist, Hank." Last Pam heard, they were up to about eight hundred songs.

"Refills?" Hank asked, then dug in the ice and pulled out fresh cans, crushing the spent ones and tucking them away in a bag. He closed the cooler, and Pam peeled the foil from the charcuterie board and set it on top. Pam raised her eyebrows when Andre passed on the carrot sticks, homing in on a cracker, slices of cheddar, and kielbasa. So much for his diet.

They sat in companionable silence. Watching other boats in the distance and sipping their drinks. After a bit, Hank disappeared into the cabin and returned with the box holding Dave's remains. Or at least, twenty-five percent of them. He set them on the captain's chair, then opened another beer. They listened to the low music and the sound of the hull gently bouncing on the water. A handful of birds flew overhead. After a few minutes, Hank said, "How do you want to do this, Marlene?"

Marlene had been following the flight path of some seagulls, but she looked over at Hank and said in a voice Pam could barely hear, "I don't want to do this at all, Hank." She paused, then said, "The family-man part of Dave is still at home. Our girls will decide what we do with that." She nodded to the box. "But that's the part of Dave that loved you guys. Whatever you think, Hank."

Hank nodded and watched a sailboat off their starboard side. Finally, he straightened, said, "Okay," and went back into the cabin. He returned a moment later with a fistful of cigars and a half-full bottle of scotch. He passed red Solo cups around and filled each with a knuckle of the amber liquid.

He offered a cigar to Larry, who said, "Maybe not the cigars, Hank. The smell makes Nancy nauseous. We can smoke them later, for Dave."

Hank tucked them back in the cabin and then instructed, "Andre, pick a song for Dave."

Hank gave Andre a minute to make his selection, then stepped to the stern, on the swim platform, held the box tight, and looked at the group. "Dave thought he had everything in life, and then he thought he lost it. But he didn't give up. You should know that, Marlene. He never gave up. And I can honestly say he used more grooming products than any man I'll ever know."

Hank opened the box, and twenty-five percent of Dave Brand arced into the sky.

Andre hit play, and Pam started, her margarita slipping over the side of her cup as the upbeat notes burst from the boat's speakers. Pam had expected soft and melancholy—Charlie Puth or Ed Sheeran—but instead, two bars of raunchy rock guitar blared, then drums joined for three, until the full band kicked in for another four. Pam couldn't peg the song until she heard Steve Earle's gritty vocals in "Hard-Core Troubadour." Then she settled back and exchanged smiles with her friends. Marlene threw her head back, laughed, and gave Andre a thumbs-up. Pam wiped away a tear, remembering Dave in so many places, so many times, dancing to this song. Moving a glowing, giggling Marlene in and out, under his arm, around his back. His hair in his eyes, his smile wide across his gorgeous face, his dimples deep. She squeezed her eyes shut to watch the memory play out.

When they reached the final chorus Marlene began the lyrics low, Nancy followed her lead, picked up volume, and then the others joined in. Belting out, their voices reaching the shore, the last lines of the song. As the notes faded, Hank fired up the engine and nosed the boat toward the harbor.

The sun's rays stretched long across the water, warming Dave's ashes on the glassy surface as they began to dissipate and disappear.

Goodbye, Dave.

All the way back to the marina Pam ran Hank's words through her mind. Not the ones about the grooming products, but the ones about not giving up.

Once the boat was secured, Pam, Nancy, Shalisa, and Marlene stepped up on the dock and took turns hugging each other. Hank stayed on board, using the pretense that there was some sort of fuel leak he needed to get looked at, and Pam partially believed him. She'd caught a whiff of gas, but that wasn't too unusual on the boat. She watched him from the dock while he coiled a line. The muscles in his forearms tensed and released with practiced rhythm. Maybe if he came home with her, they could talk. Would he come home with her if she asked?

She waited a moment, seeing if she could catch his eye, and when she didn't, she knew that he wanted to go back out on the water with Larry and Andre. To drink more scotch, smoke their cigars, and remember their friend. She turned, picked up her empty charcuterie board, and trudged up the dock. She thought she heard something and paused for a brief second. It must have been a seagull. She carried on toward the parking lot.

Pam dropped Marlene off first. They went in for a nightcap, but it was quick. It had been a long day, and Marlene was drained, ready for bed. Marlene turned the porch light on as she hugged her friends good night, and then Pam drove Nancy and Shalisa home. She pulled into her own driveway and sat in the van, thinking for a minute. She noted the weeds sprouting along her front walkway. She should pull them. Hank said Dave never gave up. If Dave never gave up, then why had Hank?

At the heart of it, wasn't that their problem? Hank had given up. On them. Him and Pam. He withdrew. If he had fought for her, maybe she'd have fought too. It was too late for Dave and Marlene. But was it too late for her and Hank? She climbed out of her van, and as she unlocked her front door her phone vibrated in her purse. Pam dropped her bag and scrambled, swiping the phone just in time.

"Claire!"

She did a quick calculation. It was ten p.m. Friday night, here, but in New Zealand it was Saturday afternoon.

"Hi, Mom! Sorry I couldn't call earlier. We've been busy. But I thought I'd try and catch you now."

Pam sank down on her front step. "Oh, sweetheart! How are you? You look amazing." Pam's pupils had to adjust to the brightness coming from the screen. Her beautiful, blond daughter was bathed in sunlight, with a glimpse of a blue ocean behind her.

"Why are you in the dark, Mom?"

"I was just getting in from the boat. We went out to scatter Uncle Dave's ashes. I just dropped everyone off and am getting home. How's Dylan?"

"He's great. Is Dad there?"

"No. He's back at the marina checking something out on the boat. He won't be home for a while."

"Well . . . I wanted to tell you both, but I can't wait. Mom! You're going to be a grandma!"

Pam grabbed her chest, sure she could feel her heart grow two sizes. Tears pricked her eyes, and she reminded herself to breathe.

"And . . . wait for it, Mom. We're coming home! We want the baby to grow up near Grandma and Grandpa."

———

Ten minutes later Pam squealed to a stop at Nancy's curb, and her friend jumped in.

"What's going on, Pam?"

Pam hit the gas before Nancy could finish her question.

"We've gotta get to Shalisa's." Pam gunned the engine.

When Shalisa opened her front door, Pam brushed by her with Nancy trailing behind. Once inside the cramped foyer, Pam waited for the door to close and then said, "We can't kill them."

Shalisa took a step forward and jabbed the air with her finger. "I knew the boat was a bad idea. We go out on the water, get a little nostalgic, the sun is setting, the music is playing, and now you're Little Miss Let's-Try-Again. It was Hank's line about how Dave never gave up, right? That's what changed your mind, isn't it? And you hoped it changed our minds too. Well, for what it's worth—it sure looks to me like Hank gave up. Where is he right now? Did he come home with you? Did any of them? No. On a night like tonight, when we scatter our friend's ashes, maybe we could use our husbands' support. But *nooo*. They fucked off and stayed at the marina. They have each other. *That's* who's important to them. They've given up on us. And you know it." She pointed at Pam for punctuation.

Shalisa was right. Pam had hoped the boat ride had softened the others up too, and that they were also second-guessing their decision. She repeated, "We can't kill them."

"We can't *not* kill them! We've hired the hitman." Nancy crossed her arms and stood with her back to the door.

"We've only paid the deposit."

Shalisa put her hands on her hips. "It's not like we're canceling the lawn guy, Pam. I doubt Hector has a refund policy. And do you really want to renege on your hitman?"

Pam held her palms up. "I don't care. We cannot do this."

Nancy looked at Pam. "It was your idea."

Pam stomped her foot. "It was not! Are you kidding me? And why do we always go to whose idea it was, anyway? Like we're in eighth grade. I wanted to hire a hitman, but killing them was your idea. You had to talk me into it."

Nancy said, "And how hard was that? All Hank had to do was eat your leftover pad thai and wham, he landed smack-dab on your hit list. I'd hate to think what would happen if he ever ate a full order. Are you telling me that's a marriage you can save?"

"If you'd remember correctly, I said I didn't want to kill Claire's dad, and you asked me, when was the last time I'd seen her. But that's the thing.

Claire's coming home! And! She's having a baby. Hank and I are going to be grandparents."

Nancy and Shalisa threw their arms in the air in surprise, and then around Pam's shoulders. They clutched each other and murmured their congratulations. When they broke apart, Shalisa wiped away a tear. "We're having our first grandchild."

Nancy squeezed Pam again. "Pam, that's wonderful news. We're so happy for you. Truly happy. But that doesn't change anything for me or Shalisa. The way Larry is, I wouldn't even be able to *see* my grandchildren, and I can't live like that. I have to do this."

Pam thought a moment. "Well, you guys go ahead. But I'm out." Of course, that would face her with another tricky moral dilemma—could she stand by and watch two of her friends have their husbands killed? Well, she'd cross that bridge when she got there. As long as she and Hank could enjoy their grandchild, she didn't care.

Nancy said, "Oh no you don't. We said right from the beginning, we're either all in or all out."

Pam grabbed their hands. "Well, let's get all out then. Please. We can't do this. This is only about money. So what? We can't give up on our husbands. We married them! We can get things back."

"I can't." Shalisa wrested herself from Pam's grip, sat down on the stairs, and put her head in her hands for a moment and then looked up at them. "Don't you see? I can't get my love for Andre back. I've tried to scrape by on the little bits I could hold on to for the past thirty years. But I have officially let go of that man. You said the other day you didn't realize my life was *that* bad. And that's the thing. I've been burying things for years, and I'm done. Since we made the decision to do this, well, I feel like *me* again. And I like it. I miss *me*." Shalisa took a breath and looked at the floor. "I know everyone's always wondered why Andre and I never had kids. I never said anything because . . . well, because it hurt."

Indeed, Pam had always wondered, especially when Shalisa and Andre were so great with everyone else's kids. But in an unusual display of restraint, she had never pried. If Shalisa wanted to share, she would. And now, finally, she was.

Shalisa rubbed her forehead with both hands. "I've been thinking about it a lot lately, and I'm done pushing it down." She took her hands away and brought her eyes back up. "We'd planned to. I wanted a family. But right after we got married, he came home one day and out of the blue said he didn't want kids. He talked about how he'd decided he didn't want the responsibility." Shalisa waved away the memory. "Oh, it doesn't matter why. But he changed my whole plan. Said I had to choose—kids or him."

Pam gasped. That fucking Andre. Maybe they should kill him.

Tears glistened in Shalisa's eyes. "I was devastated. I kicked him out, and he went to live with his mom. For eight months, I never saw him until one day he turned up on my doorstep. He looked terrible. He'd lost a ton of weight. He hadn't changed his mind, but asked if I would consider staying with him. And I knew then that I still loved him." A tear slid down her cheek. "I felt so betrayed. But I'd been with him since high school. I didn't feel strong enough to keep living without him. So we got back together. I thought I'd gotten over it, but it's been eating away at me for years. And now that I have a choice, I've decided: I can't waste another day with that man."

What could Pam say to that? No wonder Shalisa never talked about it. But wait. She had a thought.

Pam crouched before her friend. "But we don't have to kill him. We'll help you start a new life. Marlene will too, I know it. We'll figure it out. You can be *you* again. But we can still call off the hit."

Pam held Shalisa's eyes and silently said to herself, *Please say yes, please say yes.* She let Shalisa ponder her plea, stood, and turned to Nancy. "You can't have Larry killed. You can't take him away from his son."

Nancy scrunched up her face and shook her head. She sighed, opened her eyes, and looked at Pam. "Don't you see, Pam? Whatever relationship Paul and Larry had, it's dead. Larry did that. I'm not taking Larry away from his son. *Larry* already did that."

Pam rubbed her forehead. "I am so sorry you're dealing with this, Nancy. I had no idea Larry was . . . a fucking homophobic neanderthal. None at all. I guess we never talked about it. And we should have. I know for a fact, Hank isn't. Hank spoke at his nephew's wedding and welcomed his husband into our family with open arms. Hank will talk to Larry. We'll have an intervention. We'll get Paul back. You'll meet Estuardo. You shouldn't have had to deal with this alone, and now you won't. I promise. Heck. If you can get Larry to wear those shorts he had on tonight, you can get him to do anything. You love Larry. You know you do. This is a bump in your marriage— granted, it's a huge fucking bump, but you'll get over it. We'll help. He's lost his way. We'll help him find it. We'll do this together."

Nancy leaned against the wall and stared at the floor. Pam waited.

Shalisa said in a quiet voice from the stairs, "But then we won't have the money."

Pam waved that away. "So what? We'll figure it out." Pam doubled down. "Honestly. We have to stop being victims and just fucking move on with our lives. I hate to say it, but as much as we've supported each other, I think we've let each other down. We've wallowed in our loss. Or at least, I have. I see it now. Hank made a mistake. About money. Fucking money. So what? He's still a good man. He's still *my* man. I'm not going to kill him."

Where had this clarity come from? Was it remembering the feel of Hank's T-shirt under her cheek that stirred up her fight? Was that what finally nudged her out of this downward spiral of despair to an upward battle for her own life? And Hank's. A life together. Or was it learning she had a grandchild on the way? Christ. Who the fuck cared? She could do this. She didn't know how. She just knew she could. And so could her friends.

"We've ordered the hit." Nancy shook her head slowly. "I don't know much about hitman protocol." She shot Pam a look. "I couldn't google it. But I think once these things get going, there's no turning back."

"Hector will understand. As long as he gets paid, what does he care? I told him to do it Sunday, so we have two days. I'll find him tomorrow and call it off. We'll let him keep the money." Pam put her hands up to fend off the protests. "I know. I know. I have no idea how we'll repay Marlene or get the rest." Her eyebrows shot up. "Maybe we should open up that little coffee truck like we told Marlene you were doing. Maybe we could start a business. Instead of wasting our energy tearing our husbands down, maybe it's time to start building something up. I don't have the answers, but I know we can figure it out."

Nancy's and Shalisa's expressions remained unchanged. Unsure she'd said enough, Pam pushed. "We are strong, confident women. We let life knock us down, but we can get back up. Without killing our husbands. We *can* do this."

Nancy and Shalisa were silent. But they didn't disagree.

Pam pressed. "Tomorrow I'll tell Hector it's off."

Had she said enough? Nancy and Shalisa looked at each other, and Pam held her breath. After a long pause, they nodded.

Pam felt like the weight of an upright freezer had been lifted from her chest. Thank fucking God. They had stood on the brink of disaster, and she had brought them back. Her heart was racing.

Shalisa's doorbell rang. Who could be here at this hour?

Shalisa stood and looked through the peephole, and Nancy and Pam moved into the living room. Pam leaned against Shalisa's Peloton bike, looked out through the front window, and saw two police officers on the front step. A cruiser was parked in the driveway.

Pam had a clear view because Shalisa's juniper bush was gone.

Where the fuck had that juniper gone?

Twenty-Two

Some Gals Knit

P am peed her pants a little at the sight of police uniforms and was happy to be wearing the special underwear she'd ordered online. Twenty bucks a pair was beyond her budget, but in that moment, it was money well spent.

How much had the police officers heard? Had Hector tipped them off? Could he have been wearing a wire? Did Nancy google the sentence for conspiracy to commit murder, because surely that's what they were being charged with?

Oh, the shame. *My grandma's in jail.*

Now they would end up on TV, for sure. Pam looked through the newly unobstructed view from Shalisa's front window to check if there were any news cameras. At least not yet. And when had that juniper come down? Wasn't it there when she picked Shalisa up earlier? Do handcuffs hurt?

Pam perked up. If the cops *had* been listening, they must have overheard their decision to cancel the hit. Maybe Pam could blame it on postmenopause and low estrogen. Some gals knit; others pretend they're killing their husbands.

She felt faint.

There was murmuring at the front door and checking of names and notebooks. Pam had to sit down. She might need a glass of orange juice. She stumbled across the living room and sank into an armchair. She looked up at Nancy, who hadn't moved. Pam forced herself to breathe. She felt like she was floating underwater. She had a sense of something going on but couldn't quite grasp what it was.

"Pam Montgomery?"

She surfaced.

A young police officer towered over her. He couldn't have been more than thirty. Had he gone to school with Claire or Paul? Perhaps Andre had coached him in soccer. Maybe he'd go easy on them, at least be gentle when he loaded them into the cruiser's backseat. He wore a name tag, but she didn't want to pull out her readers to see if she recognized his surname.

"You're Hank Montgomery's wife?" He squatted to be at her eye level. "The same Hank Montgomery who keeps a boat at Seven Winds Marina?"

Pam nodded. The officer exchanged a look with his partner. Nancy came over, perched beside her on the chair's arm, and entwined her fingers through Pam's. The partner guided Shalisa to the sofa, and then both officers stood before them, feet splayed, hands on belts.

One spoke. "We are here with some unfortunate news." She took a breath, looked again at her partner, and then said, "There has been an incident involving your husbands." She referred to her notebook. "Witnesses report three men, identified as your husbands, took a boat out the channel to open water. Just after sunset there was a catastrophic explosion in the vicinity where they were last seen. Theirs was the only vessel in the area."

The other officer spoke. "The Coast Guard is there now with their search-and-rescue team, including helicopters. It's dark. They are doing their best, but early reports are that—"

The partner interjected, "The preliminary inspection of the site has shown a wide field of debris. They are still looking for survivors. But we think you should prepare yourselves."

In the quiet Pam heard the officer swallow.

Pam looked at him. "But it's only Friday."

"I beg your pardon?" he replied.

She'd specifically told Hector to kill them on Sunday.

Pam hated when people screwed up simple instructions.

But Hector didn't seem like the type to screw up.

Twenty-Three

A Deal's a Deal

The two police officers stayed with the three wives until Nancy's son Paul and his partner Estuardo arrived to drive them to the search command center that had been set up at the marina. As they climbed out of the backseat of Estuardo's jeep, the night air thrummed with the *chop-chop* of helicopters panning spotlights across the dark waters. In the distance, the red, green, and white lights of the Coast Guard boats traversed the surface, in a grid pattern, they were told.

But no Hank. No Larry. No Andre.

The women huddled on the marina lawn and waited. When the news crews arrived, Paul suggested Pam may want to call Claire and Dylan so they wouldn't find out about her father through social media. In all their planning, Pam hadn't thought much about that call. But she stumbled through it, and her daughter and her husband were coming from New Zealand.

As the sun peeked over the horizon and then climbed higher in the sky, curious bystanders sipped their coffees on the lawn and watched the boats come and go.

"Maybe they jumped off and swam away before the boat blew up," Pam overheard someone say.

Search parties combed the shoreline. Appeals were broadcast. Nothing.

By noon, divers retrieved some pieces of the wreckage that had sunk, but nothing larger than a steering wheel remained from the explosion that was seen and heard miles away. Officials requested their husbands' dental records.

The initial shock wore off, and Pam was flooded with emotions. Grief for the loss of her husband. Fear she was going to be charged with his murder. Anger he'd put her in this position in the first place. Pam wasn't sure she was rational. She thought it was a good sign that she was rational enough to question if she was, in fact, rational. But mostly she felt numb.

Days earlier, she, Nancy, and Shalisa had sat at the kitchen table and reviewed how they should react when the authorities knocked—but none of that happened. After the police officers delivered the news, the women all selected door number one, and remained stunned.

As the hours passed, Paul and Estuardo set up three folding camp chairs under the shaded canopy of a towering oak and waited off to the side. Pam moved toward the chairs, and she caught movement out of the corner of her eye. She turned in time to see Estuardo open his arms and Paul step into their comforting cocoon. They stood, wrapped together. How could Larry deny his son that care? That was all any parent wanted for their child: for them to be loved. Pam remembered how Hank's arms around her used to salve her soul, and she wished with all her heart she could step into them again. And now she never would.

She shook off that regret, sat down, and turned her eyes to the water. Sitting in a row with Nancy and Shalisa, Pam was reminded of the three monkeys: see-no-evil, hear-no-evil, speak-no-evil. Pam was mostly worried about the speaking monkey.

"Just don't say anything," Pam said in a low voice to Shalisa, and Nancy beyond her.

"About what?" Shalisa asked.

Pam leaned forward so she could make eye contact. "About hiring a hit-man to kill our husbands. That's what." She sat back.

"I can't believe you're thinking about that right now," Nancy said.

Pam leaned forward again. "Well, pardon me for fast-forwarding through the stages of grief to get to the one that doesn't want us to spend the rest of our lives in jail. When the police rang Shalisa's doorbell, I thought they were arresting us. I thought they *knew*. We have to be sure we don't say anything. About anything."

Nancy and Shalisa turned their eyes back to the water and nodded.

Nancy said, "You know, if this had happened five hours earlier, I would have been happy."

"You mean before we went out on the boat?" Shalisa asked.

Nancy nodded. "Five frickin' hours away from wanting something so badly I could taste it, to not wanting it and hating that it happened."

Shalisa grasped Pam's and Nancy's hands on either side of her and said, "To tell you the truth, I'm sorry for you guys. But I don't really mind that it happened to Andre."

Pam snatched her hand away and turned to face Shalisa. She took a quick look around to be sure they weren't overheard, then hissed, "How can you say that? We changed our minds."

Shalisa kept her eyes on the water. "You two changed your minds. I was just being agreeable. I decided I was going to leave Andre anyway." She looked at Pam. "You said you'd all help me. I agreed to let him live, not to stay with him." Her eyes returned to the water. "I've given too much of myself to that man. He wasn't getting any more. Anyway, my mom always said, things happen for a reason. And this way, we still get the insurance money."

Pam gasped and glanced at Nancy, whose jaw dropped.

Shalisa looked from one to the other and sighed. "Oh, all right. Maybe I am sorry for Andre. I *would* have liked it if he'd lived, but we can't do anything about it now. And you have to admit—we changed our minds, but it happened anyway. Maybe the universe is telling us something." She shrugged. "Maybe they were meant to die."

Pam sat back. Her stomach was roiling up and down like the boats on the open water. She took a deep breath. It didn't matter what Shalisa thought. That was between her and Andre. But Hank was gone, and it was because of her.

Or was it?

Another search vessel pulled away from the dock.

Pam said, "Maybe it wasn't us."

Nancy and Shalisa leaned forward to see her face, but Pam kept her eyes on the boat as it headed out the channel, beginning to bob a bit as it left the calm of the harbor for the mild chop of the sea.

"What do you mean, 'maybe it wasn't us'?" asked Nancy.

Pam took a deep breath, looked around to be sure no one had come within earshot, and leaned forward to huddle, her voice still low. "I mean, don't you remember? Hank said there might be a gas leak. The last thing he talked about was sticking around to take a look at that leak. And I smelled gas when we were on the boat. Didn't you?"

Shalisa nodded, but Nancy shrugged. "I'm not sure. I don't remember."

Pam continued, "Well, Hank said he was going to check it out. If it was nothing, they were going to head back out for a nightcap, and a cigar." She nodded toward the command center. "I heard one of the inspectors saying Hank filled up just before he went out again. Maybe this wasn't us. Maybe this *was* an accident."

"Do you think Hector will charge us the rest of his fee?" Nancy asked.

Shalisa's head snapped to her. "That's what you're worried about? Wondering if we still have to pay full price?"

Nancy shrugged. "It's a legit question."

Pam said, "If Hector didn't do it, how would we ever know? If anything, we should refuse to pay him because he screwed up and did it two days early."

"You think he's worried we won't give him a five-star rating on Yelp?" Shalisa said.

Pam insisted, "I specifically said Sunday. A deal's a deal." She sat back in the camp chair. "I just think it's something to think about. Maybe this wasn't Hector's handiwork. Maybe we're not responsible."

Nancy said, "I wish that made me feel better."

Hours later, Pam's head was bobbing as she dozed in her chair. A horn honked in the parking lot, and startled, Pam turned toward the blare. A smile broke out across her face when she saw Marlene's teased blond hairdo pop out of Estuardo's jeep. Marlene juggled a tray of coffees and a box of donuts. The women rose to greet her, and as Marlene closed the gap between them, she sped up and tossed aside the coffees and snacks, leaving a trail of debris in her wake. With mascara tears streaming tracks down her cheeks, she ran toward her friends as if pulled by a magnetic force and fell into their arms. Black tears soaked into the shoulders of Pam's sweatshirt, but Pam didn't cry. Finally, as the others composed themselves, Estuardo produced another chair and Marlene joined them, their fourth monkey. Pam strained to recall what that monkey represented, then the penny dropped. Do no evil. Well, Marlene was the only one of them who could sit in that chair.

Or maybe not. Maybe this had been an accident. Maybe the explosion was a crazy coincidence.

Finally settled, sipping fresh coffees that Pam's new favorite couple, Paul and Estuardo, had fetched for them, Marlene said, "You'll never guess who I saw at the coffee shop."

After a moment Shalisa said, "Who did you see at the coffee shop, Marlene?"

"Dave's barber."

Pam's arm jerked, and a dark patch of coffee spread across her light khakis. She straightened and held her breath, bracing for Marlene's next words.

"I don't remember his name. Victor or something. Whoa. Good-looking man. Very mysterious. Captivating eyes. Nice shoulders. Must be from working with his arms so much." Marlene inched forward in her chair and skewed toward them. "Anyway, he wanted me to pass on a message . . . What was it he said? Oh yeah. He's praying for good news. And to let him know if he could do anything else."

A chill ran down Pam's spine. "He said that? He said that, exactly?"

"What?" Marlene asked.

"He said anything *else*? Not just if he could do anything?" Pam prodded.

"Huh. I guess so. I'm just repeating the message. I didn't exactly transcribe it."

Pam sat back in her chair and, despite the raging heat, shivered.

Twenty-Four

Five Sisters

Padma was beginning to wonder if perhaps she was too preoccupied with height. Both requiring it of her prospective husband and providing the illusion of it herself. Aware of the tricks to elongate the female form, her mother had advised she always wear either vertical stripes, small print patterns, V-necks, or monochromatic color schemes and always, always wear heels. Even her bedroom slippers were wedges.

Padma stretched out her calves while the hostess confirmed her table, and then followed the perky ponytail as it cut a path through the restaurant's bar. Patrons quietly swirled ice in their cocktails as Padma passed, their eyes riveted to the silent television screen broadcasting a wide shot of Coast Guard vessels returning to the marina where Hank had kept his boat. Padma checked the breaking news banner to see if there had been any developments, but it scrolled along the bottom of the screen still declaring "Search Continues."

She took a deep breath and straightened her shoulders. With Hank presumed dead, this was peculiar timing to be meeting Akshay, the first of The Matchmaker's candidates. Padma had contemplated making an appearance at the marina in support of Hank's wife, but her mother had put the situation in perspective—Hank was probably dead and not coming back. "No point crying over spilled milk," her mother had said. Plus, assessing the marina lawn on the TV, Padma had to admit her heels would most likely sink into the grass, and she could break an ankle. She decided that was a risk she wasn't prepared to take; she needed to be in top form if she was going to outmaneuver her mother in her love life and career.

For the sake of efficiency, Padma had decided if her date was completely unattractive, she would thank him for trying and wish him good night. But as she approached Akshay's table, he stood to greet her, and her heart skipped a beat and her armpits became slick with sweat.

"Oh. We're hugging." Padma wore a fitted, low-cut, red-crepe, knee-length dress, bright-red lipstick, and her high heels.

He kissed her cheek, then bobbed to the other side.

"Oh. And kissing too." She was mortified at the sound of her own giggle.

Akshay was tall enough, his hairline was respectable, and his teeth seemed adequate, so she decided she could definitely order. She sat back, ready to be wooed.

They talked about his flight from Mumbai, his hotel, the menu.

Dinner arrived.

Then he talked about movies Padma hadn't seen, books she hadn't read, news stories she hadn't followed, and TV shows she'd never heard of. He didn't know any *Real Housewives* in any city and hadn't even downloaded TikTok. He yawned, and Padma, not to be outdone, yawned wider. The dessert menu arrived. Padma craned her neck to see if there were any updates on the bar's television screen, but programming had changed to a baseball game. She and Akshay both scanned the other diners in the restaurant.

Akshay asked, "Do you have any siblings?"

Padma waved. "I have a brother, but he's married, and I never see him anymore. His wife doesn't like me." Padma shrugged. "Most women don't, unfortunately. They can be so jealous." Padma took a sip of her wine, fiddled with her bracelet, put her hands in her lap, and looked across the table to find Akshay looking back. She started a bit. "Oh. Do you have siblings?"

He kept his gaze steady on her. "Thank you for asking. I have five sisters."

Padma gulped. Then flashed her new smile. Padma had recently realized her bottom teeth were perfectly straight, yet when examining photos of herself, she noticed those teeth were perpetually hidden. So she had been practicing widening her smile to be sure they were seen. She waited for Akshay's next question and was surprised when he raised his hand and called for the bill.

She would email The Matchmaker first thing in the morning to say Akshay was rejected.

Twenty-Five

Thorough Investigation

On the second morning after the explosion, Paul and Estuardo shepherded the four women to a meeting with the officer overseeing the search-and-rescue operation. As Pam entered the tent pitched on the marina's lawn, her eyes adjusted to the dimness. Three uniformed men stood to the side, holding their hats in clasped hands. A circular fan plugged into an orange extension cord panned the room, offering little relief in the close quarters. Four folding chairs, like you'd see at a church euchre night, were lined up in the center, and Pam took the one closest to the fan. Nancy, Shalisa, and Marlene fell in beside her, and Paul stood behind his mother with his hands on her and Shalisa's shoulders. Estuardo rested a hand on Pam's shoulders, and without thinking, she reached for it. Estuardo squeezed her fingers; his broad grip reminded her of Hank's, and Pam bit her lip.

The senior officer faced the group. A boat engine started in the distance. One of those big cigarette types that only go fast, screaming for attention. It idled and then switched into gear, and Pam could tell by its low throttle that it was headed out to sea. Against that background, Pam heard the words *catastrophic, explosion, recovery. Exhausted our resources.*

Pam lifted her head. "Wait a minute. Are you saying you're giving up and you haven't found their bodies?"

The official exchanged a glance with his colleagues. Another stepped forward and said, "Yes, ma'am. I'm afraid so. With the strength of the explosion, I'm sorry to say we've been unable to locate—"

"But surely, there's something left? You have to keep looking." Would it be gauche to say she needed proof for the insurance? "We need to find something . . . for closure. There has to be something."

The official cleared his throat. "I'm afraid, ma'am, that with the currents, and . . . other factors at play in the ocean, and, uh, currents, we have not been able to recover . . . anything. That is typical of this kind of event, I'm afraid. Especially at night. We're often unable to recover anything before the sea takes . . ."

Pam stopped listening and squeezed her eyes shut. She had fucking told Hector they needed bodies. How could he fuck that up as well as the date? There was no way in hell she was paying him full price. "Wait. How do you know for sure they were even on the boat? Maybe they jumped off?"

A third official stepped forward. "We did find fragments of . . . nonorganic material. Phones, watches, a belt, shoes, and other clothing. We've done a thorough investigation, ma'am, and there were no other vessels in the area. Even if they did jump off, their chances of survival were . . . nil. Especially now, since so many hours have elapsed."

The first official said, "We are very sorry for your loss." He turned and joined his colleagues.

Pam stood and moved toward Shalisa, Marlene, and Nancy, wrapping their arms around each other's waists, and resting their heads on their shoulders. Paul pulled out a pocket-size package of tissues and offered each woman a sheet. What an absolute prince. Fuck Larry for ever causing his boy any pain.

The officials shook everyone's hands, offering whispered condolences, and then slipped through the tent's doorway. The friends huddled a moment, and Paul and Estuardo waited, until finally the women broke apart, walking back into the sunlight, toward the car. Pam guessed Nancy and Shalisa hadn't yet realized how fucked they were. No bodies being recovered meant a seven-year wait until their husbands were declared legally dead and they'd get the insurance money. Fuck. Nancy leaned hard against Paul. Pam decided that tidbit of news could wait.

Hank had kept his boat at this marina for more than twenty-five years, and Pam couldn't count the number of times she'd lugged coolers, thermoses full of margaritas, towels, toys, sunscreen, and bags of potato chips across this lawn. She veered away from her friends and followed the familiar brick path to the dock and stepped onto its weathered planks. Seven Winds wasn't a high-end marina. It was a practical, workingman's facility with an outside stand-up fridge to hold bait. A few vending machines stood on a cement slab underneath an overhang. Pam caught a whiff of gas from the two pumps at the end of the longest dock. Hank's berth was five spots from shore. Close enough that it wasn't a slog to haul provisions, but near enough the harbor side that when the sea was rough, they could stay tied up and still have a nice view.

The dock was familiar under her feet as Pam walked to the edge of Hank's empty slip. Yellow police tape stretched from one post to the other. She was standing in the same spot as when she had last seen her husband. She had stood there and said her last words to her partner in life for the past thirty-five years. He had been coiling a rope, and talking about a cigar and a nightcap. Pam had turned and walked away, but he'd said something else. She had heard his voice one last time.

Pam could see the harbor bottom through the clear water and watched a hundred tiny little minnows sprint left, then right. Into the dock's shadow and out. She had turned and walked away from Hank, and as she had headed up the dock, she had thought she'd heard a seagull, but now she knew it was his voice that had broken the silence.

What was it Hank had said?

Twenty-Six

Inertia

Pam was so happy to hug her daughter. When she thought that Hank would never know he had a grandchild on the way, her heart cracked open, so she didn't think about that. These days, Pam didn't know what thoughts would make her happy. For the past five years she'd thought she wanted a life without Hank. Now she knew she'd been wrong.

And yet, she couldn't cry. She tried. But no tears came.

Paul and Estuardo spearheaded the funeral arrangements, consulting the new widows for confirmation on details such as music and eulogies. Claire was no help, as she was consumed with a trifecta of ailments—grief, morning sickness, and jet lag—and could barely sit upright. While Pam could offer saltines and cool pillows for two of those problems, she cringed while in her daughter's embrace, knowing she alone was responsible for her crippling grief.

She, Nancy, and Shalisa couldn't make a decision. And with all the people around, they couldn't talk about the shitstorm they were in with no bodies, and no insurance money coming their way anytime soon. After they'd met with the funeral director, Pam had briefly huddled with her friends for a hurried exchange where they agreed to shelve that problem until after the service.

There was much to do, but Pam didn't have the energy for any of it.

She'd received a plethora of texts and voicemails, many of them offering perspectives on losing a husband, but none made mention of how to cope if you'd ordered his hit. Even if you'd changed your mind at the last minute. Pam sifted through the messages and paid attention to the ones that said, "go easy on yourself," "don't expect too much," "take care of you." That was what she needed to hear.

Pam poured lemonade into her glass, topped up Shalisa's, and sat at her backyard table waiting for Nancy. She could hear the click of Elmer's nails as he roamed the townhouse, going from spot to spot, unsettled, in search of Hank.

"I sure could go for one of Hank's margaritas right now," Shalisa said.

Pam smiled. She remembered how the sweet tang hit her lips when they were out on the water just a few days earlier. She should have asked Hank years ago to show her how he made his signature, and her favorite, cocktail. She should have watched him mix that last batch in their kitchen, before they took Dave's ashes out on the boat Friday night. But even then, she thought she had more time. Two more days. Now, she'd never taste another of Hank's margaritas. She swallowed hard.

They had their reasons.

They did it because they had their reasons. Even if they did change their minds at that last minute, this whole thing started because they had their reasons. She had to hang on to that. Pam lifted her face to the sun.

Shalisa sipped her lemonade. "Thank God for Paul and Estuardo. I don't know what we'd do without them."

Pam nodded. Pam had always been a doer and had never felt this useless. She remembered the term from high school physics—inertia. Unable to move. And she was so tired. She could put her head down on this table and be asleep in seconds.

A car door slammed in her driveway. Pam jumped. Hank was home.

No.

A moment later, the screen door slid open, and Nancy stepped outside. She didn't close it behind her, just kept walking, and Elmer waddled down the step after her. Nancy approached them slowly, almost unseeing. She held an envelope in her hand. She sank into a chair.

"Nancy," Shalisa said. "Is everything all right?"

Nancy shook her head. Ever so slightly. Then looked at them, her eyes red from tears.

"What's wrong, Nancy?" Shalisa said.

Nancy slid the envelope to Shalisa, who picked it up and turned it so Pam could see that Paul's name and mailing address were neatly printed across the front.

"Open it," Nancy said.

Shalisa lifted the flap and extracted a piece of paper. Pam recognized the logo of Larry's bank on the letterhead. The note was handwritten, whatever it said.

Nancy said in a flat voice, "Paul went to the bank to collect his father's personal effects. He found this in Larry's top drawer."

A rush of adrenaline surged through Pam's veins, and for the first time since the police officers had arrived at Shalisa's door, Pam was almost herself. Her eyes felt awake. She could feel her cheeks. She could hear clearly. She leaned forward. "What does it say?"

"Read it," Nancy said to Shalisa.

"I don't have my readers," Shalisa said.

"Oh, for fuck's sake!" Pam reached across the table and plucked the paper from Shalisa's hand, held it at arm's length, and read aloud:

> Paul,
> Your dad's a jerk, but you already know that.
> I am so sorry we lost so much time. I love you with all my heart.
> Live your best life. Love anyone you want as long as he's like your mom. Because if he loves you like your mom loved me, that's all you'll ever need.
>
> All my love,
> Dad.

And finally, Pam cried.

Twenty-Seven

Thick as Thieves

The days since Hank's accident had been rough for Padma—it was as though everyone on staff had waited for him to die and then decided they needed something from her. Now her phone buzzed nonstop with bothersome questions. How would she know if payroll was approved? She had no idea who managed the dealers' schedules. And surely, they have plumbers on staff to handle that sort of thing.

She'd had an intense morning overseeing the setup for the reception that would follow Hank's funeral service at the nearby church. Her adult-onset acne was flaring up, her feet were killing her, and she was afraid she smelled.

The nozzle of the ladies' room hand dryer was blowing hard at Padma's armpit when a middle-aged customer in a crisp summer dress and flat sandals walked in, paused, and then disappeared into a stall. Padma's day had dragged on long enough by then that she didn't pretend to be drying her hands. She switched sides and raised her other arm, mildly relieved the woman hadn't arrived five minutes earlier when her black skirt had been hiked up around her waist. Pantyhose can be sweaty.

The blower stopped, and Padma tore off sheets of paper towel to blot the back of her neck and between her breasts. At the sink, she ran cold water on her wrists, then leaned toward the mirror to peer at her face. This serial

dating was tough. She had bags under her eyes, a pimple that needed popping, and her new smile strained her cheeks.

Padma pulled her black jacket down from the stall door, buttoned it up,
and headed to the third-floor reception rooms. The elevator doors opened,
and she felt as though she were being held hostage in the back of a florist
delivery van. The floral arrangements had started to arrive ahead of the
mourners who would convene here following the funeral.

The room was set up much as it had been for the slot machine tech's
reception a couple of weeks earlier. The screens were down for the slideshow;
the buffet table ran along one wall with the bar beside it. The flowers were
being arranged at one end of the room, and in front of them were two easels
with poster-size photos of Hank's friends who had been killed alongside him
in the boat explosion. Hank's photo leaned against the base of the easels.

"No, no, no, no!" Padma looked around for a waiter, a busboy, anyone to
help. Where were all the staff? She couldn't leave Hank on the floor. She had
to find him a proper easel. He deserved to be treated respectfully.

Already her feet were killing her, and she'd resolved to ration her steps to
ensure she'd have enough mileage left for her second date with Vikash—they
were going dancing tonight. She sighed. This had to be done, and she'd have
to do it. Padma headed through the upstairs kitchen to the storage closet.
She opened the door and hit the light switch. There in the far corner stood
the easel, with the video tech's poster-size photo still resting on it. Padma
paused and studied it. Dave Brand. That was his name. Man, why couldn't
she find a guy like that? Even her mother would have to admit he was a good-
looking specimen. Look at that smile, the hair, those teeth. The twinkle in
those eyes. She would have loved to have had a go at him. But he was ancient.
Although his widow was a knockout.

Widows. Widowhood. That was a tough state of affairs. You go through
all the work of landing a husband and then he up and dies. Padma set aside
Dave's photo, folded up the easel and headed back to the reception room,
working to get this new set of widows straight in her mind. Pam—Hank's
wife, whom she had already met. And Nancy and Shalisa. Apparently, the
men had been fabulous friends, and the three families wanted to commemo-
rate them with a combined triple service. The arrangements were being man-

aged by one of the sons, Paul. Padma had perked up when he and his buddy, Estuardo, had come in to discuss the details, and had been crestfallen when the two young men, both tall with good hair and dazzling smiles, had held hands.

Given the number of guests they expected, Padma had to slide open the dividing wall between rooms. But treating dead employees well was good optics. She'd figure out how to bill the other two families later.

The easel in place, Padma positioned Hank's photo in between his friends and headed outside to greet the widows. As Padma approached the casino's front doors, they automatically opened, and she stepped out under the glass canopy and into the bright sunshine. Her mouth dropped. Where had all these employees come from? Some must be here on their day off. Padma had thought she alone would meet the widows and walk them inside. She hadn't expected the staff to turn out like this. She pushed her way through the masses and from her perch on the top step, she overlooked a sea of casino uniforms, extending shoulder-to-shoulder down the stairs and lining both sides of the driveway circle at least ten people deep.

A black limousine turned off the street, and the crowd hushed. Heads bowed and hands covered hearts. The only sound was the flag, lowered to half-staff, flapping in the wind that blew off the Atlantic. Then the sharp tones of a lone bagpiper started. The car pulled to a stop at the base of the steps, and the driver jogged around and opened the car door. Pam emerged, trailed by her fellow widows. Dressed in black pumps, straight black dresses, and hats, together they looked like they were the backup singers headed for one of the casino's high-end stages.

Hank's daughter joined her mother, and the two of them led the group up the steps. Pam's lips trembled as she stooped to hug Padma and whispered over the bagpipes, "This is so thoughtful, Padma. Hank would have really appreciated this turnout. Thank you so much."

"You're welcome," Padma said.

She turned to lead Pam inside and took a last look, noting waitresses embraced in open sobs and a burly security guard wiping away his tears. Well. Hank may have been a boob, but apparently, he was a well-liked boob.

Once upstairs in the reception room, the widows stationed themselves by the door as a de facto receiving line. The space began to fill, and Padma assumed a post off to the side. She surveyed the room and was mentally weighing the pros and cons of whether she should move into Hank's office—hers was bigger, but his was better located—when a photo of Hank, when he was probably the age Padma was now, appeared on the screen. Bent over on a sports field, healthy, muscular. Shirt off. Hair. Big smile. Abs. There was so much life in that photo it was hard to fathom the boob was gone.

"Excuse me. Padma? Isn't it?"

Padma turned to find a faintly familiar, tall, slim woman at her elbow, elegantly dressed in a white sleeveless top and a black pencil skirt melded together with a wide patent leather belt. An outfit Padma would never dream of wearing yet which looked perfectly proportionate on this woman.

"I'm Sabrina Cuomo. We met at Dave Brand's funeral." The woman extended her hand, and Padma took her fingers.

"Oh yes. I'm sorry for your loss," Padma said.

"Thank you. I've known these guys and their wives forever. Our kids went to school together. I'm gutted to lose three more dear, dear friends." Sabrina blinked her dry eyes and shook her head. "The four musketeers are gone."

"Hmm mmm." Padma nodded. "Wait. Four? Hank and Andre and Larry. I'm sorry. Who's the fourth?"

"Why, Dave, of course. Dave Brand. You know him. His was the last funeral we were at. Those four guys were thick as thieves."

"They were?" Padma recalled Hank in her office, and remembered asking him, out of curiosity, if he'd known the slot machine tech. She could swear he said he hadn't. Maybe this woman was mistaken.

"Look at the photos. You can see they go way back."

Padma turned back to the slideshow and was temporarily blinded by the brightness of a shot of four men. Hank, who Padma knew, of course. Two others Padma recognized from their photos on the easels by the flowers. Even though there must have been at least twenty years between now and when the photograph was taken, she could tell they were the same men. And the fourth. Padma pinned that fourth face as the same one she'd studied earlier in the storage closet—Dave Brand, their handsome slot machine tech.

The slot machine tech Hank said he didn't know.

The slide changed. The same four men, about fifteen years ago, standing arm in arm on a dock, sun bright on their cheeks, the summer wind tousling their hair—each holding a string of fish.

Padma was confused.

She replayed her conversation with Hank. Hadn't she commented on the funeral's large turnout? Didn't she say that Dave Brand must have been a great guy? And what had Hank said? She couldn't remember exactly, but he sure hadn't admitted he knew the man firsthand.

The next photo showed the same foursome in tuxedos, more recently at a wedding. Then in a hot tub smoking cigars. On a soccer field with kids waist high. Another included their wives on a beach. A recent one of Hank, as she knew him—bald and potbellied—arm in arm with Dave in front of a barbecue of grilled hamburgers. Both smiling at the camera. Like they were best buddies. It could have been taken a month ago. How could that be? It didn't make sense. Why would Hank lie?

"Excuse me, Padma?"

Preoccupied, Padma turned to the staffer who had appeared at her side. "Yes."

"The vendor is here to switch out the slot machines downstairs. They have the new ones ready, and they're about to remove the old ones. But they wanted to show you something."

Padma nodded and turned to Sabrina Cuomo. "Excuse me. I'm needed on the floor. It was nice seeing you again."

Padma took one last look at the slides as she left the room, seeing Hank sitting in the captain's seat of a boat, with Dave on his lap, his arms around Hank's shoulders, their cheeks smushed together, wearing sunburns and smiles.

Padma pondered that photograph all the way down the escalator and across the casino floor, running the photos on a mental loop. As she approached the offending slot machines, she shifted her focus to the spreadsheet and her calculations. She knew she could be wrong; she usually was when it came to accounting. But there was also the slim possibility she was right. From what she could tell, it looked like these machines routinely paid out almost $50,000 a week more than other casinos.

The video reels were inspected by an unbiased panel to be sure they were legitimately random. And the payout percentages were government regulated. Padma couldn't change either of those things, so she hoped completely changing the machines would bring their payouts more in line. She knew it was a gamble, but she was in the right field of work to place that bet.

The vendor rep was waiting for her, a tall, slim man with cowboy boots and a white hat, wearing dark, pressed jeans and a shirt with pearl buttons. How much hair did he have under that hat, and was he already married? She could live in Texas. She'd look great on a horse. Maybe a light-colored one to contrast with her dark hair. Oh! A pure black stallion would be a perfect fit. The vendor interrupted her thoughts and opened the back of the video slot machine. Padma had no idea what she was looking at.

The man talked with a twang, and his breath smelled like beef jerky. "Our tech was inspecting the machines before we send them back to our warehouse, and this might not be anything, and just doing our due diligence, I wanted to let you know in this one machine, you can see this wire, hanging here." He pointed at it with his pen and waited for Padma to nod. "That's not our wire. We don't really know what it's doing there. For all we know it could have been put there to hold a penlight. But the onus is on us to inform the casino."

She needed Hank. The boob would know how to handle this. He'd know if this was something, or not. Hank would probably say this is an issue for security. Thankfully, that was one of the last things Hank had done before he left for the weekend and never came back. He told her he'd hired the perfect candidate as their new director of security.

Now Padma carefully teetered down the slippery cement basement hallway, past the casino bank and to the security command center. She swiped her key card, pushed open the door, and found the regular detail of people monitoring the multitude of camera feeds from around the premises. The new director stood behind them, arms folded. Padma knocked to announce her arrival.

"Excuse me, Brenda. Do you have a minute?"

Twenty-Eight

Ask the Right Way

Brenda had texted Hector that she'd forgotten her lunch in the fridge, so after the funeral service he climbed the stairs above the barbershop and grabbed her insulated bag before heading to the reception. He felt a surge of pride as he spoke to the burly security guard at the casino employee entrance. "My wife, Brenda Chavez, is the new director of security. Can someone get this to her? She said she'd be in the security command center." Then, as an afterthought, he added, "I'm going to Hank Montgomery's funeral reception. Do you think I could cut through back here?"

The guard swiped him into the elevator and told him to go to the third floor. Hector pressed the button and mused at how his mother had been right when she had told him things always work out for the best.

About a month before Hector blew up Hank's boat, he and Brenda had been sitting at their worn Formica kitchen table in their apartment above the barbershop. It was the kind of table that had been around so long it had wheeled out of style as old-fashioned and then back in as vintage. It had been in Brenda's family bungalow when she was growing up. That table had seen a lot of living with her three sisters, her stay-at-home mom, and her police-detective dad. When Brenda's parents downsized, Hector suggested he and Brenda scoop up the table for their own place. It was big for just the two of them, but he loved sitting at it with his wife.

That morning, Brenda had looked up from her laptop. "The casino is hiring."

"Uh-huh." Hector had one more chance at the Wordle game until he was officially defeated. It was hard enough when English was your first language, but when it was Spanish: yi,yi,yi,yi,yi.

"They need a director of security."

"You don't say?" Hector had looked across at his wife, her hair pulled back in a tight ponytail. Despite the wrinkles that were starting to show around her mouth and eyes, she was still youthful, with no makeup and wearing a white T-shirt. Some women didn't need any help. He had smiled at his amor. "You could do that. You should apply."

When he had first moved here, and they were binge-watching movies to get his English to the point where Hector could hold his own with Brenda's father—which wasn't easy when dealing with not only a retired cop, but one of Italian heritage, who for the past twenty-five years had been outnumbered five to one in a household of strong women—Hector and Brenda had been on the sofa sharing a bowl of popcorn, watching *Out of Sight*. It had been a good choice—a hybrid between Hector's preferred gangster movies and his new appreciation for romantic comedies. Jennifer Lopez's U.S. Marshal character had been going toe-to-toe with George Clooney's seasoned bank robber, when Hector had said, "You could do that."

"What? Rob banks?" Brenda had answered.

"No. Be a marshal, or a cop. Even a private detective. You have a degree in criminology. You're smart and tough. You have a good sense about people. You'd be good at it. It'd be better than selling life insurance."

Brenda had liked the idea but then been disappointed when she'd been deemed a fraction too short for law enforcement. But she could see herself as a private investigator. She had taken the course, passed the exam, and got her firearms license. Having a dad who had been on the job was a bonus as both a sounding board and a source of contacts. Somehow, the bulk of Brenda's clientele ended up being suspicious wives. Brenda had spent a lot of time tailing husbands to questionable meetups and made a name for herself in the divorce court circles.

She kept a pregnancy bump on the closet shelf in case she had another target with a fetish for expectant mothers. Brenda had followed up on one wife's hunch, connected with the man online and then in person, but dodged his request to touch her padded bump and flat out said no to his invitation to join him in his motel room. She had recorded the conversation, and the wife was awarded the divorce settlement she wanted.

Brenda was the most capable woman Hector had ever known, but he worried now that his suggestion for this line of work had been a mistake. He'd never let her know, but many nights he stood a silent sentinel to her stakeout. Following her, following someone else. Just in case. Nothing was going to happen to his amor, not on his watch.

Her interest in the casino job had been music to his ears. He'd sleep better knowing whoever she had to deal with now, she would have a team to support her. He had encouraged her to get her résumé together, and she sent it in to the casino, as the posting directed, to Hank's attention.

And Hank hadn't replied.

When Hank had approached Hector at the barbershop about the job he'd needed done, Hector had known Hank was panicked.

"Someone is trying to kill us. Larry, our buddy Andre, and me. We think they killed Dave." Hector had hidden his surprise as Hank had continued, "And we need you to figure out who it is and kill them before they kill us. Hire whoever you need. Whatever you need. We'll pay you well."

Perspiration had beaded on Hank's forehead. Hector had dabbed it with a linen towel and had asked only the questions he needed answers to.

After the wives' chat in the back of the minivan, Brenda and Hector had gone over the scenarios. They'd set cups of coffee on either side of their kitchen table, and two semitas—jam-filled tarts that Brenda picked up at Hector's favorite bakery as a special treat for him—and had talked it through, like they did most things.

"You think Hank will be back?"

Hector had nodded. "Things will ramp up. I'm not sure how yet, but they always do."

Brenda had picked up her pastry and had been poised to take a bite, when she'd said, "When he does come back, are you going to ask them for more money?"

Hector popped a piece of crust in his mouth. "I'm gonna do better than that. I'm gonna get you that job."

Brenda grimaced. "No, Hec-toro. I don't want to get a job that way. I want to get it on my own merit."

"Amor. You're perfect for that position. And qualified. And you know it. The casino would be lucky to have you. I bet the only reason you haven't heard from them is because Hank is so distracted right now. With thinking someone's trying to kill him and all. When he comes by again, I'll ask him to push you to the top of his to-do list, that's all." Hector licked crumbs off his fingers. "You'd be surprised what all you can get, if you ask the right way."

Brenda narrowed her eyes. "Wait. Don't tell me. George Clooney. Right? *Out of Sight*. Explaining to his buddy why he doesn't need a gun to rob banks."

Hector tapped her coffee mug with his. "Well done, amor."

She tapped his mug back. "Well, at least you didn't say you were going to make him an offer he couldn't refuse."

Hector choked a bit on his coffee, smiled broadly at his wife over the rim of his mug, and congratulated himself, again, for making the best choice, that day on the beach so many years ago.

The casino elevator doors opened, and the funeral lilies' scent snapped Hector back to the moment. Hector congratulated himself again. This time for encouraging Hank to have Brenda's position confirmed as quickly as he did. Because dead men don't hire. He walked down the casino hall and scanned the reception room for the three newly minted widows.

He hoped he didn't have to make them regret what they'd done.

Twenty-Nine

Agree to Disagree

Pam was exhausted. Bone tired. Brain tired, feet tired, back tired. She wanted to go home, hug Elmer, open a cold bottle of beer, chug it, and crawl into bed. And Pam hated beer. But it was good for Claire to see that her dad was so well thought of. All these people who came to pay their respects with a kind word. A story. People Hank had helped. Former employees he'd kept in touch with over the years.

Pam excused herself from a group of blackjack dealers and was headed for the bar when she was intercepted by Hector. "I'm sorry for your loss."

"Th . . . thank you," Pam said, conscious of people nearby. Goosebumps traveled up her bare arms.

"I was Hank's barber." Hector extended his hand, and Pam shook it. "Even though he didn't need much of one."

Hector's hand felt warm and strong around hers. Pam smiled.

"I hope to see you again." Hector lightly squeezed her fingers. "Soon."

"About that . . ."

Pam moved a few steps to the right, and Hector followed. He raised one eyebrow, a slight smile on his lips. Pam casually looked around to be sure no one was too close, then held his eyes with what she hoped was a commanding look. "We have a problem, Hector. Actually, two. First, I said *Sunday*," she hissed, then looked again to be sure no one was watching.

Hector's smile grew. "Some things you can't go by the calendar, Pam. Some things you go by feel."

Pam kept her smile frozen and spoke through gritted teeth. "Actually, I think most things you can go by the calendar. That's why there are calendars. Otherwise, there'd be chaos. And you have rained down fucking chaos on us." She leaned closer. "*We were calling it off.*"

If Hector was surprised, he hid it. His tone was conciliatory. "Pam. This was not a garage sale. Things like this don't have rain dates."

"Some things change."

"Ah. We agree to disagree." Hector raised an eyebrow. "There isn't a problem with the money, is there, Pam? Because I told you—"

"—Yes! That's our second fucking problem." She stepped closer. "We told you we needed bodies for the insurance money. With no bodies we'll have to wait. Seven years! Why do you think we specifically said we needed bodies?" She smiled and surveyed the room.

Hector smiled back. Pam remembered what Hank and the guys had said about Hector. How he had dead eyes. And while she wouldn't have described them that way—she found there was a lot of life in them—she saw steely resolve there. He said to her, "Ah, I see. Have you talked to anyone about that yet? About the insurance."

Pam shook her head.

Hector continued, "You will find that no bodies will not be a problem. The authorities have issued Presumptive Death Waivers."

Pam's mouth gaped open. "Wh-at? What are you talking about?" Her brow furrowed. Did she remember hearing one of the officials say something about that back in that tent? She couldn't be sure.

Hector bent closer to her. "If someone disappears under certain circumstances, they can be presumed dead in just a few days, provided there's enough evidence they didn't survive. And I made sure of both the circumstances and the evidence."

Pam cocked her head. "How did you know to do that?"

Hector shrugged. "It pays to know a little somethin' about the law in my line of work. Look around, Pam. How could you hold a funeral if they hadn't been declared dead?"

Oh my God. How had she not thought of that? Fuck. All this worry, for nothing. Paul and Estuardo must have taken care of it. Her shoulders relaxed, and she closed her eyes for a moment. She felt her neck muscles release. "Well, good, then. When we get the insurance money, we can pay you."

They locked eyes, and the hairs on the back of Pam's neck stood at attention. He inhaled. "I hope so, Pam. I really do."

"But you still screwed up the date. We should have been able to call it off."

"Like I told you, Pam. I'm not Airbnb. You can't just cancel your booking." Hector leaned in. "Get my money. Soon, Pam. Soon." He turned toward the door.

Pam watched his shoulders cut his way through the crowd and out the door, then went to look for Nancy. She found her, alone, in a deserted corner of the kitchen, leaning against one of the industrial-size sinks, wiping her tears with a tissue. She asked her, "Are you okay?"

"It's too much. All these people. All this attention. It's too much." She spoke in a quiet voice, then blew her nose. "We're such hypocrites."

The door opened, and Shalisa stepped inside and closed it behind her. "What are you guys doing in here?"

Nancy answered, "Drowning in guilt."

Pam said, "Well, just make sure it looks like you're grieving."

"I am grieving!" Nancy shouted.

Pam squeezed her arm. "Keep your voice down. I know you are. We all are."

"I'm not," Shalisa said.

Pam's and Nancy's heads whipped to her.

Shalisa shrugged her shoulders. "Oh, okay. I guess I'm sad. A little. Maybe I just got to the accepting stage faster than you guys. But really. It's your own fault you got all wishy-washy."

Pam rubbed her eyes. "Well, pardon us for getting wishy-washy about killing our husbands. Jeez Louise."

"Don't get snippy with me," Shalisa said. "That's how people get caught. They turn on each other. We have to keep calm. And carry on. We'll get through this if we stick together and keep our wits about us."

Pam rubbed her temples. "Hector talked to me. He wants his money. And I have to say, he was unnecessarily menacing. Didn't even apologize for killing them on the wrong day. And not leaving bodies. But he said we won't have a problem about the insurance. He said the authorities must have issued Presumptive Death Waivers. That's how we could have a funeral."

Nancy and Shalisa gasped. Nancy said, "Really? That's such a relief." Shalisa said, "I'll say."

Pam blew out a breath. "Have you seen the insurance guy? The one Marlene told us about?"

"There you are." Marlene had an uncanny knack for turning up when her name was mentioned. She closed the door behind her. She gave each of them a warm hug and then offered triangle sandwiches from her plate.

Pam selected an egg salad in honor of Andre. She closed her eyes when she tasted the gherkin pickle and the salty butter. He would have approved.

Nancy said, "We were wondering if the insurance guy is here. You said he went to Dave's funeral?"

"Hmm. Let me think." Marlene set the empty plate on the counter. "He came over to meet me before the funeral. But that's right. He did come to the funeral. He gave me his business card. Now that you mention it, I haven't seen him here. I bet I have his card. This is my funeral purse." Marlene opened her black clutch, and there beside her phone, her lipstick, and some wadded-up tissues was a small white business card. She handed it to Pam.

Pam took it. "Perfect. I'll call him tomorrow."

Thirty

A Real Looker

The first thing that struck Padma about Brenda Chavez, the casino's new director of security, was: they were the same height and Brenda wore sensible shoes. Sturdy, black leather oxfords with thick crepe soles. The kind of shoes Padma imagined those elderly female sleuths in English detective TV shows wear as they ride their bicycles around the village square on the way to the church garden party, where a corpse is tucked behind the rose-bushes.

Yet even in flat Doc Martens, Brenda exuded a calm, confident, commanding air. No wonder Hank hired her. Hank had slid the folder holding Brenda's résumé across Padma's desk, and she had glanced at it, noting the degree in criminology and her experience as a private investigator. There had been letters of recommendation from the local police chief, several area lawyers, and two judges. Well, if Hank was happy, Padma was happy. The boob generally hired well.

Having left the crowded funeral reception upstairs, Padma struggled to keep stride with Brenda. Taking careful steps, she peered into every doorway as they walked along the slippery floor, through the maze of basement hallways, past the casino bank, and to the maintenance room, where she'd had the offending slot machine hauled. Padma was impressed that Brenda, with barely a week on the job, knew her way around so well. Additionally, whenever they encountered staff, Padma noted how they greeted Brenda by name, stepped aside for her, opened the door, picked up a pen she dropped. The little things that showed she was already receiving the respect Padma kept hoping she'd find for herself.

As Brenda pushed through a fire door, she asked Padma, over her shoulder, "Are you looking for something?"

Padma flinched. She'd tried not to be obvious as she'd scanned the floor. "I, I, uh, I lost an earring down here a couple of weeks ago. I keep thinking it'll turn up somewhere."

Brenda had seemed satisfied with her answer and nodded. The two women came to stop in front of metal doors with a small, wired window that neither of them was tall enough to see through, although Padma, in her four-inch heels, had a fighting chance. Brenda swiped the lock with the key card from around her neck. There was a click, and she pushed the door open.

Padma hadn't been in the room before. It was a large, cavernous space, painted gray all around—walls and ceiling. Tiled floor. Fluorescent lights hung like piano keys along the ceiling, emitting their telltale, barely audible buzz. Padma knew this lighting made her look sallow, but fortunately, there were no potential husbands here. A few doors led off the room, and through a wall of windows to the side was a lunchroom with a kitchenette, four side-by-side vending machines, and a long table surrounded by several chairs.

In the center of the main room stood the offending slot machine. Padma frowned, folded her arms, and circled and studied it. It was just a machine. Unplugged now, merely a metal cabinet with buttons, a dark screen, and plastic signage. Yet if someone had been stealing from the casino, it held the answers. Maybe.

"How can we tell who had access to it?" Padma asked.

Brenda swung open the door. About a foot from the floor, amid a myriad of wires, a niche held a small booklet. "Dates and times of maintenance are recorded here, and initialed. Virtually all the initials are DB, that would be Dave Brand—"

Padma's head jerked up. "Dave Brand? The slot tech who died. That makes sense." She studied the pages to see if there were any other initials, but only a few here and there. Must have been when he was on vacation.

And then, of course, after his final entry, the day of his death, other initials appeared. Padma mused. "He was a real looker."

"Really?" Brenda seemed intrigued.

Padma perked up at the opportunity to dish. "Oh my gosh. I don't remember seeing him in person, but I've seen pictures of him. Tall, well built. Nice smile, chiseled jaw. He was old, like, in his sixties, probably close to retiring, but whoa, I bet he was something when he was younger. I was actually just looking at pictures of him, when he was probably about forty, upstairs at Hank's funer—"

Padma felt her scalp tighten.

If someone was ripping off the slot machines, it was probably Dave Brand. He had unlimited access. But could he have done it alone? Why would Hank lie about knowing him? Dave and Hank both died in horrible accidents weeks apart. Could the looker and the boob have done it together?

Goosebumps rippled up her arms. Padma looked to her left, then to her right. She checked the door behind her, ensuring it was only her and Brenda in the room. Brenda was thumbing through the maintenance booklet. Could anyone else have figured this out, or just her?

If Padma blew open some huge casino robbery ring, she'd be legendary. Finally, she'd be respected. Even by her mother. She'd be able to call off The Matchmaker. If there was something happening here, and if she cracked it open—after just two months on the job—there'd be no stopping her.

How to proceed?

"Can we get the inside of the machine fingerprinted?" Padma asked.

"Do you want me to bring in the police?"

"No! No police! We'll handle this internally."

If what Padma was thinking had actually happened, the police would be the last people her mother would bring in.

Padma knew how her mother would handle this. Quietly. And decisively.

Her mother would call in her professionals.

Thirty-One

This Chick Is Outta Here

Pam opened her eyes and followed the reach of her arm to her palm, lying upward, on Hank's side of the bed. It used to be, the first thing she did every morning was touch Hank's chest. Briefly, before she rose. He'd fumble for her hand, squeeze it, and then roll over.

But now his sheets were cool, his pillow plump.

He was gone. His funeral over. And she was responsible.

Cement filled her stomach, and a shiver ran from her waist into the nape of her neck. She pushed those thoughts aside. What was done was done. And she had to get on with life and put one foot in front of another down her path. She knew she wasn't processing things fully. There were emotions she should be dealing with, but they were so unwieldy she feared if she opened that can of worms, she might drown in it. And she couldn't afford to drown, not right now. Nancy was drowning enough for all of them. Pam had to keep on top of things. She had to sort out the insurance. She had to get Claire and Dylan to the airport.

Pam ran her hand over the smoothness of the mattress. Besides, she hadn't reached across to touch Hank's chest in years. And he never reached for her.

There was nothing in their bed to miss.

She rolled over, and Elmer wagged his tail, sitting on the floor beside her. "Good morning, good lookin'. Did you have a good sleep?" Pam ruffled his fur and headed to the bathroom. He followed and stretched out across the doorway.

As she brushed her teeth, in the mirror she inventoried Hank's clothes draped along the edge of the bathtub: jeans, khakis, underwear, T-shirts, sweatshirts. Everything he'd worn his last week, tossed aside in what Pam called his "wardrobe purgatory"—clothes he'd deemed too clean for the laundry yet too dirty to put away. It was how Hank lived: too lazy to fully commit to anything. She'd donate them all.

Her eyes wandered to Hank's sink. She spat, rinsed, opened Hank's vanity drawer and swept his razor, toothbrush, and dental floss out of sight. One less reminder. When she turned to leave, she found Elmer had sauntered over and pulled Hank's sweatshirt to the floor and now lay curled up on it, his nose nestled in a sleeve. She stooped to scratch his belly and brought Hank's other sleeve to her face. It felt smooth against her cheek, and she inhaled his scent and her heart started to squeeze. "He's not coming back, I'm afraid," she said to her dog.

Maybe she'd keep that shirt.

Claire's call from the bottom of the stairs, reminding her of her flight time, brought her to her feet. A short while later, after she dropped Claire and Dylan at the airport, Pam wiped away her tears and stopped by Dutton Realty to clean out her desk.

———

"Are you sure, Pam?" Mr. Dutton interrupted while she loaded her photos and spare shoes in a box. "They recommend people shouldn't make major life decisions for at least six months following a tragedy. We're happy to use temps for as long as you need."

Pam hoisted her box. "Thank you. I appreciate that, and no offense to you and Marylou, you've both been great to me, but I have hated every minute I have ever spent inside these walls, and I cannot think of anything more depressing than staying here another day." She remembered what Marlene had said about quitting her own job. "So, this chick is outta here."

As Pam walked through the office out to her van, and all the way to meet Nancy at Shalisa's, she hummed the Beatles song "Ticket to Ride."

Pam felt like she was driving away from one chapter of her life and into another. Paul and Estuardo had returned to their regular routine, and with Claire and Dylan on the morning flight to New Zealand to pack up their lives and move back Stateside, it was time to get on with the next stage of their plan—the insurance money, and then condo shopping in Boca Raton.

Marlene had flown back that morning, and Pam hoped she, Nancy, and Shalisa wouldn't be too far behind. She'd already started hinting to Claire and Dylan that perhaps a move to a new city with a warmer climate would be great for all of them and was thrilled that they seemed to be considering it. She just had to get that insurance payout in motion.

Just after lunch, Pam let herself in Shalisa's front door and found Nancy, on time for once, curled up on the end of the sofa, with a box of tissues beside her. Pam hadn't been to Shalisa's since the night the police had rung the doorbell and delivered the news about the boat explosion. It felt surreal to sit in the same chair as when the officer had knelt beside her. Shalisa brought in coffees. It was just the three of them. For the first time in days, no family or friends in the periphery.

Shalisa said, "I know I wanted this, and I said I'm good with how things turned out. But still, I didn't expect to feel so drained. I think I may actually be missing Andre. A bit." She shook her head. "I can't believe we did it."

"I can't believe we wanted to." Nancy blew her nose.

Pam had to turn this around, keep them on a positive track. What was done was done. She looked at Nancy. "We can't change the past. We have to move forward. We made our decisions based on what we knew at the time. You had no way of knowing Larry changed his mind about Paul and Estuardo. You can't blame yourself."

Shalisa said, "Pam's right. Why would Larry even leave a letter like that in his desk? It was almost like a suicide note, saying goodbye."

Nancy said, "Paul's address was on the front, so we think he was planning to mail it. It was probably easier to write the words than say them. We don't really know." She squeaked out those last words before a sob escaped. She plucked three tissues from the box, wadded them, and brought them to her face.

God. *There she goes again.* Pam searched for a way to change the subject. She looked out to the street. "Hey! Shalisa! I meant to ask you. When did the juniper come down?"

"What?"

"Your juniper bush. When did it come down?" Pam pointed past Shalisa's Peloton bike to the view of the street, which for years had been obscured by that huge, unsightly, overgrown juniper.

"What are you talking about?" Shalisa followed Pam's direction. She grabbed her chair's arms. "What the fuck?"

"I noticed it the night the police came."

"The night the police came! Really? I've walked by it a million times. I never noticed. I guess with all the family here, and everything going on, I never even noticed."

Pam's phone buzzed. "It's the insurance company returning my call." She hit accept. "Hello."

Shalisa rose, as if in a daze, and walked to the front door and stepped outside. Nancy followed.

"Hi there. I'm Pam Montgomery, and my husband has recently passed away ... thank you ... thank you, I appreciate that ... Um. I'm calling because I understand he has an insurance policy with you ... Hank Montgomery ... Yes, sure, I'll hold."

Through the window, Pam watched Shalisa and Nancy stand side by side, their hands on their hips, staring at the void the juniper had left. They looked up and down the street, as though they'd find the answer on a billboard on someone's lawn. They looked up to the roof, Pam had no idea why. Shalisa stepped forward into the garden bed. Pam moved closer to the window to get a better view. Shalisa kicked the short, ragged stump that remained, and then kicked the dirt around it. She knelt down.

Pam turned away from the window. "Hello. Yes ... yes ... I'm Pam Montgomery ... oh ... I understand procedure, but I think you'll find I'm the beneficiary . . . Yes, I understand . . . I understand a Presumptive Death Waiver has been issued. I wanted to follow up."

The voice on the other end said, "I'm not allowed, legally, to provide any information about policies." Then in a less official tone, "Listen, this happens all the time. We can't say anything, but if you have access to his email, you can check the correspondence yourself."

Pam disconnected, found Shalisa's laptop on the kitchen counter, and logged into Hank's email. They had regularly shared passwords so they could find messages in each other's mail: invitations, bills, family correspondence. It was just convenient. Could Hank have updated his? But no. His childhood phone number followed by his first dog's name still worked.

Hank had several unread emails that according to the timestamps had started arriving when they were untying from the dock on their way to scatter Dave's ashes. Interestingly, the first was from the insurance company. Pam read it.

A few minutes later, Pam held Shalisa's front door ajar, stepped outside onto the front porch, and the hot, humid air hammered her. Shalisa and Nancy were on their knees, huddled together by the juniper stump. At the sound of the door opening, they looked up.

Nancy held out a small, white business card. "We found this. Tucked in behind the tree stump. It's Andre's business card. He had it laminated."

Shalisa flipped the card over. On the back, scrawled in black marker, Pam read:

I'M SORRY. LOVE, ANDRE

Shalisa looked up at Pam. "What did Andre have to be sorry for?"

Pam let the screen door slam shut behind her, then answered, "The shitheads canceled their insurance policies."

Thirty-Two

You Don't Say

Brenda was savoring a cup of freshly brewed coffee and checking her email at their kitchen table. She had her husband's mug ready across from her, with the sugar bowl beside it.

Brenda sipped her coffee. "Any word from the wives?"

The bagel Brenda had put in the toaster for him popped. Hector slathered a pad of butter around the holes. "I spoke to Pam at the funeral. They're waiting on the insurance money. They didn't know about Presumptive Death Waivers."

Brenda nodded. "See. I told you it pays to watch *Law & Order* reruns."

In the middle of pondering the best way to take care of the husbands, and mindful of the wives' need for bodies, Hector and Brenda had been curled up on the sofa late one night, and providentially, those waivers had been a pivotal plot point in the middle of the show's rerun marathon. A widow had argued to Sam Waterston she wouldn't possibly have blown up her husband's Cessna airplane—she had cancer and was only expected to live five more years, tops. She had no motive because she couldn't claim his insurance for seven years, and she'd be dead by then. But Detectives Briscoe and Curtis had checked her computer's search history and found she'd looked up Presumptive Death Waivers. She was nailed. The next day Brenda had searched their own state laws, and Hector had his plan.

"How patient will you be?"

"I have to give them a bit more time. Normally I wouldn't, but what am I going to do? I can't get blood from a stone, and their ship is coming in." He shook his head. "That's what I like about English. You have a silly saying for everything." He pulled out the chair, sat down, and raised his mug to Brenda. "Congratulations on your first week at the new job. You stayed late last night. Everything okay?"

She touched her mug back. "Hec-toro." Brenda looked like the cat who ate the canary. Yet another English expression that made no sense. She set her mug down and leaned forward, her elbows on the table. "You'll never guess what happened."

Hector raised his eyebrows and bit into his bagel.

"We got new slot machines, and now Padma suspects someone was using the old ones to rip off the casino. She thinks it might have been going on since they got those machines four years ago."

Hector swallowed and sat back in his chair. "You don't say."

"I do say."

"And ..."

"And she thinks it might have been your husbands." Brenda raised her eyebrows back.

"You don't say." Hector took another bite.

"And I bet the wives were in on it. And they were fighting over that money. And I bet that's the real reason the wives wanted the husbands dead." Brenda sat back and crossed her arms. "To get the casino money."

Hector chewed a moment, then shook his head. "If the wives had the money, they'd have paid me already."

"Maybe they don't have it *yet*. I said, 'fighting over it.' Think about it. They're all hiring you right about the same time Padma changes out the old slot machines for new ones. Don't you think that's a strange coincidence?"

"Maybe." Hector pushed the stray sesame seeds into a little pile with his fingertip. "But even if the husbands did pull something off, that doesn't mean the wives know about it."

"Of course the wives know about it. What kind of marriages would they have if they didn't?"

Hector split the pile of sesame seeds into two smaller ones. "The kind of marriages where wives hire someone to kill their husbands, and husbands hire someone to kill their wives."

"Oh. That kind." Brenda smiled and then sipped her coffee. "Well, in fairness, maybe the husbands didn't know it was their wives who were after them."

Hector frowned and squinched an eye.

Brenda studied him a moment and then put her mug down. "Did Hank ever say *why* someone was after them?"

Hector looked at his wife and lowered his chin.

She put her hand up. "I know. I know. Some things we don't want to know." She looked out the window and then back to her husband. "I know you say that, but I don't think you mean it. I think you always want to know."

Hector shrugged.

Brenda looked into her mug and then up into Hector's eyes. "I think you just say that to shield me from nasty things."

She wasn't wrong. Hector took another bite of his bagel. "Things?"

"Yes, things. And you know, you don't have to protect me."

Hector chuckled. "You should run that by your father."

Brenda smiled. "Point taken. But I mean, I know you don't take every job you're offered. I think you only go after bad people."

"I just figure forgiveness is between them and God . . . My job is to arrange the meeting."

A furrow appeared between Brenda's eyebrows, and then she smiled. "Oh my God. Denzel Washington. *Man on Fire.*"

"Best movie ever."

"Agreed. Well, I'm not sure who needs forgiving here. What if the husbands were afraid the wives were coming after them for the casino money?" She leaned forward. "Seriously, why else would the wives want them dead?"

"Depending on how much insurance there is, that could be reason enough."

"If the husbands have tons of money from the casino, that's way more motivation for the wives to want them killed. Way more than just their insurance money. Don't you think?" Brenda took a sip of her coffee.

Hector scattered the sesame seeds on his plate. "Insurance money is usually enough."

Brenda put her chin in her hands and rubbed her cheeks. "Maybe. Maybe you're right. It wouldn't be the first time. That Murdaugh case in the Low Country. That big, red-headed lawyer killed his wife and son for the insurance money." Brenda took another sip of her coffee. "Or." Hector loved watching her brain work. "Or, the husbands *were* stealing, thought the casino caught them, and that's why they were scared. But they didn't tell you because they didn't want *you* to know."

"Why not?"

"Because they were paranoid. And they thought if you knew about the casino money, you'd try to take it."

Hector stirred three teaspoons of sugar into his coffee one at a time, then swirled his spoon. It had cooled down, just the way he liked it. "How much money are you talkin'?"

"Padma thinks it could have been about fifty grand a week since they got those machines four years ago."

"That's . . . "

Brenda slid her phone across the table, and Hector looked at the calculator readout. "About ten million dollars." Brenda tapped the screen. "What do you think about that?"

Hector gave a low whistle. "Interesting. But she's not positive it was them?"

"She knows Dave Brand had access. And she knows Hank lied about being friends with Dave, so that makes her think Hank could be involved. Although she doesn't think he was smart enough. She thinks he was a boob." Brenda smiled at Hector. "She's asked the head office in India to send help to sort it out."

Hector drained his coffee, came around to Brenda's side of the table, leaned down, and tenderly kissed her neck, then her cheek, her ear, and finally her lips. He tucked a loose strand of hair behind her ear. "Gotta go. I love you."

"I know." She smiled.

"I'll be back tomorrow night." Hector picked up his backpack on the way to the door.

Brenda called after him. "Remember—'a man's got to know his limitations.'"

Hector stopped and turned around. Tilted his head. "I'm hearing Clint Eastwood."

"One of the Dirty Harry movies. Not sure which one."

He scratched his chin. "*Magnum Force.*"

Her smile widened. "Be safe. Love you."

And their apartment door closed behind him.

Thirty-Three

It's Always About the Money

"Are you done with that?" Hank picked up the small earthenware dish that held the last of the best salsa he'd ever tasted.

He'd ask for the recipe if he thought his high school Spanish would be understood. Perhaps the sweet señora would let him watch the next time she made it. The salsa, and those things she called pupusas. Almost a quesadilla, but better. A thick corn tortilla, stuffed with a mixture of meat and spices and cooked in a hot iron skillet. Hank had a new favorite food. He ran a damp dishcloth across the rough-hewn table, wiping up the spills from dinner, and nudged the laptop out of the way. The news headline filled the screen:

Funeral Held for Local Men Following
Gas-Leak Boat Explosion

Andre pushed his bifocals up his nose. "I can't believe they spelled my name wrong. A-n-d-r-e. Journalism these days. They can't even fact-check the simplest thing."

Hank was reaching past Larry for the hot sauce bottle when there was a knock at the door. He froze. Andre and Larry quietly pushed their chairs away from the table. Another man came from down the hall and approached the door with caution. Hank, Larry, and Andre shrunk to the wall and edged back around the corner. Hank rotated the hot sauce bottle in his hand in case he needed to use it as a weapon. He tightened his grip. The man listened at the door and then put his eye to the peephole. In one movement he stood straight and flung the door open.

"Hector!" The two men embraced and spoke a stream of Spanish.

Hector's mother rushed out from the kitchen, drying her hands on a towel, and threw her arms around her son, who folded over her. Hank felt Andre's breath of relief on the back of his neck and relaxed his grip on the hot sauce bottle. They came forward to greet Hector.

"Everything okay?" Hector extended his hand and pulled each of his customers in for a hug and a slap on the back.

"Yes. Good to see you, man." Hank meant it. A lot of things could have gone wrong since they'd last seen their barber, as they slipped quietly off the side of Hector's boat into the swells of the dark, choppy Atlantic, a hundred yards offshore. Standing in the living room of Hector's mother's home in San Salvador, where every square inch of the walls was covered with family photos, alongside Larry and Andre, meant they had made it. They still had to be careful, but they were almost done.

In the six days they'd been here, there'd been no intruders, no menacing knocks at the door, no shady people lurking about. The first morning, Hank had peeked through the front curtains, in between the bars that ran vertically over the windows, and had found the other homes on the tidy street had similar security measures. The small back garden was rimmed by high cement walls, and at night when they closed the patio door, they first drew a metal gate across the opening and secured it in place. Larry had sat under the ceiling fan and checked the news on their host's laptop. There had been nothing online about anything being amiss at the casino, no indication of a theft investigation.

Their plan was working.

Hector stood back from them and smiled. "You found the keys okay?"

"Yep. On the rear tire, just like you said."

Hector nodded. "How were your flights?"

"Mine was good, no problems. Larry got delayed a bit in Chicago, and

Andre flew in from Dallas and had a bit of a scare here at immigration, but we made it."

Hector looked at Andre. "What happened at immigration?"

"They examined that passport really well. Took it into a back room. I was sweating buckets. And I was hot already. But I stayed cool. I remembered what you said. I just waited, and after a few minutes they came out and gave me the go-ahead."

Hector nodded, took his jacket off, hung it on the back of a dining table chair, and gestured to Hank, Larry, and Andre to sit down. Hank chose an armchair to avoid the plastic tucked around the cushions of the bright, floral sofa. He'd learned the hard way that the protective covering sticks to the bare skin and he didn't think he had much hair left on the backs of his legs. He was sure Larry and Andre shared the same thought but given there weren't many seating options in the neat home, they scooched forward so the plastic only hit their cargo shorts. Hank guessed the sofa was Mrs. Chavez's prized possession. It looked relatively new, and he suspected it was most likely purchased with Hector's earnings from his apparently lucrative sideline of doing "whatever needs doin'."

Hector's mother carried in a tray of what Hank had learned was chichas, and after a week of drinking the sweet, fermented-corn beverage, he was developing a taste for it. She set the glasses on the table before them, and Hector passed one to each of them.

"Salud," Hector said.

As they raised their glasses, Hank thought back to a similar toast, when he, Larry, and Andre had touched their beer cans and agreed to pivot to a new plan.

———

After Hank had overheard Padma confirm that three hitmen were coming from India in two days, on Saturday, blood had surged through his veins. His tires had squealed as he'd peeled out of the casino parking lot; his vision blurred with flashbacks to online images of other Indo-USA Gaming Inc. associates hanging from bridges. There was only one sure way out of the situation that was rapidly closing in on them. He'd given Hector the heads-up so he could get the arrangements in motion, then he'd met Larry and Andre at the marina, and they'd taken his boat out to the open water.

Hank had leaned forward from the captain's seat; music played low on the speakers to baffle their voices should the sound carry across the water in the stillness of the late morning. "We have to change the plan."

"Why?" Andre had bolted upright, defensive.

Hank had answered in an even voice, "Because now that the casino knows who we are, they'll keep coming after us until they get their money."

Andre shook his head. "But Hector will kill those guys."

Hank said, "We can hope, but then more will come. They won't quit after one try, especially when there's millions on the line."

Andre took his bifocals off and rubbed his hand across his face. "Okay, this is getting way too wild. Are you even sure the casino knows about us?"

Fuck. Hank went over it again. "I heard what Padma said. She said, 'the big, bald one.' That's me. And 'the banker.' That'd be Larry. Then she said, 'all three.' That's you. The third guy. She knows. You didn't see Dave's body, Andre. I did. Someone did that to him and left that thousand-dollar chip behind as a message. They may as well have left a note saying, *We know you stole our money and we're coming for it.* And Padma lined up those chips on her desk, so I'd know that's where that thousand-dollar chip had come from. That was *her* warning *me.* Do you want to stick around and fact-check? Do you want to end up a smashed pumpkin on your garage floor?"

Larry and Andre had considered that a moment, and then Larry asked, "What are you thinking?"

"The only way they'll stop looking for us is if they think we're dead. We're gonna have to fake our deaths."

Andre's head snapped back. He looked from Larry to Hank. "You're joking, right?"

Hank shook his head. "Dave's dead. No jokes."

Larry nodded slowly, then said, "Hank's right. If they're coming, I don't want to be here when they arrive. I think we've got to run. And as crazy as it sounds, the best way to not be chased is to be dead." Larry took a long draw on his beer, then asked, "What about the girls?"

Hank shrugged.

"What? What's that shrug mean?" Andre imitated Hank's shrug. "This whole thing was supposed to get us back to our wives. For four years I've gone along with this so I could get my queen back. And now what are you saying?" Andre shrugged again.

Hank answered, "We don't have a choice. What else are we supposed to do? Stay here and get killed? Our wives are on their own, either way. But if we run, at least we're alive. If we stay, we're putting them in danger. This is best for them too."

"Can't we take them with us? If we're faking three deaths, what's six?" Andre asked.

Hank shook his head again. "We don't have time. Hector has an idea. He's working on our fake passports now." He held up a finger. "Oh. Andre, we'll have to get photos done at your shop and get them to Hector. First thing tomorrow." He lowered his hand. "We'd never be able to get the girls on board, and keep them quiet, and get out of here in time. We'd all be killed first."

"We don't tell them anything?" Larry asked.

Hank said, "Absolutely not. For this to work, they have to believe we're dead."

Larry exhaled. Then sat back.

Andre threw his hands up in the air. "How is that even possible? Faking your death. Fuck me. Do you hear yourselves?"

"I know. But it's worked before," Hank said.

Andre scrunched his face in doubt.

Hank brought out his phone and tapped away. He turned the screen to show Andre the list of search results. Snippets of text told the tale of John Darwin, the British former teacher who'd taken his canoe for a paddle, disappeared, and been declared dead. He turned up five years later and was arrested and charged with fraud.

Hank said, "There's a TV show about it too. It was pretty good. *The Thief, His Wife and the Canoe.* Four parter. I'll email you the link."

Andre looked over his bifocals at Hank. "It says he was arrested."

"Not for disappearing or for faking his death. Believe it or not, it's not illegal to disappear. He was arrested for fraud. For claiming the insurance money. If we cancel those million-dollar life insurance policies and any other policies, there's no fraud. Plus, if there's no payout, there will be less of an investigation. We only got those policies so the girls would have something to fall back on if anything happened before we made it to ten million. But we're close enough now, we don't need the insurance."

Andre said, "But if we leave with the money, and they don't have the insurance, they'll have nothing."

"We'll get money to them. Electronically. Larry can work that out."

Andre looked at Larry. "Can you, man? Can you get them money? I don't want us to be living with millions and Shalisa to be struggling."

Larry nodded. "I'll find a way. I'll get all their bank account information. I can transfer amounts to their accounts and fake email correspondence and make it look like some kind of pension or payout. We can be sure they're taken care of."

"This is some crazy shit, man." Andre looked toward Larry. "What do you think of all this?"

Larry said, "I know. My head is ready to explode. Sorry. Bad choice of words. But I don't want to end up like Dave. I think we've gotta run. I think for right now we just need to dodge these guys from India, and the best way to do that is to die in some kind of accident before they get here. Then, I think we lay low until we see if the police are involved. If they connect us to the casino theft, and if it looks like we'll get arrested, then we'll have to stay on the run. Assume different identities. I don't know. I haven't thought that through. But maybe they don't connect us. Maybe we just live a quiet life as ourselves, somewhere else. But there are a lot of *ifs*." Larry counted them on his fingers. "*If* the casino figures out for sure they were robbed. *If* they figure out how. *If* they figure out it was us. *If* they figure out we're still alive. *If* they find us. Those are five *ifs* in our favor."

Andre brought his fingertips to his temples. "How did this get so complicated? We were supposed to cash out. Pretend we got an inheritance, won the lottery or some shit. Then retire and move to Florida like regular people. Now you want us to get into spy-movie shit. This is spiraling out of control."

Hank said, "Look. It's a complication and we have to roll with it. We have no other options. We have to stay alive. We have to work fast to get our ducks in a row. Are we in agreement?"

Larry said, "I don't think we have a choice. Andre?"

Andre bent forward, his elbows on his knees, his head in his hands. He looked up at Larry. "You have to guarantee if we cancel the insurance, you can get money to our wives."

Larry nodded.

Andre said, "Okay. Agreed."

Larry rummaged in the cooler. He looked at Andre. "We're outta light beers. You okay with a regular?"

Andre offered a small smile. "That's the one upside about this—dead men don't count carbs." Larry tossed him a can, they cracked them open and clinked them in a toast, then Andre asked, "How the fuck are we going to pull this off?"

Hank took a swig, then said, "Hector's already on it."

Andre sat straight and said, "But Rule Number Four was tell no one. Not ever. We can't let him know we're running from the casino. He'll figure out the kind of money we're talking about, and he might kill us for it."

Hank smiled to himself; he'd already thought of that. He and Larry nodded. "Agreed."

Andre continued, "So, what do we tell him?"

Hank said, "He doesn't ask a lot of questions, and I don't think we have to give reasons when you hire people to do crazy shit like this. They just want to be paid. But if we ever have to tell him anything, we tell him our wives are trying to kill us."

"Wh-at?" Andre and Larry said together.

"Think about it. People are always getting killed for insurance money."

Larry said, "It's true. It's always about the money."

———

Now, sitting in Hector's mother's living room, Hank smiled at his barber, relief washing over him. Every step of the way they'd hoped Hector wouldn't double-cross them. From when Hank handed over the first payment, to when he had changed the plan and placed the bulky envelope that would cover faking their deaths on Hector's barbershop workstation. As surprised as Hank had been when Hector had passed the envelope back and then suggested his wife, Brenda, should be the casino's new director of security, Hank had also been relieved.

Because now Hector had skin in the game too.

Hank was happy to hire Brenda. She would have been a top contender he'd have interviewed that week if he hadn't been otherwise preoccupied with staying alive. So, Hector's offer to blow up their boat that Friday night and get them out of the country, as long as Brenda got the job, was a deal Hank was good to make. But now that card was played: Brenda was working at the casino and Hank was seemingly dead—his leverage was gone.

Hank was back to square one with the barber—hoping he didn't double-cross them.

Thirty-Four

It's Starting to Rain

Larry and Andre remained side by side on Hector's mother's sofa. Hank cleared his throat. "Hector. There's one more thing we were hoping you could do for us. We'll pay you, of course."

"Of course."

"There's a business opportunity on the coast; you know the language, so we'd like you to go ahead and check it out, take some pictures. Maybe feel them out a bit on price. Be kind of our . . . you know . . . advance man."

The barber nodded. And became quiet. Hector looked from one of them to the other, then said, "Let me understand this. You're saying you feel comfortable enough to move forward with your plans. You feel you are no longer in danger."

Hank made sure to maintain eye contact and nodded. The barber couldn't know they had just over nine million casino reasons to still feel in danger.

Hector leaned back in his chair. "Yet you're nervous."

"No. We're not nervous," Hank said.

Hector tilted his head. "Really?"

Hank nodded. "Really."

"I've been here fifteen minutes, and Larry jumps every time a car door slams, Andre's leg hasn't stop jiggling since he sat down, and you, Hank, that floor fan is blowing straight at you, but you're sweating like a pig."

Hank longed to wipe his face with his T-shirt. "I'm not used to spicy food. That's all." He had to give Hector something. A diversion. The one he and the guys had talked about. "Okay, Hector. Full disclosure, we think our wives were trying to kill us for our insurance money. Who wouldn't be rattled?"

There. He'd said it. That would satisfy the barber. Hector wouldn't know how ridiculous that notion was; that Pam, Shalisa, and Nancy didn't have it in them to ever do anything even remotely that sinister. That the highlights of their wives' lives revolved around finding a new jam for their charcuterie boards and spotting a sign declaring "take an additional 50% off." Plotting their husbands' murders was totally beyond their skill set.

Hector set his drink on the table. He leaned back and crossed his legs. His hands draped over the chair's arms. "So, you know about that."

Hank's head jerked. Something was wrong here. He scrambled for a response. "What do you mean?"

"I mean, you know your wives wanted you killed." Hector picked up his drink, took a sip, and said, "I wondered."

Hank shot looks at Larry and Andre and wished they'd close their mouths. He swallowed. "Say what?"

Hector repeated himself. "You know your wives wanted you killed."

Hank's voice sounded unnaturally high. "Of course, we know our wives wanted us killed. That's what I just told you." Hank tilted his head back and peered at Hector down his nose. "But how did you know that?"

Hector smiled. "Because they hired me." He replaced his drink on the table.

Andre's knee bounced to a stop, and Hank's heart flipped.

"Say what?" Hank wasn't sure he'd heard that right.

Hector uncrossed his legs and crossed them the other way. "Your wives hired me to kill you."

Hank's heart was shadowboxing against his ribs, and he exchanged furtive glances with Larry and Andre.

Hector brushed a piece of lint from his pants. "You were right. Someone did want you dead. At first, I wondered if perhaps you were a bit paranoid. Understandable with what happened to Dave. Such a shame." Hector closed his eyes and crossed himself. Then he looked back to Hank. "But then one day I was closing up, and your wives, the three of them, pulled up in their minivan, asked me to jump in, passed me a donut, and hired me to kill you." He smiled.

What the fuck was Pam thinking? Was she out of her fucking mind? Hiring Hector to kill him. He knew things had been bad, but were they bad enough to want him dead? Then he remembered the way she had looked at him when he'd eaten her pad thai. He closed his eyes, then reopened them slowly.

Hank had the same feeling he'd had when he was a kid and a magician challenged him to follow a marble trapped under a cup as he moved a trio of identical cups about. Hank was so sure he knew where the marble was, he would have bet his whole baseball card collection. Yet when the magician lifted the cup, Hank discovered he was wrong. He was sure he had kept his eye on the marble. Yet he'd been duped. The three men exchanged puzzled looks.

Hector leaned forward. "Frankly, I was happy to so easily have identified who was after you. I would have killed your wives to complete your job, but then your job changed." Hector circled his hand, apparently meaning their faked-death situation.

Hank looked from Andre to Larry and then back to Hector, and squeaked, "What did you tell them?"

"Your wives? When they asked me to kill you?" Hector raised an eyebrow at Hank, then nodded. "I said, sure."

Hank's head snapped back, and he stared at Hector.

Hector shrugged. "It's not like we have a non-compete clause."

Hank whipped his eyes around to look at Andre and Larry. Were they hearing what he was hearing? Then Larry asked, "How much did they pay you?"

Typical Larry. Always about the money.

"Hundred and fifty grand. They've paid fifty. Still owe a hundred."

Andre gave a low whistle and looked from Hank to Larry. "Where'd they get that kind of money?"

Larry shook his head, then sat straight. "Of course! Marlene got Dave's insurance money and told them about it. They really were killing us for the insurance money." His mouth gaped in horror.

Hank considered Hector. As the barber studied him back, was he seeing a price tag hanging over Hank's head? He'd already collected fifty grand. A wave of terror traveled to his toes as he realized Hector might be here to finish their wives' job.

Hank gulped. "You don't have to kill us. They think we're dead. That's good enough. Right?"

Hector smiled. "I like to complete a job. It's an honor thing."

Larry's eyes went wide. He spoke in a calm voice. "Hector, it's not as though anyone's going to report you to the Better Business Bureau."

Hank said quickly, "You could just take their money. They already think we're dead. They'll never know you double-dipped."

"I just learned that term. Double-dip. I like it. Sounds like an ice cream cone. Sweet." Hector chuckled.

Hank thought of a better argument and blurted out, "They can't pay you! They're broke. There is no insurance money."

Hector tilted his head, and Hank felt the pressure ease up.

Larry said, "Hank's right. We canceled our policies."

Hank noticed Hector's jaw clench, ever so briefly, then the barber asked, "Why the fuck would you do that, Hank?"

Hank rushed to answer, "So there wouldn't be an investigation into the boat explosion. At least an insurance one. If someone's going to pay out three million dollars . . . that's how much the insurance would have been . . . we each had a million-dollar policy . . . they'd maybe find remnants of the explosives you planted. Maybe figure out your boat was near mine, at the same time. We didn't want to chance that kind of scrutiny. So we canceled our policies. It was smart thinking. Really." He nodded and then stilled his head when he realized he looked like a bobblehead in the back window of an old Cadillac.

The room was quiet for a few moments as Hector adjusted his watch strap, and then he looked up. "I see you have not been honest with me, Hank. At all."

Hank didn't like the way Hector kept saying his name. What was he getting at? Plus, he didn't think honesty was necessarily a prerequisite when engaging nefarious types. Hank hadn't been in a fight in a long time, but he remembered a quote he'd seen on a T-shirt: *If you're going to fight, fight like you're the third monkey on the ramp to Noah's Ark, and brother, it's starting to rain.*

Hector's mother was back in the kitchen, probably with her machete. The other man was eating at the dining table a few feet away, with a fork and butter knife. Hank could throw his drink in Hector's eyes and make a run for the door. Although Larry and Andre would probably be stuck to the sofa's plastic for a few seconds, he could create enough of a distraction, hopefully they'd catch up. Hank leaned forward and picked up his chichas glass. He concentrated so Hector wouldn't see his hand tremble.

In turn, Hector picked up his glass, took a sip, then put his drink down on the lace doily atop the coffee table and looked directly at Hank. "There's been an interesting development at the casino."

Hank's head snapped up, and he loosened the grip on his glass.

"Brenda tells me your boss thinks someone's been stealing from the slot machines. For about four years."

Hank almost made a fist pump but caught himself. Hector couldn't know it was them, but fucking hallelujah! Hank knew it! *Way to listen to your old gut, Hank Montgomery.* He caught Larry's and Andre's eyes, and they blinked their understanding. Their every conversation eventually defaulted to whether or not Hank was sure the casino knew about the theft, and if they really had to run. Or was he being paranoid? And no, he wasn't sure, but he felt it, so he'd held steadfast. That's why they were sitting in a San Salvador living room. And now he finally knew, without a doubt, he had made the right call. Thank fucking God for that. They were safe and so was their $9.3 million.

But now they had a new threat. The barber was smiling.

Is this what it was like to have money—always having to protect it from someone? Maybe Hector wouldn't connect the dots of the theft to them. Maybe he didn't know how much was stolen.

"Yep. Brenda's boss figures someone stole about ten million dollars from the casino. She doesn't know who, for sure. But she's starting to put it together."

Hank wished Larry hadn't let his eyes go so wide, or that Andre's knees weren't bouncing so fast, or that his own T-shirt wasn't sopping wet.

Hector looked from one man to the other. "Ten million dollars is a lot more than the hundred grand your wives owe me. Am I wrong?"

Hector let that question hang in the room while he went to the kitchen to see his mother. At least now Hank knew Hector wasn't going to kill them for the money their wives were paying him. Not now that the barber suspected millions might be up for grabs.

Hank might be able to make a deal here.

A noise prompted them to turn, and they watched Hector's man scrape the straight-backed chair from the table across the ceramic tiles to a spot in front of the door and sit down.

Andre leaned in and said in a low voice, "Am I the only one who gets the feeling we just went from being customers to hostages?"

Thirty-Five

Two Strikes

I am sorry, my dear, but Vikash has rejected you."

Fucking Vikash.

The Matchmaker delivered the decree in her familiar rat-a-tat-tat, from the square beside Padma's mother on the monitor in front of her.

"Rejected!" Padma was still debating whether or not she'd grant him a third date, and he'd beaten her to the punch and pulled the plug on *her*. "What did he do, Aunty, text you with one hand while he was waving good night to me with the other?"

"Miss Padma, you cannot take this personally."

If a date wasn't personal, what was? What did she ever do to Vikash? She'd been cheerful and freshly showered.

"He said you went"—The Matchmaker referred to her notes—"salsa dancing. He said you did not appear to enjoy yourself, and he has listed salsa dancing as one of his top-ten activities."

Enjoy herself? It had been hot, and outside. How could she possibly have enjoyed herself? She was sweating, and mosquitoes were dive-bombing her. If Vikash had wanted to dance, he should have taken her somewhere with air-conditioning so at least her concealer would have had a fighting chance. But at that outdoor patio with lights strung around its edges and beer served in buckets of ice, her mascara had melted so drastically that when Padma caught a glimpse of herself in the cracked bathroom mirror, she'd stepped back in horror. Of course she didn't enjoy herself. Who would?

Fuck Vikash.

"Do not be discouraged, my dear. You will see Nilesh again. Am I right?"

Padma's mother unmuted. "Oh, Nilesh. Yes. I was quite impressed with his bio data." She positioned her glasses on her nose, studied a piece of paper, and said, "Padma, you'll recall, his family is in manufacturing. They are the preeminent suppliers of bedding. He must be delightful."

Padma nodded, unsure how being from a family of pillowcase makers made one delightful. But so far things had been just that. Delightful. She'd had one dinner date with Nilesh, and while he was bald with no neck, he had a nice smile. Conveniently, he didn't have any sisters, and he'd been interested in her work, even suggesting some locations in India she and her mother might want to consider for their expansion. With all that said, although Padma would never admit it to her mother, she was very much looking forward to her second date with Nilesh. She would check his bio data for his top-ten activities and give herself plenty of time in case she needed to stretch. After The Matchmaker disconnected, her mother lingered to offer yet more unsolicited advice.

"I think we should ask The Matchmaker for more bio datas. You now have two strikes out of three. Can you not make yourself more attractive? Have you thought about highlights? Your hair is dingy. It's a hard truth." It was always the same with her mother. Padma bit her tongue and silently chanted, *I am enough.* And she thought her hair was looking pretty good these days. Her mother continued, "I think I should begin vetting the men myself."

Yikes. It was bad enough going along with this whole matchmaking process, and humiliating to be rejected only because she didn't know she should have texted The Matchmaker first, but there was no way her mother was choosing her husband. The only way out of this conversation was to switch the topic. She asked, "Mother, how do you want to proceed with the slot machines?"

Padma had hesitated before consulting her mother about the possible theft, but ultimately decided there was no downside. If there was no master-minded big rip-off, well, she looked like she was on top of things. If Hank and his buddy had indeed masterminded a big rip-off, it was before she arrived, so no blame for her. And if she had discovered a masterminded big rip-off and recovered the money, she would look like a fucking genius. Surely, she'd be promoted to lead their casino expansion across India. Maybe she'd win a company award. Padma was mentally drafting her acceptance speech when her mother interrupted.

"I've dispatched our top man and his team. He is a forensic accountant who is experienced in recovering funds. If there is an abnormality, he will find it and know how to handle things. I trust him implicitly. His name is Farid Nadir. We call him The Fiscal Falcon." Her mother tittered.

"The Fiscal Falcon?"

Her mother looked around her office and then leaned toward her computer's camera, so Padma had an extreme close-up view of one of her mother's eyes. She spoke in a low voice. "Yes. How he got that nickname is an interesting story."

Padma watched her mother's eyebrow rise and fall as she recounted the details.

Thirty-Six

The Elephant in the Room

W ake up. Wake up." Pam let herself in the door and called to Nancy and Shalisa, still asleep in Shalisa's living room, on her way to the kitchen to put the coffee on. "Get in here and bring your wits with you. We have to figure out what we're gonna do." Her dog trotted behind her. "I brought Elmer with me; hope you don't mind."

He wandered over and nuzzled Shalisa, as if he knew who he had to butter up. Shalisa gave his ears a rub. Moments later Pam set mugs of coffee and plates of toast slathered with peanut butter on the table. Shalisa dragged herself in, her cheek lined with creases from the sofa cushions.

After digesting the news about the canceled insurance policies and downing three bottles of wine, Pam had Ubered home. Nancy and Shalisa had urged her to stay, but she had wanted to see Elmer and put her head on her own pillow. She had left her friends passed out in Shalisa's living room—despondent over having returned to their familiar financial status of being poor. At least if anyone dropped by, they'd assume the widows were in the throes of grief. And they wouldn't be wrong, but they weren't just grieving the loss of their husbands—even if Shalisa was seemingly fast-tracking through the stages of grief; now they were also grieving the loss of their million-dollar insurance payouts.

Why on earth had those shitheads screwed them over again? First, when they frittered away their life savings, and now this. Why would they pull that insurance money rug out from under them? Granted, they didn't know their wives were standing on said rug, but still, why? Of all the timing in the world, why cancel their life insurance the day they died?

There wasn't even a full email chain to review, as it seemed to have been deleted. All that remained was the insurer's reply that had arrived in Hank's email while they were on the boat scattering Dave's ashes. Pam had to scroll down the thread to see the original message Hank had sent earlier in the week:

Re: Policies # 865442 / #865443 / #865444 for Montgomery, Murphy, Clooney

Please accept this as notice to cancel these policies effective immediately.

If payment is in place to cover insurance until the end of the month, please prorate that premium and issue refunds.

Please advise asap if there are any challenges completing this request.

I'd appreciate it if you could phone me asap to confirm receipt, and then you can directly speak to Larry Clooney and Andre Murphy for their authorization and to verify what is needed from them to execute these instructions.

Sincerely,

Hank Montgomery,

On behalf of Larry Clooney and Andre Murphy

The insurance agent's response indicated they had spoken on the phone, and all three policies were canceled. Pam's only consolation was that Nancy had stopped crying. Much like when Marlene was told Dave was killed by his own stupid garage door, Nancy's demeanor had taken an about-face. After the shock of discovering a million dollars wouldn't be landing in their bank accounts later that week, Pam and Nancy placed hurried calls to the Human Resources department at the bank and casino. Pam's fear was realized when a sympathetic voice told her, "Hank recently canceled the coverage and cashed out, saying he no longer believed in life insurance due to his new religious beliefs."

What the fuck? What religion didn't believe in life insurance?

Nancy heard a similar line from Larry's bank's HR. But on the bright side, they both learned they'd still receive their husbands' pensions. For Shalisa, as Andre worked independently, there was no HR rep to call. She was fucked.

Even with the pensions, about two and a half bottles in, Nancy acknowledged that Larry, and the other husbands, had left them up the proverbial shit creek without a paddle, and it was as though a steel curtain came down on Nancy's grief. Cutting it off. Reinforced by rebar.

But it was a new day and now sober, Pam planned to take a fresh look at the situation and see if they had any recourse with the insurance company—perhaps there was some loophole that hadn't closed, or maybe they could build a case of temporary insanity. Shouldn't there have been a decision-making cooling-off period? She didn't know, but she was determined to find something. She'd brought Hank's laptop and stopped by Nancy's house to pick up Larry's and some papers Nancy wanted.

"Remind me to never day-drink again." Shalisa sank into a kitchen chair and rested her head on the table.

Pam patted her on the shoulder and went back to the sink. "Honestly, we've been through so much shit lately, we're allowed to do whatever it takes to get us through the day. And if it takes drinking three bottles of wine in the middle of the afternoon, then so be it." Pam looked at Shalisa's kitchen counter. "Okay. If it takes drinking eight bottles of wine, half a pint of tequila, three beers, and some schnapps in the middle of the afternoon and into the evening, then so be it." She opened the cupboard beside Shalisa's fridge and pulled out a bottle of Tylenol and put it on the table. She filled three glasses from the kitchen tap and brought them over.

A toilet flushed, followed by running water. A few minutes later Nancy appeared, wiping her glasses with a tissue. They spent the next two hours googling insurance law, policy cancellation, and lawyers, repeatedly asking themselves the same question—why had their husbands canceled those policies?

"There's nothing in Larry's search history," Nancy said. "He didn't even watch porn. I thought he did, to tell you the truth. Especially after we stopped fooling around. But nothing shows up."

Shalisa slouched, leaning on the table. "He probably cleared it."

"Oh, he did. But that cybersecurity course I took at the library tells you how you can check." Nancy held up the dog-eared booklet of stapled pages she'd had Pam pick up along with Larry's laptop. "Maybe he used his computer at the bank." Nancy looked at Shalisa. "What about you? Any luck with Andre's password?"

Shalisa nudged Andre's laptop away and shook her head. "I can't believe you guys have this open access. I never shared my passwords with Andre, and he never shared with me."

Pam answered, "For us, at our age, and with our lifestyle, we had nothing to hide."

"Or so you thought." Shalisa nodded toward Hank's laptop. "Anything at all there, aside from the policy-fuck-over?"

Pam said, "The last email Hank read is the policy-fuck-over. Earlier than that, he deleted everything."

Pam cleared away their coffee mugs and wiped up the toast crumbs around the three laptops on the table. She stepped over Elmer, who lay stretched out beside the air-conditioning vent, and opened the fridge door. She rummaged through the shelves, peeking under the tinfoil lids covering the remaining funeral casserole dishes provided by the neighborhood, finally deciding on the one that bore the masking tape label: *Mary's Macaroni and Cheese heat on high for 5 minutes.*

She popped their lunch in the microwave.

Nancy said, "I think they mostly texted. There's nothing in Larry's inbox. He has a bunch of unread emails he's received since he died." Nancy glanced up. "That's interesting, isn't it? That you die but you still receive emails. I guess it's either spam or people who haven't heard the news. Hmm. But there's nothing from Hank or Andre."

Pam reread the email from the insurance company that blew up their dreams. "Nancy, Larry's personal email was cc'd on the policy-fuck-over. It was sent when we were already on the boat. Are you sure it isn't in Larry's inbox?"

Nancy clicked away. "No. It's not here. And the trash folder is empty."

"Would Larry have checked his email and deleted the insurance one? And his trash? While he was on the boat, just before he died."

Nancy shrugged. "Possibly. On his iPhone. What's in Hank's trash folder?"

Pam clicked. "It's empty."

Shalisa yawned. "I wouldn't think they were the type to regularly empty their trash folders."

They held each other's eyes for a moment, over their laptops. Shalisa sat up.

Nancy said, "What's in Hank's sent folder?" She began clicking.

Pam said, "Here's something to Larry and Andre. From about ten days ago." A click. "It's a YouTube link. Oh, it's a TV-show trailer. He must have recommended it. You don't see it in Larry's email?" She pushed herself away from the table to check on the macaroni and cheese.

Nancy shook her head. "No. Larry must have deleted it."

Shalisa said, "What's the show?"

Pam returned, put her readers back on, and bent down to look at the screen. "Doesn't say." She opened the drawer and pulled out two potholders.

Shalisa moved into Pam's chair. She copied the link and put it in the browser. A YouTube box appeared. Shalisa hit the triangle to play.

Pam opened the microwave door and the comforting aroma of pasta and melted cheese washed over her. She carefully placed potholders on the sides of the bubbling dish, pulled it out, and turned to take it to the table. A few notes of instrumental music played from the laptop and filled the quiet kitchen. Then a man with a British accent enunciated the words, "I'm going to fake my death . . ."

Splashes of hot cheddar stung Pam's bare shins as their lunch crashed to the floor.

The cold casserole sat in a congealed lump, shards of the white porcelain dish still scattered around it. Elmer had sniffed it, then flopped back down by the vent.

There was nothing besides the YouTube link in Hank's email. No salutation, no sign-off, no context for why it was sent. Just the link. Sent a few days before the guys had died.

If they had died.

It took Pam, Nancy, and Shalisa five hours of binge watching to see all four episodes of *The Thief, His Wife and the Canoe*, simultaneously googling and fact-checking; confirming this ordinary English man had disappeared on the water and led everyone to believe he was dead. He got away with it until he decided to fake amnesia and return. He and his wife ended up in jail because they'd claimed, and spent, his life insurance money.

As the light faded outside, the three friends sat side by side on Shalisa's family room sectional.

"That's why they canceled the insurance," Shalisa said.

"No one would look as closely if there wasn't a three-million-dollar payout," Nancy said.

"That dick in the show came back to be with his wife. Our dicks just fucked off and left us broke," Shalisa said.

The women sat on the sofa. Unable to move.

As it sank in that their husbands may have faked their deaths, the next two hours played out in a pattern of an observation voiced to the room followed by a lengthy silence until the next observation was made.

"Why?" they each asked at one point.

"That's why Larry left the note for Paul. It really was a goodbye note," Nancy said.

Silence.

"I think Andre was sorry about not cutting down the tree, but sorrier for ditching me," Shalisa said. "If he really was sorry at all."

Silence.

"I think he said goodbye," Pam said.

"What?" Nancy and Shalisa both asked, their eyes still ahead on the dark television screen.

"On the dock. After we scattered Dave's ashes. As I was walking away, I thought Hank said something, but I didn't quite catch it. I didn't bother to look back. I barely heard him, but when I think about it, as I was walking down the dock, he said, 'Goodbye, Pam.'"

"Oh."

"I need wine." Shalisa forced herself up from the sofa and padded to the fridge. Elmer lifted his paw as an invitation for a quick belly rub as she passed, and she paused to comply.

Nancy and Pam followed her into the dim kitchen and plunked themselves down at the table to wait. Nancy toyed with Larry's laptop, flipping the top up and down, finally leaving it open. She hit a key, and the screen illuminated her face. "I wish I knew if Hector really killed them in that explosion, or if somehow, the fuckers faked it."

Pam sighed. "I'd like to think they're smarter than that guy in England, and he did it. So, I think it's possible. I wish we could know for sure."

Nancy gasped. She pushed her chair back, jarring the table, and covered her mouth. Her eyes were huge. She looked from Pam to Shalisa. Was she choking and did she need the Heimlich maneuver? But she hadn't eaten anything.

"What is it? What's wrong?" Shalisa rushed over and grabbed Nancy by the shoulders. "What is it? What is it, sweetheart? What's wrong?" She stooped and held Nancy's jaw lightly in her hands.

Nancy, her mouth hanging open, pointed a trembling finger at Larry's laptop.

Pam was confused. She looked from the screen and up to Nancy. "What? What is it? It's just Larry's email."

Nancy croaked out the words. "He ... he ... read ... his emails."

"What?" Pam and Shalisa both stared at their friend. What in the world was she blabbering about?

Nancy jabbed at the screen. "They were unread. Before ... we watched that TV show, his emails were all bolded, and unread. Look at them now. You can tell. They've been read!"

Pam put her readers on and peered at the screen. There was a list of about fifteen emails, from different people, some from as recently as that morning, all unbolded and obviously read.

"Maybe *you* read them . . . and you just forgot," Pam suggested.

Nancy shook her head, hard.

They looked back at the screen, confused.

Then Nancy jumped up, knocking her chair over. Shalisa screamed and lunged for Nancy. And Pam clung to them both.

The three women stood frozen, their faces buried in each other's collars. Then, still clutching each other, they slowly inched back toward the laptop and lifted their heads. Bending closer. The three stooped shoulder to shoulder, their eyes riveted to the screen. Pam felt a jolt and jumped back. Then bent forward again as she watched one of Larry's emails change from unbolded to bold. They held their breath and squeezed each other tighter. And then the next email bolded. And the next one. All the way to the top. One at a time. Until all the emails were returned to unread status.

A wave of terror ripped through Pam as though she were witnessing a haunting ghost in action. As adrenaline surged, the wives jumped up and down, screaming and hugging each other. Pam was unsure if she was jumping for joy, or in horror. Finally, they jumped to a stop, drained and still clinging to each other.

Pam realized then: they were tears of joy running down her cheeks. Hank was alive! She hadn't killed him. Her Hank was still alive. He was alive!

And then the other shoe dropped.

Her Hank had left her. Ditched her. Left her broke, and alone.

She grabbed on to the back of a chair, steadying herself while the others wiped away their own tears.

Nancy said, "Fucking Larry."

"Fucking Larry?" Shalisa said. "Fucking Andre."

Pam joined in. "Fucking Hank."

———

Two scotches and a glass of wine each later, the three friends sat in Shalisa's dark kitchen, with only the laptop screen casting light into the room.

Pam said, "I'm so fucking relieved, and I'm so fucking mad. I don't know how I feel. My skin feels like it's crawling off my body. I can't think of anyone, at any time in the world, who has experienced this. I honestly don't know how to feel. Is there more wine?"

"The questions I have are why and how. Why would they do this?" Nancy said.

Shalisa drained her glass. "Okay. To acknowledge the elephant in the room, we did hire a hitman to kill them. I think it's fair to say none of them had a happy marriage either."

Pam stood up. "But what did we do to them? They're the ones who lost our money and torpedoed our lives!" She pointed at her chest, then at Nancy and Shalisa. "We're the ones who get to be mad. Not them."

The women thought about that while Pam went to the fridge, and then Shalisa said, "Well, if it takes two to tango, I guess it takes two to be unhappy in a marriage. If we weren't happy, how could they be?"

Nancy offered, "I never thought about them."

Pam set another bottle on the table and plunked down. "Me neither."

Nancy unscrewed the top and filled Shalisa's glass. "But then why not just leave us? Why go through all this? Why fake your death if there's no insurance money? They could have just divorced us."

Shalisa picked up her glass. "That would have taken a lot of energy, and no one ever voted our husbands most likely to do . . . anything."

"But this took energy." Pam circled a finger at the laptop and Larry's emails. She held her empty glass toward Nancy. "Maybe it wasn't about us. Maybe it had something to do with Dave's death? Do you think?" Pam set her glass down with a thud. "Dave is dead, right? Someone saw his body. Other than our husbands?" She looked from Shalisa to Nancy.

They thought a moment, then Nancy said, "Sure, the police did. And Marlene got his wedding ring back. She saw him at the funeral home. Not his head. They didn't want her to see that, but she and her daughters held his hands. She would have known if it wasn't Dave's hand. So yes. Dave *is* dead."

Nancy filled Pam's glass and set the bottle in the middle of the table. "But beyond the why, how? How could they ever pull it off?"

"It must have taken some planning. They must have been shitting themselves," Shalisa said. "That last week. Wondering if they could get it all together."

Pam looked up. "That's why they didn't want us to go out on the boat that night. To scatter Dave's ashes. They had it all planned, and we were messing it up. Remember how tense they seemed? They could hardly wait for us to get off so they could go back out."

"Larry seemed edgier all week. More irritable. I woke up one night and he was sitting in the bedroom chair, I think, watching me sleep. To be honest, my first thought was, *he's gonna kill me.* But it was Larry. So, I rolled over."

"Andre left me a cupcake. When you dropped me off after the boat ride, there was a red velvet cupcake sitting on the kitchen counter. For years he's been on me about eating healthy and keeping my weight down. I was shocked that he left me a treat. He must have rushed home to cut down that juniper before we scattered Dave's ashes and left the cupcake for me. The frosting was so beautiful. The blushest of pink. It looked like a peony perched on top of that cupcake. I love peonies. And I love red velvet."

"Hank got his hair cut something like three times that week. It wasn't even scraggly. And his neck was already shaved. But it seemed like every time I saw him those last days, he smelled like he'd just been to the barber."

Silence.

Pam rose and switched on the overhead light. Nancy and Shalisa squinted in the brightness.

"Hector," Pam said.

"Hector. Fuck, yeah," Nancy said. "They hired fucking Hector to fake their deaths."

After a moment, Shalisa said, "Wait. We hired Hector to kill them. And you're saying they hired him to *fake* their deaths?"

"Hector did a fucking double dip," Pam said.

"If they're not dead, we're not paying him that hundred grand. And he owes us our deposit back," Nancy said.

Pam and Shalisa locked eyes.

Then Shalisa said, "I nominate Nancy to tell him."

Thirty-Seven

You What?

It was hot and crowded in Hector's mother's small living room, and Hank felt as if he were living a literal game of musical chairs. Although the man Hector had hired mostly sat by the door, and Hector himself had returned to the States, Hank still had to outmaneuver Larry and Andre to avoid the skin-peeling, plastic-covered sofa.

They had gotten away.

But now they were stuck. They'd overplayed their hand. They should have arrived and moved on. Now they were vulnerable. Now Hector knew they had money. And a lot of it. Between their Duolingo Spanish lessons, they huddled around the coffee table.

"We could just walk out. Between the three of us, I think we could take him." Larry shot a discreet look to the man scrolling through his phone by the door.

"I'm more worried about his mother." Hank exchanged smiles with the compact woman at the dining table, deftly slicing peppers with a machete. "And what about our wives? We have to decide what we're going to do about them. We've gotta make sure they're safe."

"You mean if they don't pay Hector the hundred grand they owe him?" Larry asked.

Hank waved him off. "Did you not hear him when he was here? Hector's not gonna kill them over a hundred grand. Now that he thinks there's millions up for grabs, he might use them for leverage."

Larry asked, "You don't really think he'd hurt them, do you?"

"Who cares?" Andre asked.

Hank and Larry spun their heads to him.

Andre looked over the tops of his bifocals. "Am I the only one who heard what the man had to say? Our wives—Pam, Nancy, and Shalisa—paid him to kill us. And they think he did. So who the fuck cares about them?"

Larry glanced at Hank and then said, "That's a little harsh, Andre. When we decided to run, it was you who wanted to be sure the girls would be taken care of and that we'd send them money. I know they hired Hector, but there are a lot of extenuating circumstances at play here." Larry picked up a tiny tangerine from the bowl on the coffee table and began to peel it. Droplets and that sweet smell sprayed the air as he carefully piled the pieces of rind on the table's lace doily.

Andre shook his head, leaned forward, and tapped the table with his forefinger to drive his words home. "That was before I knew they paid the man to kill us. You can't extenuate enough to explain that away."

Hank sighed. "Can we blame them?"

"I can," Andre said. "I can absolutely blame them. Of all the lousy things I ever did to Shalisa, I never hired a hitman to kill her. I even got her fucking juniper chopped down."

Hank's head snapped up. "You what?"

"Before we scattered Dave's ashes, I paid that kid at the marina to run over to my house and cut down that fucking juniper bush she's been on my ass forever about. I didn't want her to be mad at me every time she looked at that fucking bush. Even had him drop off a cupcake. And I left her a note."

"Wait. You did what?" Hank had to hear it again.

"I gave him a note to leave in the dirt that said I'm sorry." Andre nodded and sat back. "Even had it laminated so the ink wouldn't run."

"Are you fucking kidding me?" Hank glanced at Hector's mom, then smiled. He lowered his voice and leaned toward Andre. "You left a goodbye note?"

"No. I left an 'I'm sorry' note. Different. She won't know what it means, but I do. She'll think I was just saying, 'I'm sorry I didn't cut the tree down the first twenty times you asked.' Not 'I'm sorry I faked my death and left you.' No big deal."

Maybe they would have been better off to have stayed home and been killed. At least then Hank would be out of this misery quickly. Now he was stuck with Andre and Larry forever.

Andre continued, "Look. I couldn't end our marriage with Shalisa hating me. She's been pissed at me for so long."

Hank couldn't speak, so he was happy when Larry did. "And whose fault is that, Andre? What kind of marriage did you think you were building? What the fuck did you expect when you didn't tell her about the cancer?"

Hank's head spun to Larry. "Cancer? What cancer? What are you talking about?"

Larry nodded at Andre.

Hank looked at Andre. "What cancer?"

Andre wrung his hands and brought his eyes up to meet Hank's. He breathed out. "Just after we got married, I found out I had testicular cancer. The treatment was gonna make me infertile, and this was back in the eighties, you know. Freezing sperm wasn't an option for me. Shalisa wanted kids. Real bad. And now I couldn't give them to her. But if she knew I had cancer, she'd never leave me. So I didn't tell her. I didn't want to ruin her life. I lied. I told her I'd decided I didn't want kids. That gave her an out. And it worked. We split up. For a while."

Hank frowned. "You could have adopted."

Andre squeezed his eyes shut for a moment, then said, "I wish we had. But I thought I was gonna die." He looked at Hank. "I didn't think I'd get to thirty, let alone sixty. I'm a walking miracle. I'm telling you—eating healthy makes a difference. Everyone gives me a hard time about it, but if Shalisa and I eat right, we could live to be a hundred. You guys and your chocolate bars and aioli, don't get me started." He shook his head and continued, "So, yes, I thought about adopting, but I didn't want to die and leave her a struggling, single mom. I saw how hard it was on my mom. I couldn't do that to my queen. I thought I'd die, and she'd still be young enough she'd remarry and have her family with her new husband. I tried to stay away. We broke up before I started my treatment, and afterward . . ." He hung his head for a moment and then looked up. "It was the most selfish thing I've ever done—I asked her to take me back. I wanted to spend my last months with her. But the cancer never came back. Every appointment, I thought I'd get bad news. But I never did. And Shalisa was stuck with me. My biggest failure in life is that I didn't die, she was saddled with me, and she never got the kids she wanted. I was young, and stupid. I thought I was doing the right thing. What can I say?"

It was a lot to process. Hank looked at Larry. "You knew about this."

Larry shrugged. "Andre and I had a heart-to-heart a while back. About fatherhood. When Paul came out and I was having a hard time with it. Andre pushed me to get my act together."

Andre jumped in. "And a lot of good that did, Larry. Your wife wanted you dead too. It's because you fucked things up with your kid. Right?"

Hank was worried. He'd been worried for years, but this was different. He used to worry about other people coming at them. Now, as he watched Larry and Andre, he was worried they could implode from within. At least they were just sniping with words. If it came to blows, Hank wasn't sure how to handle it. Out of the corner of his eye, he saw Hector's mother's machete flash.

Andre repeated, "You fucked things up with Paul, didn't you, Larry?"

Larry sighed. "I did. But I came around. I let him know I knew I was being a jerk, and I apologized."

"You did? About Estuardo?" Hank grabbed Larry's knee. "Good for you, Larry, to finally come into the twenty-first century. You never said! When did you talk to him?"

"I wrote him a letter."

Hank blinked. Then blinked again. "You what?"

Larry rubbed his hands on his knees. He tried to scooch forward. Hank could tell the hair on the backs of his thighs burned, pulling against the plastic. Larry lifted his butt a fraction and then edged ahead. "I listened to what you guys had to say. You helped me. You did." Larry exhaled. "So, before we . . . you know . . . exploded, I left Paul a note. I could not have my son thinking his father had died despising him. That's one good thing about all this. I came to grips with what's important."

Hank counted, *One, two, three, breathe. Four, five, six, breathe.*

He couldn't have heard Larry correctly. They had gone over the rules twenty times: Leave everything as if you were planning on coming home that night. Don't bring your passport. No extra money. Not your laptop. Not your father's gold watch. Delete the emails to each other. Act normal and do nothing out of the ordinary.

First Andre had some kid rush back to cut down a tree and leave an "I'm sorry" note, and now Larry wrote a goodbye letter.

Hank finally spoke. "Why didn't we just rent the billboard at the Dairy Queen and post 'Thanks for the memories, Love Hank, Larry, and Andre. Your favorite not-so-dead guys'?"

Larry ignored the comment and picked up another tangerine. "I didn't say goodbye. I made it look like I was going to mail it. I knew he'd tell his mom, and then at least Nancy could forgive me. Posthumously. I'd never get back what I lost, but at least she wouldn't spit on my grave. Anyway, I was careful to not be incriminating."

"*That* was you being careful?" Hank put his head in his hands.

He heard Andre ask him, "What did you do, Hank? What did you do to Pam that was so bad she wanted you dead?"

Staring at the floor, Hank answered, "I ate her pad thai."

He raised his eyes. Larry's and Andre's mouths hung open. He looked from one to the other. They squinted and cocked their heads. Larry finally spoke. "I don't know what to say to that."

Hank sighed. "It's her favorite food, and I ate her leftovers without asking. You should have seen her face when I told her. She crumpled. I hurt her so deeply, and I never, ever wanted to do that. But we've been in such a mess with all this shit, for so long, I don't know. So, yep. I think she wanted me dead because I ate her pad thai leftovers." He looked from one man to the other. "And I didn't get a chance to say goodbye, like you did. I didn't fuck her over with my secret cancer or disown my only child.

"The first thing I was going to do with that money was buy us one-way tickets to Claire. And rent a condo near her. Indefinitely. That was our real problem—Pam missed our girl. We both did. But once we were together again, Pam and I had a future, and I gave it up to keep us alive. So, I'm insisting"—Hank looked pointedly from Andre to Larry, so they'd understand how strongly he felt about this—"I'm insisting we make sure they're safe. We'll make a deal with Hector to leave them alone. Do you hear me? We just have to be careful we don't lose it all."

Larry and Andre nodded, then Larry said, "But it's not like the money is sitting in a duffel bag under my bed, and the last man to grab it wins. It's in secured offshore accounts. Hector's not getting anything unless we give it to him."

Hank said, "That's what I'm worried about—what he might do to get us to give it to him."

Thirty-Eight

Big Guns

Hector's stomach growled, and Brenda switched the overhead light on. The sun was setting and their kitchen was growing dim as she set the pupusa on their worn table. Hector smiled at the dish. He remembered when his mother taught his little Italian how to make it, gesturing with him occasionally translating while Brenda struggled to learn the language. Brenda knew Hector, just back from San Salvador, would be homesick. He turned his smile to her.

He often thanked his lucky stars that he had stopped in front of Brenda Palumbo's sun lounger on the beach that day. He and his buddies had sat in the shade, behind their sunglasses, sipping their Coca-Colas. Finally, once they'd zeroed in on their targets, they had jumped down from the stone wall, peeled off their shirts, and nonchalantly sauntered by the tourists. His friends had stopped at the party girls; the ones holding coconuts filled with rum and juice and topped with tiny paper parasols. Hector had kept walking, his shirt on, hiding his scars.

When Hector had joined the gang, it was a ritual that new members had the gang tag tattooed on their forearm. But Hector's mother worked two jobs in the downtown core—a hotel housekeeper during the day, a cook at night—so her sons, sus hijos, would have a better life. Her plan did not include gang membership, so Hector couldn't very well come home bearing a mark that confirmed her worst fear had come true. When he had refused to be tattooed, the gang leader had ordered he be branded—with a garden rake. They had heated the prongs in a fire, tied him down, and placed the rake's iron tentacles against his rib cage. And then they had done it on his other side. Still, Hector preferred the strips of seared skin to having that blatant label of ownership on his body. And although Hector never took his shirt off in public, he knew he'd made a wise choice.

Now, as it grew dark outside, he watched Brenda at their kitchen stove—she was his other wise choice. His buddies had flashed their smiles at the girls with delicate gold chains strung across their flat, tanned tummies and jutting hip bones. But Hector had bypassed them, somehow drawn to the only girl on the beach in a one-piece bathing suit, dressed as though she was ready to swim a race, eating potato chips, crumbs sprinkled on the navy-blue fabric, and reading a book. A textbook, at that. Things had worked out well enough for some of his buddies, but none of them had ended up with anyone like Brenda Palumbo.

Hector had won the jackpot that day on the beach.

"Tell me what the husbands said," she now prodded as she sat down.

This was why Hector flew home: to see what Brenda thought. Some guys in his line of work were impulsive and got themselves into trouble. Hector liked to think things through. Another reason he wasn't a good fit for gang life, where the men who tried to tell him what to do were as smart as his shoes. Plus, it didn't seem like Hank, Larry, and Andre were in any hurry to leave, with his mother feeding them three home-cooked meals a day plus snacks.

"They didn't come right out and admit it, but they stole the money."

"Hot dang!" Brenda slammed the table. "I knew it." She high-fived Hector. "I knew something was up with them from the get-go. Why would anyone want to kill three duds like them?"

Hector filled her in on the rest of what he'd been thinking about. Hank and his buddies were anxious to move on to the next stage of their plan. Right then they were probably sitting on his mother's plastic-covered sofa—Hector tried to convince her he'd buy her a new one if anything happened to it, but that piece of furniture was her pride and joy, and she was keeping it pristine. His mother believed once you have something, you take care of it until you die. Hector had to admit, it was a good ethos to be raised with, especially when it came to marriage. At his mother's house, the husbands were living proof of what happens when couples stop taking care of each other. But now Hector knew they were also sitting on millions of dollars.

Brenda spooned her homemade salsa, almost as good as Hector's madre's, onto her plate and said, "Padma is bringing in the big guns from Mumbai."

"To do what?"

"Well, she wants to confirm that Hank and your other customer, Dave—the dead guy—really stole the money. And if they did, she wants these guys to get it back."

"How are they gonna do that?"

"I would imagine they'll look through the surveillance videos for proof the husbands worked together. She said the lead investigator is a forensic accountant. Maybe they'll look at the husbands' banking activity. Their deposits and such."

"Oh! I didn't get to this part yet." Hector knew Brenda was going to love this twist. "The wives aren't getting any insurance money. The husbands canceled their policies."

"Shut the fuck up!" Brenda grabbed the table with both hands. She looked like she'd won the lottery. "Oh my God. This just keeps getting better! How did you find that out?"

"Hank told me. He wanted me to know the wives can't pay me to actually kill them."

"Why'd they cancel?"

"So there'd be less chance of an investigation. Not bad thinking, really." Hector paused for a moment and then said, "Did you ask your dad? Are the police looking into it at all?"

Brenda shook her head, then pushed her food to the side of her mouth. "He said they ruled the explosion was caused by faulty maintenance on the boat, and careless smoking. So no criminal charges. Case closed." Brenda chewed for a moment, then said, "I wonder if the wives have realized that yet—that there's no insurance."

"If not, they'll find out soon enough." Hector took a drink. "As far as the wives know, I killed their husbands, and they still owe me a hundred grand. If they don't have the money, they must be shittin' their skorts."

Brenda smiled. "Did you say 'skorts' on purpose?"

Hector raised his eyebrows. He loved impressing her. "I did."

"Cute. I didn't know you were so up on women's fashion. Did you give them that speech—"

"—I gave them both. The *you don't want to do this* and *don't make me make you regret this.*" Hector nodded and took another bite.

Brenda said, "You're right. They're probably shittin' their skorts right about now."

Hector added, "They should be."

They ate in silence. Then Brenda asked, "Where do you think the money is?"

Hector swallowed. "My mother said they've been talking about offshore accounts."

She cut through her pupusa with her fork and asked, "What are you going to do?"

"Same as always. I'll watch the bad people fuck each other over, and then I'll do what's right for us."

Thirty-Nine

They'll Find It

What was her mother thinking?

Padma was reviewing the details of The Matchmaker's biodata questionnaire her mother had completed on Padma's behalf and was astounded by her answers. For one thing, why was her mother so focused on profession? She'd repeatedly told Padma to have an open mind, yet her mother listed specific preferences for criminal lawyers, international tax accountants, and podiatrists. Apparently, Padma wasn't the only one with problematic feet.

For physical attributes, her mother had written *ambulatory*. For the love of God.

Brenda knocked on her door and poked her head in. "They'll be here in fifteen minutes."

Padma bounced in her chair. "This is so exciting, Brenda. Do you realize how important this is to our careers? If I'm right about this, and we've uncovered an internal theft ring, you and I can write our own tickets at Indo-USA Gaming. We'll be legends." She smiled her new smile. "Mark my words, if we get that money back, our careers are set."

Padma watched as Brenda absorbed the implications of that comment and congratulated herself on her cunning. She knew if she was going to succeed in proving and recovering this multimillion-dollar theft, she needed

Brenda to be properly motivated to be her "inside woman." She'd learned from her mother how to dangle promises of promotions in front of the ambitious. Then cut them loose because they knew too much. Like, really loose. As in, permanently loose. That's what her mother would do.

Brenda's phone buzzed. "They're here." She looked at Padma. "I'll escort them to the maintenance room. Meet you there."

Padma made a pit stop in the ladies' room. She peered at herself in the mirror. Her acne was relatively calm, thankfully, the redness covered by heavy-duty concealer. She sniffed her armpits and did a quick wipe with a paper towel. She frowned at her reflection and recalled a TikTok she'd seen where a woman had made herself *big* before she went into a meeting. Padma shrugged, bent over to her toes, inhaled deeply, and then unfolded herself, stretching her fingertips to the ceiling. She felt her lungs inflate, her shoulders broaden, and her spine lengthen. She lowered her arms. Wiggled her hips and smiled. She could do this.

She arrived at the room, swiped her key card, sucked in her stomach, and pushed open the door. Brenda stood to the right, a few feet from the group of men huddled around the slot machine. The door clicked closed behind Padma.

A face popped up. Then another. The third and fourth men slowly turned toward her. At least Padma thought it was slowly. She may have mentally turned on a slo-mo filter in her mind. She hoped she hadn't gasped out loud. She felt as if she'd mistakenly walked in on the casting call of *The Indian Bachelor*, if there were such a thing. The four men were each tall and trim in dark suits and crisp white shirts. Their hair fell in luxurious waves over liquid brown eyes. Was a wind machine blowing? She was sure they smelled fabulous.

Where had these bio datas been all her life?

Which one was The Fiscal Falcon? Any of them would do. This was the meet-cute she'd been longing for. Her life might turn out to be a Bollywood rom-com after all. Mr. and Mrs. Falcon, Padma Falcon. *Mommy and Daddy met when Mommy called Daddy to help her catch some bad guys.* Her mother could book the honeymoon.

Two of the men moved apart, and there stood a short, skinny, sallow-skinned man with thinning hair, a prominent nose, thick-rimmed glasses, and a smile of crooked teeth. He thrust his hand toward her. "Farid Nadir. They call me The Fiscal Falcon."

Fuck.

Padma wasn't used to being eye level with men. Even in heels she always had to look up. But she was eye to eye with this guy.

"So, Paddie." He rubbed his hands together. "I hear you lost us some money."

"What! No, I did—"

He put his hand up to stop her. "Right, doll." His broad smile revealed the gaps on both sides where molars used to be. His gaze moved to her cleavage, and Padma instinctively tugged at her neckline. His eyes slid down to her feet. "Heels. Nice." He licked his lips.

Ew. Padma stepped back and, struggling to maintain her balance, was grateful when Brenda spoke, calling their attention to the center of the room. Brenda began their briefing by familiarizing the five men with the room. She had set up workstations around the perimeter, each outfitted with a desktop computer and stationery supplies. A table in the middle held folders and binders.

"Each computer station has access to the closed-circuit footage we have from our two hundred cameras we have positioned inside the casino, and those outside that provide coverage within a one-mile radius of the premises. We've downloaded the past six months for a start but can go back as far as two years if required."

Four men scanned the computers. Farid scrolled through his phone.

Brenda held up a binder. "Here on the center table we have copies of the HR files on the two employees, Dave Brand and Hank Montgomery. It holds their employment records and Dave's timesheets. Hank, being management, didn't complete timesheets. Over here, we have photos of the two men for your reference." Brenda pointed to the two easels holding the poster-size pictures of the men that had been on display at their funeral receptions.

"As well—"

Farid held up his hand again, pocketed his phone, and stepped toward Brenda. "Let me stop you right there, doll. I appreciate the work you've done.

Very thorough. Now let's get down to business. Correct me if I'm wrong, but my understanding is: you have potential overpayments of ten million dollars, and you have four dead guys. Right?"

"But only two were employees," Padma said from behind him.

Farid turned and stepped toward Padma. "But the two employees knew the other two?"

Padma wanted to take a step backward but forced herself to stand still. "One employee died in an accident, and the other employee, Hank Montgomery, along with two of his friends died in a separate event. A boat explosion." Even saying the words out loud made Padma cringe at the likelihood it was a coincidence.

"And the first employee and the second employee knew each other?"

"It seems so."

"And all four dead men knew each other?"

Padma recalled the funeral photo, their arms around each other's shoulders, holding a string of fish and standing on a bright, sunny dock. "It seems so."

Farid reached in his pocket and withdrew a package of pink bubble gum. Padma watched him tear it open, unwrap a chunk, and pop it in his mouth. He winked at Padma. "I developed a taste for it when I quit smoking."

He started to chew. Padma cringed as she watched the pink blob bounce around his mouth. She was revolted but also a little mesmerized. Farid returned the package to his pocket, turned his eyes to her, tongued the wad aside to his cheek, and put his hands on his hips. "This is what is going to happen. We are going to get that money back. We start with the senior employee and the people he left behind. If they don't know where the money is, they'll find it. So the only thing I need to know from you two is"—he pointed his forefingers at Brenda and Padma like a double-barreled shotgun—"who did this Hank Montgomery love?"

Forty

No Coincidence

P am didn't know where Hector lived, otherwise they would have banged on his door in the middle of the night and confronted him about why the fuck he'd helped their husbands fake their deaths. And where the fuck were their shitheads?

Now, as morning sunlight streamed through her bathroom window, she brushed her teeth and glared at the empty vanity beside her. When was a good time to ambush a barber?

Pam spat in the sink and went downstairs.

Elmer sprawled on the floor, his eyes following Pam as she cleared away wilted floral arrangements and stacked the washed casserole dishes she needed to return to the neighbors in a box in the garage. As she passed her pup, she crouched and gave his belly a rub, and his tail thumped. For the past two years he had been the one light in her life. She squeezed his paw. He licked her hand.

"Well, it's just you and me, Elmer. And you know what? The way things have been the past few years, if I had to choose between my husband or you, I'd choose you."

There had been other dogs in Pam's life, but none like Elmer. He expected so little and loved so much. The first weeks, following his dental surgery, he'd roam from room to room, sniffing, before he'd cautiously pick a corner and curl up, making himself as small as possible. If any feet came near him, he'd bounce up and scurry to relocate. He was just beginning to settle in when the vet said he was ready to be put up for adoption. The shelter estimated he was around eight, which is fifty-six in human years. Pam had looked at him, finally comfortably stretched out beside her, and thought how hard it had been for her to change her life in her fifties. The next day she had a tag engraved with his name and her phone number.

She'd never wanted him, and now he was her everything.

Pam had just filled his water bowl when her doorbell rang. Elmer's ears twitched, the only sign he wasn't deaf.

Surely, it couldn't be more flowers or another casserole.

The doorbell rang again.

From his spot on the floor, Elmer opened one eye and watched Pam tiptoe up the stairs to peek out the window. Three short people stood on her front step. She recognized Padma, Hank's boss. She didn't know the other woman, but she held a box. The man stood a step behind the women, his hands clasped behind his back, his posture erect.

Pam wasn't up for any more condolences, especially now that she suspected she was a fake widow, so she sank down on the bottom stair and waited for them to go away. She rested her head against the cool wall wondering, again, why had Hank canceled the insurance? Why had he faked his death?

All she had were questions. She lifted her head. Maybe Padma had answers.

Pam swung the door open, and Padma said, "So sorry to intrude." Padma nodded toward the other woman. "Brenda has collected Hank's personal belongings from his office, and we'd like to have a word with you."

As they crowded into her living room, Pam scanned her front lawn, and the sight of four tall men in suits looming by the road, beside a large black SUV, made her stomach clench. She felt her heart beat against her ribs. She slowly closed her door and turned to Padma, who introduced Brenda. As uneasy as Pam felt, she appreciated the warm eyes that shone back at her above a spray of freckles, and she returned Brenda's firm handshake. Padma explained she was the casino's new director of security, Hank's latest hire, and then nodded toward the man. "This gentleman is from our head office in Mumbai. Farid Nadir."

What was going on? Who were these people, and what did they want?

"You have a dog." Padma wrinkled her nose.

Elmer lumbered over and sniffed Padma, who nudged him away with a pointy high heel, and then he sidled over to Brenda, who offered her hand. He leaned hard against her shins, his tail wagging in circles while Brenda scratched his ears and vigorously rubbed his back. "What's your name, big fella?"

"That's Elmer," Pam said.

The women sat on the sofa, and Farid remained by the door. Elmer strolled over and sat down directly in front of Pam, practically between her feet. She pulled him by his collar and pushed him to lie down beside her chair.

Padma cleared her throat. "Um. Ah." She swallowed. "We have reason to believe Hank was hiding something."

You think? Pam bit the insides of her cheeks so she wouldn't betray her thoughts. Maybe Padma really could shed some light on what the heck was going on. "What makes you say that?"

"Um. Well." She glanced at Farid and then back to Pam. "Um, for one thing. He neglected to divulge to me that he was in fact a good friend of Dave Brand's." Padma swallowed.

Pam's heart sank. That was old news. They all knew Hank and Dave downplayed their connection at work.

Padma leaned forward a touch. "The slot machine tech who died recently."

"I know who Dave Brand is."

"Oh. You do." She sounded surprised. Then she cleared her throat, smiled at Farid, and continued, but now her voice had more of an edge. "I think Hank hid their friendship at the casino."

Pam didn't think she liked that edge. She straightened her shoulders. "So?"

"To be more specific, I asked Hank if he knew Dave Brand and he said, 'not really.'"

Pam definitely didn't like that edge. She cocked her head. "So?"

"Well. Just proving the point that Hank concealed that he knew Dave Brand."

"What's your last name, Padma?"

"Um. Singh."

"Ah yes. Singh. That's what you go by, right? That's on your office door and your business cards, but Hank told me that isn't your real last name. Isn't your real last name the same as the chairwoman of Indo-USA Gaming Inc.? And yet you don't use that name. You *concealed that* from Hank. Why, Padma?"

"Um. Um. Um. That's completely diff—"

"What's your point, Padma? So what if the director of operations didn't want everyone to know he palled around with a technician. Big deal. Why are you here?"

Pam leaned back and crossed her legs. She would be polite for one more minute, and then she would boot the bunch of them from her living room. The guy at the door was creeping her out. Standing there, staring at her, trying to be intimidating. She shot him a side glance, and he looked back at her with such coldness the hairs stood on the back of her neck. She turned her focus to Padma.

Padma inched forward on the sofa and clasped her hands in front of her. "We believe your husband was involved in a scheme that misdirected funds from the casino. A lot of funds. Over about four years. Like, we're talking major. And for someone to steal that kind of money, he'd need help. We wanted to talk to you on an informal basis before we bring in the authorities to investigate—"

Pam put both her hands up. "Whoa. What in the world are you talking about?"

Padma tilted her head. "I'm talking about our belief that your husband—"

Padma had said a lot of words, but the one that popped in Pam's mind was *steal.*

"Hank. Say his name, Padma. So we're clear who you're accusing if you're saying what I think you're saying."

Padma nodded. "We think that *Hank* may have led a scheme to defraud the casino—"

Pam put a hand up again. "Let me get this straight. You're saying you're here because Hank was quiet about his friendship with Dave Brand, and you think that means they stole from the casino?" Pam couldn't think of anything more absurd that could be said to her in her living room. "You think my husband, Hank, stole from the casino, where he worked for thirty-one years?" She looked from Padma to Brenda to Farid for acknowledgment.

Only Brenda nodded.

Pam concentrated on holding her face still while she digested that. Could Hank have stolen from the casino? Is that why he faked his death? What was it Hank always said? Right. The best defense is a good offense.

Pam said, "First of all. Any conversation from representatives of the casino should have started with an acknowledgment and appreciation of my husband's years of service. I imagine he was working for the casino while you all were still pooing in your diapers. So the proper way to have started this discussion, when you were invited into Hank's home, would have been by showing proper respect."

Pam needed to get her bearings, and that seemed a good start. She liked that Brenda squirmed, and she saw blotches begin to pop up on Padma's neck. Good. The man, on the other hand, kept his cold eyes on her. She narrowed hers; he narrowed his in return. A particularly unattractive man who probably had to fight to prove himself every step of his way, and now he was trying to prove himself on the back of Hank's dead (or not-so-dead) body.

"Secondly, you think my husband stole money from the casino. If we had any money in the world at all, do you think I'd be driving that old minivan?" Pam gestured to the driveway. "Or living in this rented dump? On top of that, Hank would have had to have been struck by a bolt of lightning and made way smarter and more daring and more interesting than he'd ever been in his sixty-four years of life to do anything close to what you're accusing him of. My husband's dead, and I'm broke and counting on his pension. He didn't steal your money."

Pam looked at Brenda who looked at Padma who looked at Farid.

Farid reached into his pocket. Pam was startled to hear a low growl come from Elmer. She'd never heard her dog make a sound before. She glanced at him. He was still lying down beside her, but he held his head and ears erect. She looked to Farid, and he pulled out a package of pink bubble gum. He unwrapped a cube and placed it on his tongue. The room was quiet except for his slurpy chewing.

"Pardon me. My favorite brand." He balled up the wrapper, and Pam watched it arc through the room and land on her coffee table. She felt her jaw drop in shock. He ignored that and continued, "Well, Pam. I see your point, but it's irrelevant. Good thieves don't spend. That's a trick to not getting caught. And the best thieves are the ones who don't seem like they could do it. That's another trick. But nevertheless, they do steal other people's money, and, in my experience, their wives always know where it is."

Pam recoiled. Was this horrid man accusing her of being an *accomplice*? Was he out of his fucking mind? He put the package of bubble gum back in his pocket. Pam was mesmerized by this off-putting man's confidence. She couldn't stop watching him. But she regrouped and narrowed her eyes. "Well, I think *your* experience is irrelevant, Farid. Even if Hank did steal your money—and there's no way he did—he's dead and I don't have it."

Farid clapped his hands, and the three women jumped. "I can see we will not make progress here today. So this is what is going to happen. We will come back in a few days." He looked at Pam. "And when we do, you will give us the money. And then you will live."

Pam's head snapped back. "I told—"

Farid put his hand up and looked at her almost sympathetically before lowering it. "You will talk to your friends. Figure it out. Then you will give us the money and you will live. Simple as that."

"*My friends?*"

"The other widows, of course."

Pam's mouth hung open.

"Pam." Farid tilted his head and smiled. "It's no coincidence that four men are dead, and ten million dollars is missing."

"Ten million dollars!" Pam grabbed her chest. She may have to pick her jaw up off the floor. She shot frantic looks to Padma, then Brenda, then back to Farid. "Ten million dollars! You can't possibly mean to tell me you think Hank stole *ten million dollars*. Is this a joke?" Pam looked around to see if there were cameras or iPhones trained on her for some macabre reality show. She clutched the arms of her chair. Her heart raced. What the fuck was going on?

Farid cleared his throat. "As I was saying, my experience has shown me that ten million dollars doesn't get stolen from slot machines without help. And again, the wives always know." He moved his lips into a small smile and looked at her pointedly. Lastly, his gaze dropped to Elmer. "What an ugly dog." He turned and walked out the door. Padma scurried behind him.

Brenda rose, then crouched down to Elmer. "You're not ugly. You are a beautiful boy. What a good boy you are." She stood again, scooped up Farid's discarded bubble gum wrapper from the table, tucked it in her pocket, and closed the door behind her on her way out.

Pam was depleted. She couldn't make herself move. They could have picked up her sofa and carried it out with them and she wouldn't have budged. She heard car doors slam, engines start, and vehicles drive off. She sat, frozen, where they had left her.

How had she gone from growing up as a Girl Scout and being president of the Parent Council to hiring hitmen and being accused of grand theft auto? Well, grand theft without the auto. But still. Ten million dollars! What was happening to her life? People warned her postmenopause can be rocky, but holy fuck. Her life was spiraling out of control, and it had nothing to do with her estrogen levels.

She fumbled for her phone, and ten minutes later Shalisa's car and then Nancy's each screeched to a halt in her driveway.

Forty-One

Every Man for Himself

Pam slammed a bottle of Tylenol—their lives now called for daily doses of headache relief—and a plate of toast and peanut butter on her kitchen table, then filled Nancy's and Shalisa's mugs from the coffee pot, some drops spilling over onto the table. Her friends had barely sat down when Pam pulled out her own chair and dropped down with a thud. "I know why they faked their deaths."

Nancy stopped adjusting her bra's underwire, Shalisa took her foot away from Elmer's belly, and they both sat straight.

Pam opened her eyes wide and enunciated clearly. "Padma thinks Hank led them in some kind of scheme to steal from the casino."

Nancy and Shalisa nodded.

Where was their reaction? Pam continued, "Did you hear me? Padma thinks Hank stole money from the casino."

Nancy shrugged. "Isn't someone always stealing from a casino? I've seen all those *Ocean's Eleven*, *Twelve*, and *Thirteen* movies. Aren't they up to, like, *Ocean's Sixteen* now?"

Shalisa blew on her coffee. "The latest one went down. To *Ocean's 8*, with Sandra Bullock." She took a sip.

Nancy's face broke out in a smile. "Oh. I love her. She's so real. If there was ever a movie about my life, I'd want Sandra Bullock to play me."

Shalisa sat up, excited. "She'd be perfect. I think I'd want Niecy Nash-Betts. That girl is feisty, and I like to think I'm a bit like her." She shimmied her shoulders. "She played a nurse in that TV show *Getting On*. Just like me. Very authentic. Oh, you know who should play Marlene? Jennifer Coolidge."

Nancy slapped the table, jiggling their coffees. "Oh. My. God. She'd be fabulous. Who do you want, Pam?"

Pam had watched this exchange, her head tilted and mouth hanging open slightly. She answered, "Jamie Lee Curtis. I'll keep all this in mind when I'm negotiating our film rights from prison." She leaned forward and jabbed the table with her forefinger. "Do you not hear what I'm telling you? Padma thinks Hank, and your husbands, stole *ten million dollars* from the casino."

Finally.

Pam enjoyed seeing her friends' jaws drop. Satisfied her message was received, she popped two Tylenol, picked up a piece of toast, sat back, and said, "Mindy Kaling would be a perfect Padma. I bet she can play that mix of cute and evil." She took a bite, then reached down to pet Elmer, hoping the drugs and food would make her feel better—quick.

Nancy gave her head a couple of shakes. "You didn't say *ten million dollars*. That's not just *money*. That's a fortune." She looked for Shalisa to agree. "Wait a minute. To be clear, you're saying Padma thinks *Hank* may have masterminded stealing ten million dollars from the casino." She paused. "She's met Hank, right? And she thinks he could do that? Isn't he the guy who forgot to turn off his car while he had dinner in a restaurant? Twice."

Pam said, "To be fair, the motor was very quiet."

Pam could see Nancy's and Shalisa's brains were overloaded. This wasn't going to be easy. She added, "Padma hinted he hid his friendship with Dave because they were in on it together."

Shalisa said, "Our Dave? The Dave who, when Marlene was away, thought his daughters had been kidnapped because he forgot they were at camp?"

Nancy scoffed. "As if Hank and Dave could pull off anything." She threw out another event that still brought rounds of laughter when mentioned among them. "Marlene's fiftieth."

They started chuckling. They didn't even have to recount the story; they knew it so well. That was a good one. Dave had taken care of every detail of Marlene's surprise party himself, except getting Marlene there.

"And he blamed it on us. Like we should have known it was our job," Shalisa said. "Good thing she was home when we called."

Pam said, "That Farid guy said four men dead and ten million dollars missing from the casino slot machines isn't a coincidence."

Nancy waved that away. "But the four of them could barely plan a road trip. Remember?"

Their shoulders trembled with laughter, and Pam held her aching head in her hand. The guys' car had run out of gas on the I-10. Sure, they'd stopped at the station to fill up, but while they had been picking up coffee and donuts, they didn't notice that no one had bothered to actually pump the gas. They had piled back in, loaded with snacks, pulled straight onto the on-ramp, and cruised to a halt half an hour later. That was ten years ago, and the guys still laughed for a good twenty minutes, gasping for breath, as they relived the conversation inside the vehicle that had pieced together why they had rolled to a stop.

Maybe Padma's crazy accusation was just that. Pam shook her head. "You're right. Hank and Dave could never pull off what they're suggesting."

Shalisa took a bite of her toast, chewed a bit, and then jolted. "But if Larry helped, and Andre, they could."

Pam's head snapped up. "That's what that Farid guy said. He said it was the four of them. Together."

Shalisa dropped her toast. "Don't you see? If Dave and Hank found a way to get money *out* of the casino, I bet Andre and Larry would find a way to move it and hide it."

Pam had to think for a minute. Hank couldn't and wouldn't do anything that illicit or complicated on his own. Neither could Dave. But with Andre, the courier expert, and Larry, the bank manager, helping . . . Maybe they could. Maybe they would.

Pam could tell Nancy was starting to consider the possibility when she asked, "How long did Padma say this thing had been going on?"

"About four years."

Nancy nodded slowly. "After the investment went south."

After. Everything was always before and after with them. And now, another *after.*

Shalisa said, "After, they were different. No doubt about that."

Pam said, "I thought they were different because they were ashamed of losing our money. I never thought they were doing anything . . . illegal. I never imagined they had that kind of chutzpah. But if they stole that money, that could be reason to run."

Pam felt like she was in the optometrist's chair and the lenses in the machine suspended before her were being adjusted, her vision sharpening. Option number one, Hank was a distant dick who didn't love her anymore; and now, this option number two, Hank and his buddies had been running a casino theft scheme and faked their deaths to keep from being caught.

Nancy gasped. "Do you think Dave was *killed*?" She gasped again. "Could that be why they ran? Didn't Hank say the casino's new owners have ties to organized crime?"

Pam sat back. "He sure did. And I believe it after meeting that guy, Farid, today. You should have seen him. He stood at the door and stared me down. It was creepy. Elmer growled at him."

Shalisa and Nancy both glanced to Elmer. "Really?" Nancy asked.

Pam nodded, then continued, "If the guys thought someone at the casino had Dave killed, maybe they faked their deaths so they wouldn't be next." Pam rose, topped up their coffees, and said again, "Ten million dollars. Do you really think they could have done it?"

Shalisa gave a little smile. "A young Andre could have."

Nancy played with her earring as she said, "I could see a young Larry trying something like that." Then shook her head. "But I don't know if old, boring Larry had it in him."

Shalisa licked her lips. "Although, if they did, that could have spiced things up a bit." She raised her eyebrows. "If you know what I mean."

Pam's mouth hung open for a moment. "Are you saying the idea of Andre stealing makes him . . . sexier?"

Shalisa shrugged. "If I'd known Andre had a side hustle like that going, that could have . . . you know, helped a bit, at home. He wouldn't have seemed like such a dud. Come on, Pam. Think about it. If you knew Hank was stealing *millions* of dollars, you have to admit, there is a certain je ne sais quoi about it all." Shalisa smiled dreamily.

Pam sat back down and stroked Elmer absentmindedly. "Well, it would have been nice to know Hank had some pep in his step. That he was doing something about our mess instead of just drowning in it."

Nancy picked up the last piece of toast and took a bite. She chewed a moment, then said, "They must have done it. Why else would they run? What do you think, Shalisa?"

Shalisa closed her eyes for a moment and then opened them. "As crazy as it sounds, I have to agree. What else would make them fake their deaths? Don't you think, Pam?"

Pam scratched Elmer's ears. "I do. It makes sense now."

Nancy put her toast down. "Then the next question is, were they doing something about our mess, as you put it, or were they stealing the money and dumping us?"

Pam looked out the window. "I wish I knew."

Shalisa said, "I think we have the answer to that."

Pam and Nancy looked at her, and then Nancy asked, "What do you mean?"

Shalisa sat back and folded her arms across her chest. "They're gone, and we're here. They dumped us. They could have taken us with them. But they didn't."

Pam tapped her finger on the side of her mug while she mulled that over. Then she said, "Regardless, here's our problem: the Farid guy said we have to give the money back. He said, if we give it back, we'll live. Which I think means, if we don't give it back, the opposite will happen."

"And you think he's serious?" Shalisa asked.

Nancy piped up, "I one hundred percent think he's serious."

Shalisa slammed her hand on the table, and Pam and Nancy jumped. "It always comes back to this. Our fucking husbands. Our fucking husbands who lost all our money and ruined our lives. And now because of our fucking husbands, we could be killed. I'm sixty-three. This kind of shit isn't supposed to be happening to me." She pushed her chair back, picked up the empty plate, and headed toward the sink. "I shouldn't be hiring hitmen and dodging threats. I should be scrapbooking and playing pickleball."

"Oh! I've been wanting to try pickleball. They have a league at the community center. We can be partners." Nancy turned to Pam. "Assuming they took it, and that's why they ran, how are we supposed to get it back? And do you want to play too? We can take turns."

Pam shook her head; she wasn't the sporty type. She looked out at the empty spot on the street where the black casino SUV had sat. "I have no idea. I don't even know where to start looking."

Shalisa rinsed the plate, then turned as it dripped on the floor. "We'll never find it on our own. I think we have to flat-out ask them for it. Hopefully they feel guilty for leaving us, and they darn well should. Andre already said he was sorry. At least now I know what he was sorry for." She pulled a dish towel from the front of the stove and dried the plate as she said, "The one thing we have going for us is, they don't know we tried to have them killed. As far as they're concerned, we're still the loyal wives they dumped and left broke. I think they'd try to save us, don't you?" She put the plate in the cupboard and snapped the towel before returning it to the stove handle.

"I don't know," Pam said. "Ten years ago, I would have said yes. Maybe even five. But the way things have been, I'm not so sure. How do we even find them?"

Nancy said, "It's not like they're criminal geniuses. Larry already fucked up by reading his email. Knowing them, if we wait long enough, one of them will sign up for some happy hour discount and we can surprise them at dinner."

Shalisa sat back down, and they chuckled grimly.

Pam said, "But we don't have much time. Farid said he'd be back in a few days."

"Wait a minute." Shalisa held up her hand. "Even if we find them, and get them to give up the money, why would we give it back to the casino? If we've got ten million dollars, why wouldn't we just take it and run?"

Pam liked the idea of disappearing with Shalisa and Nancy. With that kind of money, they could pick up Marlene and run to a lot of places.

But then Nancy said, "Because if we ran, that horrible Farid dude would do the same thing to our loved ones that he's doing to us. He'd pressure Paul and Claire. And your nieces and nephews. And Marlene's daughters. That's why we're different from our husbands."

Pam said, "How's that?"

Nancy explained, "We think about who'll get hurt before we do something."

They digested that for a moment.

Shalisa said, "We could go to the police and tell them the casino's threatening us." She added, "Or the media."

Pam watched a car drive past the house. "Would the police believe we didn't know anything? What did that creep say? 'Wives always know.' Who'd believe we didn't? We can't afford good lawyers. If they investigate and find proof the guys stole, and they're not here to face trial, we could be implicated somehow. Don't you think?"

Nancy nodded. "I do."

Shalisa said, "Then what do we do if they won't give it back?"

Nancy jumped up. "I know! We tell Padma and her buddy that the guys are alive. Let the casino get their money directly from them and leave us out of it."

The room was quiet while they mulled that over until Shalisa said, "But we don't know where the guys are. And I bet Padma and her creep won't believe that. I'd be afraid he'd"—she grimaced as she said her next words—"pressure us until we told him. And . . ."

Nancy finished her sentence. ". . . and if we *can't* tell him, that kind of pressure might not end well."

After a moment, Pam's head bounced up. "But if we tell Farid that Hector knows where they are, they'll go after Hector. Let them pressure him."

Nancy pulled her glasses off her nose and began to polish them on her T-shirt. She finished and looked up. "That gets us off the hook. But it means we put targets on their backs. The casino will go after all of them—Hank, Larry, Andre, and Hector."

Shalisa said, "Hector's a hitman. Those kinds of complications come with the job. Anyway, he'd probably give the guys up to save himself. Who wouldn't?"

Pam said, "And then we're back to killing Hank, Larry, and Andre. Again. And we decided not to do that."

Shalisa said, "I think it's fair to say circumstances have changed. We made that decision before they faked their deaths, dumped us, and left us broke. I'm back on board with them being killed."

Pam looked at Nancy, who met her eyes and said, "I could go either way. Larry did mend fences with Paul. From what he wrote in that note, he's supportive of Paul and Estuardo now, and that was my only beef with him."

Pam hung her head for a moment, then brought it upright. "Well. Truth be told, I'd rather they were alive, but I think at this point it's every man for himself."

While Pam wasn't sure what their next step should be, what was mostly stacking up in her mind were the things they shouldn't do. They shouldn't go to the police. Or the media. Or run. If they told the casino guys Hector knew where to find their husbands, they'd be off the hook.

Pam said, "We have no choice. If they care for us at all, they'll give it back to save us. But that's the ten-million-dollar question, isn't it? Do they care?" Pam checked her watch. "And the barber is going to find that out."

Forty-Two

Just a Barber

Happy wife, happy life.

All kinds of men sat in Hector's barber chair, and more often than not, that's what the smart ones would say. They would catch Hector's eye in the mirror and impart that wisdom as though they were giving him the keys to the kingdom. Hector was a quick study, and he made those four words his mantra. His life was good because his wife was happy.

Brenda loved her new job at the casino, so Hector whistled while he hung a sign that said "back in 30 minutes" in the barbershop window, scanned the parking lot and, finding it clear, locked the door behind him. Three stores down the strip plaza, next to the bowling alley, he exchanged greetings with the bakery owner and purchased six donuts, four chicken empanadas, a salted caramel brownie, and a Diet Coke.

Splotches of grease began to blot the brown paper bag as it sat on the passenger seat of his truck, and the aroma of gently spiced chicken filled the cab. Moments later, Hector exchanged pleasantries with the burly casino security guard and gingerly set the bag beside the visitors list as he signed in and clipped on a guest key card. The guard pointed him toward the elevator.

Stepping into the basement corridor, Hector swung the bag and whistled as he strolled down the hallway, noting where the cameras were mounted. He passed the security command center and the casino bank and then turned the corner and was met by a young intern-type who escorted him the rest of the way and swiped them both into the maintenance room. Hector waited by the door, holding the paper bag in both hands, like an offering. The intern approached Brenda, sitting at a computer station across the room, and announced Hector's arrival.

The offending slot machine Brenda had told him about stood in the center of the room, ignored. At the far end of the space, a half wall of windows gave on to a lunchroom. Vending machines stood against the wall, and Hector could see a kitchenette outfitted with a coffee machine and microwave. Six people sat around the long lunch table. Hector surmised they were Padma and her investigators from India. Hector watched Padma, particularly. He had seen her a few times around the casino and had overheard Hank talk about her. Nothing specific, just that she was ambitious.

Now that she figured so prominently in his wife's life, Hector paid careful attention as Padma reached down and fiddled with the chair's controls until her seat rose a few inches. She looked down the length of the table, and Hector noted her dark scowl and followed her glare. As he scanned the five men in the room, he was reminded of the childhood game, *which of these is not like the other?* What had Brenda said that funny-looking guy was called? Right. Farid, The Fiscal Falcon. Hector knew men like him from his days in El Salvador. Men who adopted predator names as a badge of honor, or more accurately, a shield to hide behind.

Hector watched Farid look up from his phone and toward Padma. Goosebumps traveled up his arms when her expression instantaneously morphed from sinister sneer to sunny smile. Just like that. Her whole demeanor changed in a blink, as if she were a mythical shapeshifter. Hector took note. Ooh. She was good. Scary good.

Hector returned his gaze to the far end of the table and took in the other four men. He recognized their type. Professionals with barely perceptible bulges against their rib cages and at the hems of the pant legs he could see through the open door. Hector's shoulders tensed. This wasn't the type of team he wanted for Brenda. These men weren't here to look at surveillance tapes or bank records.

"Thank you, Hec-toro. I could have ordered in. I wouldn't have minded."

He smiled and handed her the lunch bag. "Then I wouldn't have had the chance to see you. Do you think you'll be very late?"

"I don't know. I feel as long as they're here"—she gestured to the lunchroom—"I need to stay. Just in case something comes up."

She walked him the few steps to the door and said in a low voice, "You came because you wanted to see them, didn't you?"

Hector winked. "You know me, Mr. Curious. I like to know who you're talking about."

"Who do we have here?"

Brenda and Hector turned to see Farid approach them. The small man held his shoulders back and offered a smile of crooked teeth that Hector imagined some people found disarming. Hector caught glimpses of pink gum being tossed about by his tongue. Brenda introduced her husband, and Farid extended his hand. It was wet and limp. Hector hated bad handshakes. He looked into Farid's eyes, and something twinged in Hector's gut; he'd seen eyes like them before, and he hadn't liked them. This man was no mere accountant.

"Do you work here, Hector?"

Hector kept his smile even. "Oh, no. I'm just a barber."

Brenda interjected. "He came to drop off my dinner." She held up the greasy bag as proof.

Farid ignored Brenda. "A barber. I might be in need of a trim if I'm here a couple more days. I don't suppose you make house calls?"

"Not typically. But I could make an exception."

Farid chuckled. "I like a man who sees opportunity. Nice to meet you, Hector. Excuse me. I have to make a call." He strode down the hall, and the door shut behind him.

Brenda said, "That's the one I told you about."

"I thought so." He kissed her cheek and whispered, "You be careful of them. Text me if you need me."

"I can handle myself, Hec-toro."

"Oh, I don't doubt that for a minute. I'm worried for them." He winked and took one more look at the group in the lunchroom, then whistled as he sauntered down the hall and turned away from the elevator instead, taking the stairs up to the ground floor, out the rear door, checking the locks on his way, as was his habit. Then back to the barbershop, to wait.

He turned the lights on, took the sign off the door, and busied himself sharpening his straight razor, with an eye on the parking lot. About half an hour later, he spotted Pam's van swing into a spot at the far end. He finished his task, picked up a package, and slipped out the back door.

Hector was curious about this conversation. The women owed him a hundred grand, and either they didn't have it, or that Farid dick was right and they were in with their husbands and this visit was to deliver payment. There was only one way to find out.

Hector rapped on the van's side panel and smiled at the squeals of surprise from within that rolled into giggles as he opened the door, jumped inside, and slid it closed behind him.

"I brought donuts." He offered the package.

Pam was mopping up spilled water from the front of her shirt, but Nancy smiled and selected one coated in powdered sugar. Shalisa spun around in her front seat and plucked the chocolate dip from the box.

Pam turned her knees around to face the group and settled on a Boston cream.

Hector scanned the van and didn't see anything resembling a package of cash. Okay. This should be interesting.

He sat back. Pam and Shalisa looked at Nancy, apparently waiting for her to speak.

Nancy brushed the powdered sugar from her lips and swallowed. "Um, Hector. We appreciate you taking on our little job, but we think there's been a hiccup."

Hector sighed. He set the donut box on the van's floor, stopped smiling, crossed his arms, looked hard at Nancy, and waited.

She gulped.

He kept his eyes on her. He was a patient man. But he slowed his blinks, hoping she sensed the clock was running.

She wiped her hands on her jeans.

"Hector, we paid you for a job—"

"—You partly paid me for a job."

"Um, yes. We *partly* paid you for a job . . . you *partly* did."

Hector raised his eyebrows but otherwise remained still.

Nancy picked at a seam in the upholstery. "Actually, the only part of the job you did was take our money. Um. Uh, hmmm. How do I put this? We have reason to believe—"

"—Oh, for fuck's sake, Nancy," Pam interjected. "Hector. You helped our shithead husbands fake their deaths, and you took our money. They're not dead, and you double-dipped."

Of all the things that Hector imagined being said in this van, that was not one of them. He nodded slowly, careful not to confirm their accusation. "Double-dipped?"

He'd bet it was Larry who fucked up. Tapping away on that laptop the whole time Hector had been at his mother's house. Hank had questioned Larry, and he'd said he knew what he was doing. Hector had glanced at his hired man, sitting in a chair by the front door, and he'd raised an eyebrow back to Hector.

But Pam had a point. Maybe he had gotten greedy. Ethically, it was wrong to take money for something he didn't do. But, as he often told Brenda, sometimes in the business of bad people doing bad things to other bad people, you just try to be the last bad person to make a move.

Shalisa said, "Yeah. Double-dipped. We paid you to kill them, and then we caught Larry checking his email."

Figures.

Nancy said, "Not only do we *not* owe you a hundred thousand dollars, we want our fifty-thousand-dollar deposit back."

Hector chuckled. "Sorry, ladies. I'm not set up for refunds. You wanted them gone, and they are. And I made that happen. So the fee stands."

Nancy gasped. "You can't charge us for something you didn't do."

"I'm not going to argue semantics. You wanted your husbands out of your lives. And they are. Where's my money?"

Pam answered, "We don't have it. Whether we owe it to you or not— and we dispute we do—we don't have it. Your shithead clients canceled their life insurance policies and left us fucked. For life. With nothing."

So they knew about the insurance. And really? How could those guys fuck their wives over? Some husbands. Hector felt bile rise in his throat. But then he reconsidered. Their wives had hired him to kill them, after all.

"And it's your fault," Pam added.

"My fault!" Hector was astounded. "How's it my fault?"

Pam said, "They canceled the policies because they didn't want their deaths investigated because they weren't dead. They weren't dead because you helped them fake their deaths. Ergo, it's your fault we don't have the money."

Hector had never heard *ergo* used in a sentence before.

Pam said, "Do you know why they ran?"

"Nope." No need to reveal more than he had to.

Nancy said, "You didn't ask?"

"Nope."

Pam scooched closer. "Hector, we're in a bit of a pickle. The casino thinks Hank and the guys stole a lot of money, and they want it back. Hank's boss thinks we know where it is. And she's brought in this . . . intimidating guy from Mumbai. They have links to organized crime, so we expect they won't be doing everything, you know, by the books. This guy is threatening to kill us if we don't give it back." Pam looked to Nancy and Shalisa, who nodded.

Once again, his Brenda had read the situation correctly. She told Hector that Farid's visit had rattled Pam. Brenda knew the guy was bluffing, because he had no solid proof Hank and Dave had stolen any money, let alone millions. He had no proof because, as Brenda pointed out to Hector, he and his team hadn't looked for any. They hadn't switched on a computer or opened a binder. So far, The Fiscal Falcon's only move to flush out the money had been to threaten Pam.

But she and the wives didn't have the money—if they did, Hector would have an envelope of cash in his hand, and he'd be out of the van by now. Those gals were fucked. But it wasn't his problem. "That's too bad, Pam. But I suggest you worry about me. I want my hundred grand. Get it. Nice chatting, ladies. Talk soon." He leaned forward and reached for the door handle.

Pam raised her voice. "You're going to tell our husbands to give the money back."

Hector stopped; his hand rested on the door. He couldn't have heard that right. "Sorry, can you repeat that?"

"We need you to go tell our husbands to give the money back to the casino to save us."

Hector sat back down, rubbed his jaw, and then reached for a donut. He needed time to process. He selected a plain one; that wasn't as messy as the others. He chewed. Swallowed. Took another bite.

Finally, he said, "You realize they know you hired me to kill them?"

"What?!" The women all straightened with horrified gasps. "Why?! Why would you tell them that?" Pam demanded.

"It seemed like a good idea at the time." Hector took another bite.

"Doesn't that breach some kind of confidentiality understanding?" Nancy demanded.

Hector scrunched his face. "We don't exactly have client-hitman privilege."

Nancy glared at him. "How could you do that?" She looked out the window and then back and asked in a quieter voice, "How did they take it?"

Hector shrugged. "Reasonably well, actually." He avoided eye contact. "Um. They may even have been a bit impressed with your . . . ingenuity."

Nancy sat back. Her head cocked.

Shalisa said, "Well, if they'd been more honest with us from the get-go, we may have been more impressed with their *ingenuity* too. If we'd ever known they had any."

Pam waved to stop the conversation. "None of that matters. What's important now is we've got to give that casino thug that money back or he's going to kill us. You need to tell our husbands and get the money."

Hector wiped his fingers on his jeans. "Let me get this straight. You know *they* know you wanted them dead. And now you want me to ask them for a *favor*?"

Pam shrugged. "Uh-huh."

He put it another way. "You want me to ask them to give back that money?"

Pam said, "More than ask. We want you to get it."

"And why in the world would I do that?"

The women exchanged glances, and Pam spoke. "If you don't, we'll tell that creep from Mumbai not only are our husbands alive, but *you* know where they are."

Hector could deny that. But it was one thing to *say* he didn't know where the guys were, and another to not have it beaten out of him. Hector made sure not to show it, but Pam had played a good card. He mentally lined up his own cards on the table. He knew from Brenda that Padma and Farid didn't have proof Hank and his guys had stolen the money. It was just a hunch. But if Pam told Farid the husbands had faked their deaths . . . that would be all the proof they needed to know that millions of casino dollars were out there.

That Farid dirtbag wouldn't believe the wives didn't know where that money or their husbands were, and he'd double down on his efforts to make them talk. Thirty seconds into that discussion the wives would send Farid's guys to him, no way around that.

Unless he got rid of the wives first. That could solve his problem. He looked from Pam to Nancy to Shalisa. That was one way out of this mess. Otherwise, if the wives told Farid about him, and those guys came for him, he could take care of himself, but it wouldn't be easy. Did he really want to take that on? And Brenda could get caught in the crossfire. But if he killed the wives, he wouldn't have to worry about them talking to Farid.

It didn't take Hector long to figure out his next move.

———

Hector was folding laundry when he heard Brenda's key in the apartment lock. He leaned against the doorway, lining up the seams in the sleeve of his wife's favorite pair of flannel pajamas. Cream, with a pattern of tiny dogs sprinkled across it.

She closed the door behind her, kicked off her shoes, and flung her arms around his neck. He reached down to kiss her and felt complete with her body pressed against his.

"How was my conventionally employed wife's day?"

"Oh my God, Hec-toro!" She undid her pants, stepped out of them, and grabbed her pajama bottoms from across his arm and wiggled into them. Then she whipped off her shirt and bra and grabbed her top, still warm from the dryer. She took his hand and dragged him to the sofa, where she flopped down. Hector sat at the end, and she lowered her feet—a little smelly, but not too bad—onto his lap.

She stretched. "Hec-toro, I can't tell you how nice it is to finally be living a normal life."

He rubbed her toes. He'd wash his hands later. He loved her, but jeez, she needed more absorbent socks. "You don't miss your P.I. work?"

"Not a bit. I didn't realize how much I'd like working somewhere normal. Not sitting in my car following dickweed husbands to dodgy motels. Having a desk and a restroom nearby. Not having to pee in gungy gas stations. Life is so much easier. Did you hear from the wives?"

Hector filled Brenda in on the minivan conversation. He waited for Brenda's reaction.

Brenda sat up. "It'd be good for me too. If the casino gets the money back, Padma said our careers would be set."

Hector leaned over to tuck a strand of hair behind Brenda's ear. "I'm not so sure I'd believe everything Padma says." He thought back to observing Brenda's boss at that lunchroom table, and how her expression had so quickly flipped from dark to light.

Dark and light. He looked at his wife. Hector knew he lived on the dark side of life and his amor on the light. Now that her light had shone on him, he needed it. While Brenda flirted along the edges of his dark, Hector didn't want her any closer. Ever. He was careful with that, and seeing Padma in that lunchroom made him aware of how dangerously close Brenda was to crossing that line. Padma was in an even dicier situation because good people can do bad things for only so long before they turn bad themselves. Padma seemed poised to turn. Hector hoped she would choose otherwise. But she wasn't his concern. Brenda was. And he had to be more careful with her.

He said, "Maybe we should cut our losses and walk away from this. I don't know if I can get the husbands to give the money back."

Brenda winked at him. "You always say you can get anyone to do anything, if you hold a gun to their head." She leaned in to kiss him.

He kissed her back, then Brenda rested her head on his shoulder. Hector sighed. On the other hand, he could finish this and then be done.

He pulled out his phone and opened up the airline app. "Actually, you get better results if you hold a gun to their friend's head."

Forty-Three

Since You Put It That Way

Late the next afternoon, Andre pushed his bifocals up his nose. "It's my vision that's not so great. My hearing is perfect. And I can't believe what I'm hearing." He tried to slide back in his seat, but the sofa's plastic gripped his thighs, and he had to lift his butt up and sit down again.

Hector shifted his gaze to Hank and Larry.

Larry said, "How did they figure out we're alive?"

Hank shook his head. "Larry, you're playing with fire every time you open that laptop. You must have done something. Plus, what did you expect with all the goodbye notes you guys left behind? You two are like fucking Hansel and Gretel leaving breadcrumbs for anyone and his brother to follow us."

Hank knew he was overreacting. Being cooped up in Hector's mother's house was wearing on them. But his Spanish was coming along, and the food was fantastic. Empanadas, tamales, quesadillas. He was still hoping to learn how to make pupusas.

But he, Larry, and Andre had to get on with their lives or they were going to kill each other. Hank didn't care about the money anymore. Well, that wasn't totally true. He still cared, just not as much as he had for the past four years now that it no longer was feathering a nest for him and Pam as a couple. But he didn't care enough to die for it. Or for Pam to.

Being trapped here for eleven days had made him realize anything would be better than this. Once they were out in the world, they could find a way to survive. Start over. Plenty of people did it. It would have been easier with $9.3 million, but they were smart and resourceful; they'd find a way to make a living. They had to move on or they'd die.

Larry scowled at Hank, then asked, "You're sure they know we're alive?"

Hector nodded. "No doubt in their minds."

Hank sipped his chichas. He hadn't expected this turn of events, although he was happy to see Hector arrive. Then at least he knew things were moving along. Hector would give them news from home, then, to protect their wives, they'd negotiate a fee in lieu of the hundred grand the girls couldn't pay. And finally, he, Larry, and Andre would be free to leave this house. Or Hector would hold a gun to their heads, make them give him the millions they'd stolen, and then they'd be free to go. Or they'd be dead. At this point, Hank was fine either way.

But then Hector sprung this on them.

"And the casino guys from Mumbai, they're the real deal?" Larry asked.

Hector nodded.

Hank shot glances at Larry and Andre. "Not to beat a dead horse, but you see we were right to run. The casino *was* after us. I didn't make us blow up our lives out of paranoia." Hank felt vindicated now that someone had finally laid eyes on the bogeymen they'd fled. For the past few days he'd been wondering if maybe he had misread things. Maybe Dave *had* died in a freak accident. Maybe it wasn't a murder and a message after all. Maybe Padma wasn't warning him. Hank looked around at Hector's mother's living room, his disheveled friends with their scruffy beards, wrinkled clothes, and tired eyes. But now that Hector had actually seen the casino's men from Mumbai, it was real, and he was right. He'd saved them from having their naked bodies swing from a bridge.

But what about their wives?

Andre stood. "Can I remind everyone, a few days ago we were sitting here worried he"—Andre pointed at Hector—"was going to kill us because our wives hired him. No offense, Hector."

Hector waved him off.

Andre continued. "And now we're sitting here worried some hitmen from India are going to kill our wives because we stole some money. And now you're talking about giving back everything we worked so hard for, to save them. And these are the same three women who hired him"—he pointed at Hector—"again, no offense, Hector, to kill us."

Hector waved him off again.

"Are you fucking nuts?" Andre sat down.

Larry said in a quiet voice, "If you remember, Andre, they're the reason we did all this to begin with. For our wives."

"Yeah. Well. That was before we knew our wives wanted to kill us. And, I think it's important to note, they thought they did kill us. We're just lucky we killed ourselves first. I think it's fair to say that circumstances concerning our wives have changed." Andre pushed his bifocals up his nose for emphasis.

Hank realized Andre hadn't accepted it yet.

Hank had.

Hank knew the moment Hector had found out there were more than nine million reasons for the guys to run, they weren't keeping that money. At least not all of it. They were sitting ducks in Hector's mother's house, with the bars on the windows, the walled garden, and the man at the door. They'd stayed too long, and it would cost them. He'd expected they'd be giving a chunk of the money to Hector. But he sure hadn't expected they'd be losing it all. Especially not back to the casino.

Hector said, "If you don't give the money back, the casino's men will kill your wives for the principle."

A chill traveled up Hank's spine.

Hector looked at Andre. "You may wonder why you should care—and no one's making you care about your wives—but if you don't give the money back, your wives will tell the men from Mumbai you're alive. That, and knowing you ran, will prove to them that you have their money. And they'll come for it. First, they'll come see me, and I'm not gonna die for you. Knowing the odds are not in my favor, I'm not gonna lie for you either. I may be able to take care of one or two, but probably not all five. Even if I were to kill them, they'll send more. And they'll keep sending guys until they get their money back. You'll run until you're dead."

They sat quietly for a few moments.

Hector said, "If you're not gonna give the money back, you should start running now."

Larry said, "Even if we wanted to give the money back, how do we do that? It's not like I can PayPal them. It's not a bag of cash. I have it split up in different accounts. I'd have to find a money transfer service or wire transfer system to handle it. I'd have to have an account to send it to. That all takes time."

Hank said, "You were going to send money to the girls. Before you knew they hired Hector to kill us. How were you going to do that?"

"I brought their account info with me. I was going to transfer a series of small amounts. But now we're talking the whole shebang." Larry rubbed his jaw. "I could consolidate the accounts and get a bank draft. That's as close as we'll get to cash. I suppose I could set up a virtual safety-deposit box and upload the bank draft."

"Whoa," Andre said. "Let's stop for a second. We seem to have moved right past the question of whether we want to do this, to how to do it. Can we pause?"

Larry thought a moment, then said, "What's the point of pausing, Andre? If we give the money back, the girls live, and they don't tell the men from Mumbai we're alive. So we live too." He continued, "If we don't give the money back, the girls die, but first, they'll tell those guys from Mumbai we're alive, so they'll come after us and we'll die too. Even if we run, eventually they'll catch us. We'll just die later."

All eyes were on Andre.

"Well. Since you put it that way." Andre looked up. Then chuckled. "You've got to give them credit. We fucked our wives over, even if we didn't mean to, and they fucked us right back." His chuckle grew louder, and he shook his head. "In fact, I don't think I've ever been fucked so hard. And it only makes sense if I were to get fucked that hard, that it'd be my Shalisa doing the fucking." He stood up and headed down the hallway toward the bedrooms, his laughter rolling back to the living room. "My fucking Shalisa. Man, I miss my queen." They heard his door close.

Hank looked at Hector. "How much time do we have?"

Hector answered, "I'm on the red-eye back tonight."

Hank looked at Larry, who nodded and then gingerly peeled himself off the plastic-covered sofa. He went to the table, flipped open the laptop, and said, "The bank draft will be pretty straightforward." He looked at Hector. "We'll set up a virtual safety-deposit box for you—with biometric security. Requires fingerprint and facial recognition access. I'll show you how to do it. You might want to take notes, because you'll have to show Nancy how to create her own. We'll upload the bank draft to your VSDB, then back home, you'll transfer it to Nancy's. At the handoff—" He glanced at Hank. "There's a term I never expected to use in my career at the bank." He gave his head a little shake, then turned back to Hector. "At the handoff, Nancy will transfer the draft to the casino's guy. Chances are, they're financially savvy so they'll be familiar with the VSDB. It's not rocket science."

Hank picked up his glass of chichas. "How much money does the casino think we got away with?"

"Ten million."

"Not quite. We made it to nine, and then Dave was killed. That's all we have." Hank took a sip of his drink and then asked, "What do you get out of this? You said our wives owe you a hundred grand, but they can't pay you. Now we can't pay you either. Do you get a finder's fee from the casino?"

Hector shook his head.

Hank had to know and, against his better judgment, asked, "How do we know you won't just take that bank draft and run?"

"For exactly that reason. I'd be running. That's not how I want to live, Hank. I've seen those men, and I don't want to be looking for them in my rearview mirror the rest of my life. Brenda is happy at her new job, and what I get, you can't put a price tag on."

Hank raised an eyebrow.

"I get a happy wife. And a happy life."

The men raised their glasses to each other, and Hector rose to join Larry at the table. Hank shot a look to Larry, hoping he'd overheard Hank say *nine million*. If the casino thought it was ten, and didn't have proof, they'd believe it was nine. The guys could find a use for the remaining three hundred grand.

They had to have something to show for all that work. And three hundred grand was better than nothing. He sipped his drink and as Hector sat down, Hank caught Larry's eye, and he nodded back.

Forty-Four

This Is No Dream

The sound of Hank grinding coffee beans stirred Pam from her sleep. She opened an eye to check on Elmer, who had lumbered upstairs sometime in the night and was curled up on the floor beside her bed.

Pam hated mornings. She found these early hours as the sun began its creep to the sky to be cold, lonely, and damp. If you ventured outside everything was covered in dew; pesky blades of grass stuck to the soles of your feet. Pam preferred her days to start dry and sunbaked. Even if she somehow was wide awake this early, and tempted to rise, she'd snuggle in bed until the feeling passed. And in these jumbled days since Hank's death—she'd have to reframe that in her mind—in these jumbled days since Hank fucked off and left her, she'd been snuggled in bed a lot. It was as if her pillow was emitting a magnetic field her head couldn't break free of.

Wait a minute. Hank was gone. Who was making coffee downstairs? Beneath her pajamas, a light skim of sweat broke out on Pam's skin. Could it be those Mumbai guys? The last person she wanted to see in her house was Farid, and she'd bet this was just the kind of power move he'd make. Pam carefully put her feet on the floor. Elmer bopped his head up, disturbed, squinting, his fur suffering from a bad case of bedhead. "It would be nice if you had just an ounce of watchdog in you. Just sayin'."

Elmer flopped back on his side.

Pam looked for her phone to call 911. An intruder was an intruder. She wouldn't have to explain why the thugs were there. Just get them out. But her heart sank. She'd left her cell downstairs. She should have fought Hank to have a landline. It would have been worth the extra dollars to have it now. She rolled across the bed and tiptoed to the landing. She could probably race down the flight of stairs and straight out the front door. But Elmer would never follow her; he hadn't even stretched out his groin yet. If she tucked him in a closet, he'd sleep until she came back for him later. She inched back to her bedroom.

"Pam! Are you up yet? It's Hector."

Pam fell back against the wall and peed a little.

"I'll be right down." She croaked the words out, squeezed her legs together, and scuttled to the bathroom.

In the middle of hurriedly brushing her teeth, Pam looked hard at herself in the mirror. "I hired a hitman to kill my husband, but Hank outsmarted me and hired the same hitman to fake his death, after he stole millions of dollars from his work, which I'm now trying to recover so a bubble gum–chewing thug in a nice suit won't kill me and my friends. And now our hitman has broken into my house and is apparently downstairs making me coffee. Yep. This is sixty-two."

She spat out her toothpaste.

Hector was adding sugar to his coffee. Pam counted four spoonfuls before he stirred. He must work out; he was very trim. He took a sip and nodded toward her patio door. "If I were you, I'd get a broom handle to put in the track at night."

"Thanks."

Hector pushed a mug toward Pam. She leaned against the cupboard, took a sip, and heard Elmer's nails on the floor behind her.

Hector knelt down, and Elmer sauntered toward him, tail wagging. "Hey, buddy." He rubbed Elmer vigorously from head to tail. "I've never seen a dog like you before." Elmer leaned into Hector's legs. "You're like a character in a Disney movie."

Elmer caught her eye, and Pam could swear he smiled at her. "People think he's funny looking, but I like him."

"I can see why." Hector stood. "All right. I have the money."

Pam's knees almost gave out with relief. She said, "We need Nancy. She takes care of the money."

Twenty minutes later Pam poured Nancy and Shalisa coffee from the pot Hector had made, and then topped up his mug. She set the sugar bowl on the table and was mesmerized again as Hector stirred spoonful after spoonful into the black, steaming liquid. Pam noticed no one asked Hector about their husbands. She kind of wanted to know, and she kind of didn't want to know. It was still so much to process.

Nancy put her mug down with a thud. "Okay. Enough already. How did you get the shitheads to give you the money?"

Hector watched the spoon swirl his coffee. "They didn't want to see you killed."

After a moment, Shalisa said, "Isn't that the sweetest thing you ever heard? Our husbands who faked their deaths to get away from us, and then canceled their life insurance so we'd be fucked, want to make sure we live long enough to fully understand just how fucked we are." She sat back in the kitchen chair and crossed her arms. "Well, if anyone is going to fuck me, it may as well be Andre. At least it won't last long."

Pam's head shot up. "Shalisa! Oh my God. When did you get so crude . . . and bitter?"

She waved Pam off and smiled. "I know. I couldn't resist."

Pam noticed Hector dropped another two spoonfuls of sugar in his coffee. Then he referred to some notes on his phone and tapped away on Nancy's laptop. He explained that Larry had decided to use the Virtual Safety Deposit Box app. Larry had prepared a bank draft that was in Hector's VSDB. He helped Nancy create her own box, unlocked his with his fingerprint, then transferred the draft from his box to hers and set up her facial recognition.

"I thought it was ten million," Pam said.

Hector shook his head. "Nope. They say nine is all they got." Hector referred back to his phone. "Now, Nancy, you leave it in your box and lock it with your fingerprint and your face. When the casino guy arrives, if he doesn't have his own box, he creates one, and you upload that document to his. He locks it with his fingerprint and his face. Then he transfers it to their bank account, and you're done."

Nancy took notes, although Pam was surprised and relieved it seemed relatively simple.

Hector looked at the women. "It's the payoff, except a briefcase of cash doesn't exchange hands, a bank draft is moved virtually."

Was it even legal? Given the situation, Pam didn't care.

Hector stood and dropped his phone in his pocket.

Pam said, "Um. About your hundred thousand dollars . . ."

Hector held up his hand. "It's all right." And slipped out the patio door.

Pam watched him disappear through her gate. "Do you think that means what I think it means?"

"That he's already made us regret it enough?" Shalisa asked. "I think so."

Nancy nodded. "I guess even criminals have ethics. I still think we should get back the fifty thousand dollars."

Shalisa said, "I dare you to ask him."

Pam's phone buzzed with a text from Brenda.

"They're coming tomorrow at four." She put her phone down on the counter. "We've gotta call Marlene and get her to take the next flight home. Dave was involved. It's too much to hide from her, and she'll never forgive us if we get killed without her."

"Should we call 911?"

"Maybe. Let's wait a minute. Her pulse is settling down," Shalisa said.

At noon the next day, Marlene was stretched out on Pam's kitchen's linoleum floor, her blond hair fanned out as though she were being photographed for a shampoo ad. Shalisa knelt and held her fingertips to Marlene's wrist and a hand on her forehead. Pam and Nancy were crouched on Marlene's other side.

Pam stroked Marlene's arm. "Do you think she's OD'd?"

"On edibles? I don't think you can OD on half a gummy," Nancy answered.

"I knew this was a bad idea," Pam said.

Nancy rested her hand on Marlene's shoulder. "I just wanted to give her something to take the edge off. Make her mellow."

"Well, she's mellow, all right." Pam poked Marlene's inert arm. "If she were any more mellow, she'd be dead. Oh, wait. Is she waking up?"

Shalisa leaned in and spoke in a soft voice, "Marlene, sweetheart. It's okay. We're here. You fainted."

Marlene blinked rapidly. She took a few haggard breaths. She raised her head. Squinting, her eyes darted from Shalisa's face to Nancy's and then to Pam's. "Is Dave still alive?"

Pam closed her eyes for a second and said in a soft voice, "No, sweetheart. I'm sorry. Dave's not still alive."

Marlene rested her head back on the linoleum. "That's too bad. I would have liked it if he was still alive."

Pam squeezed her arm. "Us too. We would have liked that too."

Shalisa asked her, "How are you feeling? Can you sit up?"

The women helped Marlene to a cross-legged position on the floor. "I think I peed my pants."

Nancy said, "Nooo. There were just some melted ice cubes on the floor. That's all."

Shalisa glanced down. "Nope. She peed." She rubbed Marlene's back. "Don't worry. That sometimes happens when people faint. Come on. I'll take you upstairs, and we'll get you cleaned up. Then we'll make some toast, and we'll fill you in on the rest."

Marlene nodded, then looked at Pam. "So, they're alive. Hank, Larry, and Andre are alive. This isn't a dream?"

Pam sat back on her heels and shook her head. "No, dear. This is no dream."

———

A few minutes later, wearing Pam's sweatpants and sitting at her kitchen table, Marlene said, "The funerals were fake. You knew they were alive."

Nancy answered, "No. At the funerals we thought they were dead."

"But you'd hired a hitman to kill them."

"Uh-huh."

Marlene glared at Nancy. "You cried in my arms."

Then she narrowed her eyes at Shalisa. "I made you a tuna fish casserole."

"It was very tasty."

Marlene's shoulders relaxed. "It's my mom's recipe. I can email it to you."

Shalisa put her hand on Marlene's wrist. "That'd be awesome. The crushed potato chips on top really made it."

Marlene took a breath and said, "My heart broke for you guys. How could you do that to me?"

Pam cleared her throat. "It's complicated."

Nancy reached out and took Marlene's hand in hers. "We all had marriage problems. We saw when Dave died, your problems were over. So we wanted that too. But then we realized we'd made a mistake. We tried to call off the hit, but we didn't know it at the time, but it seems they were already faking their deaths. But none of that matters. We're all alone now. The four of us. For all intents and purposes, we're widows too."

Marlene locked eyes with her. "Give me a minute to run to the drugstore and pick out the Hallmark card for the wife who hired a hitman to kill her husband and then he didn't end up dead. I'm sure there's a stack of them if I look hard enough."

Nancy grimaced and sat back. "We're still grieving. It's just a little . . . unconventional."

Marlene shook her head. "Oh, no, no, no." She wagged her finger. "You don't get to grieve. I'm the only widow here. I'm the only one who deserves any sympathy. You three just have fucked-up marriages. If there's a funeral casserole in that fridge, it's mine. You're not getting any."

Shalisa said, "Well, not to point out the obvious, Marlene, but you're also the only one who got any insurance money."

Marlene gasped. Her jaw dropped; she sat straight in her chair and pointed at Shalisa. "Oh my God. I cannot believe you just said that. I lost my husband! He's not walking around God-knows-where because he's trying to get away from me! Dave is dead! He's not coming back!" She crossed her arms over her chest. "And I'm not so sure my Dave was mixed up in any of what you've all got going on here. Thugs pulling up to your house and threatening to kill you. Whatever you've gotten yourself into here, you can count me out! My Dave would never have put me in danger. He was a wonderful husband and father. He *took care* of me and my girls." She reached for a tissue, blew her nose, and covered her eyes.

Pam squinted at her. Then looked at Nancy, who shrugged, and Shalisa, who raised her eyebrows. Apparently, death had made Dave Brand a good husband again. But Marlene was right, she was the only true widow, so Pam spoke gently when she said, "Dave had to be involved, Marlene."

Marlene took the tissue from her face and shook her head.

Pam continued, "Hank couldn't have done it alone. It had to be the four of them. Somehow, they got the money from the slot machines. So, it had to be Dave. He's the only one who worked on them. I'm so sorry, but you didn't just get Dave's insurance money when he died. You got his mess too."

Marlene sat quietly for a moment, then straightened and tucked her tissue in the edge of her bra. She scowled at each of them. "You lied to me." The others exchanged uneasy glances and looked to the floor. "That's not cool. We can't be doing that."

They shook their heads and murmured, "No."

"Seriously, Shalisa." She looked from one woman to the other. "As if you'd ever open a yoga studio. You can't even hold the tree pose. And Nancy running a coffee truck. Who did you think you were kidding? You're the last person who should be in the service industry. For one thing, you'd never open up on time. For another, you're so cheap you'd probably buy day-old baked goods and overcharge. You'd have zero stars on Yelp." Marlene shook her head. "I wasn't sure exactly what you all were up to, but . . . well, it's safe to say I never imagined I was financing a mass murder."

The room was quiet for a moment, and then Marlene added, "Well. I forgive you. Even though you haven't asked me to, I know you want me to. So I will. We're in this together. Whatever this is, even if you've all lost your minds. We'll do what we always do. We'll stick together, and we'll be okay. We have each other." She reached for Pam's and Nancy's hands, who in turn grasped Shalisa's. "That's what matters."

Forty-Five

A Real Dog

The four friends were waiting in Pam's living room when two vehicles pulled up to the curb. They huddled to the side of the curtains to peer out for a better view and watched Padma emerge from the driver's side of her white BMW and Brenda step onto Pam's lawn from the other side. Behind them, a large, black SUV with tinted windows parked. Farid bounced down from the passenger seat. The other doors opened, and the four men in suits, who looked like they could be walking off the set of a Bollywood gangster movie, stepped out and, this time, walked toward Pam's house. Nancy and Shalisa each put a hand on Pam's forearm. Pam felt goosebumps ripple up toward the base of her neck.

"The smaller one, that's Farid." Pam gulped.

"Holy heck," Nancy said in a low voice.

"Why are there so many?" Shalisa asked.

"To intimidate us and make sure we pay up," Pam said.

Marlene gave a low whistle. "What have you gotten me into?"

"Us? This is what our shithead husbands got us all into," Nancy answered.

Marlene said, "That one on the left is crazy handsome. Actually, they're all pretty good-looking. But kinda scary."

Pam tried to wet her lips, but she'd run out of saliva. She had to keep her nerves in check and get through this. Her voice cracked a bit as she said, "We'll be okay. We're giving them what they want. We'll be totally fine. There won't be any problem. We've got nothing to worry about. We're good."

Shalisa kept her eyes on the group of men. "Do you have any more self-talk you want to share?"

Pam shot her a quick smile just before the doorbell rang.

Marlene grabbed Pam's arm. "Don't offer them snacks. Let's get them in and out."

Pam opened the door, and the group crowded into Pam's cramped living room. Padma and Brenda took a seat on the sofa; Farid stood by the doorway, his hands folded in front of him, with his four men behind lining the wall near the entry. Pam sat forward in the armchair with Nancy perched on its arm, and Marlene and Shalisa sat straight in kitchen chairs beside her.

Elmer, surprisingly, was interested in the guests and sniffed around their pant legs until Pam feared he might lift his leg and pee on a Gucci loafer, so she lightly whistled for him to join her. Thankfully, he liked that idea and lay down beside her chair with a thud.

Their guests' bums had barely creased the seat cushions when Pam said, "We have the money."

Padma looked like she was about to clap, but instead tucked her hands under her thighs. Brenda didn't seem surprised, and Farid's face was so still he could be in the middle of a poker tournament.

Nancy said, "I just need to transfer it to your Virtual Safety Deposit Box."

Farid's expression turned dark. "What? You don't have it here?"

"How would we ever get nine million dollars here?" Pam was puzzled. How much space did that kind of money even take? Fifty thousand fit nicely in her purse, she knew that from hiring a hitman. But nine million? She had no idea. Oh my God. The things she now wondered about.

Farid frowned. "Nine? We were talking ten."

Pam shook her head. "Nine is all there is. We have everything they took."

"And where is that, exactly?"

Nancy answered, "I have a bank draft in a Virtual Safety Deposit Box. I can upload it into yours if you have one."

Farid nodded. "Let's do it." He cocked his head to the men at the door, and one handed him a laptop.

"We can use the kitchen table." Nancy stood, and Farid trailed her.

Padma began to push herself up off the sofa, but Farid put his hand up to stop her. "No worries, doll. I've got the accounting. That's what I do." He winked, and Padma froze for a moment, then slowly lowered herself back into the cushions beside Brenda. Pam noticed the flush make its way up her neck.

Pam remained seated and felt more uncomfortable in her living room than she ever had before. They waited. Padma scrolled through her phone, and Brenda sat straight with her hands folded on her knees, occasionally exchanging uneasy smiles with anyone who made eye contact with her. Pam noticed end-of-day traffic begin on her street as people headed home from work. The only sounds in the dreary townhouse were Elmer's snoring and murmured voices and laptop keys clicking coming from the other room. A few minutes later Farid returned and stood beside his men, still lined up by the front door.

Nancy appeared in the kitchen's threshold. "Okay. I uploaded the draft, and he's transferred it to the bank." She gave two thumbs up. "We're done."

"Not quite," Farid said.

Nancy dropped her thumbs. "What do you mean? You have the money. We're done."

Farid's cool gaze swept the room until it landed on Pam. "I've initiated the transfer, but it can't be completed and verified until the bank opens." He shrugged. "For all I know, you created that document at bank-drafts-dot-com and kept the money for yourself." He checked his watch. "Our bank in Mumbai opens in six hours. Midnight here. If it clears, *then* we're done."

Pam swung her head to Brenda and Padma. Her stomach sank when Padma nodded in agreement. Pam heard the panic in her own voice. "Don't you have a local account you could use?"

Farid replied, "Banks are closed here. Then we'd have to wait till morning. Which do you prefer?"

Fuck. Six hours. He couldn't possibly be planning to sit in her living room for six hours. Pam had nothing in the fridge. Marlene had just finished the last of the funeral casseroles. Were they vegetarian? She may have some nachos and salsa, and possibly a bit of Hank's favorite trail mix. But nothing to properly entertain people for six hours. They'd have to order in, and she couldn't pay for it. Her credit card was maxed, and her bank account empty. Then she remembered what Marlene had said. She wasn't offering snacks; she wanted them gone.

Farid put his hands in his pockets and seemed to be weighing his options. He looked around the room. "We'll go back to the casino."

Thank fuck for that.

"And we'll take that dog."

"No, you won't." Pam put her hand on Elmer's collar and looked to Padma, hoping she'd intervene. Brenda moved forward in her seat and Padma raised her hand in a gesture that stopped her, and they both remained quiet. Pam looked back to Farid.

"For insurance," Farid explained.

"Insurance against what? We've done everything you asked for. We've given you everything you wanted. What do you need insurance for?"

Farid smiled, raised his eyebrows, and brought his forefinger to his lips. "Hmm. Let me think about that. I think we need insurance to ensure that the people who ripped us off the first time aren't ripping us off again." He shrugged. "Call me crazy but I don't trust you." He gave a wide, toothy smile that didn't reach his eyes but showed the gaps in his molars. His four colleagues remained soldier-still behind him. He tapped his watch. "At midnight, when we've confirmed the draft is legitimate, we'll bring the dog back. If it's not legitimate . . . *then* your furry friend has something to worry about."

Pam's heart was at the bottom of her stomach. It was hard to breathe. She hadn't cared one bit about giving them the money, because it wasn't hers, never had been. But to trust these thugs with her Elmer. She checked on her dog. He was stretched out on his side, oblivious to the commotion about him. Pam looked at the four large men.

Pam jumped up. "I'll go too." She took a step toward Farid. "I'll sit quietly in a corner until you have the money. You won't even know I'm there."

Farid squinted at Pam, then said, "Frankly, I'd rather spend time with just the dog." Farid squatted. "Elmer, want to go hunt some wabbits? I bet you like car wides. If we get along, maybe we'll even take you for a plane wide. Have you ever flown pwivate?"

Pam's head spun to Farid.

Farid stood up. "Relax. I'm joking. If I wanted a dog, I'd get a real dog."

One of Farid's men pulled Elmer's leash off its hook by the door, and seeing it dangle, Elmer bounced up, his rear end vibrating, his tail wagging. He hopped around, seemingly excited to head out on his routine walk, then politely sat down and waited for his leash to be attached. The group started out the door, and Elmer pranced two steps, then stopped and looked at Pam. Farid's man tugged on the leash. Elmer took a half step, his eyes on Pam, then spread his front paws wide and hunkered down. The man pulled, and Elmer slid a few inches. Then another man bent down, scooped Elmer up in his arms, and strode out the door and across the front lawn. Elmer peered around his shoulder, his eyes locked on Pam's.

Brenda said to Pam on her way out the door, "Elmer will be fine."

Pam's words caught in her throat. "He better be."

Forty-Six

You Should Stay

Even though Padma was mere hours away from reclaiming the nine million dollars no one but her had even noticed was missing and being officially hailed as Indo-USA Gaming Inc.'s conquering hero, at the moment, she faced two problems.

The first was that her mother may have been right. Not about her being frumpy—hard truth, her ass, she was fucking awesome. But that this matchmaking thing may have been a good idea. When she'd walked through the doors and spotted Nilesh waiting for her at the counter her armpits had immediately felt sticky. If that wasn't a sign she was in love, she didn't know what was. They'd had two great dates, and this third one could seal the deal. She had been practically floating as she'd considered her career and personal dreams could finally be coming true. And that brought her to her second problem: Nilesh wanted to go bowling.

Padma made sure her smile included her perfect bottom teeth. "I'm not doing that."

Nilesh tapped his fingers on the counter. "I don't know how else you expect to bowl."

His last word narrowly missed being drowned out by a crashing noise from behind them, followed by an eruption of cheers. And then another crash, and another wave of cheers. The teenage attendant stood on the other side of the counter beside a hot dog–rolling machine as a dozen browning frankfurters continued their slow spin. He held a pair of flat bowling shoes he'd pulled from the rental shelf. The teen stood still, except for his head swiveling back and forth from Padma to Nilesh.

"I told you. I'm not wearing *used* shoes." Padma sniffed.

Nilesh didn't need to know Padma didn't mind they were used; she was refusing to wear them because they were flat. Padma liked Nilesh—a lot—and she couldn't take any chances. She had to nail this. He could be the one. He came from a prominent family of bedding manufacturers, was an international tax specialist, and like her, he hated outdoor patios and salsa dancing. And he'd made her laugh. Twice. Bottom line, when he looked at her, her toes tingled. And not because their circulation was cut off. Before meeting him at the strip plaza bowling alley, to be on the safe side, Padma had reviewed his requirements. Nilesh had specifically noted that he wanted his prospective bride to be five-four and above. Padma came in at maybe five-two, in heels, on tiptoes. Padma had never been bowling before and was pleasantly surprised when she'd checked the website photos and saw there was plenty of seating. But somehow, she'd missed the part about the required footwear. There was no way she was shedding her shoes in front of him. That would be matchmaking suicide.

"But everyone wears bowling shoes when they go bowling. And they disinfect them between wears. Don't you?" Nilesh looked at the attendant.

The teen nodded mutely.

Padma sneered at the footwear.

"Look, Padma, I like you. But I haven't seen these friends since college, and they're waiting for me. You decide if you'll wear 'used shoes' or not. As you choose." He spun on his heels and walked away.

Padma watched Nilesh go and gauged the likelihood of surviving a courtship without ever taking her heels off, lest he reject her. There would be no swimming, no running, no horseback riding, no sex . . . well, maybe, if he had a fetish. She weighed her options and decided, regrettably, in the dog-eat-dog world of Indian matchmaking, she had to cut her losses and reject before being rejected. Her mother had warned her, if she was presented with a third strike she would be taking matters into her own hands. And Padma couldn't have that.

She scanned the bowling alley for one last look and spotted Nilesh reaching into his pocket. He pulled out his phone. Padma rifled through her purse for hers and glanced back to see Nilesh waving his arm, in the telltale search for a signal. She checked her device. Damn. No signal either. She looked back at him, and for a split second their eyes met and held. Then Nilesh turned and speed walked toward the emergency exit. Padma sprinted for the front entrance and pushed her way through the door. Once outside, a bar appeared. Padma frantically texted The Matchmaker.

Padma Singh: Sorry, Aunty. Nilesh is very nice, but it did not work out.

Three dots . . . then:

The Matchmaker: Yes. He told me he has rejected you.

"Fuck!" Padma threw her phone to the ground. "Fuck!"
There was nothing Padma despised more than being outmaneuvered.

———

Twenty minutes later Padma swiped herself into the maintenance room and wrinkled her nose in disgust. Dog. She scanned the room and spotted Pam's mutt curled up in a corner, on the cement floor. Was the mangy thing still alive? She watched him and saw an ear twitch.

The room was quiet, except for the hum of the fluorescent lights and Farid, sitting at the table Brenda had set up in the middle of the room, tapping on his laptop. The materials Brenda had prepared for the investigation were piled at the end, never having been opened. What a waste of time that had been. Brenda had completely misread the situation's needs. As if this team flew over from India to screen surveillance footage. Ha! Coupled with Brenda's badgering that Padma should have stopped Farid from taking the dog "hostage," babbling on about it until Padma had recounted her mother's tale of precisely why Farid was called The Fiscal Falcon—that had shut Brenda up pretty quickly.

Her mother had already cautioned Padma to be sure to tie up her loose ends. Padma knew what that meant. She wanted Padma to cut her new director of security loose. Permanently loose. Well, these were the hard truths she'd have to deal with if she intended to climb over her mother on that *Forbes* list. She'd get Farid's men to take care of this piece of business. But she pushed that task aside for the moment, as she observed The Fiscal Falcon. He sat at the table, his leather briefcase closed beside him.

When those millions landed in the casino bank account at midnight, Padma would surely be booted up the corporate ladder. She was on the rise, and she was finally wresting her career out from under her mother's thumb. Now if only she could do the same for her love life. She checked Farid's ring finger. It was bare.

Farid looked up and smiled. As soon as her mother found out about Nilesh's rejection, she'd start vetting anyone with a penis. Padma studied Farid for a moment. Her mother said he was practically legendary. Maybe it was a case of "better the devil you know than the devil you don't." Padma smiled back. Maybe the two of them could work hand in hand as she expanded their casinos across India. They could be a lethal, take-no-prisoners type of couple and have their own Wikipedia page. He was short and unattractive, but Padma had to admit there was something about the way he commanded a room. All eyes on him.

Her mother could have anyone warming up in the on-deck circle. He was worth a shot.

Farid pulled a pack of bubble gum from his pocket. "Care for one, doll?"

Padma nodded, looked at him through her lashes and leaned forward to accept the offered piece, thankful her third-date mode had called for a pushup bra. Farid's eyes swept across her cleavage while he returned his gum to his pocket.

She unwrapped her piece, held it between her teeth for a moment in what she was sure was a sexy look, started chewing, and then tucked the wad into her cheek. "You should stay in town a few extra days, Farid. Seeing as we got the money back so quickly. I could show you around." She flashed her new smile, including her bottom teeth.

He chuckled and leaned back in his chair, spinning his knees toward her and spreading them wide. "And why would The Fiscal Falcon do that?"

Padma liked to think she was a practiced flirt. She perched on the edge of the table, crossed her legs, and dangled a stiletto a few inches from him. "I thought we might get to know each other better. We could make a good team, you and me." She rolled her shoulder and licked her lips.

"Ha! Doll. The Falcon's a ten. Even with your mom as part of the package, The Falcon would never be seen with anything less than a six." Farid turned back to his laptop.

Padma gasped. Straightened. When she realized her mouth was hanging open, she forced herself to close it.

"Besides"—his eyes were on his laptop screen—"The Falcon is already planning on sticking around. You should read your email."

Padma's mouth sprung back open. "What?"

Farid was typing. "I briefed your mom on the situation here. She emailed you explaining everything. If you'd had your eye on the ball instead of prancing around in your come-fuck-me shoes, you'd be up to speed. Since I've cleaned up your mess so spectacularly, my guys have packed up and headed home."

Padma looked around the room. She had assumed the other four men were getting dinner or coffees, but now she noticed their luggage and personal items were gone. "Don't you need them until you're sure you got the money?" She studied him. That was the whole point of having that stupid dog. Waiting until the Mumbai banks opened and confirming that bank draft was legitimate.

He chuckled. "Doll. The Falcon always gets the money. The moment those old gals let us walk out of there with that mutt, I knew I had the money. *That* was the test. Not waiting around until midnight to see if some deposit goes through." He glanced at her and then back to the laptop. "See, that's the difference between you and me. I know how to read the room. The guys' work here is done, and the company jet should be"—he looked at his chunky gold watch—"wheels up any minute. But The Falcon is staying put." He swiveled around again, spread his knees wider, put his hands in the air, and smiled broadly. "Say hello to your new boss."

Forty-Seven

Just a Bean Counter

Hector Chavez's least favorite part of any day was when he had to sit in a car and wait. Like he was now, in the casino's back parking lot. It was dark, and hot and still. Hot enough he had to leave his window open more than a crack, or he'd incubate to death. And still enough he kept swatting mosquitoes. He hated their buzz near his ear. He was fumbling through his glove box for bug repellent and almost missed Brenda's text:

Amor: B there in 5 minutes

Hector decided he could survive that long without dousing himself. He scrolled back through his earlier conversation with his wife. He'd been re- turning to their apartment after paying the guy who had rushed to provide him with Hank's, Larry's, and Andre's fake passports a couple of weeks ear- lier. When Hector had turned into the barbershop's strip plaza and scanned the parking lot, he had noticed a white BMW parked outside the bowling alley. Hmm. Brenda said Padma drove a white BMW, although he couldn't imagine that woman bowling, not with the footwear she favored.

Hector paid attention to people's vehicles. Brenda teased that he was more likely to know what someone drove than their last name. Hector ex- plained, if you're the kind of guy who lives with the possibility of sometimes being surprised by people—also interpreted as sometimes being jumped by people—it's wiser to know what your would-be attacker is driving than to know how to properly address his Christmas card.

Hector found the first text he'd sent Brenda from outside the bowling alley after he had watched Padma throw her phone to the ground and peel out of the parking lot.

> **Hector**: just saw P at bowling alley. very upset
> **Amor**: really? said she had a personal matter tonight
> **Hector**: don't think it went well
> **Amor**: hmm. Mumbai guys drove off an hour ago
> **Hector**: all?
> **Amor**: no Falcon guy still here. But no explanation. They just left
> **Hector**: dog?
> **Amor**: with Falcon

There had been a break while Hector had considered his next move. Then:

> **Hector**: K. I'll get dog now.
> **Amor**: K
> **Hector**: can u let me in back door in 20?

Brenda had sent a thumbs-up emoji, and when he'd arrived at the casino, he'd texted:

> **Hector**: here
> **Amor**: wait. P just left Falcon. I saw her in hall on TV. Can tell she's mad. She took her shoes off and ran!
> **Hector**: who's with Falcon now?
> **Amor**: no cameras in there but I think he's alone with dog. Will let u know when clear. dog's name is Elmer

Now it was two hours until midnight, when, according to Brenda, Farid was expecting the bank draft to hit the casino's account. He'd said if it went through with no hitches, he would release the dog. Hector had known enough guys like this Falcon dude, back in his gang days, that he wasn't going to wait around and see if this one would keep his word. Not after Brenda relayed how he'd come to be called The Fiscal Falcon.

Seems a man had once owed Farid's employer money and had offered his prized falcon as insurance. But apparently, the man hadn't paid quickly enough, and Farid had maimed the bird—clipped its wings so the majestic creature would never fly again. Just to send a message. Just because he could.

Hector had to get the dog out of there. If anything happened to Elmer, Brenda would be devastated, and he wasn't about to let that happen. Plus, he liked that dog.

His phone dinged:

Amor: good to go

Hector turned his phone to silent, got out of his car, put his windbreaker on, and patted his pockets, double-checking he had everything he needed. He trotted across the parking lot, and Brenda let him in the casino's back door, gave him a quick kiss on the cheek, and handed him an employee ID and key card. He took the door to the right, the same one he'd left through the day he'd delivered Brenda's chicken empanada dinner, and went down the stairwell to the basement floor, while she went upstairs to the offices to keep an eye on Padma.

Hector strung the lanyard with the employee ID and key card around his neck and pulled on a baseball cap. Brenda had put still shots up on the cameras in this area so nothing would look amiss on the monitors in the security command center, but if he ran into anyone, he could obscure his face behind the brim. He stepped out into the hallway, walked a few doors down, swiped, and entered the maintenance room.

It was set up as it had been when Hector was last here. Hector scanned the room and found the dog lying on the cement floor to the right, his leash draped across a nearby chair. Elmer raised his head and wagged his tail.

Perfect.

Hector crossed the floor, grabbed the leash, and Elmer pulled himself up, stretched, and took a step toward Hector. At the sound of a voice they both stopped and turned.

"What do you think you're doing?"

Farid rose from behind the table, in the center of the room.

"Sorry. Didn't see you there," Hector said.

Hector scanned the table, saw the laptop and briefcase, and reasoned the man must have been sitting behind the stack of binders, hidden from Hector's line of sight.

Farid said, "Do I know you? Oh, right. You're the barber. Guess what, it looks like I am sticking around, and I could probably use that house call after all."

"Sure. Let me know when. I'm just here to pick up the dog." Hector took a step toward Elmer.

Farid edged down the table. "Sorry. You can't take the dog. I need him."

Hector shook his head. "Meh. I don't think you do."

Farid said, "I told the owner I'll give him back at midnight." He trailed his fingers along the table, toward the leather briefcase.

Hector tilted his head. "I'm not so sure you will."

Farid raised an eyebrow and gave a small smile. "Why would I want to keep that dog?"

Hector glanced at Elmer, who now sat a few feet away and seemed to be following the conversation, his eyes going from speaker to speaker.

Hector exhaled. "Oh, I'm not worried about you keeping him. I'm worried a man like you might want to use the dog to send a message."

Farid scoffed. "What kind of message would I send? I'm an accountant. Just a bean counter. I push money here and there."

Hector studied him a moment and said, "Then you don't need the dog. What's he gonna do? Figure out your taxes? I'll take him home now. Get him outta your hair."

Farid toyed with the briefcase clasp. "Actually. Come to think of it, there's a lot to be said for messages. I've found they can be an effective way to get people to pay attention, especially when coming to a new city. Listen.

This is what's gonna happen. You are going to back out of this room and go away. At midnight, I'll give the dog back. Trust me."

A broad smile spread on Hector's face, and he chuckled. "In my profession, you trust too much, you don't celebrate many birthdays."

Farid's eyebrows furrowed together.

"John Wayne. In *The Shootist*."

"Ah. A movie. It's lost on me." Farid shrugged. "Sorry."

Hector's smile dropped, and he sighed. "This is what's gonna happen. I'm leaving with the dog." Hector shifted so his left shoulder was angled toward Farid. He stretched the leash in both hands before him and gently twirled the metal fastener at the end, moving his right hand closer to his windbreaker's pocket.

Farid eyed the leash's heavy, spinning fastener. His lips twitched into a tight smile, and he brought his eyes back to Hector. "Why do I get the feeling you're not just a barber?" The lock on his briefcase clicked.

"Probably the same reason I get the feeling you're not just an accountant."

Farid lifted the lid of his briefcase. "Why would someone like you come for a *dog*?"

Hector inched his hand to his pocket. "I'm guessing you've never seen a John Wick movie."

Farid shook his head. "Again. Movies."

Hector said, "You should watch one. There's four in the franchise. Gotta love Keanu Reeves. Start with the first one. Then maybe you'll understand why you don't mess around with someone's dog."

And there it was.

Farid was not only stupid enough to point a gun at Hector, but also stupid enough to not pull the trigger.

Farid clocked his arm to the left and leveled his gun at Elmer. "You know what? I'm tired of talking about this fucking dog."

The pop of the gunshot reverberated through the room. Hector's ears rang, and the spicy smell of gunpowder stung his nose.

Elmer scurried over and buried his head between Hector's legs. Hector crouched down and hugged the trembling dog close. From that position, he studied Farid's body, crumpled on the floor. The bullet hole between his eyes looked clean and crisp, and the blood seeping from the back of his head formed a circle that creeped larger.

Hector stood and returned his gun to his windbreaker's pocket.

He had to move swiftly. He checked the doors off the room and, finding a janitor's closet, moved an industrial bucket aside and dragged Farid's body to rest by the closet's drain. He threw some rags down to wipe up the blood, bagged them and tossed them in the closet. He gathered Farid's belongings and stowed them with the corpse. He ran a mop over the area where Farid had fallen. It wouldn't pass close inspection, but for now, looking around the room, if anyone did stumble in, Hector was satisfied nothing looked amiss. It would do until he returned for a proper cleanup.

He sniffed the air, checked the janitor's closet, and had just pulled a can of air freshener from the shelf when he heard a voice. He returned the air freshener, stepped out of the closet, and pulled the door closed behind him.

Forty-Eight

Know Anybody?

P adma couldn't recall exactly which route she had taken back to her office from the maintenance room, but she knew she had kicked off her heels and carried them as she ran down the hall and up some stairs. Of all the times to be without her phone.

Fuck.

After receiving The Matchmaker's reply that Nilesh had rejected her, Padma had smashed her device against the sidewalk outside the bowling alley and had watched it bounce up in the air and then disappear down through the bars of the sidewalk grate. She couldn't have aimed it through that gap if she'd tried a hundred times, but just her luck to have had it hit the opening on that one throw.

Now in her office, she tossed her shoes on the floor beside her desk, powered up her laptop, pulled her backup phone out of her drawer, and plugged it in to charge while she waited for her email to load. Sure enough. The fucking Fiscal Falcon—what a ridiculous name—was right. There was a message from her mother:

Padma,

The Fiscal Falcon has updated me on his spectacular accomplishment.

Given his great success, and the unfortunate debacle you have made of both your position at the casino and The Matchmaker's efforts, we need to refocus your energy. Really, Padma. This is for your own good. To have three rejections . . .

Regardless, The Falcon is to be commended for recovering nine million dollars—that is an amazing achievement. Thank God I sent him when I did. I told you he is something else. (I wonder if he found you attractive at all? Did you wear dresses and heels? That is your most flattering look. And again, I strongly urge you to consider highlights.)

I'm sure you'll agree he demonstrated the ability needed to run the casino, and I should not have put you in a situation beyond the scope of your skill set. It is best we abandon that plan immediately and bring you home before there is any further embarrassment.

Ensure a smooth handover. I trust you'll take care of the loose end we talked about, and I want you back in Mumbai by the end of the week.

Your mother,
Amrita Kulkarni

Padma was incensed. *She* rejected Akshay, it was technically a mutual rejection on Vikash, and she only missed rejecting Nilesh first by seconds. And she couldn't help it if she was short. It was her mother's fucking genes. Padma slammed down her laptop. That fucking Falcon. He took her credit. He stole her job. He called her a six.

Brenda popped her head in Padma's office door. "Everything okay?"

"Farid said my shoes say 'come fuck me.'"

Brenda came in and sat across from her. "You know what? Your shoes could say 'come fuck me up the butt and hang me from a tree,' but if you want to wear them, you should just go ahead and wear whatever you fucking well want to."

Padma's head jerked as she took in that reply.

Brenda sighed. "Sorry. I have three sisters and we have strong opinions on this. Our mom taught us early, as women, we cannot worry about what anyone says about us, our body, what we wear, or what we do. *We* are the masters of ourselves. My mom says we should do and wear whatever makes us comfortable."

"Your mom says that?"

Brenda nodded. "She sure does. That and a lot of other stuff I hated hearing as a kid, but now as a woman, and wife, it makes sense."

Padma thought about that, then asked, "How long have you been married?"

"Ten years."

That's what Padma wanted. She wanted to just think about someone and get that spark in Brenda's eyes. Padma sighed. "To be honest, heels kill my feet."

"Then why the fuck wear them?"

Padma sat back in her chair and pondered that. Then she thought of her mother, and that fucking, condescending Farid. The Fiscal Falcon. More like The Fiscal Fuckface. She studied Brenda. "You've lived in this town a long time, right?"

"All my life," Brenda answered.

Padma tapped her fingertips together in front of her. She looked at her whiteboard mounted across from her desk and studied the words *CAUSE* and *EFFECT* she'd written there. It was time for her to cause her own effect. She redirected her gaze to Brenda and asked, "Would you happen to know anybody who does whatever needs doing?"

Forty-Nine

Emergency Stash

Hector nudged Farid's dead foot aside, stepped out of the janitor's closet, and quietly closed the door behind him to find his wife kneeling, rubbing Elmer's belly, a blue duffel bag on the floor beside her.

She jumped up when she saw him. "Hec-toro! Where were you? How did it go? Where's Farid?" Brenda often did that—pepper him with questions without giving him the time to answer. He knew she'd re-ask what was important. She looked around and, apparently satisfied the room was empty, said, "You'll never guess what Padma wants to do now."

She unzipped the duffel bag, and Hector peeked in. He raised his eyebrows at Brenda.

"She says it may be the one good lesson she's learned from her mother—always have an emergency stash."

Hector peeked at the bag again. There were strapped bundles of hundreds, each worth ten grand. He guessed there were fifty bundles. "Half a million dollars? That's her emergency stash?"

Brenda shrugged. "I think Padma's emergencies are bigger than paying cash to the plumber when the hot-water heater leaks. And Hec-toro, guess what emergency she needs taken care of." Brenda opened her eyes wide and nodded, presumably encouraging Hector to guess.

"The Falcon."

Brenda's face dropped. "How'd you know?"

It was Hector's turn to shrug. "It was only a matter of time. Someone like her and a guy like that. It's not gonna end well." He grimaced.

Brenda filled him in. "Padma is so pissed. He went to her mother behind her back, and Padma's beside herself. She wants him gone. Oh! And when you saw her at the bowling alley, she was on a date, and she knew the guy was going to reject her just because she's short." Brenda stood up. "So much drama. I kinda feel sorry for her."

This is what Hector worried about: Brenda got to know people and warmed to them, overlooking the fact that they're thieving, two-faced lowlifes. Brenda saw the best in people, and while Hector didn't want to ruin that for her, he also didn't want her to be hurt by that either. And now Padma was dangerously close to harming his amor.

Hector poked a toe at the duffel bag. "She just handed this over to you?"

Brenda nodded.

"What did she say?"

"She asked me to find someone to take care of The Fiscal Falcon."

Hector rubbed his jaw. "That's not good, Brenda." He looked at his wife. "She's dangerous to you. You see that, right? This is not what we wanted for you."

Fucking Padma. Handing Brenda that money was pushing his wife into a hole she wouldn't be able to climb out of. Padma would always have something on her.

Brenda's smile dropped. "I know. But can we not discuss my career right now?" She wrinkled her nose. "What's that smell?"

Hector sniffed. The gunpowder aroma lingered. "Elmer farted." Hector waved his hand and eyed the dog. "Elmer, bud. You need to control that."

Brenda, her hands on her hips, sniffed again. She tilted her head and zeroed in on her husband. "Somebody's fired a weapon in here."

Hector braced himself. Brenda was like a dog with a bone, and she wouldn't let up. He considered his options, and usually, when he was in this position, the best thing to do was come clean with her. He led her to the janitor's closet and opened the door.

Brenda's head snapped back at the sight of Farid's corpse. "Whoa. This is an interesting turn of events."

They stood shoulder to shoulder in the doorway and looked at The Falcon. He'd had his last flight.

Hector swallowed. "He killed himself."

"No!" Brenda spun to Hector, her eyes wide.

Hector tried to match Brenda's look of shock. Then he remembered the life they'd built together and that the reason it flourished was because it stood on a foundation of truth.

He shrugged. "Okay. I killed him. He was going to kill Elmer."

"Oh. Good call." Brenda nodded sharply, then turned toward Padma's duffel bag holding half a million dollars. "What are we gonna do about that?"

Fifty

Something Like That

It was ten thirty p.m., and Pam had waited long enough.

She wasn't going to sit around until that bubble gum–chewing psychopath decided he was good and ready to bring Elmer home—Pam was getting her dog. She, Nancy, Marlene, and Shalisa jumped in her van.

"What's your plan?" Marlene asked.

"I don't have one. I just have a gut feeling. We'll work it out when we get there."

Pam turned into the employee parking lot around the back of the casino and pulled into Hank's old spot, his name still emblazoned across the post. She led the way up the concrete walkway, pushing aside the memories of other times she'd made this journey, always with the goal of meeting her husband. In good times and in bad, he had always been on the other side of that door. But not now. The air-conditioning blanketed them with relief as they ducked through the carpeted vestibule, escaping the night's stickiness.

"Sorry, ladies. This is employees only. Patrons use the—" The guard stood up. "Oh. Sorry, Mrs. Montgomery." He frowned and cocked his head.

Pam didn't know the burly man's name but recognized him from her years of coming and going. He had been a skinny teenager when he'd started, now he was filled out and over thirty. She decided to lay her cards on the table. "I've just come to pick up my dog. I don't suppose you've seen him?"

"I did see a dog down on B2. I think they took him into the maintenance room."

The maintenance room. That was fabulous news. Pam couldn't imagine Farid and his pals hanging around within a utilitarian space. Maybe Elmer was alone, and they could just grab him and run. That would be perfect. "Do you think you could let us in there to get him?"

The guard grimaced and shook his head. "I'm sorry. No one's allowed access unless previously authorized. The rules are very strict. Especially now, with the new management. I could ask Ms. Singh, though—" He reached for the phone.

Pam put her hand up. "No. No. I don't want to disturb her." Pam chewed her lip, and wished her gut could give her some further direction. She tapped her fingers on the security station and was startled when the guard spoke again.

"I didn't get a chance to talk to you at the funeral, but Mr. Montgomery was really good to me."

"Oh?"

The young man came around the side of the desk and glanced at Nancy, Marlene, and Shalisa, who took a few steps back and turned to look out the door. He continued in a low voice, "I used to have a substance abuse problem." He shot his eyes to her, and then down to the floor and back up. "I got caught a few times, you know, working while under the influence. I was just a kid, and I was so stupid. I was being fired, but I, I, uh, I talked to your husband. I told him I had a new baby, and I needed this job. He looked at me and said, 'Yes, you do.' I'll always remember that. He told me, my most important role in life now was to take care of my wife and child. Nothing else mattered. Not drugs, not booze. He got me into rehab and got the casino to pay. I never could have swung that on my own. He told me as long as I stayed clean, I'd have a job here. It's been eleven years." He smiled at Pam, tears glistening in his eyes. "I have three kids now. And a happy wife and life."

Pam threw her arms around the young man's broad shoulders, held him a moment, and then stepped back.

He wiped away a tear. "I really miss him." He cleared his throat, then said, "I have to do rounds now. It was nice seeing you again." He turned, swiped his key card, and disappeared down the corridor.

As Shalisa, Marlene, and Nancy joined Pam, Nancy asked, "What's that?" She gestured to the dark patterned carpet. She stooped, picked up a key card, and turned it over to show the words stamped across the front—*all access.*

Pam glanced down the hallway, but the security guard was gone.

"Game on." She smiled.

A few minutes later, the elevator doors opened, and Pam made her way down the hall, following the signs. She glanced over her shoulder and saw Nancy and Shalisa were creeping along, hugging one wall, and Marlene was plastered up against the other. Pam wheeled around. "Will you guys stop? If anyone saw you on camera, they'd call in a SWAT team. We're not committing a crime. We're getting Elmer."

Pam held the key card up to the maintenance room door and when it swung open, she jumped at the sight of Hector and, a few feet away, Brenda, crouched down and zipping up a blue duffel bag. Pam's heart skipped as she considered the bag was the perfect size to carry Elmer. Brenda froze, her eyes wide, her mouth gaping open. She sat back on her heels.

Pam braced herself. Her heart raced. Why had she ever let her dog go? Why had she not come earlier? She whispered, "I came to get Elmer."

Brenda and Hector both looked toward the corner of the room, and Pam followed their line of vision. Elmer's tail thumped as he lazily pulled himself up, stretched, then waddled toward her. Pam sank to the floor with relief.

Brenda said, "He's fine. I'm really sorry Farid took him."

Pam hugged Elmer, whose tail swirled in circles. She wanted to get out of there before anyone tried to stop her. "Where is Farid? His men?"

Brenda said, "Um. They all left."

"What do you mean, 'they all left'?"

Brenda exchanged a look with Hector. "They've gone back to Mumbai."

"All of them? You're kidding me. That 'wait till midnight' stuff was a bluff? They're gone?" Pam, still holding Elmer tight, peered at Brenda and then at Hector. "Do you two know each other?"

Brenda exchanged another glance with Hector, then answered, "Hector's my husband."

"Your husband!" Pam cocked her head. She glanced at Nancy, Marlene, and Shalisa for their reaction and was gratified to see they seemed as surprised as she was.

Nancy looked from Hector to Brenda and then back again, circling her finger at the two of them, and said, "This has something to do with our husbands, doesn't it?"

Oh. That hadn't occurred to Pam, but Nancy could be on to something.

Nancy asked, "Did they hire you as a team? You"—she looked at Hector—"to fake their deaths, and you"—she looked at Brenda—"to spy on Padma?"

Pam noticed Hector and Brenda exchange yet another look.

Hector said, "Something like that."

Pam stood. "Well, I don't know if it worked out for them or not, and I don't care. I am so done with this shit." She pulled the leash off the chair and clipped it to Elmer, then said to Brenda, "You tell that Padma bitch our business is done. I don't expect to see her again. Ever."

Brenda nodded.

The wives had started toward the door when Elmer tugged his leash from Pam's grip and lunged toward Hector for a last pet, then moved on to Brenda. He leaned against her, and Brenda bent to give him a full-body scratch. Elmer's back end vibrated with pleasure.

Pam thought a moment, then said, "You know, Brenda, I don't know if you legitimately have a job here or not, but Elmer's a good judge of character. This was a great place to work when Hank ran it, but I don't think it's so good now. If I were you, I'd think about getting out of here while you can."

Brenda scratched Elmer's chin and looked up at Pam. "You might be right about that. And you know, I never met Hank, but I can tell you everyone loved him. I'm sorry whatever happened between you happened."

Pam looked to Nancy, Marlene, and Shalisa and shrugged. "It's the same story with anything—you've got to nourish a marriage if you want it to survive. Otherwise it shrivels up and dies."

Pam looked at Hector. How could Hank ever have said this man had dead eyes? They were so full of light, they were almost blinding. Pam had another question. She asked it with a quiet voice. "Do you think we'll ever see them again?"

Hector blew out a breath, shook his head, and answered, "Only if they want to be seen."

Nancy stepped toward them. "And for sure they know we hired you to . . . you know?"

Hector nodded. "Oh yeah. They know."

The women nodded in understanding, and then Pam tugged on the leash and said, "Come on, Elmer. Let's go home."

Fifty-One

Old Before He's Forty

Padma was drafting an email to her mother as she watched the clock tick closer to midnight. As soon as Brenda could confirm plans were in place for The Fiscal Fuckface to be taken care of, she would hit send. The email would inform her mother Farid Nadir had inexplicably disappeared and beg her for another chance at running the casino. She would promise to get highlights in her hair and to date any other candidates her mother and The Matchmaker wanted to send her way. She just needed one more chance to prove to her mother she could run a business as well as her.

Finally, Brenda walked in, dropped the duffel bag on Padma's desk, and took a seat across from her. "Farid is gone," Brenda said.

Good. Padma could send the email.

But wait a minute.

"Gone. Gone? Like, mission accomplished, gone?" She squinted at the duffel bag. It looked as full as when Brenda had carried it from this office an hour earlier. That couldn't be good.

Brenda shook her head. "Gone, like, left the building. Drove away. Disappeared. Took all his things. Are you sure he didn't head back to Mumbai with his guys?"

"No. The company jet was wheels up around nine p.m., and I saw him after that. Why would he leave? He got my job and all the credit. The cocky asshole says the money will transfer to the bank at midnight. Do you believe it? He says he knew as soon as we left Pam's house that he had the money. Once that nine million lands, he'll be crowned my mother's new prince. Why would he walk out on that?"

Brenda shrugged. "Who knows why anyone like that does anything."

Padma looked at the clock. Banks opened in Mumbai in one minute. She was logged into the bank account—the casino CFO had walked her through it earlier, and she'd seen the pending transfer. She checked the account activity; it was still pending. She waited an extra minute just to be sure, then refreshed. Not yet. She waited, then refreshed again. Still not there. A third time.

Transaction canceled.

Padma jolted. She thought a moment, and then she knew.

Down in the maintenance room, he must have stolen the money. The Fiscal Fuckface had redirected Nancy's bank draft to his personal account. That was the real reason he'd sent his guys home before the money landed in the casino account at midnight—because he knew it never would. He'd left Pam's house smug that the wives had handed over the money. And then he'd grabbed it for himself.

That fucker.

A slow smile crept across Padma's face. Good thing she hadn't sent that email to her mother yet. Her rewrite would be even juicier. She'd inform her mother that she didn't care what lies The Falcon had been spewing, Padma was the true driving force behind recovering the nine million, not him, thank you very much. And that Padma was perfectly capable of running the casino, and finding her own husband, if and when she wanted. Again, thank you very much. She could hardly wait to add in the line that her mother's prized prince had not only disappeared, but he'd taken her nine million dollars with him.

"What? What is it?" Brenda asked.

Padma sat back and grinned. "Turns out I didn't have to worry about The Fiscal Fuckface after all. He has singlehandedly just destroyed his life."

"What do you mean?"

"The money's gone."

Brenda's eyes widened. "Gone. Gone? Like not in the account, gone? Are you sure?"

Padma turned her screen toward Brenda so she could read the *transaction canceled* notification for herself. Brenda leaned forward to study the account page.

Padma continued, "Yep. Farid took the money and ran. The little twat. Making us wait until the Mumbai bank opened at midnight was just a ruse to give him time to make his getaway. He sent his team home and then hightailed it himself. He's probably halfway to the Maldives with my mother's nine million dollars." Padma chuckled.

Brenda's mouth hung open. She blinked repeatedly.

"Brenda, what don't you understand? That dude had slimeball written all over him like a face tattoo. Remember how he said at Pam's, 'I've got the accounting. That's what I do'? Ha! Sure he does."

Brenda frowned. "I ... I ... suppose so. I guess he must have run off with the money. What will you do now? Will . . . you bring someone else in to look for him?"

Padma checked her phone's charge. "Nope. Don't you see, Brenda? This has worked out perfectly for me. What do I care about the money? It was gone before I ever got here. Now that The Fuckface Falcon has fucked my mother over, she can deal with him. Though the way my mother operates, she'll decide he never existed—less embarrassing than admitting she got outmaneuvered. I bet my mother puts her own nine million in the casino account just to be sure no one will ever know Farid The Fiscal Fuckface got the best of her. But he doesn't know that. He'll be looking over his shoulder until the day he dies. He'll be old before he's forty." Padma smiled at Brenda. "But the best thing about this is, my mother knows I know. That's what matters now." Padma leaned forward. "I couldn't have planned this more perfectly if I'd tried." She shimmied her shoulders and leaned back.

Brenda frowned and chewed her lip.

Padma studied Brenda. What should she do about this woman her mother called her loose end? She asked, "Is there anything else?"

Brenda folded her hands in front of her. "I don't think this is going to work out, Padma."

Padma sighed. Women never liked her. She couldn't help it. "I don't suppose it is." She looked at the duffel bag. It would have been a different story if Brenda had taken that cash and either hired someone or kept it for herself. Then Padma could control her. But the moment Brenda plopped that full duffel bag back on her desk, Padma knew Brenda was trying to walk away while she could. Padma had to admit, Brenda was making the smart move in the situation. But should she let her? Padma tapped her fingers on her desk. One call and she could get those Mumbai guys back here. That was how her mother did business.

Padma made her decision.

Fuck her mother and her hard truths. The real hard truth was it would be sweeter to get on that *Forbes* list on her own terms. She was enough. She was fucking awesome. She motioned toward the blue duffel bag. "If you tell anyone about this, I'll deny it."

"Oh. I don't doubt that for a minute. But I won't be telling anyone." Brenda rose and walked to the door, then turned and said, "I left something in the bag for you, Padma. Good luck."

Padma watched the door close and, curious, unzipped the bag, and smiled.

———

A few minutes later Padma strode down the hall, out the door, and across the parking lot to her car, feeling more confident and comfortable than she had in a long time, taking powerful, commanding strides in Brenda's Doc Martens combat boots.

She stopped for a moment and sent a text:

Padma: Hey Nilesh. If it's not too late I'd love to go bowling with you. Used shoes are fine. But full disclosure—I'm short.

Three dots appeared, then:

Nilesh: That was obvious. And I'd really like that. I'll text u tmr. And full disclosure—I'm bald.

Three dots appeared again, then:

Nilesh: I can tell The Matchmaker that I made a mistake rejecting you.
Padma: It's okay. I don't care what The Matchmaker thinks.
I don't care what anyone thinks. Now.

Nilesh replied with a heart emoji, and Padma sent one back.

Fifty-Two

Don't Mean to Be Rude

H ank set the bowl of salsa on the coffee table. "Tell me what you think." Hector dipped a tortilla chip and tasted it. He raised an eyebrow. "It's almost as good as my moth—"

"—She showed me how she does it. There's a secret herb." Hank winked and sat back. Hector's mom promised she would finally teach him how to make pupusas later that afternoon.

Andre brought over a tray of glasses, and Larry poured the pitcher of Hank's margaritas. Hector took a sip, then a bigger one, smacked his lips, and smiled. "Very tasty."

Hank was blatantly buttering up the barber in the hopes he'd let them go. The money was returned to the casino—well, except for the three hundred thousand they'd held back, and they were sorting out the best way to get that to their wives. Everybody seemed to be safe. Even Elmer. And according to Hector, his wife thought Padma could be in love. Brenda had dropped by the casino to pick up her personal belongings, and Padma's office was draped in bedsheets. Apparently, she was leaving the casino business, moving back to India, and becoming a VP of some big bedding company. As for the man who'd threatened their wives—The Fiscal Falcon—Hector had told them once the nine million dollars had landed in the casino's account, he'd gone back down whatever hole he'd crawled out of.

So, Hector had no reason to keep them here. Yet, still, his man sat by the door.

Once released, the husbands weren't completely sure where they were headed. From what they could tell, legally they could return home. There were no criminal charges against them—not for the casino theft, or the boat explosion. They would just have to navigate the awkwardness of being declared dead, then they'd be free to live their lives as they wanted. But was there anything left for them in the States?

As Hector reached for the chips, Hank asked, "Did they say anything? You know. About us." He felt like he was in ninth grade all over again and asking a friend about a girl. How did he go from being sixty-four to fourteen again?

Hector's eyes widened, and he crammed four chips in his mouth. He held up his finger and chewed slowly. Hank knew that maneuver. The barber was buying time until he broke the bad news. They wouldn't be going back. He looked at Larry and Andre, and they nodded.

Hank let Hector off the hook. "It's okay. Had to ask. We realize we pretty much burned our bridges."

Finally, Hector swallowed. "Burned bridges? What does that mean?"

The men remained quiet for a moment, and then Andre spoke. "It's when something magical anchors two people together in this unwieldy world we live in, and then one of them is so stupid he literally torches that connection, and it burns to the ground, and he can't get back across to the best thing that ever could have happened to him."

Larry said in a quiet voice, "Andre. There are two ends to any bridge. They did try to kill us."

Andre looked at the floor, nodded slightly, and finally smiled. He looked up from Hank to Larry, with tears in his eyes, and then shrugged. "After we lied to them for years. It's us. We lit the match."

He gingerly peeled himself off the plastic-covered sofa and walked down the hall. They heard his door softly close behind him.

Hector watched him go and then said, "Well, Pam did tell me it used to be really good for all of them. And then a few years ago, it got not so good." He shrugged. "She did ask if I thought they'd ever see you again."

"Oh!" Larry's head snapped up.

Hank's eyes widened. "Really?"

Hank and Larry exchanged a glance.

Hector added, "For what it's worth, I think they were really impressed with what you did. You know, the theft, and then giving the money back to save them." He reached for another chip. "I heard they're moving in with Marlene in Boca Raton."

Hank smiled. Larry chuckled. "They're the fucking *Golden Girls*."

Hank laughed. "I bet they all think they're Blanche. No one will want to be Sophia and carry her purse everywhere." He sat back in his chair and looked at Larry. "That's good. They have each other. They'll be good."

So now they'd move to Plan B. They had been thinking their best bet would be to head to a resort town where their English could come in handy in the tourist industry, while they improved their Spanish. If Hector would let them go.

As Hector reached for another chip, he spoke in a low voice. "Look. I don't mean to be rude. But my mother is wondering how much longer you guys will be staying."

Hank glanced to the man guarding the door. "What do you mean?"

"I mean, I told her you'd be here a few days. A week, tops. And it's been almost three. She's hoping you might be ready to move on. Her sister wants to come visit."

Hank closed his eyes for a couple of seconds, then opened them. "Sure. Sure. We can probably be on our way tomorrow. Right, Larry?"

He rubbed his face to hide his smile and noticed Larry's brow was furrowed.

Larry motioned to the door—he'd want to be sure of the details. Although, it was a little late in this case. "So, Hector, why the guy at the door?"

Hector dipped more salsa and tilted his head back as he dropped another chip in his mouth. He pushed the food aside to answer. "Him? The extra help in case you needed it."

"You mean, he's not guarding us?" Larry asked, his voice rising.

"Guarding you?" Hector laughed. "Why would anyone guard you?

He's here in case you needed a ride somewhere, or a translator. He's part of your fee. I told you that when you hired me. Don't you remember?" Hector reached for another chip. "Now I have a question for you. Remember the first time I came down to see you. You wanted me to check out a business opportunity you were interested in on the coast. What exactly was that?"

Fifty-Three

Everybody Knows

Pam backed her van up to the Goodwill donation door, and when the three young men saw how full the vehicle was, they blew out breaths. She stood to the side as boxes holding thirty-year-old wedding gift china and bridal shower cookware were carted into the building.

So much stuff.

George Carlin had a great routine about stuff. How you spend the first part of your life accumulating it—the herb muddler you thought you'd use regularly, or the cornucopia horn that sits in a closet for fifty weeks of the year—and then you spend the last part of your life ditching it all. Marlene told them not to bring a thing. She'd bought everything new and didn't want one chipped platter, sentimental silver spoon, or tattered towel in her condo. Even Claire didn't want Pam's crap.

So here it was. Boxed and donated. The guys started to pull out the clear bags full of clothing, tossing them to each other like a relay chain.

"Wait!" Pam called. "Sorry. That one. Can I see that one, just for a sec?"

The teen leaned the bag against the wall and Pam pried open the knot. She dug down through Hank's shorts and T-shirts until her fingers brushed familiar, heavy cotton. She dragged Hank's worn sweatshirt through the crush and brought it to her cheek. She breathed in, hard, for a moment, and then set the shirt gently on the backseat of her van, climbed in, and put the key in the ignition.

"Hey, Pam! Yoo-hoo! Is that you, Pam? Pam Montgomery!"

Pam whispered under her breath, "Oh, for fuck's sake." She glanced at her dog, curled up on the passenger seat. "Better buckle up, Elmer. This ride could get rocky." She pasted on a smile and turned to face Sabrina Cuomo as she approached the driver's window. The coolest mom who loomed over her during her daughter's school years and was now decked out in head-to-toe linen with her face shaded by a wide-brimmed straw hat, extra-large gold hoops dangling from her ears. Sabrina leaned against Pam's van window, her Cartier gold-and-diamond love bracelets clanging up against her Apple watch.

"Sabrina! Hi! How are you?" Kill her with kindness and get rid of her.

"I'm fabulous." Then her smile turned upside down to a pout and her bracelets jangled as she reached out to pat Pam's arm. "How are youuuu? You've been through soooo much. You're here shopping? At the thrift store. You poooor thing."

"I'm actually making a donation."

"Of course you are." Sabrina scanned the interior. Pam was sure she was looking for purchases, and Pam was grateful it had been too hot to leave Elmer in the car, otherwise she might well have had a whole new, discounted wardrobe stuffed into the backseat. Sabrina moved to the next item on her agenda. "I hear you're leaving. You're all moving in with Marlene. Well, we'll miss you. But you know what they say: things always work out for the best. Anyhoo. I'm sure you gals will love Florida—"

Pam stared straight ahead a moment and watched a young couple navigate the sidewalk while she digested that. She tilted her head, then turned to squint at Sabrina. "I find it hard to understand how my husband being killed in a horrific boat explosion could be *things working out for the best*."

Sabrina squinched her face into what Pam bet she imagined to be her sympathetic look and rubbed Pam's arm. Then she said, "Pam. Everybody knows."

Pam shook off Sabrina's hand and crossed her arms. She pivoted in her seat to better face her. "Knows what, Sabrina?" There were so many things to know. What exactly did Sabrina know?

Sabrina lowered her chin and spoke as though she were soothing a child. "We know you're broke. We know you said you were downsizing all those years ago, but face it, Pam. Everybody knows you and Hank had money problems." She moved to pat Pam's arm but then withdrew her hand. "There's nothing to be ashamed of, Pam. Some husbands aren't good providers, like my Gene. At least now you have a second chance. You still have some of your looks." Sabrina glanced downward. "You still have great legs. Now you can find someone better."

Pam blinked as she tried to hold Sabrina's gaze. *Everybody knows.* Her heart hit the inside of her chest. *Someone better.* But everybody didn't know everything. They didn't know Hank masterminded stealing nine million dollars. They didn't know he faked his death. They didn't know he gave up that money to save her. Granted, she had to threaten he'd be killed first, but still, he gave up the money for her. That's the kind of man Hollywood makes movies about. What would Sabrina say about that? What was it Hank always said? Right. Offense is the best defense.

"Sabrina, you let on like your husband is self-made, that he's some investment whiz, but *everybody knows* you got your money when he found vermin in his burger. He sued Big Bobby Lew's and settled out of court. Your cleaning lady told *everybody.* And she thinks he planted that mouse tail. That's right—she found the tail-less body." Sabrina looked like she'd been slapped. Good. "So shut your face. You don't know anything about Hank. My Hank was something else. And I would take my Hank without a penny to his name, over your douchebag Gene any day of the week." Pam started the ignition. "Who cuts tails off dead mice? Ew." She put her van in gear and drove the hell out of there.

Dusk was falling as she passed the casino and her pulse returned to normal. She slowed down as the streetlights came on and took a sharp right down a street she usually avoided. Elmer sat in the passenger seat, with his head on the armrest.

"Why don't you hang your head out the window like other dogs?" Pam asked.

He pointed his nose toward the air-conditioning vent.

"Ah. Sure. Makes sense."

Pam pulled to a stop in front of the pretty, colonial home and turned the engine off. The boxwoods had finally reached the height Pam had hoped for when she'd planted them. Window boxes and a basketball hoop had been added since she had last been here, the day they moved out. The living room light was on. The fireplace had been painted white, and it looked elegant.

She sat in the quiet and listened to the crickets, like she used to, on a night like this, in the backyard, beside her pool. She breathed in the night air and could almost feel the warm water rush over her. How she missed this tranquility. A mosquito buzzed her ear. Another bit her cheek. And then her neck. She swatted her forehead. Then her arm. And her ankle. Her other ear. She turned the car back on and put the windows up.

"I'm done, Elmer."

His ears perked up.

"I'm done being mad and sad. It's only money, Elmer. It's only fucking money. So I don't have any anymore. Or a husband. I don't know why he left me behind, but he did. It's time to move on. I've got my health. I've got my friends. I've got a daughter and a grandchild on the way. Apparently, I've still got great legs. And I've got you."

She took one more look at her old house. It was smaller than she remembered.

"From now on, Elmer, we're only looking forward. Deal?"

She reached over and squeezed his paw, put the van in gear, pulled into the road, and didn't look back.

Fifty-Four

You Couldn't Have Mentioned It?

The past six months, it had been more and more challenging for Hector to decide which part of the day was his favorite. He loved them all.

He poured the kibble into the troughs, then checked the board and saw four more dogs had been placed in homes that day, and even better, only two new rescues had arrived. The way Brenda's model was working, it was only a matter of time before every stray around had found a forever home, and in the meantime, they were safe and cared for.

Hector waved adios to the staff and walked down the path and through the gate to the resort side of their property. He passed the row of casitas and caught the sun on the horizon, quickening its descent into the Pacific. Live music from the patio wafted through the coconut trees, and he checked his watch. Happy hour was in full swing. Hector skirted the entry fountain, cut through the open-air lobby, and slid two pieces of paper across the front desk to Andre. They lifted a bit off the counter in the breeze from the ceiling fans. "The couple in 4C are adopting Ranger, the black lab mix. They're taking him back to Philadelphia, and Casita 6 are taking the beagle mix, Scout, to St. Louis."

Andre nodded, pushed his bifocals up his nose, and studied the papers. "Cool. That'll make Brenda happy. I'll get the paperwork going and line up the arrangements with the airlines." He turned back to the computer.

Hector rounded the end of the counter and ducked his head in the office. He waved and moved on, not wanting to disturb Larry, who was readying a deposit and in the middle of counting money.

Money. It's always about the money.

When Brenda had first told Hector that Padma suspected there was money—and millions at that—missing from the casino, and the husbands had something to do with it, Hector had thought that even a barber, a guy who did whatever needs doin', and his wife could use a retirement plan.

Back in his mother's living room, Hank had asked why he didn't put a gun to the husbands' heads and take the money and run. Hector had considered it, but then he'd have a target on his back, and that was no life for Brenda. Plus, he'd spent a lifetime around bad people doing bad things and he'd learned it pays to be patient.

With one look at Padma he'd known not only would she never follow through on any career promise she made to Brenda, but she could even be dangerous to his wife. He loved that Brenda couldn't see it. And she didn't need to. That's why she had him. Then, when he'd met Farid and smelled his sickly breath and felt the weak squeeze of his handshake, Hector saw that Farid and Padma would either fuck each other over or expect to be fucked. All he had to do was wait on the sidelines.

That was the one thing Hector liked about working with bad people— or in Padma's case, essentially good people in the habit of doing bad things: they're predictable. While he hadn't exactly predicted Farid would level his gun at Elmer, he hadn't been surprised. And in that moment, Farid had opened up another line of possibility. Now if the money didn't make it back to the casino, Farid wouldn't kill the wives—because dead guys can't do anything.

Opportunity had knocked, and Hector had been patiently waiting by the door. When Larry had walked him through the Virtual Safety Deposit Box and the subsequent bank transfer Farid would have to set up, Hector had paid close attention and asked the right questions.

Farid should never have messed with the dog.

While Hector had comforted the quaking Elmer, he had looked from the dead creep to his briefcase, and when his eyes had landed on Farid's laptop, he had done a quick risk assessment. Then he had done what he always did. He had done what was best for him and Brenda.

He'd stood, picked up Farid's laptop from the table, lifted the corpse's finger to unlock it, and then he'd clicked on the Virtual Safety Deposit Box icon. When it had called for facial recognition, grateful for his clean shot, he'd held the laptop in front of Farid's dead face.

Bingo.

The VSDB had opened, and there sat the nine-million-dollar bank draft, its transfer to the casino bank account pending. Hector had used Farid's dead face again to cancel the transfer, and then he had signed into his own anonymous email account, the one he kept for times when he, well, needed to be anonymous. He had attached the nine-million-dollar draft and had sent it to a numbered company that owned another numbered company that owned the San Salvador Animal Rescue. He had tucked the laptop on Farid's chest and later destroyed it when he returned to clean up the body.

The husbands and wives thought Padma and the casino had the money.

Padma thought Farid took the money and ran.

Farid was going to kill a dog. Fuck him.

And that's the nice thing about doing whatever needs doin'. No one really knows what kind of money that pays, or how much there is in the offshore bank accounts. People can speculate, but they don't know. So, when a barber looks like he's worked hard and has been able to cobble some funds together to buy a rundown resort on the coast of El Salvador, and he's able to make cash deals for renovations, and hire people who he knows can take care of things, and build a community, no one asks where his money came from. They may wonder, but they don't ask.

But most importantly, for Hector: happy wife, happy life.

He looked for her now and found Brenda at the far end of the dining room, standing in a swath of setting sunlight, watching over happy hour by the pool.

It was still early for dinner service, and the dining room was deserted as Hector walked by the louvered windows that gave onto the patio, when a familiar voice filtered through the slats and the hairs on his arms stood up.

"I had a close call one time. I had a break-in but didn't have my phone with me. So, after my husband died and the girls and I—you met Nancy and Shalisa, right? They're in the pool. That's Nancy doing laps, and that's Shalisa, floating on the rubber ducky. She's on the phone, probably talking to Bob, he's her new boyfriend. Look, she's waving. Cheers!" A pause and the voice continued, "When we moved to Boca Raton, with our friend Marlene—she said you're taking her to dinner later. She loves to dance. Do you dance? Oh, great. You'll have fun. Anyway, I insisted on a landline. About a month ago I answered the phone . . ."

Another pause and the clinking sound of cocktails arriving at the table.

"Gracias. You know how it is—you answer the phone and either they want to clean your ducts, or you've won a cruise."

Hector could hear the response of a male chuckle. He sidled up to the other side of the shutters and stood still. He checked, and Brenda was still at the far end of the room, arms folded, focused on the patio.

Hector sighed. What the fuck had she done now?

The voice carried on. "Well, this time when I picked up the phone, they told me I'd won an all-expenses-paid trip for four, to this place. *Sure*, I thought. But I'll go along with it. We're doing okay, but we're on a budget. We each got a cash settlement of a hundred grand when our husbands died—we didn't even make a claim, just got an email from the boat manufacturer and a deposit in our accounts. And Nancy and I have a bit of a pension. Oh my God. I'm talking so much. Well, we sure could use a vacation, so I said to the woman on the phone, send the tickets. And they showed up by courier. When we went to the airport this morning, we weren't even positive there'd be a flight. Or what it'd be like when we got here. What kind of resort has an animal rescue attached to it? There aren't any pictures online, you know. No social media presence at all. So it was a real leap of faith, but here we are. Voilà. Cheers to you, Manuel. How long have you been a widower?"

Hector heard the clink of glasses and then the slurp of straws.

The man's voice, heavy with a Latin American accent, said, "My. I've never had a margarita this good. Have you?"

There was no reply.

Hector heard a chair scrape against the flagstone, and he pushed back the shutter to take a peek. Yep. There they were. Marlene was under an umbrella, her nose buried in a tourist brochure, and Nancy and Shalisa were in the pool. A handsome, older man sat alone, sipping a margarita with an empty chair beside him, the partially full glass and straw hat his companion had abruptly abandoned sitting on the table in front of him.

Brenda slipped her arm around Hector's waist, and he put his around her shoulders. He raised an eyebrow, then jumped when something brushed his shin. He crouched down. "Elmer! They brought you too! Good to see you, bud." He looked up at Brenda. "An all-expenses-paid trip for four, plus a dog. What have you done?"

"I've just put some people with a shared history in the same geographical area to see if there's still any chemistry."

Hector shook his head. "You sound like you're lining up your high school course schedule, but you're messing with people's lives." He ruffled Elmer's fur as the dog leaned hard against him. He looked up at his wife. "And you couldn't have mentioned it?"

Brenda smoothed her husband's hair. "You guys would all have said no. Your mother approved."

Hector gave Elmer's chin a final rub, ran his hands over his own face, and stood.

Their greeting completed, Elmer trotted out through the dining room doorway to the patio. His nose high, he sniffed and then followed Pam's scent along the pool's edge. He was closing the gap behind her when he caught another smell. His ears popped up, and he sniffed again, turning his head in time to catch Hank coming out from behind the bar, drying his hands on a white linen towel. Elmer's rear end vibrated, and he bounded three quick steps toward his old friend before forcing himself to brake, wait, and watch.

Seeing Pam, Hank jerked to a stop. Elmer sat down, and his tail cautiously swept stray grains of beach sand left and right across the flagstones while his eyes traveled from Hank to Pam and back again. His tail stilled as Pam slowed and then paused ten paces from her husband.

The couple locked eyes for a long moment, and then Pam said, "You remind me of someone I used to know."

A corner of Hank's mouth turned up. "Funny. I was thinking the same about you."

Pam crossed her arms. "The man I'm thinking of left me. A while back."

Hank gave two slow nods. "I bet he had a real good reason to leave someone like you."

Pam raised an eyebrow. "You think?"

"I do." Hank crossed his arms. "Mind you, the woman I'm thinking of did some crazy shit to me. Like cray-zee."

Pam nodded twice. "I bet she thought it was a good idea. At the time."

Hank raised an eyebrow back. "You think?"

Hank looked off and squinted into the setting sun. Pam gave a subtle shrug and a small smile. Elmer had never seen Pam look like this. Happy and sad at the same time. He could tell she wanted something. And he did too. But he wasn't sure they were going to get it.

Then Pam said, "I bet she wishes none of it ever happened."

Hank brought his eyes back to her, and they glistened as he said, so softly that Elmer could barely hear, "I bet he does too."

Hank tossed the towel over his shoulder, smiled, and opened his arms wide. Elmer bounced up, and his tail whirred like a helicopter rotor. Pam held Hank's gaze; she waited half a beat and then sprinted to her husband, stretching her arms around his waist, nestling her cheek against his chest, and slipping into place like the final piece of a jigsaw puzzle that had been sitting unfinished, for too long, on a dusty card table. As they embraced, Elmer pushed his way between them, his tail tickling their bare legs.

In the dining room, Brenda slid her finger in Hector's belt loop and leaned into him.

Hector's eyes lingered on Pam and Hank. "You realize that could have gone sideways."

Brenda rested her head against his shoulder. "Hec-toro. You, especially, know everyone deserves a second chance."

"I guess." He tucked a strand of hair behind Brenda's ear. "Ay, Dios mio, amor. Fasten your seatbelts. It's going to be a bumpy night."

She looked up at him. "*Airplane!*?"

"No. Bette Davis in *All About Eve*." Hector grabbed her hand and led her away. "Let's get out of here quick. We don't want to be around when Andre and Shalisa see each other."

Epilogue

Another Six Months Later

I Do Now

Pam scanned faces as guests drifted down the aisle, taking their seats in front of the floral arbor overlooking the Pacific. But still no Nancy. She pursed her lips, then remembered how that deepened the lines around her mouth and smoothed her expression—another skirmish in the battle against aging. There was only so much Pam could do about both her wrinkles and Nancy. If Nancy couldn't be where she was supposed to be, too bad.

Marlene's warning rang in her ears. Early on, she pulled Pam aside and whispered, "I'll be the perfect silent partner, but we know what Nancy's like. She'll research everything and get you the best prices . . . but she'll never be on time. And wedding planners need to be on time."

Pam checked her watch, and as if on cue, the band transitioned from cheerful welcome music to sentimental ceremony. Footsteps prompted Pam to turn and see Hector coming down the path. Behind him, Elmer hugged the wall, keeping his paws to the cool strip of shade. He eyed the baskets of flowers lining the aisle, and Pam would bet her share of the business that as soon as people left, he'd pee on each of them—just to be sure the other dogs knew they were in Elmer-Town.

"They made it." Hector nodded toward the pool.

Pam shifted her attention across the lawn to where Brenda supervised two men carrying a three-tiered wedding cake along the patio. Señora Chavez, her sturdy body wrapped in an apron, stood by the dining room door, waving them her way with a towel, like a matador attracting a bull. She noticed Pam and blew her a kiss, and Pam blew one back.

Hector squinted into the setting sun. "Did you know Bob's not coming?"

"What?!" Pam spun to face him.

Hector nodded. "Yep. Dylan picked Shalisa up at the airport. She told him they split up."

Pam gasped. That must have been the news Shalisa wanted to tell her. "Does Andre know?"

Hector nodded again. "Dylan texted Claire so she'd give him the heads-up."

"That's good. He doesn't like surprises," Pam said. It was even better that she wasn't the one who told him. It was awkward being in the middle. Pam tried not to talk about Shalisa around Andre anymore. They weren't officially divorced—that's tricky once a death certificate has been issued—but they told everyone they were.

Hector continued, "She said she's staying longer."

Pam's heart sank. While she treasured every minute she spent with Shalisa, an extended stay, with Bob now out of the picture, would get Andre's hopes up. Well, she couldn't worry about them. "You haven't seen Nancy, have you? I looked all over for her. I even went by Marlene's casita, but her shutters were closed."

Hector chuckled. "Manuel arrived an hour ago."

"Ah. That explains that."

Whenever Marlene visited, Manuel would drive over from San Salvador. She'd giggle like a teenager around him, but it was good to see her smile. Pam swallowed the lump in her throat that settled in whenever she thought of her old friend. Dave had been gone just over a year, and it hurt to think how he'd started everything but never got to see how it ended.

When Hank had come out from behind the resort's bar that first day, Pam's heart had somersaulted. As soon as his arms were around her, she knew she was home. A few days later, over a pitcher of margaritas and a bucket of beer, Nancy had filled everyone in on how the scene had played out from her perspective—how she and Shalisa had been puttering around in the pool, and without her glasses, she could see Pam was embracing a man, but she couldn't make out who it was. She'd sidestroked to Shalisa, who was floating on an inflatable rubber ducky, a wide-brimmed straw hat shading her face, her phone lying on her chest, and a fruity cocktail lazily held in her hand. Nancy had nudged the raft. "Shalisa. Who's the guy Pam's hugging?"

"Huh?" Shalisa had languidly lifted the hat's brim, then jerked upright so fast she'd tumbled on top of Nancy. They'd thrashed in the water, paraphernalia flying, until they grabbed the duck, gasping for air. Shalisa spat out water and finally croaked, "Hank! Pam is hugging Hank!"

Shocked, Nancy had leaped on Shalisa's shoulders like a synchronized swimmer doing a stack lift. She sank them both and underwater they fought each other off, scrambling for the side. Nancy clambered out of the pool, dripping, and bellowed, "Larry! Larry Clooney! I know you're here! It's me. Larry! Where are youuuu!"

Poor Larry had rushed from the office, with no idea what the hell was going on. As soon as he was close enough that Nancy could recognize him, she sprinted across the patio, sopping wet, and catapulted herself into his arms. Pam had witnessed that herself, and doubted she'd ever be able to purge the image of Nancy's fleshy white thighs wrapped around Larry's waist, and him, knees bent, hands gripping Nancy's bum, struggling to keep his balance.

Some things you can't unsee.

No one heard from Nancy and Larry for the next two days. When they finally emerged from Larry's casita, Nancy announced she was moving to El Salvador and urged Pam to join her, saying, "Remember how gutted we were when we thought they'd died in that explosion? This is our second chance, Pam. We've got to take it. We have to."

Pam quickly fell in line with the idea, and as things settled down the friends spent hours together, around a table for eight, just like old times. An empty chair sat in unspoken commemoration of their missing pal. They went over all they'd done and why. As the clock ticked, secrets dropped, and laughter returned. When the conversation inevitably turned to debating whether Dave had died in a freakish accident or if Padma really had him killed, Pam, tired of hearing about it, would change the topic.

Ultimately Shalisa's second chance took her in a different direction. She and Andre had quietly reunited by the pool that day—nothing like the spectacle Nancy and Larry had put on—and while they had considered reconciling, Shalisa was already seeing Bob. She took some time and eventually asked Andre for a fresh start, without him. Although the bottom dropped out of his world, he'd said, "Anything for my queen," wanting her to have the *fucking fantastic* life she deserved.

None of their retirement plans had panned out quite as they'd envisioned, but they'd worked out. Although Pam still puzzled over how the husbands ended up being employed by their barber. But then she reasoned, with the kind of money they were paying Hector, he had an impressively lucrative side hustle. And she came to accept she'd never know everything.

Pam glanced at Hector. "You staying for the ceremony?"

He shook his head. "I'm gonna give Brenda a hand. I know how you and Nancy get when things don't go right." He winked. "And I wouldn't want you to make me regret anything." He flashed a smile and headed across the lawn.

Pam chuckled and watched him exchange a fist bump as he crossed paths with Hank, who, finished at the bar, had changed into a freshly ironed guayabera shirt. Waiting for him to join her, Pam studied her husband. Had he changed, had she, had they both? Or had they just not known each other as well as they thought they did?

She used to think it took all of Hank's mental fortitude to finish a game of Wordle, yet somehow, it was Hank who'd come up with their Plan B. He was the one who realized Dylan's scuba diving and tourism experience made him a perfect fit to run the resort's watersports. And that Claire could pitch in anywhere, when she wasn't busy with the baby. Even the destination wedding business was his idea.

Shalisa had opted out, wanting to build her new life Stateside, away from Andre. And it was no surprise that Marlene didn't want to leave her condo or move too far from her daughters. But she forgave their $50,000 loan in exchange for part ownership. The rest of their startup funding had arrived the morning after they'd shared their plan with Hector and Brenda. The retired barber had dropped by at breakfast and nudged a box of donuts and an envelope holding their disputed $50,000 down payment across the table, saying he and Brenda would buy in too. Their investments were paying off; Pam and Nancy were doing so well they'd just paid Hector and Marlene their first dividend and were now drawing good salaries themselves. Ha! Maybe they'd be rich bitches after all.

But who cared about money when you had family? Henry was a familiar sight at the resort, strapped to his grandfather's chest as Hank mixed cocktails, continually corralling the chubby six-month-old's curious fingers. They'd all played fast and loose with the facts when they'd filled their relatives in on their escapades—outlining a scenario where the men had been framed by the casino and had to run for their lives. And while they were now safe, they still needed discretion. They'd skipped any mention of hiring a hitman. Some things were best left unsaid.

As Hank met her in the shade of the palm tree Pam's cheek brushed his shoulder, warm through the crisp cotton. She inhaled, taking in his scent of lemon, saltwater, and sweat because it was always so fucking hot. She closed her eyes, flashing back to the moment outside Goodwill when she'd buried her face in his shirt, believing he was gone to her forever. How lucky she was. She squeezed Hank's hand and pulled him forward to fall in with the other guests and take a seat.

The magistrado stood in front of the arbor. Pam felt a rustle at her elbow and turned to be wrapped in Shalisa's arms. She squealed, "You made it!" And then, "Oh my God, are you okay? Your skin's on fire."

Shalisa waved her off. "I'm not used to the climate."

Over Shalisa's shoulder, Pam was surprised to see Andre drop into the next chair. She raised her eyebrow to him, and he winked, then took a handkerchief from his pocket and mopped his brow. Pam straightened, a touch perplexed, as everyone rose to face the foot of the aisle. In the distance, Marlene and Manuel held hands and laughed as they scurried across the lawn. They skirted the chairs and came along the side, scooting into the seats behind Pam.

The music swelled, and from around the corner Estuardo appeared, walking along the flower-lined path, with his mother and father on either side. Pam blinked away tears as the trio made their way toward the arbor. A moment later Paul, with Nancy—at least she had arrived here on time—and Larry, rounded the same corner. Nancy looked pale beneath her tan. Where had she been all afternoon? Could a problem have arisen? Larry's jaw muscles clenched and unclenched as he passed their row.

The magistrado motioned for the guests to be seated. Estuardo kissed his mother then shook his father's hand, and his parents took their seats. Paul kissed Nancy's cheek then reached for Larry. Pam held her breath. Hank leaned into her shoulder, his muscles tensed, as though he was willing his friend to do the right thing. Paul's hand, suspended in air, looked as if it was photoshopped against a canvas of Pacific blue, waiting to be encased in his father's grip.

And finally, it was.

Larry grasped Paul's hand with both of his, then pulled his son in for a bear hug. When he stepped back, the sun reflected off his tear-strewn cheeks. Paul wiped his own eyes as he joined Estuardo.

The magistrado gave the expected warnings about sickness and health, good times and bad. Pam squirmed when he talked about richer or poorer, but then decided that in the end she'd come out on the right side of that equation.

He said, "Today, you stand with the partner you have chosen to walk beside you in life. For whatever reason you made this choice, tuck it away in your heart so you can pull it out when you need it. Because, as every married person here can tell you—you will need it."

Ain't that the truth.

———

The sun disappeared into the Pacific, and the patio lights twinkled. The band played, couples danced, waitstaff replenished cocktails, and candles flickered on the tables around the pool. The four girlfriends sat, as they had so many times over the years, under the night sky. Pam emptied their third bottle of champagne into Nancy's flute and asked, "Where were you this afternoon? I looked all over for you."

Nancy cast her gaze to the table. "In the cabana."

"The *cabana*? What were you doing in the *cabana*?" Even in the darkness Pam saw the red flush creep up Nancy's neck. Pam set the bottle down with a thud. "You and Larry were fooling around. Right before you walked your son down the aisle. Ew. That's so gross! Someone could have seen you!"

Nancy kept her lips tightly closed and toyed with the stem of her flute.

Marlene smiled at Nancy. "There's nothing wrong with the parents of the groom getting a little frisky. I think it's sexy."

Pam recoiled. "If you're David and Victoria Beckham, maybe! But not when you look like King Charles and Camilla." She stifled a gag. "No one wants to see *them* doing it."

Nancy sat up, indignant. "Come on. We may not be Posh and Becks, but we've gotta look better than Charles and Camilla."

Pam did a double take. "Who do you think you look like during sex?"

Nancy thought a moment and then brightened. "Kurt and Goldie."

Pam reeled in disbelief. "You're not even blond."

Marlene murmured, "Good choice. Goldie's pretty limber. She used to be a dancer. Or Tom Hanks and Rita Wilson. I bet they still look good doing it. Maybe Denzel and Pauletta. I'd say Kevin Costner, but he's dating younger these days, so that's not fair. Oh! I know! Matthew Broderick and Sarah Jessica Parker. I bet they have great rhythm. They're both very fit." She sat back in her chair and smiled. "That's who I want to look like."

Sometimes Marlene amazed Pam. She shook her head and said, "But still, it's downright off-putting for the parents of the groom to be doing the deed, right before the wedding." Shalisa had remained surprisingly quiet. Pam turned to her for support. "Am I right?"

Now it was Shalisa's turn to keep her lips tightly closed and toy with a flute's stem.

Pam leaned across the table and hissed, "You had sex with Andre. Shalisa!" She fell back in the chair. "That's why you were all hot and bothered at the ceremony." She surged forward again. "You couldn't have been here ten minutes before you were in his pants. You've kept that man at arm's length

for a year. You better not be leading him on. He's just starting to be himself."
It wasn't Pam's business, and she hadn't defended Andre before. But if this
were a fling he'd be shattered and she'd have to help pick up those pieces.

Shalisa looked around and said in a low voice, "Sometimes you have to
let something go before you know you want it."

Nancy and Marlene both jolted upright. Then Nancy said, "Whoa.
Shalisa. You need to be sure you want this for *you*. Remember. *You* deserve
your life to be fucking fantastic."

Shalisa smiled and said, "I know I do. And it is. Or it will be. Andre and
I belong together. I know that now."

Pam rubbed her temples. This was a turn of events she hadn't seen coming. She looked around the table.

Marlene straightened in her chair and said, "You'll never guess what I've
learned from all this."

Pam could only imagine the multitude of lessons any of them had
learned *from all this*. Like how much room fifty grand takes up in your purse,
or the going rate for a hitman, or how about when you do or don't need bodies to collect insurance money. She blew out a breath.

Finally, Shalisa replied with a smile, "What have you learned from all
this, Marlene?"

Marlene glowed as she answered, "I've learned to seize the day. Manuel
calls it carpe diem. He speaks Spanish, you know. But that's what we've gotta
do, gals. Love hard today, 'cuz who knows what will happen tomorrow."

She lifted her flute to the center of the table, and the others joined.

Then Marlene added, "I've also learned we should toss these back like
shots."

———

After the toasts to the new husbands, Pam and Hank sat side by side by
the pool, and Pam watched with envy as Manuel whirled Marlene around the
dance floor. Her blond hair flew as she fell in and out of his arms. Next to
them, Larry and Nancy swayed with his hands on her bum as though they
were in eighth grade. Pam smiled. Beyond the twinkle lights, she caught a

glimpse of Shalisa and Andre slipping away. Andre carried Shalisa's high heels in one hand, with his other entwined in hers. Maybe they'd make it after all. Pam hoped so. Farther around the patio, at another table, sat their saviors. Who knew a barber could have so much influence in someone's life? And Pam didn't mean for the good grooming.

Brenda perched on Hector's lap, probably telling everyone a private investigator story, with Elmer sprawled on the flagstones beside them. Across the pool Hector caught Pam's eye, and he raised his glass to her. She raised hers back. Pam watched him tuck a strand of hair behind Brenda's ear, then scratch Elmer's belly. Brenda kissed Hector's forehead and delivered her punchline. Everyone laughed, and Hector beamed. The first notes of a Michael Bublé love song played, and Brenda stood, pulling Hector to his feet. On the dance floor he folded around her, and she looked like she was in heaven. Pam remembered that long-ago feeling of dancing with the one you love.

She took a sip of her margarita, licked the salt from her lips, and smiled at Hank. She searched for a glimpse of the man she'd married so long ago, and when he smiled back, she found it. Not every couple has to dance.

Hank nodded toward the others. "Do you want to?"

Who was he kidding? "You don't dance."

"I do now."

Pam raised a skeptical eyebrow.

Hank stood and held out his hand; his smile stretched across his face. "I've been taking lessons."

Pam was stunned for a moment, then she tossed her head back and laughed. She jumped to her feet, threw her arms around her husband's neck, and kissed him. Yep. Her life was fucking fantastic.

Again.

Post Script

How Dave Died

After that hot, Saturday night at Pam and Hank's, back in July when all their trouble started, it took Andre about twenty-two hours to realize how much shit he was in with Shalisa for suggesting she didn't *need* that piece of chocolate mousse cheesecake.

The Uber ride home was quiet, but that wasn't unusual in itself. Andre trailed his wife up the driveway, and she stepped aside and waited by that contentious juniper bush while he unlocked their door and let her pass. Wordlessly, she pushed the empty springform pan into his chest and went upstairs. He listened for the decisive click of their bedroom door closing, then went to the kitchen and poured himself a nightcap. An hour later he wandered up the same stairs and closed their guest room door.

Shalisa was still in bed the next morning when Andre left for the marina to meet up with Hank, Larry, and Dave for a day of fishing. He didn't see his wife until the next evening, when he returned home, his skin tight from the hours in the wind and sun. His stomach grumbled as he came through the door and was greeted by a whiff of grilled steak, and he smiled. Maybe there was some life left in his old girl after all. He dropped his gear and sauntered into the kitchen, rubbing his belly, his mood light and bright.

He found Shalisa sitting at the table. Before her, a fresh gingham tablecloth was laid with flowers, the perfect plate of steak, sauteed mushrooms still succulent and sizzling from the cast-iron frying pan, and a baked potato peeking out from under a scoop of sour cream sprinkled with chopped chives. Andre's smile dropped when he noticed the table was set for one.

"Where's mine?" he asked.

He scanned the counter and peeked through the oven window to see if it was warming inside. It wasn't. He looked back to his wife. Shalisa gently pierced a juicy cube of ribeye with her fork and raised it to her mouth, pausing to consider it before she turned her big, brown eyes on him and said, "I didn't think you *needed* it."

She sucked the steak into her mouth with a quiet pop.

They'd been married thirty years, so even though Andre wasn't able to recall exactly what he'd said the previous evening around the table in Hank and Pam's backyard, he knew enough to apologize. "Hon, I was just trying to help."

Shalisa chewed, then swallowed. She pointed her fork at Andre. "You want to help, Andre?" Then she pointed her fork to their living room. "If you want to *help*, you would chop down that juniper bush like I asked you a year ago. And show me the proper respect my requests deserve." She brought her fork back to Andre. "*That* is how you can help." She pierced another piece of meat.

"Juniper bush?" Andre scrunched up his face. "What's a bush have to do with anything?" He put his hands on his hips.

"A year ago, I set that goddamned Peloton bike up in front of the window so I could look outside while I rode that goddamned thing. Only, that old, overgrown juniper is in the way. I've asked you a hundred times to get rid of that bush. How can you not remember that?"

Oh, yeah. *That* bush.

"What do you want to look out the window for? The whole point of a Peloton bike is that you watch the screen for a better workout."

Shalisa held his eyes a moment, then said, "If you don't cut down that tree, as God is my witness, you will regret it for the rest of our marriage." She picked up her knife and cut another piece of steak.

Andre had heard empty threats before, and he pondered exactly how empty this one was as he opened the fridge to grab a beer in defeat. Reaching in, he noticed Shalisa had stocked the shelves with grilled chicken, fresh salmon, and homemade fruit salad. As Andre scanned the dishes, he knew he wouldn't be eating any of that food unless he chopped down that fucking bush.

And that's why Andre texted Dave and asked to borrow his ax.

—————

The next morning Dave was driving to meet Hank for their regular Monday drop when he remembered Andre needed his ax. "Fuck!"

He made a U-turn, drove the few blocks to his house, turned into his driveway, stopped his car with a squeal, and jumped out. He should have gone to the garage and set the ax out the night before, but that would have meant a conversation with Marlene. And he hadn't been up for that.

Marlene would have kept her eyes on the TV and said, "You know what Larry and Nancy do with their garage, Dave? They park their car in it. Same with Hank and Pam. Right in the center of their garage. You know what's in the center of our garage, Dave? Our Christmas tree stand."

Marlene would have kept going. "Everything in Larry's garage has a spot. His tools hang on hooks. You know where our snow shovel is, Dave? It's leaning against the wall. It's July. How much snow you expecting tonight, Dave? And Larry has an automatic garage door opener. Almost like they're living in the 2020s. And we pull our garage door down with a rope. Like the cavemen. I swear to God, Dave, that garage door is gonna kill one of us someday."

Dave wouldn't have bothered pointing out to Marlene that cavemen didn't have garages.

So that's why Dave was in a hurry that Monday morning. He'd saved himself from that conversation with Marlene the previous night by staying in his chair and shouting out the answers to the TV screen—"What is the capital of Argentina?" and "Who are the Rolling Stones?"—instead of going to the garage and getting his ax.

He would be late to meet Hank, but Andre had texted he needed it

ASAP; he had some crisis brewing with Shalisa, so Dave had texted back that he'd hand it off to Hank that morning.

And Dave was the kind of guy who did what he said.

The sun beat down on the back of Dave's neck as he bent over, grabbed the garage door handle and heaved the heavy, hinged sections upward, rolling them back on their track. He stood with his hands on his hips, his eyes adjusting to the dimness and then darting about the clutter until he spotted the ax, leaning against his tall red toolbox. He picked a quick path around the lawnmower, snow tires, and hockey sticks, snatched the ax by its handle, reached up to grab the rope to bring down the garage door, and then stopped.

Wait. What was the other thing he needed? He planned to give Andre two things. The ax, and . . . He stood still while his brain fired on all cylinders. Two things. He'd told himself to pick up two things. What was the second? Did it have something to do with . . . coffee? His head snapped up.

Right.

Three days earlier Dave had been walking along the casino basement hallway, enjoying the coffee he'd just grabbed from the maintenance room, when the new boss, Padma Singh, had pushed past him from behind, like the self-important piece of work she was rumored to be, and jostled his arm. She'd flung open the door to the casino bank and disappeared inside. So preoccupied she hadn't glanced back to apologize for the mess she'd made of Dave's shirt and the floor.

Dave had just been chatting with the janitor in the lunchroom, so knew he wouldn't be around this way for a while, and that puddle of coffee was just the kind of thing someone could slip on and crack open their skull. And Dave Brand wasn't the kind of guy to let that happen. So, he'd ducked into the men's room, stopped to pee, admired his new haircut in the mirror—thinking maybe it was time to up Hector's tip, he liked that guy—and then wadded up some paper towels to wipe up his mess.

Back in the hallway, he'd squatted and was doing a final pass across the tile, satisfied the halls were once again safe, when he'd noticed it. Peeking out from the tiny space between the bottom of the casino bank's door and the tiled floor, one lonely casino chip had winked at him.

Dave had rolled forward on his knee, passed the paper towel along the edge of the door, then rocked back on his heels. He'd stood and taken deliberately calm strides back to the men's room. He'd discarded the soggy paper towels and had opened his palm to examine the casino chip, wishing for a hundred dollars.

He'd gasped as his fingers had unfurled—one thousand dollars!

The corners of his eyes had creased as he'd laughed.

The belt on his finances had been tight the past few years. This chip was pennies from heaven. Andre would get it cashed, and with those thousand bucks, they could take the girls out for a proper good time. Maybe that's when they'd finally tell them about their retirement plan. A pre-celebration. Maybe even champagne, because, *hello good life—we're comin' for ya'!*

When he had arrived home that Friday night, he'd tucked the chip into the top drawer of the toolbox.

That hot, Monday morning, his smile was broad and his dimples deep when, still holding the ax, Dave pulled the chip from its hiding spot. He tossed it high, debating at which waterfront restaurant he should make their dinner reservation. He snatched it from the air, kissed it, and then he flipped it again, reached up to grab the rope to bring the garage door down, and tripped on his snow shovel.

His six-foot-four-inch frame rocketed toward his heavy-duty Christmas tree stand—solid steel construction, the best money could buy (Marlene was done with the tree tipping over). His skull connected with the cylindrical base, and as his momentum rolled him over, the casino chip somersaulted through the air, heads over tails over heads. He reflexively gripped the ax as the garage door continued its descent and the casino chip finished its arc, landing softly on the middle of Dave's chest. It bounced once and then fell flat on his sternum. The door crashed down toward him, and Dave Brand had his last thought:

My wife was right.

Acknowledgments

First of all, I'd like to thank Bruce Springsteen.

I've never met The Boss, but back in the eighties he talked a lot about dreams. When I was twenty and sitting second row from the rafters in Maple Leaf Gardens, I promised him that I'd never give up on my dream to write a novel.

Then life got in the way—kids, mortgage, meal-prep. But Bruce doesn't go away: he's on Broadway, he tours, he writes a book. And every time he resurfaced, I remembered my promise.

So, thank you, Bruce, for inspiring me back in my glory days, and for not fading away, but instead giving me a reason to believe that somehow, my later days could be my better days.

Now, you don't start something new in your sixties without support. My husband, Andy, in addition to giving me mounds of material just by being, well, Andy, never minded the hours I'd shut myself away to write—even if he did say "working" in air quotes. He would always mute the TV or put down his Wordle to bounce an idea about.

The heartbeats of my life are my sons, Jack, Luke, and Walker. I didn't need to be published to feel I've accomplished something—I've raised three stellar young men. They've made me the luckiest mom around and they will always be my best work. And as it turns out, excellent sounding boards for plot points—kudos to Walker for coming through in the clutch.

An honorable mention to my son's buddy David Hopfer who created my website and wasn't alarmed when our dinner conversations turned to murder and hitmen.

My sister Jan Banting and sisters-in-law Frances Hincenbergs and

Kim Gilbert were my first readers. (Even if Kim pawned unread drafts off on her friends.) My nieces and nephew Jessica Sperry, Kate Banting, Loulie McMaster, and Angus McMaster, and brothers-in-law Gord Banting and Al McMaster, whose support ranged from asking polite questions at Thanksgiving—sometimes even a follow-up—to giving tips on Word doc edit mode.

If this book made you laugh you can thank my brother, Bob Gilbert. Almost from birth, I've been teased relentlessly and had to fine-tune my sense of humor. He's still at it. Case in point, a few years back I borrowed his car and had to ask how to start a push-button ignition. Picture my startled passenger when I stepped on the brake, pushed the button, and clearly said "start, start, start" to the rearview mirror. That tells you everything you need to know about Bob and me.

Much like his father, my nephew, Dane Gilbert, has always kept me on my toes. I have to admit I stole a couple snappy lines from him. No, I don't use a sundial to tell time, I just travel with your uncle Andy, who perpetually runs late. (And that confession isn't legally binding so I'm not cutting you in—although I know I'll hear about this forever.)

Friendships are the fabric of this book, and the threads that weave through my life are Suzanne and Karl Brand, Sharon and Jamie Howe, and Laurie and Jerry Sobie. We've had so many laughs over the years, it was only fair that I shared some with the world. I don't know who of us will die first—but I'll make sure they serve a perfect egg salad sandwich at your funeral.

And then there are the new people who made Bruce's and my dream come true. I queried 198 times before I found my agent, Rachel Neely. I'm eternally grateful that Juliet Mushens liked my pages and sent them her way. Rachel hit the ground running and the path to publication was a sprint where I'd expected a marathon. I'd pass my baton to her anytime, anywhere. The Mushens Entertainment team of Alba Arnau Prado, Liza DeBlock, and Catriona Fida is the gift that keeps giving. Jenny Bent of The Bent Agency took me on for North America, and Anna DeRoy and Sanjana Seelam at WME championed the film rights.

I think the true heroes of any novel are the editors who, where others see word counts, they see books on bedside tables, passed into friends' hands.

I wrote as good a story as I could, and all I wanted was expert guidance to make it better. And that's what I had from Danielle Dietrich of William Morrow in New York, Jennifer Lambert of HarperCollins Canada, and Ed Wood and Tilda Key of Little, Brown Book Group in the UK. A top five moment of my life was learning you liked this book.

It takes a village to raise children, and one comes in handy when writing a book. Bianca Marais opened the door to the community in her podcast *The Shit No One Tells You About Writing*, and then connected me with my writing groups. Those Zoom calls were my first objective feedback, and their encouragement and critiques helped me find my voice: Donna Curtin, MaryLou Galyo, Kristina Johnson. Then Emily Bean, Genevieve Lyons, Jessie Ann Squires, Amanda VanOpdorp. Also Trish DiStefano, Holly Dunn, Vicki Gladwish, Heather Hooper, and Kate Todd. All coming soon to a bookstore near you.

I have to backtrack to family, because that's where everything starts and ends. The downside of achieving something later in life is that those who loved you first aren't here to see it.

My parents, Barbara and Howard Gilbert, always had books around them. I'll never know anyone as curious, or who enjoyed life more than them. And my mom passed her love for reading on to me. But mostly they told me I could do anything I put my mind to. (Although my dad would add, the challenge was getting me to put my mind to it.) I'd say they'd be proud, but then, I know they always were.

And to you, the reader. Thank you for giving me your precious time. If you found any heart or humor in this book, it's because I'm lucky to have so much of both in my life.

Thank you all.